Rea(

SUE

Frankie & Al

"This is a lovely easy read with the gentle, slightly sarcastic humour that Sue Brown does so well."

—Prism Book Alliance

"An entertaining story with an amazing character that kept me completely engaged from start to finish."
—The Romance Reviews

Ed & Marchant

"Fest paced, far too short just because I want more Ed and Marchant! I haven't made myself familiar with Frankie's series, now I certainly will!"
—MM Good Book Reviews

Anthony & Leo

"I liked this story a lot… a great addition to the series…"
—Love Bytes

"…the journey the book takes the reader is gripping with several unanticipated twists and turns… a very captivating book and I hope to see these characters again in the future."
—Hearts on Fire

By SUE BROWN

Chance to Be King
Falling for Ramos
Final Admission
Grand Adventures (Dreamspinner Anthology)
The Layered Mask
The Night Porter • Light of Day
Nothing Ever Happens
The Sky Is Dead
Stitch (Multiple Author Anthology)
Stolen Dreams
Waiting

FRANKIE'S SERIES
Frankie & Al
Ed & Marchant
Anthony & Leo
Frankie & Friends (Author Anthology, Print Only)

THE ISLE SERIES
The Isle of... Where?
Isle of Wishes
Isle of Waves

MORNING REPORT
Morning Report
Complete Faith
Papa's Boy
Luke's Present
Letters From a Cowboy
Letters From a Cowboy (Author Anthology, Print Only)

Published by DREAMSPINNER PRESS
http://www.dreamspinnerpress.com

FRANKIE
& FRIENDS

SUE BROWN

Published by
DREAMSPINNER PRESS

5032 Capital Circle SW, Suite 2, PMB# 279, Tallahassee, FL 32305-7886 USA
www.dreamspinnerpress.com/

Frankie & Friends
© 2015 Sue Brown.

Cover Art
© 2015 Paul Richmond.
http://paulrichmondstudio.com
Cover Photo by DWS Photography.
cerberuspic@gmail.com
Cover content is for illustrative purposes only and any person depicted on the cover is a model.

Frankie & Al Cover Art © 2014 Cover photo by DWS Photography,
cerberuspic@gmail.com. Cover design by Paul Richmond.
Ed & Marchant Cover Art © 2014 Paul Richmond. http://www.paulrichmondstudio.com
Anthony & Leo Cover Art © 2015 Cover photo by Ethan James Photography,
ethanjamesphotography.com. Cover design by Paul Richmond.

ISBN: 978-1-63476-489-6
Library of Congress Control Number: 2015911861
First Edition September 2015

Printed in the United States of America
∞
This paper meets the requirements of
ANSI/NISO Z39.48-1992 (Permanence of Paper).

Table of Contents

Frankie & Al 1

Ed & Marchant 97

Anthony & Leo 195

FRANKIE & AL

SUE BROWN

To Lisa Worrall and S.A. Meade: friends, talented authors, my shoulders to cry on, and the girls who keep me sane.
I love you.

Prologue

FRANKIE MASON got dumped two days into a holiday with his friends. He stared at the text his boyfriend had sent him, trying to make sense of the words.

We're over. Don't come back. Your gear is at your mums.

Jonno flopped down beside him on the sunbed and stretched out luxuriously. "Hey, party pooper, why aren't you dancing?"

Frankie stared at the guys dancing on the makeshift dance floor on the beach and then back at the phone. The words hadn't changed. "Chaz dumped me."

"What the fuck?" Jonno frowned and snatched the phone out of Frankie's hand. He squinted at the screen. "Bitch! What are you going to do?"

"What can I do?" Frankie swallowed against the sudden lump in his throat. "It's his house. I was just his boyfriend. I didn't even pay rent."

"Key his car," Jonno said promptly. "You always said he loved that more than you. Or cut up his clothes. Or post pictures of his wiener on Tumblr."

"I'm going to regret ever showing you those photos."

"The bloke's built like a chipolata. How could you not show the world?" Jonno rubbed Frankie's back soothingly. "Fuck, babe, where're you gonna stay?"

"Not with my mum, that's for sure. We'd kill each other within a day." Frankie laid his head on Jonno's shoulder. "Can I stay with you?"

Jonno hesitated. "You know I'd have you like a shot, but Will…."

"Doesn't like me."

"It's not that he doesn't like you." Jonno was crap at lying. "He was just…."

"Forget it. I'll stay at a hotel." Frankie sat up, scrubbing at his eyes. What he wanted to do, what he was going to do in the next ten minutes, was step into a shower and bawl his eyes out. He'd not seen this coming. He loved Chaz and he'd thought Chaz loved him. Why the fuck had his boyfriend dumped him? The bastard owed him an explanation.

He texted Chaz and then wished he hadn't when the answer flashed up ten seconds later.

Found a younger model.

"Fuck it. I may be nearly thirty but I'm not too old to have some fun." Frankie got to his feet and pulled Jonno up with him. "Come and dance."

Jonno kissed him on the mouth, smearing cherry lip gloss across Frankie's lips. "That's more like it." He slapped Frankie on the arse and ran onto the dance floor, dragging his friend behind him.

Frankie plastered a fake smile on his face and ripped off his T-shirt. He had a body worth showing off, and now he was young, free, and single. Well, one of those three. He wasn't free to anyone.

He danced until his feet hurt more than his heart, grinding against Jonno, dancing with anyone who approached, but he ignored all the offers and the cards stuffed into his pockets. Tomorrow maybe he'd look at the meat, but today the twink who was too old closed his eyes and let the music take him.

AFTER JONNO dragged him to the bar and made him down shot after shot, Frankie's pain dulled and his world was woozy. He stumbled along the corridor of the hotel, squinting as he tried to focus on the room numbers. He wasn't even convinced he was on the right floor. Jonno, the bitch, had deserted him to go to another club. He'd tried to persuade Frankie to go, but Frankie knew his limits.

"Room 245, room 254," Frankie muttered.

"Which one is it?"

Frankie tried to focus on the man standing next to him. It wasn't easy. The man kept swaying. "Stand still," he ordered.

"Christ, you really are drunk, aren't you? I am standing still. You're the one doing the swaying."

Frankie shook his head and then wished he hadn't. "Gonna hurl." He heard the man groan.

"Why is it always me? Hold on for two minutes. Give me your keycard."

After that, Frankie's whole focus became not humiliating himself in front of a complete stranger. By some miracle, the first door the stranger tried was the right one, although Frankie still wasn't sure of the number.

He was pushed into the bathroom, and what followed was the worst fifteen minutes of his life—since the last time.

To his surprise, once he'd got his stomach under control, he realized that the man hadn't left. He sat on the floor next to Frankie, his hand on Frankie's back.

When the retching ceased enough for Frankie sit back, the man offered him a drink of water. "Sip it slowly," he warned.

Frankie used it to clear his mouth and then sipped it, feeling his stomach rebel at even the small amount of liquid.

"Feeling better?"

"Much." Frankie wiped his mouth. He squinted at his savior. "Thanks."

"I suppose there's no point me saying you shouldn't binge-drink."

Frankie groaned. "You're not a teetotaler, are you?"

"Would it be an issue if I was?"

"It is if you're going to give me a lecture." Frankie was so not in a mood for a fucking lecture.

"Bad day?" The man sounded more sympathetic at least.

"Yeah." The worst fucking kind of day.

"Have you finished puking?"

"I think so." Frankie would reserve judgment until he stood up.

"Come on. You don't want to spend the night here." The man helped Frankie to his feet and led him into the bedroom. "Lie down on the bed." He pushed Frankie onto the bed and removed his shoes. "Here, I'll leave the bin next to you in case you feel sick again. And more water."

Frankie curled into a ball and wished he could die. "Thank you," he whispered.

"You're welcome." Frankie felt a ghost of a caress over his hair. "Go to sleep."

Obediently Frankie closed his eyes, wishing he could ask the stranger to stay and hold his hand.

But you don't ask strangers to hold your hand while you fall asleep, and as he heard the door close behind his Good Samaritan, Frankie let the tears fall.

Chapter 1

ONE OF the joys of working in a large insurance company was that Frankie had a Monday-to-Friday job processing new insurance policies. He waved good-bye at five o'clock Friday evening and didn't have to think about work or his colleagues until eight thirty Monday morning.

Until the day Frankie opened the e-mail from Human Resources. "You've got to be fucking kidding me."

Charlotte looked over from her desk. "What?"

"They're sending me on a team-building exercise." He didn't appreciate Charlotte's chuckle. "*Winning Ways*? What the fuck is that?"

"You've been caught. They get us all in the end. You get to spend the weekend in a swanky hotel, building egg wombs and sucking up to managers. Don't sweat it. You'll enjoy it."

"Don't bank on it," he muttered. "Wait, egg what?"

"Egg wombs. You know." At Frankie's frown, she said, "You have to drop the egg out of a window without it cracking, using only a plastic bag and a cup."

"Is that what they really call it?"

She shrugged. "Who knows? That's what you've got to do. And the sucking up to the managers. They give you the 'We're all equal here. Call me Jeff' speech but you know they're just spying on everything you do."

It was Frankie's recurring nightmare—to be stuck in a small room with his colleagues and not be able to get away. He got that five days a week but at the weekend as well? "Karma's a bitch."

"What have you done?"

"Do you want the list?"

"You've been that bad?"

"Probably worse," he admitted.

She smirked at him. "Frankie's been a bad, bad boy, and now he is going to get his bottom spanked?"

"I wouldn't mind if it was *that* sort of weekend." Frankie grinned as Charlotte's cheeks crimsoned. "Gotcha!"

"You're wicked," she said. "My mother warned me about boys like you."

"My mother warned me about boys like me too. They sounded much more fun than the good, church-going boys she wanted me to meet."

She gave him an odd look. "She knew you were gay back then?"

He rolled his eyes. "Girl, look at me. Could anyone not realize I'm gay?"

"You have a point."

Frankie's mum said it was obvious he was gay from the moment he came out of the womb. According to her description, Frankie flounced out to the song on the radio. Frankie thought that being born to Kylie must have been prophetic. It could have been worse—he might have been born to Meat Loaf.

"When are you going on the exercise?"

Frankie scanned the e-mail. "Next month. They've got a dropout and they want me to fill in."

"Can you go?"

Frankie shrugged. "It's not like my calendar is full or anything." It would give him something to do. Since Chaz had thrown him out, his social life consisted of clubbing with Jonno or staring at the walls in his tiny flat, eating ready meals he could ill afford and wishing he had Sky TV instead of Freeview. "It might be fun."

She gave him a dubious look. "Your life really is boring at the moment, isn't it?"

"You have no idea."

"Why don't you come out with me and the girls? We're going to try that new club in town."

"Uh, gay, remember?"

"Uh, gay club, remember?"

He frowned. "There's a new gay club in town? In this dump of a town?"

"God, Frankie, you really are out of it. It opened a couple of weeks ago. It's near Primark, over the slappers' shop."

"I didn't know. Anyway, why're you going to a gay club?"

"Ignorance is no excuse, and I'm going to a gay club because most of my mates are dykes and the rest of us are married. It suits us fine not to be hit on by sleazebags. Anyway, the booze is cheaper and the music's better."

"How did you end up with lesbians for friends?"

Charlotte grinned at him. "Some of us aren't narrow-minded little pricks like some people I could mention."

"You mean...."

"Uh-huh."

She did a dramatic head roll to their manager who sat not ten feet away, oblivious to their conversation. Ed Winters was a 1950s Tory poster boy. He disliked women, black people, anyone from the Indian subcontinent, curry, the French, the Irish, dogs, and particularly *hom-o-sex-uals*—he always enunciated the word as if a bad smell was under his nose.

Frankie grinned at her. Taking the piss out of Ed was one of the few joys in his life. "I'm on for the club. You say where and when."

Maybe he needed a change from the scene with Jonno. Those clubs were hook-up sites, and much as he needed action, he needed fun. God, he *really* needed some fun.

"Done. Don't worry. I'll make sure the straight girls don't treat you like their pet poodle for the evening."

He shrugged. "They can be my bitches."

"They'll love it. Do you want to bring the leashes?"

"I worry about you sometimes."

Charlotte tossed her hair. "You love it."

"Hell yeah!"

"Mr. Mason, Ms. Tiller, is something wrong?" Winters peered over his frameless glasses to stare at them.

They shook their heads and smirked at each other when he scowled and turned away.

Frankie looked at the files on his desk, and the e-mail telling him he had to play nice for a weekend. Charlotte was one bright sparkle in a sea of beige and gray. He pecked disconsolately at the keyboard. "Okay, I've confirmed my attendance at the egg womb thing. Now you take me out."

Charlotte looked up from her phone. "Friday? The girls can't wait to meet you."

Frankie nodded. "I'm all yours."

"Ah baby, if only that were true." Charlotte blew him a kiss and turned her attention back to her own work.

Hmmm, a new club, potential new meat. Frankie needed something new to wear. He might be short of cash, but he could work that budget. Frankie rocked at the vintage look.

THE FOUR girls whistled when they met Frankie outside Primark. He twirled for them, shimmying his arse for a show. He was wearing black: tight, tight black, the shirt displaying every asset he owned.

"Very nice, Frankie." Charlotte kissed his cheek and slapped his denim-covered arse.

"Hey!" He rubbed his buttcheek and glared at her.

"It's such a nice arse, sweetheart." She slapped it again before hooking her arm through his and leading him to the club.

A petite redhead fell into position on his other side. "Hi, Frankie, I'm Joan."

He grinned at her, awkwardly shaking her hand with his left as Charlotte had a death grip on his right. "Hey, Joan."

"That's Tina, Jane, and Lindsay," she said, pointing at the others. "Jane's my girlfriend, and Tina's married to Lindsay's brother."

Joan and Jane? Frankie knew he'd never remember who was who, but he smiled at everyone.

"Julie and the gang are going to meet us in the club," Charlotte said. "I hope you've got your dancing shoes on because we are going to par-ar-tay!"

She wiggled her behind, and the girls cheered her on. Frankie grinned, feeling lighter for the first time since he'd received the text from Chaz. There was no pressure to hook up or do anything except dance 'til his feet ached and his body craved a bacon sandwich.

"Did you say bacon sandwich?" Charlotte looked confused.

"Did I speak out loud?" At her nod, Frankie said, "Post clubbing I want a bacon butty."

"I thought you preferred sausage," Jane said, a wicked smirk on her face.

The girls cackled as he poked his tongue out. "Tonight bacon trumps sausage."

"I'll go with that," Lindsay said. "Bacon sandwiches and cups of tea at Greasy Joe's after the club."

"The best bacon butties ever," Joan said reverentially.

Frankie moaned just a little. This was going to be an awesome night.

QUEENS, DYKES, pretty gay boys—the new club was a real mixture. Frankie spotted one or two straight men looking like deer caught in headlights, but at the door the bouncers had been turning away large groups of straight girls and their boyfriends. He felt comfortable here; it was a place to have a good time rather than hook up. The club was heaving, and Frankie felt the sweat beading on his forehead within minutes of arriving. He didn't care because almost as soon as they'd hit the dance floor the girls had him arms-up and grinding his hips to "Dancing Queen." He really hoped they were going to get past the seventies classics. Still, the night was young.

The girls were up for everything, and they didn't let Frankie leave the dance floor until he threatened to pass out from dehydration.

"Make sure you come back," Charlotte said when he pleaded to be allowed to get a drink.

"Promise ya," Frankie stumbled off to get a drink from the bar. Christ, he thought he had stamina, but the girls hadn't stopped dancing the entire night and they were all wearing heels that could do serious damage.

The bar was packed, and Frankie wasn't tall. He waited in the scrum until it was his turn to be served and then beamed at the barman, who was short, blond, and really cute.

"Two bottles of water," Frankie said.

The barman blinked. "Still or sparkling?"

"Still, please."

Frankie admired the guy's arse as he bent to get the bottles from the chiller. Cute *and* a nice butt! Not Frankie's usual type, but never let it be said he wasn't flexible... except for women—he wasn't that flexible.

"I get off at three," the barman said, obviously reading Frankie's admiration.

Frankie licked his lips, pleased to see the barman's eyes tracking the action. "See you then."

"Mark, if you've finished flirting with the customers...." A woman dressed in the club's uniform leaned across him to serve another customer.

"Yeah, sorry, Sarah." Mark smiled at Frankie. "Later."

Frankie nodded and backed away. Later sounded good enough for him.

He chugged back an entire bottle of water to slake his thirst, then followed up with half of the second.

"There you are," Charlotte said. "I thought you'd escaped."

Frankie smirked at her. "Cute barman."

"Name?"

"Mark."

"Vitals?"

"'Bout my height, big eyes, probably blue, and a tight arse that's waiting for me to plough it."

Her eyes widened. "You top?"

"Don't sound so surprised. It's been known to happen."

Charlotte plucked the water bottle out of his hand and downed the rest of it, ignoring his outraged "What the fuck?" When she'd finished, she wiped her mouth and looked at him. "Thought we were going for breakfast after the clubbing."

Frankie leaned forward to kiss her on the cheek. "Babe, we'll have breakfast."

"Are you bringing him with us?"

Frankie shrugged. "We'll see. Leave the details to me. Now let's get back to the dancing."

She whooped and dragged him back on the floor. The music changed to George Michael.

"Jesus, get in this century already," Frankie yelled.

Jane shimmied against him. "He's a classic."

"That's one way to describe him," Frankie agreed. He could think of others.

MARK'S MOUTH tasted of mint as Frankie explored it, pressing Mark against the door so that he controlled the kiss. That was odd in itself. He was usually more than happy to be in Mark's position, but this time… damn, the blond made him hot and horny.

Frankie had presented the problem to the barman during the evening. He wanted to fuck Mark, and he wanted to have breakfast with his friends. Mark was welcome to be present at both.

Mark had taken a long time to reply, and Frankie was sure he was going to say no. Then he'd looked at Frankie. "My break's in ten minutes. Maybe breakfast another time?"

So yeah, hot and horny and in a store cupboard. Frankie roamed under Mark's shirt, pinching his nipples and making him groan loudly.

"I haven't got long," Mark said, but as he worried a hickey onto Frankie's neck, he obviously wasn't that bothered.

"Wanna fuck you," Frankie said.

"Condoms?"

Frankie held up a foil packet.

Mark turned around and pushed his trousers around his thighs. Then he slapped his hands flat on the wall.

Okay, then. They were short of time, so Frankie didn't waste a second, rolling on the condom and lubing Mark's arsehole, grunting as it closed like a vise around his fingers. Damn, he was tight.

"Relax," Frankie whispered in his ear.

"Trying." Mark sounded strained.

Frankie wasn't going to hurt the kid, and he took a few minutes gently preparing him until the blood supply was flowing to his fingers and Mark was panting, his head down between his shoulders.

Mark turned his head. "Get a move on."

Sound advice that Frankie was happy to take. He lined up his cock and pressed in, still taking his time for Mark's body to adjust. When Mark was obviously ready, Frankie pumped his hips several times, drawing a groan from him.

Frankie held on to Mark's hips, changing position to peg his prostate, and grinned when Mark yelled. He set up a rhythm, thrusting hard enough that his balls slapped against Mark's, and Mark was reduced to grunts and moans. As Frankie's balls tightened, he leant against Mark's body and wrapped his hand around his leaking cock. Three more thrusts and come shot over his fingers and splattered the floor. Frankie hammered into Mark's arse, pulsing into the condom as he climaxed.

He could feel the sweat prickling his chest as he rested against Mark's back.

"Fuck," Mark said.

Frankie frowned and pulled back, slipping out of Mark's body. The barman hissed at the movement. "You okay?" Frankie asked.

"Due back at work five minutes ago." Mark pulled his trousers around his hips. "Boss'll kill me. Gotta go."

Before Frankie could decide if he was meant to apologize or even pull up his jeans, Mark was out of the door. Frankie stared after him, then pulled off the condom and headed for the gents.

Charlotte gave him a knowing look when he returned.

"What?" Frankie asked.

"Hooked up with your little barman?"

"Yeah. Then he ran back to work."

"Aw, baby, no spark?"

Frankie shrugged. "I've had better. Dance with me, girl." He wrapped his arm around her waist and dragged her onto the dance floor. The music was from a decade ago. At least they'd made it into the twenty-first century.

JANE STARED at Frankie openmouthed. "How can you shovel that much food into your mouth? Don't answer that until you've chewed!"

"Frankie's got a huge gob," Charlotte said.

Frankie chewed obediently because Jane was scary. Charlotte, he would have just sprayed with crumbs. "It's a gift," he said and took another huge mouthful.

"Ugh!" Jane pulled a face. "You like this man?"

Charlotte grinned at Frankie. "I love this man. He makes my day at work bearable."

"Ditto." Frankie loved her and her husband, David. "Otherwise I'd have to put up with Edward Shitbag all by myself."

"You'd have killed him by now," Charlotte said.

"Fucking right I would. That man deserves to be hanged by his own polyester tie."

"He can't be that bad," Jane protested. She was cuddled next to Joan, quiet and sleepy. Tina and Lindsay had gone home after the club, protesting their exhaustion.

"This is the man that believes all lesbians haven't been porked by the right man," Frankie said.

"Kill the bastard painfully," Jane said flatly.

He grinned at her.

Charlotte moaned as she put the last of her sandwich in her mouth.

"Good?" Frankie asked.

"The best. Breakfast at Greasy Joe's in the morning with my favorite people. What could be better?"

"I'll remind David you said that," Joan said.

"*Most* of my favorite people." Charlotte licked her fingers. "He is my soul mate."

"Aw, isn't that sickening." Frankie pretended to gag.

"Just because you haven't found your soul mate, you don't have to knock mine."

"You really believe in soul mates?"

"You don't?" Joan asked.

Frankie looked at the couple, huddled as close as they could in public, and Charlotte, who adored her husband passionately. "Maybe for some people, sweetness, but not for me."

"Why not?"

"Because guys like me have fun and sex, not cuddles on the sofa and walks with the dog on the common. We don't get the beige life." Frankie had seen heteronormative life described in a book as "beige," and he liked that description. So many of his straight friends seemed happy to settle for dull and boring.

"You don't get it or don't want it?" Jane asked.

None of the girls seemed offended by his rejection of their lives.

"I…." Frankie had to think for a moment. "I don't want it."

Charlotte nodded. "You never want to settle down?"

He shook his head. "Not me. I just want to have fun, you know?"

"I know, sweetie," Charlotte patted his arm. "But at some point even that gets old and the sofa looks real comfortable."

Frankie didn't need reminding that he was too old to be a twink. He beamed at the girls. "I'm going home to get my beauty sleep. I'll see you on Monday."

"What are you doing this weekend?" Charlotte asked. "We've got a barbeque if you want to come."

Frankie tried to think of a way of declining without saying he'd rather gouge his eyes out with a red-hot poker. A couple of hours in the company of happy couples and their brats was his idea of hell.

Charlotte burst out laughing. "Frankie, if you could see your face! Don't worry, I won't be upset if you stay at home and count your ingrowing hairs."

"I don't have any ingrowing hairs," he said, thoroughly offended.

"Course you don't. See you on Monday."

Frankie kissed them on the cheek and headed for the door. Dawn had arrived with a pale pink-and-blue sky, and thankfully no rain. He decided to walk home, relaxed and full, and ready to sleep. At this time of the morning, he could cut off a few minutes by walking through the station concourse without negotiating hundreds of tourists.

He stepped off the curb, and after that, he wasn't sure what happened except his world spun crazily out of control. He heard the sound of a car horn, and Frankie was thrown off his feet, only to land on the ground, an excruciating pain in his hip.

What the fuck?

"He just stepped out in front of me. You saw that, didn't you? He didn't look at all. He was probably after a score."

Frankie opened his eyes and glared at the man standing over him. "Thanks for your concern, arsehole, but I'm not a druggie. Give me your phone number, address, and insurance details," he said brusquely. At least, he aimed for brusque rather than weak and feeble.

The man sniffed and vanished out of sight. Frankie contemplated getting up. On the other hand, the ground was comfortable and he had nowhere to be.

"An ambulance is on its way. You have a habit of getting into trouble, don't you?"

Frankie turned his head to deny the charge and was fixed by the most beautiful green eyes he had ever seen. "Take me home," he said and was rewarded with a smile from the man.

"Huh, a faggot. Might have known."

The driver was really getting on Frankie's nerves. "Give me the details, and then you can get lost."

A hand squeezed Frankie's, and Green Eyes said, "Give *me* the details. You can talk to the police and I'll look after my boy here, before he gets into any more trouble."

"Frankie," Frankie said.

"What?"

"My name's Frankie." Frankie gave a melting smile to the nice man with dark hair and gorgeous green eyes. Then he glared at the driver. "That's Mr. Lawsuit to you."

"Listen, you little—"

Green Eyes sighed. "How the hell did you manage to get to adulthood, Frankie? The ambulance is here, thank God."

Frankie was really pleased because fuck knows the pain in his hip was hurting like a bitch, and no one seemed to give a shit about him, and his mum would wash his mouth out with soap and water if he kept swearing, and....

His brain shut off as Green Eyes kissed him.

"What the...?" he said faintly.

"You were talking again, Frankie. It seemed the best way to shut you up."

Frankie was about to ask if he could do it again when they were interrupted by a woman wearing a green monstrosity. Seriously, couldn't they find anyone to design better uniforms than this boiler suit?

"What's happened here?" she asked perkily.

Oh great, a perky girl. Even her ponytail swung in a perky fashion. Frankie hated her on sight.

"Frankie got hit by the car. He's been conscious all the time."

The girl smiled at Frankie. "How are you feeling, Frankie?"

He rolled his eyes. "How do you think I feel? Like I've been hit by a fucking car."

Her smile didn't fade, but Green Eyes said, "*I'll* wash your mouth out with soap if you don't start being nice to the lady."

"You could always spank my arse," Frankie suggested hopefully.

"You'll have to spank your boyfriend later," the paramedic said. "We need to get him to hospital."

"He's not my boyfriend," Green Eyes said. "I was on my way to meet my mum and I saw the incident."

"Ah, sorry. I thought I saw you kissing him."

"You did. It's a remarkably good way of shutting him up."

"It only works with hot men," Frankie said hastily in case the paramedic got any ideas.

"Understood," she said with a completely straight face and then ruined it by grinning at him. "Way to go to pick up a guy."

She held out a hand for a high five. Frankie tried hard to respond, but the pain was making it difficult for him to move.

The paramedic frowned. "Where does it hurt, Frankie?"

"Everywhere." Frankie swallowed back the rising nausea. "I feel like shit."

She was all professional now, feeling down his body. "We're going to get you to hospital now."

Frankie tried to nod, but she stayed the action. "Just stay still and let us move you. We're going to put a collar on you so don't move."

Green Eyes loomed over him. "I've got to meet my mum, Frankie, or I'm in trouble. I'll leave you with the ladies." He bent down and brushed Frankie's mouth with his. "My mum is seriously ill, or there is nothing that would keep me from coming with you. I'll see you again. This is the second time, and things like this always run in threes. Try not to drink so much next time."

Frankie frowned. The second time? Next time? What the hell was he talking about? What was his telephone number? But he didn't get a chance to ask as he was loaded into an ambulance. The doors closed on hot Green Eyes, and Frankie was left with Ms. Perky Green Boiler Suit.

Someone up there had a sick sense of humor.

Chapter 2

FRANKIE'S WEEKEND sucked huge fucking lime-green donkey balls. He spent five hours in Accident & Emergency to find he was bruised, battered, and hurting like hell, but had no broken bones and no concussion. In other words....

"You were very lucky," the doctor said as he agreed Frankie could be released from living hell. Frankie and hospitals did not make a good combo.

Frankie didn't feel lucky. Frankie felt like living shit. He said as much.

"You could be dead," the doctor pointed out unsympathetically. "Go home and rest. Next time stop drinking so much and look where you're going."

"I don't drink that much," Frankie protested.

The doctor gave him *that* look, and immediately Frankie felt twelve years old again, when his father had caught him and Jonno smoking behind the shed. He'd just been damn lucky his father hadn't caught them ten minutes earlier. He and Jonno were early starters in everything.

Frankie called a taxi and limped up the stairs to his manky flat, his hip aching with each step. He collapsed on his bed and closed his eyes, too damned tired and hungover to get undressed.

He woke up around 10:00 p.m. in the same position, his hip still hurting like a bitch, his mouth feeling like a mouse had crawled in and died there while he was asleep. His stomach rumbled loudly.

For a moment he contemplated calling his mother and asking her to come over, but firstly, his mother lived five hours away, and secondly, his mother? That would be like asking a heavyweight boxer to babysit a little bunny. Not that Frankie was a bunny, except in the sack, but the thought of his mother caring for him.... He really needed an alternative.

Jonno.

Moving swiftly on....

Charlotte? The poor girl was stuck with him all week. She and David deserved their weekend of rest.

That left no one, not one solitary person to look after Frankie Mason. A tear rolled down his cheek. He was alone and no one gave a damn about him.

Unbidden, a pair of green eyes popped into his mind.

"Where the hell are you when I need you?"

Eventually Frankie managed to roll off his bed. He took care of bodily needs and the mouse in his mouth. Once he'd scrubbed his teeth and tongue, he contemplated a shower because he was still covered in grit from the road. He undid the buttons on his tattered shirt, dropped it into the bin, and pushed down his jeans, yelping as he brushed his hip.

Fuck! His hip and thigh looked like a map for the tube, multicolored and completely incomprehensible. He winced as he touched the swollen flesh.

"Not so gorgeous now, are you, doll?"

Frankie took a deep breath, slammed on his radio that he had in the bathroom, and held on tightly as he got into the shower in case he slipped. Was this what it was like to be old? Because it sucked balls.

The water stung his cuts and scrapes, but by the time he'd finished, Frankie felt like a new man, if not up to feeling a new man. He gave up on the idea of getting dressed and wrapped up in his dressing gown.

While he was in the shower, he'd missed a call from Jonno, and so he sent him a text saying he wouldn't be at the club. His phone rang immediately.

"Why not, bitch?"

"Collision with a car."

"Do what?"

Frankie sighed. "I got knocked down by a car this morning and spent the day in hospital. I can't come out to play because I can barely move."

"Girl!" At least Jonno sounded concerned. It was more than Frankie had expected. "Can't you just, like, stand or something? I need you."

"Jonno, I can't get down the stairs, so no, you'll have to go solo. Or take Will."

"I want to have fun. Why on earth would I take Will?"

"Because he is your husband."

"Now I know you've been hitting too many painkillers. Oh well, have fun doing nothing. *Ciao.*" Jonno disconnected before Frankie could respond.

Frankie snorted and threw his phone onto the sofa. He needed food. He needed soup and ice cream. Frankie opened his kitchen cupboard and contemplated his selection of soup. Frankie did soup like other people did… whatever they did.

He'd tried every brand of soup he could find, and these ones were his favorites. Frankie pursed his lips as he contemplated his selection and his fingers danced over the tins. Mushroom soup, that's what he wanted.

A few minutes later, Frankie curled up on the sofa, sipping at mushroom soup in his "Take it like a man" mug.

His phone beeped.

Breakfast 12 ur bed

He grinned at Jonno's message. Maybe someone liked him just a little.

FRANKIE FELL asleep on the sofa and later woke in agony, his muscles frozen in place as he tried to move. Each movement was so painful he could only let out a string of expletives. "Jesus shit, Jesus fuck!"

"You're awake, good. Eggs?" Jonno poked his head around the kitchen door.

Frankie's jaw dropped. "How the hell did you get in here?"

Jonno rolled his eyes. "Please, you've kept your spare key in the same place since you left home."

"I haven't."

"How did I get in, then?"

The evidence was irrefutable, and Frankie shut up.

Jonno came in with two mugs, handing one to Frankie. "Coffee a la Jonno."

Frankie stared at the contents suspiciously. "What's in it?"

"A pick-me-up."

"I'm on enough pills. I don't need any more."

"Brandy, you turkey, not drugs."

Frankie contemplated the coffee. It smelled divine. He could dump the coffee or take the pills. He decided to drink the coffee and take the pills later. "I thought you were coming here later."

"I said midday. It's two now."

"Bloody hell, is it?" Frankie looked at the clock on his phone. "I've been asleep since eleven last night." He tried to move again. It was no less painful, but at least this time his joints and muscles tried to cooperate. "I think I've been hit by a truck."

"What did hit you?"

Frankie shook his head. "I've no idea. The driver was a prick, though. If it hadn't been for Mr. Green Eyes—"

"Mr. Who?"

Frankie shut his mouth.

Jonno arched a perfectly plucked eyebrow. "Francis Daniel Mason, who is Mr. Green Eyes?"

"I don't know," Frankie muttered.

"What do you mean you don't know? Where did you meet him? I thought you were going out with the girls."

"I did go out with the girls," Frankie said hastily hoping to avert a Jonno sulk. "He looked after me when I got knocked over."

"Tell me more."

"There isn't much more I can tell you. He kissed me—"

"Wait, you were bleeding on the road and he molests you?"

"He was trying to shut me up."

Jonno shook his head. "You pick 'em, Frankie. Scrambled eggs?"

"Granary bread?"

"And smoked salmon."

Frankie sighed happily. Jonno knew how to look after him.

He was almost through his breakfast when Jonno raised the subject again.

"So when are you going to see Mr. Can't Keep His Lips to Himself again?"

Frankie shrugged and then wished he hadn't because it hurt like hell. "Can't talk to him. No phone number."

"You didn't get his details? You're slipping, Frankie."

"I'd just been knocked over."

"No excuse. Now how are you going to see him again?"

Frankie opened his mouth to tell him about Green Eyes's weird comments as he was loaded into the ambulance, and then he hesitated. It had been such an odd thing to say, and he hadn't had time to process it. "It's in the hands of the gods," he said eventually.

Jonno snorted. "You don't half talk bollocks, mate."

"At least I don't talk like a reject from *EastEnders*."

"Touché." Jonno got to his feet and took Frankie's plate. "More food?"

Frankie shook his head. "I think I'm just going to sleep—in my bed this time. Thanks for breakfast."

"Better we do this in the office. Now, please," she said briskly.

Frankie looked over at Ed, who was looking smug. "Fine."

He stood up, smiling reassuringly at Charlotte. "HR want to see me."

"What the hell for?"

"Probably to give me a bollocking for not coming in."

"You were run over, for Christ's sake." She stood up. "I'm coming with you."

"It's okay. I'll call you if I need backup." Frankie limped away, praying the lifts were working.

By the time he reached HR on the fifth floor, Frankie had to swallow hard not to puke on their nice faux-oak desks. He knocked on Jenny's door, waiting for her call.

Her professional smile faded as she looked at him, and she rushed around the desk to help him into a seat, more comfy than the one at his desk. "Sweet Jesus, what the hell happened to you?"

"I got hit by a car at the weekend." He frowned. "You didn't know that?"

"Winters said you'd taken time off without giving a reason." Jenny sat down again behind her desk. "Did you tell him what happened?"

"Of course I did, and he only had to ask Charlotte."

"He asked that you be given a formal warning about your behavior."

Frankie pressed his lips together, because if he spoke, the words were going to involve lots of swearwords, and Jenny was a lady.

"Fucking bastard!" she exclaimed.

Frankie revised his opinion of her ladylike status.

"What happened? Wait, coffee or tea?" Jenny picked up the phone. "Tina, can you get me a tea and—" She looked at Frankie, who mouthed "tea." "—another tea as well."

Frankie waited until she'd put the phone down before he said, "Thank you."

"No worries. Now tell me what happened."

"I stepped off the curb without looking and got hit by a car. No broken bones, but my hip was badly bruised."

She looked at him shrewdly. "Is that code for 'I want to cry like a little girl every time I walk'?"

"Something like that. I won't be running any marathons this week."

"And Winters knew this?"

Frankie nodded. "I told him on Monday. What's the problem, Jenny? Don't you believe me? I'll show you the injuries, if you want." Did he want to shuck his trousers in the middle of the office? No. If it would stop this shitfest? Yeah, hell, he would.

"I bet you've taken pictures of it already," Jenny said thoughtfully.

"I can show you if you want." He handed his phone over as Tina, Jenny's secretary, walked in with the tea.

"Jesus, Frankie." She tapped on the screen to bring up more photos. Frankie prayed she couldn't see the ones of him and Jonno at last month's party.

"Send these to me and nothing more will be said. At least not to you."

Jenny tilted the phone to get a better look, then handed it to Tina, who smirked at Frankie.

"Nice present."

Frankie sighed as he took his tea. He'd been tied up with a big rainbow ribbon as a present for someone, stark-bollock-naked aside from a large bow. Oh well, two hundred guests had seen him too. What was two more?

Tina leant closer to the screen. Jeez, he wasn't *that* small. She tapped the phone. "Is that why you are limping? It looked like you took a huge knock."

"I got knocked down by a car at the weekend."

"Should you be here?"

Frankie sighed. It was going to be a long, long day.

Jenny shook her head. "No, he shouldn't. Go home, Frankie. Tina will call you a cab. I don't want to see you until you can jump from a cake again. Get a doctor's note if you have to."

"I'm fine to work, really."

"Uh-huh." Tina rolled her eyes. "Sure you are. Nice bow, by the way. Very nice."

Frankie blushed.

Chapter 3

BY THE time Frankie returned to work, he was going (had gone) stir-crazy. He'd counted the cracks in his bedroom ceiling, shouted at every stupid, crying girl on *Britain's Next Top Model*, watched all of *Supernatural* to see the rare glimpses of the guys with their shirts off, eaten enough Ben & Jerry's to make himself sick, and decided he needed an entire new wardrobe for Womb Weekend, as he was now calling the team-building event. He was that bored; he'd watched an entire documentary on tie-dyeing and was seriously considering jazzing up his wardrobe in fetching shades of cerise pink and sunset orange. Just in time, he'd realized he was gay, not desperate.

The only piece of good news was that Ed Winters had been severely bollocked for his behavior over Frankie's accident. Frankie wasn't meant to know this, of course. He'd heard it from Charlotte, who had been told by Tina as they repaired lipstick in the ladies' loo. Frankie had grinned in satisfaction at the news. The downside was that Winters was going to hate him even more, but on the upside, HR knew that Winters had it in for Frankie, and maybe they'd keep a tighter leash on him. Frankie spent a few minutes thinking about Ed Winters naked, cuffed, and on the end of a leash. He liked the thought. The guy wasn't bad looking, despite the fact he was a bigoted arsehole and he'd look even better in chains.

"FRANKIE!"

Frankie winced as Charlotte shrieked his name across the office. So much for slipping in unnoticed. He'd returned to work after a week. His hip was still painful, but he could walk without feeling sick and sit for longer than a few minutes without falling asleep.

He smiled at her, pretending to be unaware of the glare aimed in his direction from his manager. "Hey, beautiful. Miss me?"

Charlotte bounced from her seat and pulled Frankie into a huge hug. "You don't know how much. It's been no fun here without you."

"It's been no fun at home. I almost tie-dyed my entire wardrobe."

"There ain't enough dye in the world for that, sweetcheeks."

"Heh." He heard a familiar tut behind him. "Is he watching?"

Charlotte glanced over his shoulder. "Winters? Yep. Eyes like icy daggers our way."

Frankie grunted and made sure he limped pathetically to his seat, Charlotte cooing over him.

Naz, who was part of their team, looked up. "So you're not dead, Frankie."

"Not today, Naz."

"Good. It's been far too quiet around here. Mind you, at least we've been able to work."

Frankie flipped him off and looked at his desk. He sighed. "Has anything been touched since I left?"

"Do you really need an answer?" Charlotte asked.

"No, not really." He sighed and pulled the first batch of files toward him.

"Mr. Mason."

Frankie looked up to see Ed Winters standing by his desk. "Ed, what can I do for you?" he said with all the fake enthusiasm he could manage.

"How is your leg?"

"It's… better, thanks." Frankie was taken aback by the question.

"Good." Winters looked as if he was about to face root-canal work. "I'm pleased to see you back."

Frankie had to give the man credit for doing his best not to look as if he was spouting the biggest lie of his life. He smiled brightly at his boss. "Thank you, Mr. Winters."

Winters's eyes widened, and then he nodded and walked with his back ramrod straight, to his desk.

Charlotte rolled her eyes at Winters behind his back. Frankie just grinned. It was good to be at work.

Even receiving the information for Womb Weekend didn't put a dampener on his day.

"You're going to go insane," Charlotte predicted as she read the itinerary over his shoulder.

"Stark raving bonkers," he agreed. He snorted as he read activity four on the list. "Raft building at nine thirty in the morning. Seriously?" His voice went up a couple of octaves.

Charlotte snorted into her coffee. "Why, Frankie, that'll be just your thing. Don't you just lurve getting up at seven a.m. to eat your porridge and yomp across the fields to the stream to make a raft?"

"I stopped listening after seven."

"Sweetheart, it'll be so good for you. Fostering all that team spirit."

"The only spirit I like is vodka."

"I've got to see pictures. You promise you'll take pictures?"

"Haven't you got work to do?" Frankie asked sourly.

Charlotte kissed him on the cheek and flounced back to her desk still snickering. Frankie looked at the torture they were going to put him through. Perhaps he could claim his injury prevented him from taking part, and then just prop up the hotel bar for the weekend.

He yelped as something hit him squarely on the forehead.

Naz grinned. "Just want you to get into practice for the trebuchet."

"What the fuck is a trebuchet?" It sounded like a fancy bread roll.

"It's a siege engine that hurls projectiles at castle walls. You have to make one."

Bewildered, Frankie stared at him. "Can't I just throw Winters?"

"Once you've built the trebuchet."

"I'm going to find another car to throw myself under," Frankie muttered. There was nothing in the world that was going to make this shit bearable.

JONNO INSISTED on dragging him out to the club the Saturday before Womb Weekend.

Frankie protested that he wasn't physically capable of dancing.

"You can get it up, can't you?" Jonno said.

"Yeah."

"We can go dancing, then. You can just stand there and let them rub against you."

"They have poles for that sort of thing."

"Warm bodies with dicks are much more fun."

Frankie scowled at him. "Do I have a choice?"

"Is the Pope a Catholic?"

Frankie gave in as he always did. Jonno would force him out on his deathbed.

TWO HOURS later, Frankie was regretting his decision. Despite the amount of virtually naked eye candy on the dance floor, nothing could distract him from his hip, which had been steadily aching since he'd arrived.

Jonno had disappeared as soon as they arrived to wrap around a fresh young thing called Gemini. Seriously, who called themselves Gemini? The explanation was even worse. He had a twin. Frankie had rolled his eyes and limped away to find a pillar to lean against in an attempt to take the weight off his feet and have a chance to rub his temples. The thumping bass that Frankie usually lost himself in when he danced was just provoking a headache today.

If this was what getting old was like, it fucking sucked.

"You look like you need a drink."

Frankie looked at the man: fifties, potbelly, comb-over, and reeking of desperation. He smiled as nicely as he could. "No, thanks."

"How about a blowjob?"

"No, thanks. I don't want one."

"Hah, funny," the man said. "Come on, I'll pay."

"Good for you. I'm not for sale. Piss off." Frankie looked away, not expecting the man to grab Frankie's shoulder as if he was going to push him down.

Frankie shrieked as pain shot through his hip. "Take your fucking hand off me."

The man stepped back as if he'd been electrocuted. "What's your bloody problem? You were asking for it."

"By standing still?" Frankie asked incredulously.

"You better get it while you can, sweetheart. I can get younger and prettier than you."

"Then piss off and find one," Frankie spat.

The dick leaned in, and for one moment, Frankie thought he was going to have serious trouble. There was no way he could defend himself at the moment.

"Frankie, there you are. Where did you disappear to?" For the second time in five minutes, a stranger put his hand on Frankie.

Frankie tensed, ready to fight off another unwanted grope, and looked up to see a pair of gorgeous green eyes staring at him. "You!"

A smile curved Green Eyes's mouth. "Who were you expecting?" He looked at the middle-aged guy, who was twitching angrily at being thwarted. "Get lost."

"Who the hell are you?"

"His. Now piss off." Green Eyes turned his back on the man and looked at Frankie. "Isn't that right?"

If Frankie had been remotely aroused, he'd have creamed his jeans on the spot. "That's right," he said, and if he sounded breathless, that's because he was.

Green Eyes looked over his shoulder, and whatever the man had been about to say, he obviously changed his mind and scuttled off.

Frankie sagged with relief. It wasn't that he'd been scared by the guy, but he'd been only too aware of his frailty.

"Are you all right? I heard you cry out." Green Eyes gripped Frankie's biceps.

"He caught me by surprise, that's all."

Green Eyes frowned. "Are you in pain? Should you be here?"

Frankie bit his lip. "Not really. Jonno wanted to go out and I've missed the last two weeks."

"I'm sure Jonno is a big boy. You should be at home."

"What's your name?"

"What?"

"I don't know your name," Frankie said. "I can't keep calling you Green Eyes."

"Al Stoneham. Alan really, but everyone calls me Al. Did you really call me Green Eyes?"

"I was hardly going to call you Blue Eyes, was I?"

"I suppose not. Now, do you want to stay here or shall I take you home?"

Frankie looked around. "Are you with anyone?" Hell, it hadn't occurred to him Al might be with a boyfriend.

"I'll call them later. I'm just here with some friends. Shall we go?"

"I need to find Jonno."

Al looked doubtfully at the heaving, writhing mass of bodies on the dance floor. "I don't think we're going to find him in this crowd."

"I know where he'll be." Frankie placed his weight on his bad leg and stumbled under the sudden pain.

Immediately Al's arm went around him, holding him steady. "We're going to find this Jonno, and then I'm taking you home."

Frankie leaned into Al, swallowing hard against the nausea. "Just give me a minute." He took a few deep breaths until he was ready to walk again. "I'll text Jonno. I just want to sit down."

"Good idea. I'll get you a cab."

Frankie looked up. "Me? Just me? Aren't you coming with me?"

"Do you want me to?"

"I'm not letting you out of my sight for a second time," Frankie declared, his fingers curling into Al's navy shirt.

"Third."

Frankie furrowed his brow. "What?"

Al snorted. "You don't remember, do you?"

"Remember what?"

"I'll take you home and we'll talk. Are you ready to walk?"

Frankie took a deep breath and nodded. Each step was painful, but with Al to hang on to, he could make it—or faint. He wasn't laying bets on either at the moment.

As they were almost at the exit, Jonno appeared with Gemini plastered to his side. "Where are you going, Frankie?"

Frankie stopped and leant against Al, his body a reassuringly solid presence. "It fucking hurts, Jonno."

"Poor Frankie," Gemini cooed. "Do you need a Zimmer frame?"

Frankie scowled.

Ignoring Gemini, Jonno said, "Who's this?"

"Jonno, Al. Al, Jonno."

Jonno glared suspiciously at Al. "Why're you leaving with him? Fuck me, Green Eyes!"

Frankie ducked his head to avoid Al's amused expression.

"It is, isn't it? Is this your guardian angel?" Jonno was all excited, pumping Al's free hand.

"Put him down, Jonno. Yes, it's Green Eyes. Now I've really got to sit down." He wanted to get Al away, not only from Jonno's questions but also from Gemini, who was eyeing him with a distinctly predatory look. Frankie had to resist the urge to stand between Al and Gemini. Al was Frankie's meat.

The twink smirked at him as if he could read Frankie's thoughts. "Let him go, Jonno. You promised me we'd dance." He clung tighter to Jonno, showing off his muscles for Al's benefit, no doubt.

Al, who had kept quiet up to now, smiled at Jonno, ignored Gemini, and looked at Frankie. "Let's go, hmmm?"

"Call me," Jonno yelled as they left.

Frankie made a phone sign and breathed a sigh of relief as they got out into the night air. He paused on the pavement, not sure what Al wanted to do.

"You're leaving early, Frankie."

Frankie looked over to the speaker and grinned when he saw Brian and his boyfriend, Kurt, in the queue to go in. "Hey guys. Yeah, it's too much tonight. My hip hurts."

Kurt frowned at him. "I told you to come and see me." He was a physiotherapist with a private practice.

Frankie made a noncommittal noise. Kurt had made the offer over the phone the previous week, but Frankie had just enough money until payday, and he couldn't afford to see Kurt.

"Call me," Kurt insisted, breaking the line to come over to Frankie and Al. "Don't worry about the bill, Frankie. We can sort it another time. Just make an appointment."

"I'll make sure he does," Al assured him.

Frankie raised an eyebrow at Al. They hadn't even fucked, and the man was already making decisions for him. Al just stared back, and it was Frankie who broke their gaze.

Kurt made a snorting sound, and Frankie was sure he heard him mutter "Whipped."

"Come on, Frankie. We need to get you to bed." Al urged Frankie forward. "We'll call you."

"Make sure you do," Kurt said and jogged back to Brian.

Frankie stopped, ignored Al's noise of frustration. "Is it always going to be like this?"

"Like what?"

"You making decisions for me?"

"Yes."

"What if I don't like it?"

Al's smile made Frankie shiver. He leant and brushed his lips against Frankie's ear. "But you do like it, don't you?"

Frankie swallowed, the sound loud in his ears. "Yeah."

"Well, then." Al pressed a kiss to Frankie's neck, provoking another shiver. "Taxi!"

Frankie blinked at the sudden change as Al hailed a passing black cab and helped Frankie into it.

"Where are we going?" the driver said.

"King Street," Frankie said.

Frankie's home was only a few streets away, but the way his hip was hurting, it was beyond him to walk.

Al sat back and gathered Frankie into his arms. Personal space didn't seem to occur to him. Normally Frankie would be crowded by so much touching. He *should* be crowded. The fact that he wasn't freaked him out.

"Relax," Al said, holding him closer, and Frankie did as he was told, resting against Al's chest, listening to the steady beat of his heart, until the taxi pulled up outside his house.

Frankie was relieved to reach the landing to his flat. He dug into his pocket for his key, then leaned against the doorframe to unlock the door.

"Here." Al plucked the key out of Frankie's hand, opened the door, and stood back to let Frankie limp to the sofa.

Frankie collapsed onto the sofa and closed his eyes. "Fuck me, that's better."

"I don't think you're capable today." Al sat down next to him.

"Sadly, I think you're right. Tomorrow, perhaps."

"I'll leave you to get some sleep."

Frankie opened his eyes in a panic, fumbling for Al's hand. "You're not going?"

"I'm going away tomorrow for a few days. I need to get home to pack my suitcase."

"I don't believe this. You're leaving me again?" Frankie sat up, hissing as pain shot down his leg.

Al pressed him back. He looked as fed up as Frankie. "I know, sweetheart. It's my mum. She's... she's got cancer. It won't be long now, and I'm trying to spend as much time with her as possible."

And didn't that make Frankie feel like a selfish shit?

He wriggled around so that this time he was the one holding Al. "I'm sorry." He kissed the top of Al's head and held him as close as he could.

Al pressed his face against Frankie's chest in a reverse of their position in the taxi. "I am too. She's the best mum ever."

Frankie held him for long moments until Al sat up, his back to Frankie as he collected himself. Frankie rubbed a soothing pattern on Al's back to let him know he wasn't alone. "Do you have time for a coffee before you go?"

"Yeah. I'll make it. You need to rest that leg."

Al turned and smiled, and if the smile was fake, Frankie didn't call him out on it.

"I'll have chamomile tea," Frankie said. "Coffee makes me buzz at this time of night."

"You're a mass of contradictions, you know that?"

"What do you mean?"

"You're a party animal who drinks chamomile tea."

Frankie wasn't sure what to make of that. "I like cuddling on the sofa and long walks in the park too. Oh wait, no, I don't. Yes, I'm a party animal, but I have to sleep sometimes."

"You don't like cuddling on the sofa?" Al's lips twitched, and Frankie suddenly remembered what they'd been doing for the past ten minutes.

"Perhaps I haven't found the right person to snuggle with."

Chaz hadn't been much for snuggling. He'd preferred playing computer games.

"Perhaps not," Al agreed and left him to make the drinks.

Frankie took the opportunity to change into a T-shirt and pajama bottoms, sighing with relief as he stripped off the tight jeans and threw them into the washing basket.

"That's a good view," Al said, coming back into the room as Frankie pulled up the pj's.

Frankie tugged the T-shirt over his head and smiled at Al. He wasn't in the business of false modesty. He knew he had a great body, no matter if he was old.

"Do you need any painkillers?" Al asked.

"They're on a shelf in the bathroom." If Frankie took them now, it would give him a chance to relax before bed.

When Al returned, Frankie said, "When will you be back?"

"End of the week, probably." Al sat next to Frankie. "But I've got to work next weekend."

Frankie pulled a face. "So've I. Bloody Womb Weekend."

"What weekend?"

"Womb Weekend." Frankie explained Charlotte's description of the activities, and Al burst out laughing.

"You're really looking forward to this, aren't you?"

"As opposed to having my balls cut off? Yeah, I suppose so."

Al laughed again, and Frankie openly stared at him, admiring the way his eyes crinkled around the edges and his huge beaming smile.

"Do they know what's about to hit them?"

"I hope not, because I wouldn't want to spoil their fun." Frankie slurped his tea happily at the thought of the people he was going to piss off next weekend. He startled as Al stroked a finger along his jaw. "Hey."

Al took the cup from Frankie's hands, slid onto the floor between Frankie's legs, and cradled his jaw. "Stay still," he ordered. "I want to kiss you, but I don't want you to hurt yourself."

Frankie held his breath as Al paused, tilting his head as he stared at Frankie, as if he was wondering which way to fit their mouths together.

Then Frankie was being kissed, and coherent thought dribbled out his ears.

Frankie had been kissed once or twice in his life. He had been kissed by men who knew what they were doing with their mouths. Chaz had been… average. Al was not average. Al demanded Frankie's full attention.

Frankie gave him his attention and more. Frankie held on to Al and was never letting him go.

"I'VE GOT to go," Al murmured.

He lay beside Frankie on his bed, looking mussed and tousled and, in spite of his words, like he wanted to stay there forever. That was fine with Frankie.

Despite the fact Frankie wanted to rip his hip and leg off his useless body because it was so painful, there was nowhere else he'd rather be.

They hadn't got further than kissing because Al refused to let Frankie move in any way.

"You could give me a blowjob; you could straddle me and stick your dick down my throat. There are endless possibilities," Frankie suggested helpfully.

"You could wait patiently until we have the whole night to make love."

Frankie's heart skipped a beat. Make love? It was too soon for the L word. They hadn't got to the F word, the B word, or the 'it's your turn to drive' word. "I'm just saying—"

Al kissed him.

It wasn't that Frankie minded being kissed, but he realized Al used it to shut him up.

"You can go off someone rapidly," he whined when he got his mouth free.

"Um."

"You're not listening, are you?"

Al didn't respond. His whole attention was focused on Frankie's mouth. For a man who had somewhere else to be, he wasn't in a rush.

Frankie gave up and lifted his face to be kissed again.

Chapter 4

WOMB WEEKEND approached all too rapidly. Frankie's only consolation was that he was physically incapable of doing some of the activities, and propping up the hotel bar was looking more of a possibility.

Jenny from HR had approached him about changing the date for when he was more physically capable of taking part. He'd smiled sweetly at her and suggested that if she changed the date he would do unspeakable things to her person.

"Honey, the only unspeakable thing I can think of you doing is mixing spots with stripes," she drawled.

Frankie shuddered. Just the idea set his Gok Wan–wannabe cells into a frenzied quiver.

She patted his shoulder. "I'll tell them you're walking wounded, and they can decide alternative things for you to do."

"Alternative?" he said suspiciously. "Can't I just... cut up the oranges or something?"

"I'm sure they'll find something suitable."

Jenny's smug expression left Frankie with a nasty feeling in the pit of his stomach. He didn't trust the look on her face as she walked away and was seriously contemplating a case of dodgy prawns when Charlotte returned from wherever she'd been hiding for the last half hour.

She grinned at Frankie. "You look as pale as you did when Naz tried to feed you flies."

"They were crickets, you daft cow," Naz called out without looking up.

Charlotte waved her hand in a dismissive gesture. "Flies, crickets, what's the difference?"

"Several billion years on the evolutionary ladder," Naz said.

"Whatever. Anyway, what's the matter, dumpling?" she said to Frankie.

"Jenny's got plans for my weekend and I don't think I'm going to like them."

Charlotte furrowed her brow. "I thought you were going to Womb Weekend."

"I am, but I can't do the physical elements and so she was thinking of 'alternatives.'" He made it sound like a dirty word.

"Cheer up. You might get to gunk the losers or massage the winners. Oooh, you could oil their legs like they do with cyclists before races, or oil anything else that might need a hand."

Frankie stared at her. "Where does your brain go, Charlotte?"

"I don't know what you mean," she said haughtily. "It's logical to me."

"That's the worrying part."

"Circumvent her," Naz said as he paused to drink something green and revolting, to Frankie's mind, from the glass on his desk.

Frankie frowned at him. "What do you mean?"

"Volunteer to do things before they come up with alternatives. You'll please the bosses and get out of doing something you don't want to do."

Frankie and Charlotte stared at each other.

"This is why Naz will rule the world and we'll still be stuck at these desks," Frankie said.

Charlotte hummed her agreement. "When you're the boss, will you still be friends with us?"

Naz flipped them off. "No chance. If you won't eat my crickets, then you're out of the running for chief brownnose."

"It's just you and me, dumpling," Frankie sang to Charlotte. If he'd been able, he'd have twirled her, just to annoy Ed Winters.

She spun anyway, because she was Charlotte, and launched herself toward her own desk.

"When are you getting to the hotel?" she asked.

"Friday night. The powers that be agreed I could stay an extra night rather than rushing down Saturday morning. I can't drive and I'd have to take a taxi rather than the train. Someone from Accounts was going and they're going to drive me, but they are going Friday." And wasn't that fun? Stuck in a car for two hours with a bean counter.

"You'll have fun," Charlotte said.

"Define fun."

"You never know, you could hook up with some gorgeous guy while you're there."

Frankie made a scoffing noise. "I've got more chance of getting syphilis."

"Probably," Charlotte agreed cheerfully.

Frankie sighed and went back to the work he had been doing before Jenny interrupted him. "Prawns," he muttered. "Definitely prawns."

FRANKIE'S FACE was frozen in place from having kept the same polite, interested expression for the last two hours. His transport to the hotel was very friendly. One might say overly friendly. As far he knew, "Dick from Accounts" was happily married, but if the man touched Frankie's thigh one more time, Frankie was going to break his wrist.

Dick from Accounts also talked incessantly about everything: the upcoming weekend, the state of the company they worked for, the price of frozen bloody peas. Frankie spent much of the journey thinking of neat ways he could torture Jenny for putting him with Dick. Frankie was very fond of dick—small d—but being stuck with Dick with a capital D was like watching gay porn with his mother in the room.

"So what do you think?"

It was the lack of talking that clued Frankie in that he was supposed to answer. He had no idea what Dick had been talking about. He ran through a number of answers in his head and in the end stuck with the partial truth.

"I'm sorry, Dick, I was dozing. What did you say?"

"Do you think we need to go down the country roads or stick to the motorway? The traffic report said there's congestion on the main road after the next junction."

Stuck with Dick in a car, standing still on the motorway.

"Take the country roads," Frankie said hastily.

"You'll need to navigate. My satnav is broken."

"I'll look it up on my phone." Frankie's map-reading skills were legendary for being dire. He'd once directed Chaz a hundred miles out of their way because he mistook Broadstairs for Brighton.

To Frankie's relief, the directions were simple enough, and within half an hour, they were pulling in to the hotel. Frankie got out of the car, feeling like he'd been set free from a life sentence. He rubbed his hip, stiff and painful from staying in one position for so long.

Dick bounded out of the car and opened the boot. "Do you need me to carry your case?"

Frankie shook his head. "I'm fine. It's got wheels."

"We could meet at the bar as soon as we've settled. I could do with a beer."

"Sounds good." The last thing Frankie wanted was to go drinking with Dick, but he'd agreed to be sociable, and sociable he would be even if it cost him his sanity. *"Drama Queen!"* He heard Charlotte's voice in his head, only for some reason it morphed into Al's reproving tone. Frankie heaved a great sigh. He'd managed to speak to Al once during the week, and then not for long. Al's mother had taken a turn for the worse, and they were considering moving her to a hospice. Frankie wasn't sure what to say or do, but he made sure Al knew that he was available day or night if Al needed to talk.

Frankie had to hold back a cry of pain as he lifted his suitcase up the steps to the entrance of the hotel. Things were easier once he could roll the suitcase, and he was pleasantly surprised to find that the hotel knew he needed a room on the ground floor.

The young guy who processed the check-in smiled at him brightly. "The room has a wet room, sir, so you should manage just fine."

Frankie stared at him blankly. Wet room? Was he supposed to sleep in the swimming pool?

"Usually we keep these rooms for our disabled guests, but your company requested one of these rooms for you."

Frankie resisted the urge to punch the twink on the nose for yet another reminder that he was old. He felt old and crippled. God, he needed to hide and get drunk.

It became clearer once he reached his room and discovered that the wet room was the bathroom. There was a chair he could sit in to take a shower if he needed it.

"Skippety doo-dah," he muttered.

He'd promised Dick he'd meet him in half an hour in the bar, begging time for a shower. Frankie stripped off his clothes and limped into the bathroom. He glared at the offending chair, but after he switched the shower on, he decided to try it out just because his hip ached. After five minutes, Frankie shook his head. "I have got to get me a wet room." He patted the arm of the chair. "I like you!"

Frankie limped into the bar five minutes late, relieved to see Dick wasn't anywhere to be seen. He scanned the beers on tap. The barman smiled at him and waited.

"I'll have a Bud," Frankie said, awkwardly sitting on the barstool.

"Drinking already?"

Frankie stiffened. Anyone else, he would have shredded them for questioning his right to drink right the fuck now. "You?"

"Me," Al agreed, sitting on the next stool. "I'll have the same, thanks," he said to the barman.

"What the hell are you doing here?" Frankie sounded more aggressive than he actually felt, because what the flaming fuck?

Al raised his eyebrow. "I told you I had to work this weekend."

"You didn't tell me what you were doing." A horrible thought struck him. "What are you doing here?"

"I work for Team Elements."

"Team Elements?"

"Hmmm, we're here running a team-building weekend."

"Womb Weekend?" Frankie said faintly.

Al beamed at him. "Womb Weekend."

"You knew I was going to be here?"

"Once you told me about Womb Weekend, I checked the list of participants and saw one Francis Mason."

"You let me go on and on and you never told me what you did for a living."

"Well, to be fair, I didn't know we were on the same one until afterwards, and I was having far too much fun hearing you rant. By the way, my colleagues love 'Womb Weekend.'"

"I'm glad you find me so amusing," Frankie said icily, standing up.

Al seemed to notice for the first time that Frankie was not a happy boy. "Hey, where are you going?"

"I'm waiting for a colleague. Excuse me." Frankie looked at barman. "Can you add it to the room?" When the man nodded, he gave him the room number.

Al caught Frankie by the sleeve. "Frankie, I thought you'd be pleased to see me."

"I was until I discovered you were laughing at me."

"You're such a princess."

So the wrong thing to say to a pissed-off Frankie. "That's Mr. Princess to you." He stalked away, ignoring Dick as he entered the bar.

Fuck Al. Fuck Dick. Fuck the whole fucking lot of them. He was going to call a cab and go home.

He had the key in the lock when someone pressed in behind him. It didn't take a rocket scientist to realize who it was.

"Go away."

"Not until you give me a chance to apologize." Al took the key out of the lock and pushed Frankie into the room.

"Quit bloody manhandling me. I'm not a fucking dog." Frankie pulled away, refusing to give Al the satisfaction of seeing him wince.

"If you were a dog, I could collar you," Al snapped, and Frankie had a flashback to his image of Ed Winters, collared and leashed.

Frankie bared his teeth. "Just try it."

"Are you growling at me?"

He was? Maybe he was a dog. He was panting like one, from pent-up emotion.

Al stepped into his space and slid his hands though Frankie's hair, tugging him in, their lips almost brushing when he murmured, "God, what did I do before I met you? My life was so boring."

"Beige," Frankie supplied.

"Beige."

Frankie let Al kiss him because that's where he wanted to be, not angry and snarly. He licked his lips when Al pulled back, tasting the beer.

"If I'd known getting knocked down would bring you into my life, I'd have done it sooner."

Al paused. "You really don't remember the first time we met, do you?"

"You keep saying that. Was it at a club?"

"Let's just say I've seen you at the worst of times."

At Frankie's blank look, he said, "Palm Hotel? A couple of months ago? You had problems remembering your room number."

The blood drained out of Frankie's face. "You were the bloke who looked after me when I puked? I didn't know it was you. How could I not know it was you?"

"Sweetheart, you were so trashed you couldn't focus on anything."

Frankie thunked his forehead onto Al's shoulder, colliding painfully with his collarbone. "Ow!"

"Well, don't do it again."

Frankie raised his head. "Are you stalking me?"

"Stalking you?"

"What about getting run over? Did you push me in front of the taxi so you could *rescue* me again?"

"A bit drastic, don't you think?" Al sounded overly amused for a man accused of stalking.

"Well, why were you there?"

The amusement slid off Al's face. "I was visiting my mum."

Frankie slapped his head. "Jesus, sorry. Your mum, how is she?"

"Not good, to be honest. There isn't much time left."

"What the hell are you doing here?"

Al shrugged. "My job. I work most weekends and visit her during the week. My Aunty Vi, Mum's sister, visits at the weekend. She doesn't approve of me or my 'lifestyle.'" He made air quotes around the word.

"Oh babe." Frankie's suspicions were forgotten in response to the obvious pain on Al's face.

"It's okay. I've known this day was coming for a while."

"It's anything *but* okay. This is your mum!" Frankie said, drawing Al's head down to his shoulder as Al's face crumpled. He rubbed Al's shoulders as they shook, feeling awkward because comforting people really wasn't Frankie's bag, but he had an uncommon desire to protect Al, as the man had looked after him.

After a few minutes, Al stilled in his arms but didn't move immediately. Eventually, he raised his head, his eyes red and puffy, and a look of acute embarrassment on his face.

"I'm sorry. I didn't mean to do that."

Frankie kissed him lightly on the mouth. "This looking-after thing… it works both ways."

"I've not had that before."

"What?"

"Someone who wanted to look after me." Al sighed and ran a hand through his hair. "I like taking care of people. Mum always said I should have been a woman because I mother everyone."

"Not a mother. More like a Dom. Or a guardian angel."

Al grinned. "I thought a guardian angel was meant to keep you out of trouble."

"Are you a Dom, then?"

"Dominant with a small d."

"Not so small," Frankie muttered.

"Not so small," Al agreed. He looked at the time on his watch. "There's a meeting scheduled in half an hour. I ought to prepare for it."

"And I need a drink and a sit-down." Frankie rubbed his hip.

"Lay off the booze this weekend, yeah?"

Frankie frowned at him. "Are you nagging, 'cause I gotta tell you, I don't respond well to nagging."

Al quirked an eyebrow. "You like being looked after but not nagged?"

"You got it."

"Tough. One comes with the other." He bent to kiss Frankie on the mouth, only this kiss wasn't so light or chaste. It was, however, far too brief.

When Al stepped back, Frankie licked his lips. "You need to do that again."

Al tapped him on the nose. "Not now. Got to prepare for that meeting, remember?"

"Later?" Frankie wasn't going to let go of him until he got a cast-iron guarantee that Al was going to warm his bed later.

"Definitely later."

"And sex?"

Al's lips twitched. "We'll see. I shouldn't be fraternizing with the participants."

"I can always refuse to participate."

"Knowing you, you bloody well will."

Frankie smirked because Al had him sussed. "I'm not so much refusing, as suggesting alternative activities."

"I won't let you get away with it," Al warned.

"Was that a challenge?" Frankie loved a challenge.

"Frankie...." Al curled a finger in Frankie's T-shirt and pulled him closer. "No trouble-making or you will suffer the consequences."

"Like what? You gonna tell my boss? 'Cause I have to tell you my boss already hates me and HR think I'm golden."

Al leant forward to whisper in Frankie's ear, his warm breath making Frankie shiver. "I could refuse to let you come for the entire weekend."

"You wouldn't be that cruel."

"Try me," Al said flatly and stepped back. "I've got to go." He left without giving Frankie the chance to respond.

Frankie and certain parts of Frankie's anatomy were extremely turned on by this show of dominance, even if orgasms were at stake. Besides, the man had to be joking. He'd said dominance with a small *d*. Denying Frankie the chance to come was a bloody big D!

Chapter 5

THE MEETING had been going for fifteen minutes by the time Frankie made an appearance. His tardiness wasn't entirely his fault as he'd slipped in the bathroom and banged his hip, then retched from the pain as he lay on the tiled floor. Nonslip floor, huh!

By the time he'd got over the wish to die and the embarrassment of thinking he'd be found by some twinkie bellboy, he'd be an old dude unable to frickin' move, and the meeting would be well underway.

He limped into the conference room, aware of all eyes upon him—including Dick, who scowled at him from across the room—and Al's icy look as he stopped addressing the group.

"Mr. Mason, you finally make an appearance," Al said. "Kind of you to join us."

Snotty bastard. Frankie opened his mouth to explain and then shut it again. The whole fucking world didn't need to know he was a bloody cripple at the moment. "Sorry," he muttered and limped to an empty chair, biting back a moan of pain as he sat down.

Al's eyes narrowed as he watched Frankie sit down, and seemed to hold back whatever snide comment he'd been about to make.

"As I was saying, the actual course starts tomorrow at eight thirty. We'll meet here for the first exercise. Tonight is just a chance to get to know each other and for us to run through what we are going to be doing. If you have any concerns now is the time to vocalize them. Don't worry if you feel you can't participate in one of the exercises, we have alternative torture… fun planned for all of them."

"I'll bet you do," a woman muttered sotto voce next to Frankie. "I bet you've got a whole weekend of torture planned."

Frankie snorted and cast a look at her out of the corner of his eyes. She was older than him, maybe in her late thirties. He vaguely recognized her, but she didn't work in his building—that he was sure of. He'd have spotted the gorgeous red hair before.

She grinned at him. "Sorry."

"Nothing to be sorry about," he whispered, ignoring Al who'd carried on talking. "I agree with you."

"I'm Carol."

"Frankie."

Al scowled at them both. "If you could give me your attention for another five minutes, then you'll be free to introduce yourselves."

Frankie rolled his eyes at Carol, then put on his best innocent look and fixed his eyes on Al.

"I predict fireworks ahead," Carol said for his ears only.

"You have no idea, darling. No idea at all."

FRANKIE DIDN'T move immediately when Al dismissed them to dinner, partly because he knew he owed Al an apology, and partly because it hurt too fucking much to move.

"I'll see you in there," he said to Carol. "Save me a seat."

"Sure." She looked at him, concern in her eyes. "Do you need a hand?"

"If I'm not there in ten minutes, send a search party."

"I'll do that," she promised and slipped past him.

His back to Frankie, Al was talking to another man and a woman, all of them dressed in polo shirts and trousers with the company logo. Frankie decided to move while Al's attention was distracted. Over the previous few weeks, Frankie had become adept at learning how to get off chairs with the minimum amount of pain. He wriggled to the front of the seat and pushed off using the arms. Normally he was young and fit enough to compensate with his uninjured leg, but the shock of falling had made every part of him ache.

Frankie gritted his teeth and stood, clutching the back of the seat in front for a moment.

"What the hell happened after I left you?" Al hissed, by his side in an instant, his hand on Frankie's lower back.

"I fell in the bathroom."

"You did what?" Al exclaimed. "For heaven's sake, Frankie, can't I leave you for five seconds without you injuring yourself?"

"Hopeless case. I was late because I couldn't get up for a while."

"Go and get dinner before you do yourself another injury."

Frankie's reply was forestalled by the girl from Team Elements joining them, her expression rife with curiosity.

"Is everything all right, Al?"

Al gave a brief nod. "We're fine, Jill. Frankie damaged his hip again."

She looked at Al and then at Frankie. "You two know each other." She snapped her fingers. "Womb Weekend. You're Mr. Womb Weekend."

"That's me." Frankie pasted on a bright smile.

"Al's not stopped talking about you for weeks."

"He hasn't?" He looked at Al, who'd gone an interesting shade of red.

"Hell no. I've never seen him so besotted."

"You can shut up now, Jill," Al said, but Frankie held up his hand.

"Tell me more. You say he was besotted with me?"

Jill grinned at him. "Big, bad Al's like a little schoolgirl where you're concerned. I'm not kidding, every time he mentions your name he just melts."

They shared a mutual mischievous grin as Al turned puce.

"Shut. Up. Jill."

She ignored him and called over to the man who was frowning at the sound system. "Len, come over here and meet Mr. Womb Weekend."

Len trotted over and held out his hand to Frankie. "Good to meet you finally. Al's been almost pleasant to work with the last few weeks."

"I hate you both," Al said. "You should go to dinner, Frankie. It's not professional for me to beat up my staff in front of clients."

"Aren't you joining us?" Frankie asked.

Al shook his head. "Not this evening. We've got some work to do setting up the course."

"When are you eating?"

"Oh, look. Frankie's just as bad as Al." Jill made a cooing noise, giggling when both men scowled at her.

"I'll get room service later. You go in and cause trouble with that redhead."

"You're going to regret saying that."

"As soon as I saw you two together, I knew there was going to be trouble. I'll see you after dinner." Al kissed Frankie. "Now go. From the look on Len's face, we've got a PA system to wrangle."

Frankie grinned at him and said good-bye to the others, limping out of the conference room. In the dining room, he was intercepted by a waiter, but when Frankie pointed to Carol, waving at him from the far end, he was allowed to go through.

"Hey you," she said as Frankie approached, "I thought we'd lost you."

"I thought I'd better apologize to Al."

"Mr. Tall Dark and Handsome?" she said, moving up so Frankie could join the table, thankfully at the opposite end of the table to Dick.

"You mean the scary dude at the front?"

Frankie looked at the balding thirtysomething man sitting opposite Carol. "Scary? Do you really think he was scary?"

"You don't?"

"No, I don't."

"But you do think he was tall, dark, and handsome?" Carol teased.

"Well, yeah."

The man groaned. "Just what we need, a fag and a faghag."

"What did you just say?"

The man blanched at Carol's icy tone. "I… was joking. I didn't mean to upset anyone."

"Don't ever let me hear you using those words again," Carol said, not bothering to lower her voice.

Frankie squirmed as other people looked over. "It's okay, Carol," he said quietly.

"No, it's not. No one demeans you in front of me."

The man looked at Frankie. "Sorry, man, I didn't intend to piss you off."

Frankie nodded and held out his hand. "It's cool. I'm Frankie. I can't get up because of my hip."

"Ray." Ray stood and shook Frankie's hand over the table, while Carol scowled at him.

Ray held out his hand to Carol. "Peace?"

Unseen under the table Frankie kicked her ankle when she didn't look like she was going to move.

Reluctantly Carol shook his hand. "Peace," she said.

"Do you know him?"

Frankie hesitated, not sure whether he should admit that he had a prior relationship with Al.

To his surprise, Ray said, "Don't worry, we won't hold it against you."

They were interrupted by the waitresses bringing food to the table. Frankie got his the same time as everyone else.

"I told them you were coming," Carol said when Frankie mentioned it.

"I'm starving," he said.

"So?" Ray asked. "Do you know the scary dude?"

"Yeah," Frankie admitted. "He's almost my boyfriend."

Ray's eyes opened wide. "He's a poofter too?"

"You just can't help yourself, can you?" Carol said, but this time she sounded more resigned than angry.

"I'm sorry."

Frankie laughed. "No offense taken, but Ray, if you want to keep your teeth, do not call our glorious leader a poofter. I haven't known him that long, but I can't see him being very happy about it."

"And that goes for the rest of you," Carol growled, scanning the rest of the table.

Frankie took the grunts and nods as assent. He took the time to assess the rest of the course participants. It was almost split down the middle: ten men and twelve women, all varying ages. He knew one or two from his office and a couple from the Manchester office whom he'd met on another course.

"You're a good guard dog," he said to Carol as he finished his dinner.

She grunted as she chewed. "I hate demeaning words. I hate the fact we know not to use the N word but using the F word is just fine."

"To be fair, people eat faggots," Frankie pointed out.

Ray choked on a mouthful of food.

Frankie smirked at him. "Need some water, Ray?"

"I'm going to smack you," Carol said.

"No damaging the crippled guy."

"What did you do?" Ray said. "I saw you walking earlier and you weren't limping as much."

"I slipped in the bathroom and fell on my bad hip. I damaged that by getting hit by a car a few weeks ago."

Ray whistled. "You're a walking disaster zone."

"I know. Believe me, I wish I wasn't."

"How long have you known Al?" Carol asked curiously.

"Not long."

"That's cryptic."

Frankie didn't want to talk about his relationship with Al. For one thing, he wasn't sure he had a defined relationship, and for the other.... Frankie wasn't sure if there was another, but the one reason sounded lame.

"There's not much to talk about at the moment. Ask me again in a month."

"I thought you fa—" Ray stopped as Carol and Frankie glared at him. "—guys didn't do relationships. It's all gay pride and clubs."

"How many gays have you actually known?" Frankie asked.

The fact Ray had to think about it told him all he needed to know, but the answer surprised him.

"Five—no, six. Uncle David and Uncle Paul, the old lesbos down the road, you, and Al."

"Who are Uncle David and Uncle Paul?"

"My uncle and his flatmate. My mum made me call Paul 'Uncle' since I was a kid. They've shared the same house for thirty years."

Frankie rolled his eyes at Carol. Some people were so sweetly oblivious.

"And the lesbos down the road?"

"Gina and Lisa. They share a flat together."

Carol burst out laughing. "Ray, are you blind, honey? You've just mentioned two couples you know."

Ray shook his head. "They're not together. Mum said they were just sharing because of the costs."

"Do you think she might have been trying to avoid telling you they were a couple?" Frankie asked gently, because the man looked like someone had pulled the rug from under his feet.

"Don't know," Ray mumbled.

"If it's any consolation, my friend Jonno is exactly the gay you're talking about. He wouldn't shack up with anyone if they paid him." He paused for a moment. "That might be the only reason he shacks up with someone."

Carol frowned at him. "That doesn't make sense."

He shrugged. "I know. You have to meet Jonno. He is the biggest tart, but he's been with Will for years."

"I gotta wazz," Ray said and escaped from the table just as the waitresses came back to the table with desserts.

"Don't be too long. We might eat yours before you get back," Carol called after him, then grinned at Frankie. "Poor bloke. You've just wrecked his entire life."

"Telling him his uncle was a happily married queer? Oh, come on, I bet he knew and just didn't want to admit it."

"I wonder if he still lives at home with his mum?"

"Ask him when he comes back." Frankie said.

He'd eaten his cheesecake and was eyeing Ray's untouched dessert when he saw Carol doing the same thing. "It's mine, girl."

"Hell no," she said emphatically. "That cheesecake is all mine. It's fucking orgasmic."

"God yes. We'll share. If we take it now he'll never know."

Unfortunately Frankie's nefarious plans were foiled by the return of Ray.

"What do you do?" Carol asked Ray when he'd sat down.

He looked relieved to be talking about something neutral. "I work in IT in the Manchester office. You?"

"I've just got promoted. I'm the assistant director of administration in the Birmingham office."

Frankie whistled. "Congratulations, Carol, or should we call you ma'am? Should we be talking to the big boss?"

She shoved his shoulder. "What happens here, stays here."

"Yeah, yeah, that's what they all say."

"What do you do, Frankie?" Ray asked around a mouthful of cheesecake.

"Admin. I work in the Wimbledon office."

"Who's your boss?" Carol asked.

"My immediate boss is Ed Winters." He pulled a face, and both Ray and Carol groaned. "You know him?"

"We looked after a couple of his clients," Ray said. "He was... particular." It seemed Ray had taken a lesson in how to be diplomatic.

"If that's code for 'he was a complete arsehole,' then yeah, he was particular," Carol said. "He used to be my boss."

Frankie snapped his fingers. "That's why I know you. You used to come into the office to talk to him."

"Try to clear up his messes, more like. We cheered when he left."

"He hates me," Frankie admitted.

Carol rolled her eyes. "Well duh. You're everything he wants to be and never will."

"Young, good-looking, smart, well-hung...."

Ray blushed as Frankie listed his attributes. "Easy, tiger. I did not need to know that."

"*Gay*, dipstick. You're out and he never will be."

Frankie stared at her openmouthed, seeing a matching expression on Ray's face.

"Ed is g-gay?" Ray stuttered.

"You mean you've never thought the same thing?"

"Once or twice," Frankie conceded, "but I thought he was just a prick."

"He was that and more. I wish he'd just come out and have done with it. But seriously." Carol fixed her gaze on Frankie. "If he was that much of a shit, you've got to say something to your director."

Frankie added milk to the coffee that had just been placed in front of him. "No need. HR has got his number now."

"Got to feel sorry for the bloke really," Ray said, taking Frankie by surprise.

Carol shook her head. "He was a dick."

"But he's conflicted," Ray argued.

"Who are you and what happened to Ray when he went to the loo?" Carol said.

Ray shrugged. "I don't have a problem with… gays. I'm just crap at being PC. I feel sorry for the guy if he's a dick because he's jealous he can never come out. It's an empty life."

"That's really sensitive," Carol said quietly.

Ray grinned at her. "I'm not a total tosser."

Frankie's attention was distracted by Al walking into the dining room. Fuck, the man looked edible. Frankie wanted to bend over the nearest table and let Al fuck him senseless.

"Frankie?"

"Huh?" Frankie looked at Carol.

"What do you think?"

"I wasn't listening."

Carol saw Al coming over. "You're forgiven. What can we do for you, Al?"

Al smiled at them, reserving a longer smile for Frankie. "Time to come back, folks." His lips twitched when one or two people groaned. "It's not that bad. You only have to be polite to each other tonight. You've managed so far."

Frankie sighed and struggled to his feet. He'd much rather stay chatting to Carol and Ray, particularly if Carol was going to dish the dirt on Ed Winters. Each step was like a red-hot poker through his hip, but he tried to keep his face passive as he limped toward the conference room with Ray and Carol.

"You okay, Frankie?" Carol said.

"Yeah."

"You don't look okay."

"And there I thought I was wearing my best poker face." He gave Carol a brave smile.

"Why don't you go to bed?" Ray suggested.

Because I'm hoping to finally get laid.

"I should have taken painkillers before I came down."

"Do you want me to go to your room and get them?" Carol asked.

Al frowned at them by the conference room door. "Hurry up, please. We've got a lot to get through."

"Frankie's in pain," Carol said before Frankie could stop her.

Al's attention immediately switched to him. "What do you need?"

"He needs painkillers."

"I'll go get them," Al said. "You go and sit down."

Frankie handed over his room key because God knows he really needed to take the weight off his hip. He was so bloody tired of hurting.

Chapter 6

BY THE time the evening finished, the painkillers had taken effect, but they left Frankie tired and more than willing to hit the sack.

He waited at the lifts with Ray and Carol and said good night when the doors opened. Dick walked past them into the lift, very obviously ignoring him.

Out of sight of Dick, Carol raised her eyebrow. The doors closed as Frankie shrugged. He turned to go back to his own room only to fall into Al's waiting arms.

"Steady, babe." Al held on to his arms.

Frankie looked at him. "Take me back to my room and fuck me senseless."

"Your hip...."

"Endorphins are good for pain."

Al pressed his lips together.

"Why aren't you slinging me over your shoulder and dragging me back to the room? What the hell is stopping you?"

"Quiet down. I'm supposed to be working, remember."

Frankie took a careful step back, not convinced his leg would support his weight. "I'm going to bed. If you don't join me, then it's over."

"What?" Al stared at him. "I refuse to screw you tonight when I'm working, and that's it? We're finished?"

"I can't keep waiting for you, Al. I keep asking and you keep saying no."

"I had my reasons. Good reasons."

"Sure you did, but you've got the whole night now and I'm tired of waiting."

Al looked stunned. "Fuck you!"

"That's the idea!"

Frankie turned on his heel and walked away, knowing he was being unfair and not caring in the least. He reached his door and shoved the keycard in the slot, but the light remained stubbornly red. He tried again, and again, but it didn't work.

He rammed it into the lock. "Work, damn you."

A warm, solid weight pressed against him. "Here, it's the wrong card." Al plucked the card out of Frankie's hand and used another one.

Frankie watched the light go green with a mixture of excitement and resignation. "Am I ever going to open a door by myself?"

"No." Al pushed open the door and steered Frankie into the room. "Strip."

"What?"

That really irritating eyebrow that Al used to such good effect shot up. "Do I have to repeat myself? It's not that difficult to understand."

"You want me to strip naked here?"

Al stayed where he was, that bloody eyebrow still elevated. Frankie undid the buttons of his shirt, but as he went to take the green cotton off, Al said, "Leave it like that."

He undid his jeans, hearing the sharp hiss that he took to mean that Al had just discovered he wasn't wearing any underwear.

"Wait. Let me help you." Al knelt at his feet and looked up. "Hold on to my shoulders and I'll pull your jeans off so you don't have to bend."

Frankie swallowed and did as he was told.

"Do you normally go commando?"

"It was so painful I could only manage my jeans," Frankie explained. He heard a choked noise and looked down to see Al pressing his face into Frankie's belly.

"You need a minder." Al kissed from his navel to the exposed sensitive skin around his cock, devoid of any hair, and then kissed his hip, muffled through the denim. Then Al finally pulled his jeans off to repeat the action. Frankie's cock twitched in appreciation—and desperation.

"I've got to taste you," Al said, looking up at him with huge eyes.

Frankie suddenly thought of a problem. "Have you got a rubber?"

"No."

"I haven't either. I wasn't expecting to see you."

"I'll blow you without."

"Not this time. I'm not going to come in your mouth. I've not been tested for months." Frankie curled his fingers in Al's hair and tilted his head back to make sure Al looked at him. Frankie was safe; he knew that, as he was paranoid about the use of condoms even with blowjobs, but this was Al, and he wasn't putting him at risk.

"I could pull off before you come and we can get tested next week," Al insisted.

"No deal. Suck my balls and give me a hand job and suck me tomorrow."

Al scowled at the list of instructions but he nodded. "Lie on the bed and get comfortable."

Frankie almost whined in exasperation.

"Lie on the bed," Al repeated. "I'm not risking you falling again when I make your knees give way."

Frankie raised an eyebrow. "You're that confident?" He made himself comfortable on the bed, refusing to show how relieved he was to be off his feet.

Al, the bastard, smirked at him. "Better now? Do you need a pillow for your hip?"

"I'll be even better when your mouth is around my cock," Frankie pointed out.

"Do you always bottom from the top?"

"Always. Get used to it."

Al shook his head. "If I'm topping, you shut up."

Frankie opened his mouth to argue but then Al jacked his cock sweeping a thumb across his cockhead, and every coherent thought in Frankie's brain melted into a *moreyespleasemore* at the simple touch.

"I wish I could taste you," Al said, fisting Frankie's cock.

Frankie squinted at him, because since his first sexual encounter he'd never really cared whether he tasted a guy or not, but he could feel Al's need and desire for this to be more, and he realized that he wanted that too.

"You're going to stay still. Do not move your hips."

And back to the orders again. Frankie looked up at the ceiling and tried to do what he was told. In truth, it was too painful to wriggle.

Frankie did not shriek like a girl when Al sucked one of Frankie's balls into his mouth, but it was a close-run thing. His fingers curled into the duvet as Al licked and explored his sac, rolling each ball until they were tight with the need to explode. Frankie had no clue what Al was going to do next. Just as his climax was curling in the base of Frankie's spine, Al ignored his balls and played with his cock. Frankie begged Al to let him come, but he changed it up again, spending time on his perineum and behind his balls.

"Please, please," Frankie begged, his fingers curling in Al's hair, but the bastard played with Frankie's dick like a cat with a mouse. Maybe that wasn't the right analogy, but he stroked the head of Frankie's cock for what seemed like hours, until Frankie was whining in frustration, trying to pump his hips to get some extra action.

"Stay still," Al growled, cupping Frankie's hips with his warm hands.

"Fucking let me come, then," Frankie fucking growled right back.

Al naughtily kissed the tip of his cock in reply and finally started jacking him so that he quickly had Frankie at the edge of his climax. He tugged Al's hair to warn him. Al pushed Frankie's shirt up. "Come now."

Frankie couldn't have held back if he'd tried. His cock pulsed in Al's hand, and he came, spurting over his bare belly. He felt like his nuts were turning inside out with the intensity of his orgasm, and all the time he was aware of Al's eyes on him, watching his reactions.

"What about you?" Frankie asked when he could speak again.

"I don't need—"

Frankie placed a palm over his mouth. "What about you?"

"I could hold on to the headboard and jack off over your face, or—"

"Do it."

Al undid his trousers enough to release his cock. Nice and thick and Frankie just wanted to get his mouth around it. Al straddled Frankie's chest and leaned over to hold on to the headboard with one hand. He smeared the precome over the head and groaned deep in his chest.

"Fuck, nice." Frankie wanted to open his throat muscles and let Al sink right in, but instead he watched in frustration as Al set up a fast rhythm and pumped come over Frankie's face.

Frankie closed his eyes and felt the warm spurts across his face. He resisted the urge to lick them off his lips but promised himself once they'd been tested, he'd be sucking Al's come down his throat as fast as he could.

When Al's breathing returned to normal, he climbed off the bed and returned from the bathroom with a flannel to wipe Frankie's face and belly. Frankie lay back and let his lover take care of him. This was what he'd wanted, and now he'd got it, he felt king of the heap.

"I'LL LEAVE you to sleep," Al said as he came back from the bathroom.

Frankie frowned. "Aren't you staying the night?"

Al shook his head. "I've got to work a bit longer before I sleep. I'll see you in the morning." He bent down to kiss Frankie on the mouth. "Do you want me to undress you?"

"I'm not a kid."

"I wasn't sure how painful your hip was now."

His hip. Ah. Frankie had been ignoring it for the last half an hour because he knew one hint of being in pain and Al would stop their fun.

"It's okay."

Al hummed. "Yeah, right. Well, I'll be by in the morning to see how it was. I'll be honest, you're not physically up to this weekend."

"I thought you had alternative exercises," Frankie snarked.

"They're not as much fun."

"Fun? You have a weird idea of what's fun, Al."

"You don't think a weekend like this is fun?"

"I think being stuck with my work colleagues a whole weekend is hell on earth. A whole weekend with Dick? I'll rather poke my eyeballs out."

"You can have a weekend with my dick as compensation." Al waggled his eyebrows suggestively.

"I hope that's not an offer you make to everyone."

Al shook his head. "Only the hot ones." Before Frankie could respond to that, Al kissed him again and said, "And you're the only hot one I've found in months."

"Glad to hear it," Frankie said huskily. He pulled Al down for another kiss and explored his mouth thoroughly.

Al was panting again by the time he pulled back. "Got to go before I end up fucking you." He sounded really reluctant.

Frankie lay back and stretched, the pain in his hip negated by Al's hot gaze, which was sweeping down his exposed belly and groin to his legs. Despite his monumental orgasm, Frankie's cock responded to the heat, hardening under his gaze.

"You are not being fair." Al stood up to put some distance between them. "I've got to work."

"I know." Now it was Frankie's turn to smirk at him.

"I'm going." Al backed away toward the door, looking at him the whole time.

Frankie huffed because he'd got a hard-on and he expected Al to deal with it. Oh well… he wrapped a hand around his cock.

"Bastard." Al was back on the bed before Frankie could draw another breath, knocking Frankie's hand away and replacing it with his own.

Before he thought deeply about it, Frankie thrust up and couldn't hide the wince of pain.

"Stay still," Al barked, one hand on Frankie's lower belly.

Frankie did as he was told because Al was working Frankie's dick like a pro, and no way did he want Al to let go. When he came finally, it was more of a slow roll than a thunderclap, the release taking all his body.

He was still recovering as Al headed for the door. "Go to sleep." Al was gone before Frankie could respond.

Frankie closed his eyes and smiled. He fell asleep before he had time to think he ought to get under the covers.

Chapter 7

AL WAS fucking Frankie over a tree branch in the middle of a field of cows. The cattle seemed singularly unbothered by the noisy sex, and Frankie was too busy working his way to a noisy climax to care who was looking.

The alarm was an unwelcome intrusion into an interesting dream, and he swiped viciously at the phone to shut it up. It shot off the bedside table, and Frankie had to fumble on the floor to find it, his eyes still half-closed before the sounds turned from unwelcome to fire-engine obnoxious. He rolled over onto his back to glare at the ceiling, conscious that his hip hurt like the proverbial bitch and that he needed to shift if he wanted breakfast. Then he frowned, because as far as he remembered, he had fallen asleep before he set an alarm.

He picked up his phone and noticed a text.

U better b awake

Frankie fired off a response to Al.

U call me?

:)

Bastard

U no me.

"Yeah, and I'm beginning to realize that is a huge mistake," Frankie muttered. He scratched his belly lazily, picking at the flakes of dried come that Al missed the previous night.

His phone beeped again. "What?" he snarled. Frankie was not a morning person.

Get up

Frankie's response was short and not so sweet.

I'm outside the door. Open up.

"For fuck's sake, can't I even clean my fucking teeth or take a piss before you order me around," Frankie said, getting up really slowly and limping to the door.

Al stood on the other side with a large takeaway cup of….

Frankie sniffed. "I love you," he said, reaching eagerly for the cup.

"Teeth, piss, then you can stock up on caffeine."

"Huh." Frankie headed toward the bathroom. "You heard?"

"You weren't whispering. Are you always such a grump in the morning?"

"Always." Frankie relieved himself with a sigh.

"I thought you drank chamomile tea and stuff."

"Does that have to make me Mr. Happy?" Frankie had a mouthful of toothbrush and toothpaste by this time, so his reply was probably unintelligible.

"Take a shower. You stink of come."

Frankie spat and cursed. "I want my coffee first."

"All right, but it's going to taste foul with the toothpaste." Al grinned at him from the doorway.

"I don't care." Frankie held out his hand for the coffee.

Al handed it over, and Frankie swallowed half the cup without stopping.

While Frankie moaned in appreciation at the smooth latte rolling down his gullet, Al prepared the shower.

"You've got twenty minutes before breakfast."

"I'm not hungry. The coffee was enough."

"Attendance is mandatory."

Frankie gave him the hairy eyeball. "Being on the course was mandatory. It said nothing about having to attend all the meals. I checked." Frankie *always* checked the fine print.

"The staff make it mandatory. As we speak, Jill and Len are waking everyone up and forcing them to breakfast."

"With gifts of coffee and leering at their cock?" He was pleased to see the crimson on Al's cheeks.

"This was just for you." Al leant forward and kissed him. "Minty coffee, my favorite."

"Have you got time for a shower with me?"

"I wish I could, but I need to wake up a couple of others. Strictly just knocks at the door," Al added hastily.

"Good, because this—" Frankie took Al's hand and pressed it into his groin. "—is just for me."

Al squeezed gently, then let go. "I've got to go, babe. Fifteen minutes, otherwise you're on the naughty step for a spanking."

Frankie rolled his eyes. "Yeah, yeah, later."

He turned to step in the shower and received a slap on the arse for his trouble.

"Fourteen minutes and counting. Don't be late."

Frankie wondered if he answered back, would he get another smack? But Al was out the door before he could find out. He sighed as he scrubbed his belly with the floral shower gel provided by the hotel. He was not looking forward to the coming day.

THIRTEEN MINUTES and fifty seconds later, Frankie entered the dining room to find Al looking at the clock. Frankie poked his tongue out at him and headed toward Ray and Carol who waved him over. He hesitated a second because he wasn't sure if he should go to Al's table. Then he realized Al was sitting with the rest of Team Elements and wasn't expecting Frankie to sit with them.

"Morning, sunshine." Carol beamed at him.

Frankie scowled at her. "If you're going to be cheerful, I'm going to find somewhere else to sit."

"Well, who's a grumpy bunny this morning," she cooed.

"Oh God," he moaned.

"Have a coffee," Ray said sympathetically. "She's easier to deal with after caffeine."

Frankie poured a coffee from the pot on their table, downed it, and refilled it straightaway.

Ray chuckled. "Oh dear, is it that bad a day?"

"Worse. What do we have to do this morning?"

Frankie nodded at the waiter (cute, unfortunately straight) who asked him if he wanted a full English. Unfortunately, Frankie hadn't woken up sufficiently to think of a euphemism for the term and stuck with a "Yes, please," and a sweet smile. The boy didn't blink.

"Oh, goodie," Carol said, "one that bats for my team. I was beginning to think all the gorgeous ones were gay."

"All gays are gorgeous, not all gorgeous men are gay." Frankie must have been feeling better if he could manage that.

"Is being gorgeous a prerequisite?" Ray challenged Carol.

"No, but it helps."

Frankie was about to join the conversation when he noticed the eye contact going on between them. "Uh, is there something I should know about?"

They both turned pink, which was adorable and sickening. Surreptitiously, Frankie checked their left hands. No rings adorned either of their hands: not obviously married, then. Although that didn't mean a thing, as Frankie had found out on past courses. He'd been targeted by married men considering the course as an awayday from their marriages.

"Do you want me to find somewhere else to sit?" he asked.

They both said "no" really quickly, and Carol grabbed Frankie's wrist.

"Stay right where you are, mister. We're the Three Musketeers."

"Two and a lame queer," Frankie suggested.

"It's you or Dick on our team. I know which one I'd rather have," Carol murmured.

Frankie looked over to where Dick was sitting with two middle-aged women. He looked uncomfortable as they talked animatedly together, making no effort to include him.

"I can't ignore him all weekend. I am the only person he knows," he said.

"How sweet. He still can't be on our team," Carol said.

"She's fierce, isn't she?" Ray sounded almost proud.

"That's one way to describe her," Frankie agreed. "I can think of others. Don't you dare kick me," he warned, thinking Carol was about to lash out. "Think of my hip."

Carol snorted derisively, but their breakfasts arrived and any retaliation was thankfully postponed.

Two of the course participants, both young women, slunk into the dining room, hoping to sit down unnoticed by the Team Elements crew. Al frowned at them both.

"Not a good start, ladies. You have ten minutes to eat breakfast."

They groaned and their hands clashed as they both headed for the coffeepot at the same time. Fortunately, the staff had obviously been primed, and their breakfasts appeared in front of the latecomers.

"I got promised a spanking if I was late," Frankie said.

Ray snorted. "I'm surprised you turned up at all."

"He can get breakfast and get the spanking later," Carol said. "Damn, this bacon is good."

It was good, really good, and under other circumstances Frankie would have asked for more, but Al and the Team Elements were already leaving their table.

Al smiled at the course participants. "We'll see you in ten minutes in the conference room. Don't be late."

"Womb Weekend, here we come," Frankie said.

Ray and Carol looked puzzled. "Womb Weekend?" she asked.

Frankie got himself another coffee and explained the origins of the name.

"I can't wait to throw the sucker off the building," Carol said. "The more mess that egg makes, the better."

"I don't think you've grasped the idea," Ray said.

"She has," Frankie said. "She just wants to make a mess."

Carol grinned wickedly. "You know me so well. We ought to go. Our glorious leader is getting impatient," she said as Al coughed at the doorway.

Frankie shrugged. "Fuck it, he can wait five minutes."

"I need the ladies'. See you in there, guys." Carol headed for the door.

Frankie grinned at Ray's rapt attention of her retreating figure. "You really like her."

"What? Yeah, she is great, isn't she?" Ray's expression told it all. He was totally bowled over by the redheaded ball of fire.

"She is." Last night Frankie had thought Ray was your typical homophobe, but now, he really liked the guy.

"She's got a gay cousin she is very close to. That's why she was so protective of you," Ray said.

"I thought it might be something like that. Most allies have gay relatives or friends."

"You're the first gay person I've ever met at work. I never had to think about what I said before."

"No, I'm not."

"Not what?" Ray looked puzzled.

"The first gay person you've met at work. I'm just the first that's openly out to you. Not everyone is out to their family and friends, let alone work colleagues."

"I never thought of that."

"I know five people at the Birmingham office that are LGBT but are not out."

"They are?" Now Ray looked frankly bewildered. "Why aren't they out?"

Frankie wiped his mouth and got to his feet. "Because their work colleagues call them all queers and poofs."

Ray looked down at the remains of his breakfast. "Fuck."

"Yep. But now there'll be one less idiot making crass remarks, won't there?" Frankie smiled at Ray. "Come on, before we get the Al glare."

Frankie was very conscious of Al's eyes on him as he walked into the conference room, and he did his best not to limp. He hadn't forgotten Al's remarks about his level of fitness.

Once everybody was gathered, including the two latecomers from breakfast, Al smiled at them. "Morning, everyone. I know we did all the introductions to Winning Ways—"

Frankie snorted, which made Carol laugh.

Al scowled at them and carried on. "—last night, but this morning we're going to find out a bit more about each other." He rolled his eyes at the groans. "I know, but you've done this before. Turn to the person next to you. You've got one minute to find out five facts about them. Go." His order took the participants all by surprise, and they hesitated. "Fifty-seven seconds and counting."

Frankie turned to Carol. "Tell me five facts about you, gorgeous."

"Uh.... I hate Marmite, love terrapins, eat peanut butter out the jar, can pee up a wall, and once voted for the Monster Raving Loony party." She finished on a gasp.

"Why am I not surprised by any of that? So let me repeat that back: you hate Marmite, love turtles—"

"Terrapins."

"Terrapins. You eat peanut butter out of the jar, you can pee up a wall—way to go, girl—and you once voted for the Monster Raving Loony party."

She nodded. "Yep, well remembered."

"Swap over," Al called out.

Carol looked at Frankie expectantly. "Five facts from you now."

"Fuck me, what can I say?" Normally an open book, Frankie struggled to think of anything interesting about himself. "I drink chamomile tea at night, I broke my collarbone jumping off a cliff, I once got bitten on my arse by a dog, my ex dumped me by text, and a TV chef taught me how to cook boeuf bourguignon at his Thames-side mansion."

"Wow! Which one?"

"Can't tell you. I promised never to mention his name in case his wife found out. She would have his balls for toast." He leant closer to Carol. "But we cooked naked and he's got a really small dick."

She made a laugh-cum-snorting noise, which attracted Al's attention again.

"I hope you've remembered each other's facts," he said.

"Chamomile tea, cliff, arse, shitbag, nude cooking," Carol recites.

"That's about it," Frankie agreed. "Marmite, terrapins, peanut butter, pee, and a really peculiar desire to waste your vote."

Carol shrugged. "The alternative was UKIP, and you'd have to poke my eyeballs out before I voted for them."

Frankie actually shuddered at the mere thought. "Christ, yes. That's never going to happen."

"Time to introduce your partners," Jill called out.

Frankie realized Al had disappeared, and Jill was now leading the exercise.

Everyone obediently recited the five facts about their partner. Frankie was surprised to hear that Dick liked amateur moviemaking. He wondered if that was a euphemism for porn.

There were a few nervous chuckles when Carol mentioned Frankie's cooking exercise with the TV chef. To his relief, she refrained from mentioning his wife or penis size.

Five facts from twenty people seemed to go on forever, but eventually they were released for a fifteen-minute coffee break.

"I gotta hit the head and get some painkillers," Frankie said.

Carol nodded. "I'll get you coffee. Choccie biscuit?"

"Does mouse shit roll?"

"Can't say I've played with mouse poo, babe."

Frankie walked as evenly as he could toward the door, conscious of Jill's eyes on him. He hoped it was because he had an awesome arse and not because she was assessing his capability to do the next exercise.

He had just zipped up his trousers when Al walked into the gents. To his shock, Al backed him into one of the two stalls and locked the door. Al went to his knees, unzipped him, rolled on a rubber, and gave him the filthiest, fastest blowjob he'd had since ever.

When Frankie drew breath again, he looked down at Al. "Where did you get the rubber?" he hissed as quietly as possible.

Al raised his eyebrow. "Got a problem?"

"No, but—"

"Endorphins. You said they'd help. They sell condoms in the machines in here." Al wiped his mouth and got to his feet.

Tricky bastard. Frankie was starting to realize that he couldn't predict Al—one minute he was a shoulder, the next a total dick. Frankie loved this man.

And that there, made Frankie still. *Fuck!*

Al got to his feet, oblivious to the Tilt-A-Whirl in Frankie's brain. "We'd better get back."

Frankie nodded dumbly because the revelation that he was in love with Al had short-circuited his speech.

Al looked at him curiously and then bent to kiss him. Frankie wasn't fond of latex breath, but it was Al kissing him and he really didn't care. His fingers slid through Al's hair, and he held him close while they kissed.

By the time they got back to the table, everyone had sat down and Carol was rolling her eyes at him.

"Your coffee's cold by now."

"It's okay," he muttered.

"Hope it was worth it."

Frankie didn't pretend not to know what she was talking about. "That man can suck dick for Britain." He swallowed a cup of lukewarm coffee… and yes, it was worth it.

"Lucky boy." She patted his knee.

He caught Ray staring at them, a burning look in his eyes at the way Carol was touching Frankie.

"Sorry," he mouthed to Ray, because he didn't want trouble.

Ray shrugged, and then he smiled wryly, to Frankie's relief.

Carol was oblivious to the exchange, too busy looking at the next exercise on the sheet. "Oh look, we get to kill the eggs now."

"Welcome back, guys." Len held up a sheet of paper. "We're going to change things around because of the impending bad weather. Now we're going to divide you into two groups: half of you will follow Al and Jill to the river for the raft-building exercise, and half of you will stay with me for Toxic Waste and Minefield. Then we're going to swap. This afternoon we're going go-karting. For those of you not up to go-karting, we have an afternoon of activities planned. Tomorrow we'll do the indoor exercises. And don't forget this evening is the wine tasting before dinner."

"Couldn't we just skip to the wine tasting?" Frankie muttered.

"We could hide," Carol suggested.

"They'll find us."

"Damn, was that my name?" Carol sat forward. "Shit, I've got to get wet and muddy."

"Wish it was me," Frankie said.

She looked at him dubiously. "You want to build a raft?"

"Don't be stupid, I want to spend more time with Al."

"That's more like it."

Frankie sat back in his seat, chewing on his bottom lip. "I expect he'll be doing the go-karting as well."

"He did seem the type," Carol agreed. "I bet he was a Boy Scout."

"Raft builders, meet back in the foyer in fifteen minutes. Remember you're going to get very wet. Al and Jill don't allow any slackers. The rest of you can grab another coffee and meet me in the garden for Minefield in ten minutes," Len said.

"Have fun," Frankie said wistfully.

Ray came over and looked at Carol. "Ready?"

"If I must." She looked around. "Who's staying behind?"

Frankie wasn't surprised to see it was mostly the older women heading for the coffee pot. "Time for me to lay on the charm."

"Go win the WI over, big boy. My man and I have a raft to build."

Ray went pink but held out his arm. "Shall we go?"

"Onward!" She hooked her elbow through his, and they wandered off, leaving Frankie to contemplate what exactly he was supposed to do for the next couple of hours.

Chapter 8

HAVING MORE fun than he expected. That's how Frankie spent the rest of his morning. He was adopted by the older ladies the minute they heard of his "war wound."

A couple of the women were a little standoffish until Len explained the first game, which was to "loosen them up." Frankie felt sufficiently loose enough without having to play kids' games. Minefield started, and he was paired up with one of them to guide her through the obstacle-ridden minefield. Initially, Lynn stood apart from him until Len put the blindfold on her and she panicked.

"It's okay," Frankie said soothingly. "Just leave it to me."

Lynn clung to him, her pink-tipped nails digging into his arm. "I don't like the dark."

"I won't let you trip," Frankie promised.

He and Lynn negotiated the course successfully, and she ripped off the blindfold with a gleeful grin, her gray hair tousled. He vaguely recognized her as one of the women from Accounts.

"I bet you rock at navigation," she said.

"I'm crap, but I know my left from my right. That helped," he stage-whispered, giving a grin to a pair of women who had stumbled over so many obstacles because the guide couldn't remember which way was which.

The women poked their tongues out, and the group laughed. Len swapped them around, and this time Frankie was the one blindfolded. Now, he wasn't about to admit to any of these ladies that he was used to being blindfolded and playing games, but when the scent of the woman next to him changed, he realized they were playing a little game with *him*, and from the whispers, Len was joining in.

"Be careful, ladies, if I fall or trip I'm going to hurt, and Al will not be a happy boy." Frankie decided a gentle reminder wasn't a bad idea.

The giggles increased, and then his guide stopped. He waited patiently, and then someone lifted his chin and kissed him: a very male someone. When they pulled back, Frankie said, "Lynn, darling, I think you need a shave."

"Cheeky git," she said from behind him.

He was smiling as he was kissed again, and he sank into Al's embrace. How Al had got here and why he wasn't looking after his rafting group, Frankie didn't give a flying fuck. Al ended with a soft kiss to a cacophony of wolf whistles and catcalls. Who knew ten women could make so much noise?

Frankie blinked as the blindfold was taken off, and he got used to the light. He looked around to see everyone grinning at him, including Al. "I thought you were down at the river?"

Al shrugged. "I wanted to be with you. My boss turned up, so I strong-armed him into taking the river exercise, and I've come to help Len. We'll swap shortly."

"By helping you mean snogging me."

Al grinned. "That's just an added bonus."

A cough by Frankie's ear reminded him that they weren't alone, and he looked up to see Len waving what looked like one small and one large coffee tin, a bicycle-tire inner tube, and several lengths of rope.

"Ladies and gentlemen, it's time for Toxic Waste."

The group gathered around Len as he read out the game information.

"A can of highly toxic popcorn"—Len shook one of the coffee tins—"has contaminated a circle eight feet in diameter. The toxic area extends upwards." He pointed toward the sky. "If the poisonous popcorn is not transferred to a safe container for decontamination, the toxic popcorn will contaminate and destroy the population of the entire city. The popcorn is estimated to have a safe life of exactly twenty minutes before it explodes. Obviously, there is insufficient time to contact the authorities and evacuate. The lives of thousands of people are in your hands."

"No pressure, then," one of the ladies said.

"None whatsoever, Barb," Len agreed. "You're going to be split into two teams. You have to find a way to safely transfer the toxic popcorn from the unsafe container to the safe container, using only the materials provided. This includes a piece of rope for each person and a bicycle-tire tube. You can see we've marked out the two areas for you with rope and a tarp. You cannot pick up the toxic tin with your hands, and you cannot step into the danger zone or you will die. Any body part in the danger zone and that person is out of the game. You have twenty minutes to work it out."

"Oh dear Lord," Lynn muttered. "Isn't it time for coffee yet?"

Frankie agreed with her, but with Al standing next to him, he could hardly run away.

"If you even think of bolting, remember I can catch you," Al murmured in his ear.

Frankie ignored him and joined his group. Lynn beamed at him like he was an old friend. "So what do we have to do? Get the little tin into the big tin?"

"I'm having a *Die Hard* moment," Barb said. She looked like Frankie's Auntie Nora, but she had a mouth on her like his Uncle Doug. Doug was a sailor; he knew how to curse up a blue storm. Frankie thought Barb could give Doug a run for his money.

"Ah, Bruce Willis."

The women sighed. Frankie looked at Al, who just shrugged.

"Do you know what they're talking about?" Frankie said.

"Not a clue. Time's ticking, guys. What are you going to do?"

Al stepped back as the group surveyed the area. Frankie did his best to ignore Al and concentrate on the task at hand. He'd seen something like this before, but he couldn't remember where.

"I haven't got a clue," Barb admitted.

Lynn nodded. "Nor me. We could just give up."

Frankie looked at them, horrified. "I haven't sacrificed my weekend just to give up at the first hurdle."

One of the other two women, whom Frankie thought was called Dawn, frowned at him. "Have you got any ideas?"

"Not yet." Frankie looked at Al. "Is there any chance of a chair? I can't stand for much longer."

Al nodded. "I'll go and find one."

"Five. Five chairs. We need to sit and think this through."

The women smiled broadly. Frankie was getting the hang of this management thing. Al gave a put-upon sigh but went to find the chairs, and Frankie looked at the women.

"Now he is gone, there's to be no more talk of giving up, okay?"

They all nodded obediently. He smiled at them. They had a little over fifteen minutes, so the chances of finding a solution were slim, but what the hell.

"We have to get the little tin into the big tin using the ropes," Dawn said.

"And the inner tube," the last woman in the group reminded them.

Frankie nodded. "Yep."

"It obviously involves moving the little tin into the big tin, and we've all got to get involved."

"One of us could be sacrificed for the greater good," Lynn suggested.

"And I thought you were a nice girl," Frankie said.

"Oh, honey, I've never been a *nice* girl."

Barb grinned wickedly. "All hands for Lynn being sacrificed?"

Four hands shot up.

She poked her tongue out at them.

"Alternatively we could work out what the hell to do with the inner tube," Frankie said.

"I think it goes around the tin. It's less likely to slip than the rope," Dawn said.

Once they actually applied themselves, the answer was relatively simple, although its actual execution took time as they suspended the toxic tin and maneuvered it into the larger tin. Frankie did the directing from the chair that Al had placed in front of him with a flourish. There was some mild grumbling—that it was typical the women were doing all the work—but it was obvious he was in pain, and they were content to leave him in the driving seat.

His team succeeded with five minutes to spare, and after a cheer and a team hug, they collapsed on the chairs to watch the other team's progress. Although both teams came to the same basic idea, it seemed to take the other team longer to negotiate the maneuver.

Frankie walked over and smiled at the team. "Ladies, may I help?"

"If it means this torture is over and I get my gin and tonic, be our guest," one of the women said.

Frankie issued a few directions, and within a couple of minutes the toxic popcorn was contained and the world was saved from total devastation once more.

The women issue a ragged cheer, and one kissed Frankie on the cheek.

"You don't mind, do you?" She grinned at Al.

"As long as that's all you do with him," Al said.

Len clapped enthusiastically. "Well done, ladies. Give yourselves a round of applause." He waited until they'd clapped and cheered, then he said, "Go and get yourself a drink, and then you can go down to the river for the raft exercise."

They all groaned and Frankie heard Barb threaten to mutiny, but they headed toward the hotel.

Before Frankie could go, Al's arms went around him. "You are going to stay here and help Len and me."

Frankie tilted his head, frowning. "Why?"

"Don't ask stupid questions, babe. You can have the afternoon off while the others come with us to the go-karting."

"But—"

"If you argue, I'm taking you to A & E."

"I'm fine."

Al held him firmly. "You're sweating and pale."

"I'm not."

"Yes, you are. In fact, go and rest now. If—and only if—you turn a better color by lunchtime, you can come with us to watch."

"This is embarrassing."

"Suck it up, lover. Next time watch where you walk."

Frankie wanted to argue, but he wanted to sit down and take the weight off his feet a whole lot more.

Al led Frankie back to the hotel, an arm around him. Frankie was ashamed to admit he needed Al's help. His legs were wobbly enough as it was. At Frankie's door, Al held out his hand for the keycard. Frankie snorted but handed it over without a word, realizing that this man had his own quirks.

Once inside, he sat on the bed with a sigh of relief. "I think I'm going to sleep for a while."

"Wait 'til I give you some painkillers," Al said, kneeling to remove Frankie's trainers. "I'll save you some lunch if you don't appear."

Frankie managed to take the pills, then yawned and lay on the bed, his eyes closed.

"Sleep tight, sweetheart."

Frankie felt a brush of lips over his forehead, and then the door closed. He yawned again. Hell, what a weekend.

FRANKIE WOKE up to the feel of his bed dipping and a warm body spooning him from behind.

"Is it time for the go-karting?" he mumbled, praying he could still sleep for another few minutes.

Al snorted in his ear. "You slept through that. I thought I'd better wake you up before you miss dinner as well as lunch."

"What's the time?"

"Six thirty."

"Christ, is it?" Frankie pushed back into Al's warmth, seeking comfort from his closeness.

"Do you want to get up for the dinner?"

"Have I missed the wine tasting?"

"Yeah, or most of it."

"It's not worth getting up. I wish I'd driven myself down here," Frankie admitted. "I don't think I can keep this up."

"Well, hallelujah, the man has finally seen the light."

"I came with Dick the dick, remember? I still can't get home."

"I'll drive you home now or in the morning."

"You've got a job to do."

"My boss is here. I called him this morning and asked if he'd take over for me as one of the participants was a right pain in the arse and needed to go home." Al kissed the back of Frankie's neck, sending a shiver down Frankie's spine.

"And your boss just dropped all his plans and said sure?" Frankie asked skeptically.

"He owed me. I cancelled a holiday to help him a few months ago. The least he could do was help me with this weekend." Al stroked Frankie's hair. "When do you want to go home?"

"In the morning. You go to the dinner. I'll stay here in the warm and sleep some more."

"You need some dinner."

"Um…." Frankie wasn't hungry, and Al was warm and cozy around him and didn't seem anxious to move. He stayed where he was until he fell asleep again.

THE DOWNSIDE was waking up at two thirty in the morning ragingly thirsty and with a belly growling so loudly Frankie was surprised the noise hadn't woken up the whole hotel.

He fumbled for the light, not surprised to see Al wasn't there, but there was a note, and a bottle of water, and—Frankie drooled when he uncovered it—a sandwich large enough to quell the ravening beast inside him. He sat on the bed, stuffed his face until he was satisfied and then ate the crisps, homemade and drenched in sea salt, and Frankie could have eaten another plateful. He downed the water in one gulp and belched loudly.

Immediate needs satisfied, Frankie remembered the note. Al's scrawl looked like a drunken spider had wandered across the page, but with some squinting he realized it said Al would be ready to take Frankie home after breakfast.

Frankie wondered whether he should just stick it out and finish the course. As he padded into the bathroom, the dull ache in his hip reminded him that he really needed to go home and probably get his hip X-rayed to see if he'd done more damage in the latest fall.

He wondered why Al hadn't stayed the night with him. Perhaps he was concerned that he'd disturb Frankie, but it was a stupid idea because he could think of nothing better than being disturbed by Al. Preferably with his dick.

Frankie stared at himself in the mirror. He looked like death warmed up, and he didn't feel much better. He sniffed his armpit and almost gagged. Damn, he smelled like death too.

With a mental apology to the occupants of the rooms to either side of him, Frankie started the shower, figuring he could use the cleanup. This time he'd sit on the seat and stay there. Frankie moaned in pleasure as the hot water slaked over his skin and he started to feel better. He scrubbed his hair and skin, determined to get rid of eau de rancid man sweat.

"Why're you having a shower at three in the morning? You should have waited for me to help you."

Frankie yelped, nearly smacking his head against the tiled wall—in shock at someone talking to him. "What the fuck? Are you trying to kill me?"

Al leaned up against the sink out of the range of the spray, his arms folded, an amused, exasperated expression on his face.

"What are you doing here?" Frankie asked.

"We got chucked out of the bar."

"You don't seem drunk."

"That's because I'm not. I thought I'd come back and see how you are. I didn't expect to find you in the shower... putting on a show."

Frankie wanted to protest that he wasn't putting on a show, but then Al's expression changed, became heated, and Frankie *wanted* to display himself for Al. His movements became slower, languorous, and he was aware of Al's eyes tracking him as he swirled the shower gel across his skin. He smoothed the bubbles down his cock, feeling it harden and swell in his hand. Al's moan was like an aphrodisiac and Frankie wanted more.

"Join me," he begged.

Al shook his head, softening his rejection with a smile. "I want to fuck you but not in the shower." He held out a towel. "Come here."

Frankie turned off the water, stood, and allowed Al to dry him, holding on to the sink as Al crouched at his feet to dry his legs. Al slid back up with the towel to wrap his hand around Frankie's cock. Frankie's loud moan was smothered by Al's mouth.

"Ssh, you'll wake the neighbors."

"Fuck the neighbors."

Al arched his eyebrow. "You want an orgy?"

Frankie shook his head. "Just you."

He was rewarded with a brilliant smile from Al, and then he was lifted off his feet and carried into the bedroom to be dumped onto the bed. Frankie watched Al strip and stroked his cock, his legs falling apart as he got more aroused.

Al didn't take his eyes off Frankie the whole time he was undressing, watching as Frankie jacked himself, using his thumb to spread the precome over the head.

"I wish I could pound you through the mattress," Al growled as he climbed onto the bed.

"So do I."

Frankie wasn't sure how they were going to do this, because pretty much every position hurt. He accepted that this time they'd have to take it easy, but one day Al would fuck him against every hard surface in his flat, and Frankie would love every second.

Al opted to spoon behind him again, and Frankie lay on his good hip and relaxed against Al's body, feeling Al's hard dick nestle between his arse cheeks.

"I wanna be buried in you already," Al said.

"Lube and rubbers?"

"All ready and waiting."

Frankie heard the *snick* of the cap and hissed as cool jelly slid down his crack.

"Sorry," Al apologized. "It slipped out of my fingers."

Frankie's chuckle morphed into a low moan as Al rimmed him slowly with his fingers.

Despite the fact it was the middle of the night, Al took his time to take Frankie apart nerve by overloaded nerve. He ignored Frankie's pleas for him to goddamn fuck him already and pressed in one finger.

Frankie looked over his shoulder. "I'm not giving you my bloody cherry. I don't need this three-finger bullshit. Get in here and fuck me."

To his annoyance, Al calmly slid his finger out, resting his hand on Frankie's arse.

Frankie pushed back to get some action, but Al didn't move until Frankie went limp. "I thought you weren't a Dom," he said.

"Only with you." Al accompanied the admission with two fingers sliding into him.

Warmth bloomed in Frankie's stomach even if he didn't believe him for a moment.

Al fingered him to the brink of climax before he was pushing in with his cock, filling Frankie until he was pressed hard against Frankie's arse. His arm went around Frankie and pulled him close as he thrust his hips, gently at first until Frankie was begging for more.

Frankie held on to Al, trying to stave his climax, but it was too late and he came untouched, shooting onto the sheet as he yelled with relief.

Al grunted, pounding through his own orgasm, until finally he collapsed hot and sweaty against Frankie.

"I should have waited for my shower," Frankie said with a grin.

A rumbling snore was Al's only response.

Chapter 9

BREAKFAST WAS a rushed affair because they both overslept, Frankie only waking when a door banged outside his room. He jumped, which startled Al, as he was still wrapped tightly in Al's arms.

"Wassup?" Al mumbled.

Frankie relaxed back into Al's embrace. "Just a door banging, nothing important."

Al snuffled and kissed the back of Frankie's neck, making him shiver. Just as Frankie thought about a repeat performance of last night, Al sat up.

"Oh shit! Fuck! It's nine o'clock."

"Yeah?" Frankie rolled onto his back. Considering he had spent most of the last twenty-four hours asleep, Frankie was quite happy to go back to sleep for another couple of hours.

"Breakfast finishes in thirty minutes, and I need to talk to my boss before we go."

"Okay." Frankie was talking to himself because Al had sprung out of bed and rushed into the bathroom.

"Morning, Frankie. Did you sleep well, Frankie? Yes, I did, thank you, Al."

"Do you always hold conversations with yourself?" Al asked, coming back into the bedroom.

"Only when the person I'm sleeping with rushes off without saying good morning," Frankie said tartly.

"Sorry, babe." Al bent down to give Frankie a kiss before he got dressed.

Frankie forgave him because he kissed very nicely. "You go ahead and order me breakfast. I'll have a quick shower and join you. Have I got time to shave?"

"No. Be careful, okay?"

"Yeah, yeah." Frankie groaned as he stretched out tired muscles. "I'll be good, Mum."

"Heh. I don't want you to be good. I want you to be careful."

Frankie headed for the bathroom, leaving Al to get dressed. He wanted breakfast, so the cleanup would have to be brief.

"I'm going," Al called out as Frankie scrubbed his teeth.

"'Kay," he mumbled around the toothbrush.

"Don't be long. And no shaving!"

Frankie wrinkled his nose at his stubbly reflection. "If we're going to make a go of this, you have got to stop nagging, dude." He made sure Al had left the room before he spoke, though.

TO FRANKIE'S surprise, most of the participants were still at breakfast, and a lot of them were nursing very sore heads. A few of the women from yesterday's group waved weakly at him.

Carol had her head in her hands as he sat down next to her.

"Dear me, does the assistant director have a hangover?"

"Piss off," she moaned.

"I missed a good night, then."

"I thought you'd gone home," Ray said as he sat opposite them.

"I was asleep. I missed the whole day."

"You look better now."

"I feel better, unlike Carol who wishes she could die quietly."

"There's nothing quiet about her," Ray said.

Frankie raised his eyebrow. "Oh?" He smirked as they both turned red. "You two finally bumped uglies?"

Carol finally looked up. "Bumped uglies? What are you? My grandmother?" She was still crimson, so Frankie figured that the answer was yes.

Frankie's breakfast arrived, along with the cute and sadly straight waiter. Frankie didn't bother trying to flirt this morning. Why waste his time when he had a sure thing a few seats down?

The sure thing looked at him and smiled, and Frankie did that melting thing that he only did with Al.

Carol nudged him in the ribs. "Eat your breakfast. You can jump his bones later."

"No jumping until you've been checked out," Ray said.

Frankie looked at him and shook his head. "No more nagging. I get enough of that from Al." He scratched at his chin.

"Are you going for the caveman look deliberately?" Carol asked as she surveyed his stubble.

"He," Frankie pointed at Al, "didn't give me permission to shave."

Carol's eyes widened. "Permission? Blimey, the next thing you know you'll be waiting for permission to breathe."

"It's not that bad," Frankie protested.

"No?" Carol leant forward. "Who's the top?"

"Uh…." Frankie squirmed under her intense gaze.

"Thought so."

"It's not like that. We overslept and he wanted to make sure I got breakfast."

"How sweet." Her tone suggested she thought anything but.

Frankie scowled at her. "You're a cynical old bitch, do you know that?"

"Frankie!" Ray sounded outraged.

Carol patted Ray's hand. "He's right, though."

Ray sighed. "What am I going to do with you two?"

Frankie fluttered his eyelashes. "Why Ray, I didn't realize you were into an open relationship. So it'll be you, me, and Carol topping us both." He and Carol burst out laughing as Ray choked on a mouthful of coffee.

"What? No! Never!"

Frankie grinned, and then he caught Carol's speculative glance. "Whatever you're thinking about, lady, the answer is no. I'm strictly a one-man kind of guy."

"You mean you've never thought about more than one?"

"Well, yeah, but they all had dicks. Adorable as you are, I'm not into boobs."

"Such a shame. We could raise hell as a threesome."

Ray gave her dubious look. "Is that what you want? I'm not sure I could do a man."

"Nice turn of phrase," Frankie said.

Ray blushed. "I mean… I…."

Carol laughed. "Relax and take a deep breath. As much as I've had my fantasies about three in a bed, I am more than happy with just you."

"How sweet." Frankie mimicked Carol's previous tone.

She smacked him over the head. "Cheeky bugger."

"Well, yeah! And go easy with the cripple."

They were interrupted by Jill from Team Elements.

"Fifteen minutes, guys, then we need to get started." She winked at Frankie who grinned back.

"I guess Jill didn't stay up drinking last night?" Frankie said.

Carol snorted. "She drank most of us under the table and walked out of the bar looking sober."

"Gotta admire a girl who can do that." Frankie wished he still could. Once of the prices for getting old, he supposed. It suddenly occurred to him that he had not thought about Chaz since Al had started dominating his thoughts.

"We're murdering the eggs this morning," Carol said as she perused the schedule.

"The eggs aren't alive," Ray pointed out.

"Well, they won't be after we've thrown them out of the window."

Frankie snickered. "I wish I could, but I'm going home with Al. I guess they'll make me do this course again."

"Not for a while. I heard one of the others saying this was the last course the company's booked."

"Thank God for that." Frankie was relieved enough to finish his breakfast. He looked slyly at Ray and Carol. "So what's happening with you two? Was it what happens in Guildford, stays in Guildford, or are you carrying on when you get home?"

"We don't live that close to each other," Carol pointed out.

Frankie could see the sadness in Ray's eyes. "It's not that far. Not like you were having a relationship with me."

Carol burst out laughing. "Heaven forbid."

"I'm not that bad."

"Babe, you and me would be like crack and speed together. I'm much better with someone like Ray." She smiled across the table at Ray, who melted and smiled goofily back.

"Well, then," Frankie said. "Not that far apart."

"Not that far," Ray agreed.

Al waved to attract his attention. "I'm going to talk to Jimmy, then I'll take you home."

Frankie nodded. "Cool."

Carol grabbed his arm. "You can't go yet. The old dears were all fluttery because you weren't around last night. You need to say good-bye to them."

"I'll say good-bye to everyone, even Dick. How was the go-karting?"

"It was fun," Ray said. "The other team won. Did you know Barb was a champion driver?"

Frankie's jaw dropped. "Barb? The gray-haired old dear with the foul mouth?" On the other hand, why did it surprise him? She had to have learnt the language from somewhere, and it definitely wasn't extreme jam-making.

Carol nodded. "Before she joined the firm, she worked in a Formula One team and her hobby was go-karting."

"Fuck me," he said. He stared at Barb who was gossiping with Lynn and Dawn, oblivious to their conversation.

"She's not your type, love." Carol reached over for a piece of toast. "But she was a demon on the track. Cut up that young kid over there. He was really pissed off. He tried to get back in front of her but she wasn't having any of it." She waved the toast at a young guy whom Frankie hadn't paid much attention to. "He's more your type, of course."

"Because he's got a dick, you mean?" The guy wasn't anything like his type.

She nodded.

"I'll have you know I'm choosy about who I hook up with. I am!" he protested at her skeptical expression. He felt a kiss on the top of his head.

"Yes, you are." Al scowled at Carol. "Isn't it time you joined the others?"

To Frankie's surprise, she didn't protest, although he was pretty sure from the way Carol jumped, that was to do with the kick Ray aimed at her shin. She kissed Frankie's cheek and left, still munching on her toast. Ray followed her after shaking Frankie's hand.

When they'd gone, Frankie grinned at Al. "Did you just protect my honor, lover?"

"She was calling you a slut," Al grumbled, his fingers tightening on Frankie's shoulders.

"I am many things, but I'm never a slut." Frankie said, tilting his head so he could have a kiss. "I'm not like Jonno. If I'm in a relationship, I'm monogamous."

Al nodded. "Me too. And I won't dump you by text if it goes wrong."

"You'd better not because I'll have your balls if you do. No one does that to me again." Frankie wouldn't let any bastard do that to him again.

"Now we've established the boundaries of our relationship in the middle of the restaurant, can we go home?" Al asked.

"Yeah." Frankie smiled at him softly. "We can do that." He stood up to leave, but Lynn forestalled them.

"Not before I give him a hug." She held out her arms and pulled Frankie into a hug.

"My turn." Barb tugged him out of Lynn's arms and into her own before Frankie had even drawn breath.

"Shouldn't you ladies be in the conference room?" Al asked, a possessive edge to his voice that Frankie was starting to recognize. He apparently did not like other people mauling his boy.

Lynn squeaked, but Barb snapped, "Oh, give it up, big boy. You can have him back in a minute." She squeezed Frankie one more time, kissed him on the cheek, and followed Lynn out of the restaurant, completely ignoring Al.

Al spat on his thumb and smeared it across Frankie's cheek.

"Nice," Frankie said. "Is there something wrong with soap and water?"

"Lipstick doesn't belong there," Al grumbled, rubbing at the mark.

"Oh, darling, you have got to spend more time with Jonno. He'll have you wearing lipstick in no time." Frankie snickered at the horrified look on Al's face.

"Tell me you're joking."

Frankie shook his head. "He loves makeup. Will has a hard job convincing him not to wear it all the time. He wears lipstick, eyeliner, and mascara to work, but he works in a boutique so they don't care."

"Let's go home before I have to prize another female off you." Al laid a hand on Frankie's lower back to guide him out of the restaurant.

Frankie paused in the lobby. "I ought to say good-bye to Dick." He felt guilty at the way he'd ignored Dick all weekend.

Al broke into a broad smile. "I don't think you need to worry about him. Dick has his hands full this morning."

"What did he do?"

"Let's just say he got jumped by one of the women last night, and he's busy trying to get over a hangover and avoid her persistent attentions."

"She does know he's married, right?"

"So's she."

Frankie smacked his forehead. "I don't get it. One weekend away and they're in anybody's briefs. He had his hands all over me on the way down."

Al growled at the news. "He did what?"

"Down, tiger. I wouldn't give a man like that a millimeter of encouragement." He patted Al on the chest.

"He touches you again and I'll make him wish he'd never been born."

Of course, Frankie rolled his eyes and made noises about his born-again caveman, but his dick perked up at being so possessively wanted. And when they got back to Frankie's room, he pushed Al on the bed and blew him as thanks just for being Al. Then Al returned the favor, because he could.

AL LOADED his jeep with their bags while Frankie checked out of his room and bought takeaway coffee for both of them.

He breathed a sigh of relief as Al drove away from the hotel.

"You sound pleased to be away from there," Al said.

"I shouldn't have come this weekend. I'm not up to it."

"Yeah, I think we worked that one out yesterday."

"I just wanted to get it over and done with."

Al snorted loudly. "Most people find any way they can to get out of it. You wouldn't believe the excuses we get."

Frankie grinned at him, admiring Al's profile as he drove. "I'm not most people. I'm me."

"You're one of a kind," Al said. "I knew that from the moment you puked up on me."

"I didn't," Frankie protested.

"I thought you didn't remember anything about that time."

"I don't. Well, not much. But I know I managed to hurl into the loo."

"Well, mostly," Al agreed, "you had a better aim than I thought you would. You were so drunk you couldn't remember your room number."

Frankie grinned at the memory, or what was left of it. "I still don't remember what it was."

"Nor do I. At least I didn't have to take you to hospital."

"What were you doing there? It doesn't seem like your scene."

"Team Elements was contemplating running one of our courses there. I was sent to scout out the hotel, not realizing it was their gay weekend."

"Did you have fun?" Frankie looked at Al when he didn't respond. "Al?"

"I played with a couple of guys," Al said guardedly.

Frankie frowned at him, a nasty suspicion forming in the back of his mind. "Why do I get the feeling you're hiding something?"

"Because… because if I tell you, I don't want it becoming a problem between us."

"Like that isn't going to immediately make me worried."

Al huffed. "Like I said, I was at the hotel, and after I got you back to your room and into bed, I went clubbing."

"Yeah?"

"I ended up in a threesome with a couple of guys."

"That's the way it usually works," Frankie said tightly, wishing Al would just spit it out. He was trying hard not to show how he felt about Al playing with other guys while he'd been sick and miserable.

"I met one of the men again. Not for another fuck," Al added hastily, "and he doesn't remember me."

"Is it Dick?" Frankie asked because Al was obviously worrying that Frankie might be upset.

The look of horror on Al's face nixed that idea. "Fuck no, give me some credit for having better taste than that. I meant Jonno."

Frankie turned to look at him. "You? Fucked Jonno? My friend, Jonno?"

"Well, yeah. Do you know another one?" Al's hands were white-knuckled as he drove.

"And he doesn't remember?"

"He didn't even blink when we met."

"Fucking awesome!"

Al took his eye off the road to stare at him. "What?"

"Road, look at the road," Frankie said hastily.

Al snapped his attention back in front of him. "You don't mind?"

Frankie shrugged. "Why should I? We've shared enough men over the years. But don't let Will know. He'll go mental."

"Will is Jonno's partner?"

"Yep, and a real possessive son of a bitch. He can live with the twinks, but you are way off-limits."

"Uh… why?"

"Too much man for Will. He'd think you were trying to take his place."

"Do you want to tell Jonno?"

"Oh hell no, at least not yet. He might think he can have another threesome, and that is never going to happen. I don't share my meat. Who was the other guy?"

"Hell knows. Just some twink Jonno had already picked up. Short, blond, brainless. Big cock."

"What did he do with the big cock?" Frankie asked, his tone low and dangerous.

"Shoved it down Jonno's throat."

"And you?"

"Plugged Jonno's arse with mine. I don't bottom for any twink."

"Was it a good fuck?"

"If I say never as good as you, is that the right answer?"

"Definitely." Frankie chewed on his lip for a moment. "Would you bottom for me?"

Al sighed and scrubbed through his hair. "We can talk about it. I'm not promising anything. I haven't been fucked by anyone since I was a teenager, and nothing goes near my arse."

"Not even a plug?"

"No."

"Fair enough." Frankie rested his hand on Al's thigh, squeezing it lightly.

"No playing while I'm driving," Al warned. "You cannot give me head or we'll end up in a ditch."

"We could stop." Frankie was all for stopping if it provided a little relief from the tension in the car.

"How about we get home and I fuck you properly?"

"We could do both."

Al groaned. "I am never going to keep up with you."

"Said the man who indulged in a threesome."

"You're not going to let that one go, are you?"

Frankie picked at a piece of fluff on his jeans. "Not for a while."

"What annoys you the most? The fact I had a threesome or the fact it was Jonno?"

"The fact it wasn't me." Frankie threw caution to the wind and admitted how weak he'd felt that night. "I wanted to ask you to stay and hold my hand that night."

Al laid his hand over Frankie's. "I would have stayed if you'd asked."

"I know that now. You're the most caring man I've ever met."

"Not too bossy?"

"You're bossy and you're dominant with a big D, but as long as you remember who it is you're dominating, I can live with that." Frankie leered at him.

"So it's just us, then?"

"Definitely. I don't share my toys." Frankie yelped as Al pinched the back of his hand. "Be careful of the cripple."

"Sorry."

"Try sounding sincere next time."

Al chuckled. "And you call me bossy?"

"Someone has to remind you that you can't get away with everything. I still remember you kissing me as a way of shutting me up."

"It worked."

"Yeah." He went quiet as he remembered the feel of Al's mouth on his as he lay dazed on the road. From the reflective look on Al's face, he was having the same memory. The peace was broken by Al bashing the steering wheel.

"Damn."

"What's the matter?"

"I promised I would visit my mum this evening."

"What's the problem?"

"I want to spend the day with you, but if I go to Mum's, I'm going to have to leave as soon as we can get home."

Frankie patted Al's thigh. "You spend as much as time as you need with your mum. I can wait, she can't."

"Are you sure?"

"I'm sure. I'm not going to have a tantrum about you spending time with your mum at this stage. Give me credit for being more of a grown-up than that."

Al looked over at him briefly. "Twenty-nine and all growed-up."

"Heh, look, Mum, it happened finally. How old are you? I never asked you that."

"Thirty-five, thirty-six next July."

"So you've had a birthday since I knew you."

Al flushed again. "It was my birthday the night we first met. I figured the threesome was a great present for having to work on my birthday."

"Not so beige after all," Frankie murmured.

"What did you say?"

"Never mind." There was time to explain the life of beige later. It was bad enough that he'd succumbed to snuggling on the sofas but he was blowed if he was going to go for long walks in the park.

WHEN THEY got to Frankie's place, Al carried Frankie's bag up the stairs and came back down again to give Frankie an arm. Frankie's legs weren't cooperating after the drive.

He leant against Al, grateful for the support. "Dammit, it was just a bruise."

"Which you compounded by falling on it again."

"Yes, thanks, doc," Frankie said sourly.

Al held him tighter. "Come on, you'll feel better once you're sitting down."

Frankie made it up the stairs by sheer force of will and the seven times table.

As he fumbled with his key, Al plucked it out of his hand (as usual) saying, "You got that wrong."

"Got what wrong?" Not that Frankie cared because all he could think of was "Ow! Shit!" as he placed one foot in front of the other.

"Eight times seven is not fifty-four. It's fifty-six."

"Do I care?"

"I was just pointing out your error."

"What a helpful little Alan you are." Frankie collapsed on his sofa with a huge sigh of relief, ignoring Al's eye roll by closing his own eyes. He wasn't moving from here for the next year if he could help it.

"I'm going to sleep. Wake me up when you leave."

"You don't want any endorphin-releasing fun?"

Frankie opened his eyes reluctantly. "I never thought I'd hear myself say this but not really."

Al looked disappointed, but he sat down next to Frankie, careful not to jog him. "I'll call the hospice. Let them know I'll be on my way soon."

"Can't you just go in when you want?"

"Yes, but I like to check in every day." He frowned as he looked at his phone. "I think they called me while we were driving. I've got a missed call."

Hearing Al's voice crack at the end, Frankie held his hand while he waited for the hospice to answer. It wasn't hard to guess the nature of the call from the anguish in Al's voice.

Al put the phone down, refusing to look at Frankie.

"When?" Frankie asked.

"An hour ago. She went more suddenly than they expected. They rang me to say it was imminent, and she died about fifteen minutes after that."

Frankie tugged Al into his arms, ignoring the resistance. "Come here, you idiot."

"I've got to go. Mum…." He struggled to find the words.

"She is sleeping now, love. She won't mind if you take a little longer to get your head together. I'm not letting you drive yet," Frankie said, prepared to barricade the door if necessary.

Al finally let Frankie hold him, burying his face in the crook of Frankie's neck, his shoulders shaking as he mourned for his mother. Wetness soaked Frankie's skin as he held Al as close as he could, and he had to bite his lip against tears of his own that threatened to fall.

Epilogue

IT WAS a week before Frankie saw Al again. Funeral arrangements and clearing out his mother's house had taken all of Al's time. Frankie wasn't able to offer his assistance as his hip was still healing and he had been warned by Kurt, the physiotherapist, to stick to his exercises until he had fully recovered.

They'd spoken every night. Frankie had stared at the phone like a teenage girl, waiting for Al's phone call. Not seeing him was chafing on Frankie's nerves. He was thrilled when Al called after work on the Monday following his mother's death and asked if he could come around to see him.

"When?" Frankie said immediately. "Now? Where are you?"

"Standing outside your door," Al said, sounding sheepish.

Frankie opened the front door and hauled Al into his arms before he could even speak. Al collapsed against him, his shoulders shaking. Frankie slammed the door shut with his leg, not wanting to let go of Al, and maneuvered them so he could rest against the wall and bear Al's weight. They stayed like that until the storm of Al's grief had lessened and he could raise his head. Frankie cupped Al's jaw, now covered in a short dark beard, and wiped the tears away with a tissue he'd had in his pocket, just in case it was needed.

Al sniffled. "Sorry."

"Nothing to be sorry about, idiot. Blow." Frankie waited until Al had blown his nose, and then he kissed him. "Ready to come and sit down?"

"Could we lie down on the bed? I'm shattered, and I haven't slept in days." The lines around Al's eyes and mouth were testament to how tired he was.

"Sure." Frankie took Al's hand and led him into the bedroom. Al stood, acquiescent, as Frankie undressed him like a child. "Get into bed."

Al grabbed his hand. "Will you stay with me for a while?"

"Course I will." Frankie stripped himself, leaving the clothes where they fell. In bed he wrapped himself around Al, kissing whatever patch of skin he could reach.

Al shuddered and held on tight. "I've missed you so much."

"Ditto." Frankie wasn't going to let go of Al until he loved away some of the misery and grief.

Al rolled them over so he lay with his head on Frankie's chest, one leg slung over Frankie's waist. "I'm glad she's gone. She was in so much pain and so brave."

Frankie didn't have a clue what to say, so he just held on to Al, stroking his hair and murmuring soothing noises. Al didn't seem to expect anything more and relaxed against Frankie, his slow breathing gradually changing into shallow snores.

Frankie dozed for a while as Al slept, but eventually he had to move, spurred on by bodily needs and the weight of Al's leg bearing down on his bad hip. To Frankie's relief, Al didn't wake as Frankie wriggled out from underneath him. He grumbled and snuggled back into the warm patch Frankie had left behind.

"Love you," Frankie whispered and kissed Al's neck. Then he headed for the bathroom because, fuck, he needed a piss.

Al emerged about eleven o'clock, just when Frankie was wrapped in his dressing gown, drinking chamomile tea, and thinking about going to bed because he'd seen this episode of *Law & Order: SVU* too many times, and the fact he was repeating the script along with the delightful Detective Elliot Stabler was not a good sign. On the other hand, drooling at the good detective was never to be missed, and *Castle* wasn't on.

"Hey." Al flopped down next to him, still naked, and picked up the remote to see which episode it was. "He did it," Al said immediately as a generic bad dude of the week appeared.

"Spoiler much," Frankie said without heat.

"Yeah, I do that a lot." Al curled into Frankie's side.

"Want a drink?" Frankie asked.

"Yes, but not right now. I need a cuddle first."

Frankie put his arms around Al and relaxed, half watching the TV and mostly concentrating on keeping Al safe.

"Would you come to the funeral with me?" Al asked after a few minutes.

"Are you sure, babe? I didn't know your mum." The last funeral Frankie had attended was his Auntie Mabel's, and that had been a riot, her bingo crowd like a flash mob with Zimmer frames and walking sticks.

"I haven't got anyone else to ask. She didn't have many friends, and we only had each other and Aunty Vi, and she wants to send me to hell. Her brother died five years ago."

"I'll be there."

"Thanks."

Frankie kissed the top of his head, and they watched to the end of the episode.

"Told you it was him," Al said as the credits rolled.

"Yeah, yeah, I have seen it before." Frankie stretched his arms above his head, trying hard not to wince in front of Al.

"How is your hip really?" Al held up his hand as Frankie opened his mouth. "I will know if you lie."

"Don't need to tell you, then, do I?"

Frankie limped with fucking dignity over to the kettle. "Tea or coffee?"

Al grimaced. "I don't need caffeine. Have you got any cocoa?"

"Er…." Frankie rooted in the cupboard. "Here we are." Christ knows why he had cocoa, he didn't drink it.

"How old is it?" Al asked suspiciously.

"I've only been here a couple of months. Jonno must have brought it over when he stayed."

"He slept with you?"

"Not in the biblical sense." Frankie poured some milk into a saucepan. "He took care of me after the accident for a few days. Besides, you can't be jealous as you actually *have* slept with him."

"I should have got your phone number," Al said.

Frankie nodded. "I wanted you here to hold my hand again. I can't believe I didn't ask you for it."

"You were in pain."

"Didn't stop me clocking you were gorgeous."

"I noticed that." Al smirked. "I think we freaked the driver. I can't believe you threatened him with a lawsuit when you stepped out in front of him."

"Huh. It shut his homophobic arse up."

"I'm sure that's not even English."

Frankie flipped him off. "You know what I mean. Do you want any sugar?"

"Two, please."

Frankie made himself another tea and brought the mugs over to the sofa. "You're not going back tonight, are you?"

"Not unless you want me to." Al wrapped his hands around the mug of cocoa.

Frankie tried hard to dispel the image of those hands wrapped around his cock.

"Frankie?"

"Huh?" Frankie looked up.

"Do you want me to go home?"

He shook his head. "Stay with me as long as you like."

"You haven't seen my place yet."

"We can go there if you like." Frankie was curious to see what sort of place Al lived in.

Al leant back against the sofa and closed his eyes. "I'm happy here."

"I can call in sick tomorrow if you want to stay," Frankie said, feeling all melty again.

"I have to go in to your office tomorrow. I promised my boss I'd do this meeting."

"Is that why you came over?"

Al tapped him on the head. "I came over because I needed you."

Frankie kissed him on his lips, sweet tasting and infinitely lickable. "Glad you did. I was going to come over to you if you hadn't called."

"Wish you had." Al slumped against Frankie, and it was obvious he was flagging.

Frankie downed the rest of his tea and smiled at him. "Drink up. We'll go back to bed."

"I'm fine," Al lied.

"Fine, you stay up. I'm going to bed because I'm shattered."

"I'm not going to stay up on my own."

"Then come to bed with me." Frankie held out his hand. "If you're awake enough, you can fuck me through the mattress."

Al's eyes lit up, but then he yawned. "Can we take a rain check on that? I can't think of anything I want more, but I'd like to stay awake long enough to enjoy it."

Frankie smiled sweetly at him. "You're on." He tugged Al to his feet and into his arms. "I love you."

Al nosed Frankie along the line of his jaw. "You need a shave—everywhere."

"I'll go for a wax. And so do you by the way." Frankie tugged on Al's beard. "What's all this about?"

"I couldn't be bothered to shave."

Frankie licked his lips because the thought of getting up close and personal with Al's throat was a real turn-on. "I'll shave you."

Al's eyes widened slightly. "If you promise not to slit my throat, you're on."

Frankie tangled his fingers through Al's. "Come to bed, love. We can play with each other tomorrow. Tonight we'll sleep in each other's arms."

"Are you always so poetic?"

"Only when it involves parts of your anatomy."

"That's all right, then. You can go to sleep holding one part of me in reserve for tomorrow morning."

Frankie dropped his gaze to the other part of Al he definitely had plans for. "My pleasure."

ED &
MARCHANT

SUE BROWN

To T.J. Masters. You have a big heart, my friend. Much love, Sue xx

Chapter 1

FROM THE isolation of his cubicle, Ed Winters watched over the top of his rimless glasses as two members of his staff twirled around the office, and his lip curled. "One day soon, Mr. Mason, you will get what you deserve."

It was wishful thinking on Ed's part. Frankie Mason was Teflon-coated. He could waltz in late, flirt with all the women, and screw up, but nothing touched him, and everyone worshipped the ground he walked on. Even the bitches in management thought Mason had golden balls. The bollocking Ed had received for snitching on Frankie still rankled bitterly.

Ed hated his job… and his staff, including Frankie Mason. Especially Frankie Mason.

Of course the feeling was returned in spades. Ed knew exactly what his staff at the insurance company thought of him. He had once heard Frankie describe him as a 1950s Tory poster boy who disliked "women, black people, anyone from the Indian subcontinent, curry, the French, the Irish, dogs—" and after that damning (and stunningly accurate) indictment, Frankie had minced across the room with a limp wrist, enunciating "—*hom-o-sex-uals.*"

Frankie was a screaming queer (his words) and didn't give a flying fart what Ed Winters thought about him (also his words).

Ed despised him.

It's not as if anything Frankie said was incorrect. Ed hated all those things and more. If anyone had asked him what he did like… well, no one asked him. No one talked to him at work unless they had to, which was exactly the way he preferred it, and he didn't have any friends or family.

In Ed's pristine ivory home, nothing and no one disturbed his peace. He could shut the door behind him, place his shoes neatly in the shoe rack, hang up his jacket, and forget about the idiots and lowlifes that infested his existence.

No one knocked at Ed's door or called his phone. His flat was his castle, and there he found peace. His sanctuary soothed his soul. It kept him going through the eight-and-a-half hours of the miserable drudgery of work.

If he lived close enough, he would escape back home at lunchtime, but it was just too far away to make it feasible. Instead Ed ate his spinach salad and sparkling water at his desk every day, looking out the window to the park beyond and wishing he was there. Not in the park. The park was fine, but the other occupants—the screaming kids, filthy dogs leaving their shit over the paths, and shrill mothers—were the bane of his existence. But the park was on his route. A place of joy at five thirty in the evening and doom and despair at eight thirty in the morning as he approached the office.

Ed looked down at the files on his desk, and his lip curled. "How on earth did I end up here? I had *plans*."

He'd planned to set the world on fire with his dancing. Instead he'd ended up in a dead-end job that drained his soul. Not just his job. His life. Ed refused to admit, even to himself, the soul-sucking loneliness of his existence.

Ed looked over at Frankie now engaging in an obscene tango with that slut, Charlotte, also a member of his team.

"You think you can dance?" he muttered. "*I* can dance. I could make you cry with my paso doble."

But the world was never going to weep tears over his paso doble, and Ed was going to shuffle papers, hating his life until he died, bitter and alone.

Chapter 2

WAKING UP on Saturday mornings was a rare shining moment of happiness in Ed's miserable existence. He didn't have to go to work. He didn't have to suck up to the coven in management, and he didn't have to see Frankie Mason. God shined down on him on Saturday mornings.

Ed followed a strict routine of housework, laundry, and shopping so that he could spend the rest of the day free to do what he wanted. Once he'd removed the dust from his flat and laundered and neatly ironed his shirts, at eleven fifteen Ed braved the crowds to purchase his food for the week.

This particular Saturday he was fifteen minutes earlier than usual and, for some extremely annoying reason, unable to park in his preferred row in the supermarket car park. He had to park ten rows away, which annoyed him intensely. However, it was Saturday, and Ed had to take a deep breath, because he wasn't going to let anything ruin his peace.

One moment Ed was dodging a 4x4 as it launched out of a parking space toward the supermarket, and the next he stood in disbelief as sticky brown liquid dripped from his hair and glasses, and ice slid down his skin inside his shirt. "What the hell?"

A tall man with dark hair waved a now empty cup at him. "Oh shit! I am so sorry. I tripped."

"You should be more careful!" Ed snapped, gasping as a cube of ice slithered down his breastbone, followed by a wake of goose bumps.

"It was an accident," the man said, an edge to his voice.

Ed managed to tear himself away from the tantalizing feel of ice sliding down his body to focus on the man ineffectually dabbing at his chest with a handkerchief. He blinked at the sight of the square of linen. He thought he was the only person who bothered with such an anachronism. The hand attached to the handkerchief was large, with thick blunt fingers.

"You've got large hands," Ed blurted out.

The man narrowed his eyes. "I throw Coke over you, and you look at my hands?"

Ed swallowed nervously. Unguarded comments like that were asking for trouble, and this man was huge, in proportion to his hands. "I'm sorry... I...." He sucked in a breath as the ice finished its sticky trail to his navel. "Just a sliver of ice," he explained weakly. "It caught me by surprise."

"You liked that."

"I... no... it was a shock."

"You're getting off on the ice on your skin."

Ed didn't need complete strangers judging him. "Be more careful in the future."

He fled before the stranger could say anything else.

What had been pleasurable was now sticky and horrible as the ice melted. Away from the judging eyes of the stranger, Ed hesitated, not sure whether to purchase a fresh shirt from the supermarket or retreat back home. He didn't wear anything as cheap and formless as supermarket shirts, but needs must, and he didn't want to dirty his car with Coke stains.

Ignoring the amused eyes of the shoppers as they took in his dripping form, Ed headed toward the clothing section of the supermarket. He looked at the small variety of shirts as he rubbed the soda off his glasses and replaced them. Under normal circumstances he wouldn't be seen dead in any of these badly made garments. Ed only wore expensive formal shirts, whether it was weekend or weekday. His only concession to the weekend was the lack of a tie.

"Needs bloody must." He picked out a pale gray shirt and headed to the till.

The woman clucked at him as she scanned the shirt and removed the security tag. "Had an accident, did you? Clumsy fingers?"

Ed scowled at her. "It was done to me," he snapped, resenting the amused, knowing tone.

"It was my fault." Ed stiffened as he heard a voice behind him. "I'll pay for the shirt."

Ed looked over his shoulder to see the Coke-throwing, morning-disrupting annoyance smiling at him. "I'm quite capable of paying for a cheap shirt."

The smile faded, but the man said, "I know, but it was my fault. I should pay for it."

"There's no need," Ed said, searching through his wallet for his card.

"I insist."

"Someone pay for the sodding shirt," a woman behind Ed shouted.

To Ed's fury, the man handed over his card, and the cashier processed it before Ed could object again.

"Come on, let's get you cleaned up." The man took the shirt and walked away without looking to see whether Ed was following him.

"Is there anything else, love?"

Ed realized he was gaping after the stranger who was making off with his shirt, and he was holding up the queue. "No, sorry."

He hastened after the man, who hadn't looked back. "Wait!"

The man paused outside the toilets. "Is there anything else you need to clean up?" Ed shook his head dumbly. "Good boy. Go and get changed, and then I'll take you for a coffee to apologize."

"But...."

"Is there a problem?"

The man raised an eyebrow, and Ed had the sudden feeling he would take Ed into the toilets and undress him if Ed didn't regain control of the situation.

"No." Ed snatched the shirt out of his hand and rushed into the gents.

To his relief the stranger didn't try to follow him.

It took a few minutes to clean up to Ed's satisfaction. He was a sticky mess, and even after he'd washed his torso and scrubbed his hair with the cheap soap, he was uncomfortably aware he still smelled of Coke. He shoved the ruined shirt into one of the bags he used for shopping. It was one of his favorites and too expensive to ditch.

He hoped the man would have given up waiting for him, but his wish wasn't to be answered, as the man was leaning against the wall outside the door as Ed emerged.

The man smiled broadly at him. "I was about to come in and fetch you."

Ed wanted to snap that he wasn't a dog, but he didn't have a chance to respond because the man walked away. Once again Ed was faced with the choice of following him like a naughty schoolboy or running away. The urge to flee was great, but he had the feeling the man would retrieve him. Reluctantly he followed, conscious his entire day was out of kilter. Ed did not like this at all.

The supermarket café was on the first floor. Ed had never been up there. He didn't frequent cheap restaurants full of the type of people he didn't like. When he reached the café, he discovered it was as bad as he expected, and he had to negotiate three buggies before he could even reach the annoying stranger.

"What do you want to drink?" The man didn't look at Ed as he approached, his gaze fixed on the menu board. "Coffee or tea?"

"I don't drink either."

The admission did make the man look at him in surprise. "Really? I couldn't live without coffee. I'll have a large latte, and you?"

"Sparkling water."

"Please."

Ed frowned. "I'm sorry?"

"That's quite all right... this time. Next time say please." The man went back to studying the board. "It's almost lunchtime. I can't decide whether to have a cake or an early lunch."

Ed's eyes widened as he realized a total stranger was chastising him for his lack of manners... one who had disrupted his entire morning. He walked away, his gut churning with anger.

"Hey, where are you going?"

Ed ignored him, negotiating the people coming out of the lift, and headed down the stairs. He was stopped in his tracks by a hand on his bicep. For a second Ed teetered on the edge of a step, and he was afraid he was going to fall. Then he was yanked back.

"What the hell are you doing now?"

"Leave me alone," Ed yelled. "You've ruined enough of my day." He was aware of people looking at him as they went up the stairs, but he'd had enough—more than enough.

The man ran a hand through his hair, and Ed noticed the red glints as sunlight sparkled on them. "I was trying to apologize by buying you a drink."

"I don't need a drink, and I don't need a lesson in manners."

"Oh." The man grinned. "That's what got your knickers in a twist. It is polite to say please."

"I don't need to be told by a man half my age. And I'm not a kid you can order about."

"But you are a sub, aren't you?" the man said, his voice quieter than before.

Horrified, Ed took a step back and missed his footing. For a brief second he flailed before being hauled to safety again.

"Jesus, let's get off these stairs before you kill yourself or someone else."

The man stalked downstairs. Ed stared after him, knowing he expected him to follow.

As he reached the landing, the man looked over his shoulder. "Well?"

Ed pressed his lips together and followed him downstairs. At the bottom of the stairs, the man said, "Look. We seem to have got off on the wrong foot. Let's start again." He stuck out his hand. "My name is Marchant Belarus. I'm sorry for throwing Coke over you, and I'd like to buy you a drink to apologize. I really need a coffee now."

Ed didn't respond immediately. The twitch of Marchant's lips told him that he not only expected a response, but Ed was going to get another lesson in manners if he didn't reply. "Ed Winters."

He shook Marchant's hand. The man—Marchant—had a firm, dry handshake.

"Nice to meet you, Ed. Shall we get that drink?"

Ed would much rather have run home and hidden than spend more time in Marchant's company, but he gave a brief nod.

"Good boy."

Ed seethed at his condescending tone as Marchant turned to walk up the stairs.

Back in the café, the queue thankfully had died down. Marchant ordered a large latte and a sparkling water. "Do you want anything to eat?"

Ed shook his head, as his spinach salad was waiting for him at home. Then he saw the expectant look on Marchant's face. "No… thank you."

Marchant looked at him approvingly. Ed thought that if Marchant said "good boy" one more time he would be the one wearing the drink.

Within a couple of minutes, Marchant seated them in a small area thankfully away from kids and buggies.

Marchant took a noisy, long swallow. "That's better."

Ed sipped at his water, trying hard not to curl his lip. He hated sloppy eating.

"You freaked out when I called you a sub."

"I…." Ed's hand clenched around his glass. "I didn't know what you meant."

"Yes, you did," Marchant said, his eyes trained on Ed.

"I'm not a sub."

That was true. At least not in Ed's life… maybe in his dreams. And once, just once, he'd given in to his desires. But he had to push those thoughts away.

"If you say so." Marchant's tone told of his doubt. "Tell me about yourself, Ed Winters."

"I'm an administration manager for an insurance company."

Marchant nodded. When nothing more was forthcoming, he said, "Boyfriend? Husband?"

Ed choked on his water. "I'm not… you can't… you don't…." He coughed violently as the water he had drunk threatened to make a return appearance.

"Whoa, easy, tiger." Marchant was out of his chair and rubbing Ed's back before he could stop him. "Breathe… breathe."

Ed was mortified and coughing and wishing the floor would open up and swallow him whole.

"Better?" Marchant waited for him to stop spluttering before he returned to his seat.

Ed grabbed his drink and sipped at it desperately, coughing again as the water hit the back of his throat.

"Easy. Sip it slowly. You don't want to do that again," Marchant said. "Now, let's get one thing straight."

Ed looked at him.

"Don't treat me as stupid, Ed."

"I'm not. I don't *know* you."

"That's true. But I know *you*, or people like you."

"You don't." Ed shook his head. "You can't."

Marchant leaned forward, his expression intent. Ed felt like a small rodent under the gaze of a snake. "But I do. You're gay, and you're a sub."

Ed stood up, his chair falling over with the force of the action. "Thank you for the drink. I've got to go."

Marchant stood. "Ed, don't go."

"Ed? Mr. Winters? What a surprise to see you here."

And with that, Ed's Saturday slid into the toilet. Frankie Mason smirked at him. Frankie's boyfriend stood behind him, scowling at Ed. Presumably this was Al. Ed knew his name because Frankie never bloody stopped talking about him. Why did they have to look so… *together*? The rest of the world didn't need to know they were mooning over each other.

"Mason." He attempted a polite smile, although it was probably more of a grimace.

"I didn't realize you used this supermarket," Frankie said perkily.

Ed refrained from pointing out it was the only one in town. "I'm just...."

He trailed off as Frankie's attention strayed to Marchant, who for some reason now stood next to Ed.

Frankie smiled brightly. "Hi, I'm Frankie Mason. I work with Ed."

For Ed. Not with. Ed kept his mouth shut.

Marchant shook his hand. "Marchant Belarus."

"Wow, that's an unusual name."

Marchant snorted. "Blame it on the arty parents."

"Great name. This is Al, my boyfriend."

Al leaned forward and shook Marchant's hand. He didn't offer to shake Ed's hand, and Ed could tell by the way Marchant stiffened that he was deeply unhappy about this. Ed was half expecting Marchant to deliver a lecture on manners to Al when Frankie started babbling.

"So how do you two know each other?"

Ed was about to tell him to mind his own business when Marchant chuckled.

"I tripped, and my Coke landed over Ed. He kindly agreed to let me buy him a drink by way of an apology."

Frankie's eyes widened. "You covered him in Coke?"

Ed gritted his teeth. That morsel of gossip was going to be around the office before he'd taken off his coat on Monday morning. He also saw the satisfaction on Al's face. It was bad enough having to take it from his underling, but Ed wasn't going to take it from Al.

"I have to go," he said.

"I'll come with you. Good-bye, Frankie. Al." Marchant grasped Ed's arm and steered him to the door.

"Wait, Mr. Winters."

Ed looked over his shoulder to see Frankie waving a bag over his head. "My shirt."

Marchant let him go, and Ed went back.

To his surprise, Frankie held on to the bag. "Mr. Winters, Ed, are you all right? We saw what happened. Do you want us to come with you or run him off?"

Ed stared at him.

"Is he hurting you?" Al asked.

Slowly Ed shook his head. Marchant was confused about a lot of things, but he seemed to be a good man. "He's not hurting me. I'm fine."

"Are you sure?" Frankie asked.

He looked genuinely concerned, and Ed was unwillingly touched. "I'm okay. I need to get my shopping completed."

Frankie didn't look convinced, but he let go of the bag. "Okay, then." Then he smirked again. "I'd have given anything to see the pristine Ed Winters covered in Coke."

Any softening of feelings Ed might have been harboring toward Frankie vanished, and he scowled. "I'll see you on Monday, Mr. Mason."

He stalked away, conscious of Marchant staring at him and the all-too-seeing eyes of his nemesis behind.

"Will this day never end?" he muttered.

At the base of the stairs, Marchant pulled Ed to one side and didn't let go of his arm. "What did Frankie say to you?"

"What?"

"What did he say?"

"He asked me if you were hurting me."

Marchant nodded. "Good. It's good you have friends looking after you."

"He's hardly a friend," Ed said without thinking.

"He took the time to see if you were all right," Marchant pointed out. "That implies some degree of friendship."

"I'm his boss, and Frankie Mason is a...." Ed pressed his lips together.

"Ah, that explains the hostility from his boyfriend."

Ed reached the end of his patience. "Thank you for the drink, but I have to do my shopping now."

"We can go around together," Marchant said cheerfully.

"I don't want to go around with you," Ed said, aware he sounded petty and childish. "I have a routine."

Marchant raised his eyebrow. "A routine? Well, I can fit in with that."

Ed gaped at him. "What the hell? What don't you understand? I've let you ruin my morning. I've put up with you telling me to sit, stay, and come. Now I want to do my shopping and forget this day ever happened."

To Ed's chagrin, Marchant didn't seem at all bothered by his outburst. Instead he leaned forward, and unconsciously Ed mimicked his action.

"I haven't told you to come yet, but when I do, you'll obey."

The breath knocked out of Ed's chest. He stumbled back. "Leave me alone. Don't come near me again."

Ed fled the supermarket as if the hounds of hell were after him, all the time waiting for Marchant to drag him back. He reached his car without intervention, fumbling as he tried to press the button on the keys to unlock the door. Inside the car he clutched the steering wheel, the blood pounding in his ears. He'd been seen for what he was.

Deviant! Abomination! Pervert!

He could hear his mother and grandmother huddled around, whispering names about him as he sat at the table and tried to do his homework. They knew what he was from the moment he was born, and they took every opportunity to tell him. He'd spent a lifetime building a barrier between him and the world so he wouldn't be tempted to sully someone with his perversion. He'd tried to hide himself for so long, and yet a complete stranger had seen him for what he was from the moment they met.

Deviant! Abomination! Pervert!

Ed leaned his head on the steering wheel and tried to block out the sound of their voices, closing his eyes until he was together enough to drive again.

It was only when he got home that two things became evident. Firstly, he needed food. His lunch was waiting for him in the fridge, but he needed food for the coming week. And secondly, he'd lost his expensive shirt, dropped somewhere in the flight from the supermarket.

As he ripped off the hated, cheap-and-nasty shirt, Ed gritted his teeth so hard his jaw ached. He threw it into the bin and stripped down, only realizing how Coke-stained his trousers were as he took them off. The shower was always turned to hot, but this time he turned the temperature high enough that it was on the point of pain.

Deviant! Abomination! Pervert!

Ed leaned against the tiles and closed his eyes. Never a day went past but their voices were in his head, telling him exactly what he was.

"Deviant! Abomination! Pervert!" Ed curled his right hand into a fist and smacked it against the tiled wall in time with each hurtful word. "Deviant! Abomination! Pervert!"

It was a mantra that Ed had been repeating since he was a child.

The hot water streamed over his hair and down his back. Ed slammed up the temperature even further, gasping at the pain, because he couldn't take pleasure at it. Couldn't. Wouldn't. It was wrong.

Deviant! Abomination! Pervert!

Chapter 3

ED WALKED to work on Monday morning, his footsteps lagging as he approached the office. It was hard to explain, if anyone had cared to listen, how he had got to thirty-seven and boxed into a place he hated.

He could leave, search for another job, but what could he do? He was piss-poor at this one, but it paid the bills. How was he going to explain to a prospective employer that he'd only stayed in his current role because he was too afraid to leave?

For all his failings, Ed wasn't stupid. He knew that employers were looking for dynamic managers. No one had ever called him dynamic except on the dance floor.

Ed put aside the image of him dancing. That was in the past.

He walked through the main entrance and nodded at the security guard. "Morning, Chris."

"Morning, Mr. Winters. How are you?"

"Fine, fine."

He was always polite to the security guards. He'd seen what happened to people who pissed them off or ignored them. Ed took care to avoid the day-to-day bag searches or the "Oh my, you have a flat tire again."

Pleasantries aside, he headed for the lifts. As he stepped inside, he spotted Frankie. Ed stabbed at the button, hoping the doors would close before Frankie arrived, but as in all things, he was doomed to disappointment.

Frankie squeezed in between the doors, grinning at him. "Morning, Mr. Winters."

"Mr. Mason."

"I… have…. Marchant asked me to give you this."

Frankie drew out a bag. Ed's bag, containing his shirt.

"I'm surprised he bothered." Ed took it gingerly as if it was about to explode.

"Look, I don't know what happened on Saturday, but it was obvious you were upset. You know you can talk to me—anytime."

Ed stared at him. Talk? To Frankie Mason? He'd sooner have each hair follicle pulled out by tweezers. But Frankie was the golden boy, and Ed knew if he said one more wrong word, he'd be out of a job. "I'm fine, thank you. It was just a disagreement."

Frankie bit his lip. "Marchant seemed really unhappy when he found us. He stayed for a coffee."

"He discussed me with you?"

Could this Monday get any worse?

"No, no, not at all. It turns out he knows Al through some club they both belong to. He left his phone number in the bag in case you want to ring him."

Ed took a deep breath as the lift doors opened. "I have no intention of calling Mr. Belarus." He stalked out of the lift, only too aware of Frankie dogging his footsteps.

To his relief Charlotte and Naz intercepted Frankie before he could speak again.

"Jesus, did you have to come up with Tory Boy?" Charlotte didn't even attempt to keep her voice down.

Ed waited for Frankie to spill the beans about Ed's Saturday morning, but to his surprise, Frankie merely said, "Morning, darlin'. Don't worry, he didn't have time to convert me. I'm still one hundred percent queer-queer-queer."

Ed pressed his lips together, words burning on his tongue. He hated the way Frankie flaunted his perversion—in the office, in the supermarket. There was no rest from it. Don't ask, don't tell had been perfectly acceptable before. Now it was in the papers and homosexuals could get married, for heaven's sake. His mother and grandmother would have been turning in their graves.

He sat down at his desk and looked out the window. The urge to run was so strong. One day he would start running and not stop until he was hundreds of miles away from here.

His phone disturbed his musing.

"Winters?"

Ed bit back a sigh as he heard the clipped tones of his director. "Yes."

"Is the report for the Baker case finished?"

"Almost. I have the conclusion to type up."

It was a lie. He hadn't started it. Yet another thing he'd failed to do.

"I want it on my desk by ten o'clock."

Ed listened to the ring tone for a few seconds before he realized the director had hung up. "Happy bloody Monday to you too, dick."

He looked at the Baker folder, spilling over with paper. It would take more than an hour just to read it. He looked over at Frankie and Charlotte, gossiping by the coffee machine.

"Mr. Mason?"

Frankie glanced over with a look of surprise. "Yes?"

"I have a job I'd like you to do." This was mean and petty. It wasn't Frankie's job at all, but Ed didn't give a flying flamingo.

Frankie came over with two cups in his hands. "Sparkling water." He handed one to Ed, who blinked, shocked by the courtesy.

"Th-thank you. I need your help." That wasn't what he'd been about to say. He'd been about to dump a huge report in Frankie's lap and tell him to get on with it.

"What can I do?"

"I have a report that's urgent, and I need the stats. Would you find the information for me as I type it up?"

Frankie pursed his lips, and Ed thought he was about to tell him to take a hike.

"I can type faster than you. How about you find the info, and I'll type."

Ed nodded, because it was logical. He pulled the file toward him. "Joseph Baker, date of birth November 25, 1949."

An hour later Frankie typed the last sentence of the conclusion. "Done. And done. I'll print a copy so you can look for errors."

Ed sat back in his seat and breathed easy for the first time since he'd stepped out of the lifts. The report was done, it looked professional, and it proved conclusively that Ed and his team were not responsible for the shitstorm that had happened last Thursday.

When the phone rang, he knew who was on the line. To his surprise Frankie answered the phone.

"Mr. Winters's phone. No, sir, it's Frankie Mason. Mr. Winters is at the printer. Yes. Your report. He's asked me to check it before he brings it up. Don't want any mistakes, do we?"

Ed listened to the conversation, envying the easy flow Frankie had with a man who'd barely spoken to Ed since he joined the department.

Frankie put the phone down. "All sorted. Let's check the report and get it up to him."

"Thank you."

It was Frankie's turn to blink. "Thank *you*."

Ed realized today was probably the first time he'd ever thanked Frankie for anything. "You taught me a great deal about producing a report."

"It's simple enough when you know how. Tell me next time you have one to do, and we'll run through it."

"I will."

Fifteen minutes later the report was in the hands of the director, who gave him an odd look when Ed praised Frankie for his help.

"Are you feeling all right, Winters?"

"Yes. Why?"

"Because you've been positively pleasant about Mason, and usually you don't give him the time of day."

"I couldn't have done this without him. He deserves the praise. He also helped to prove that we weren't responsible for last week's... issues with Mr. Baker's account."

"Glad to hear it. The last thing I need is another PR disaster. Good work, Winters."

"Thank you."

Ed walked away from the director's office on a high. It was the first time the man had praised him for anything. As he sat down at his desk and Frankie smiled at him a little tentatively, Ed smiled back. Frankie looked shocked, but he gave Ed a thumbs-up and went back to his work.

Ed looked out the window at the park. For the first time in a long while, he didn't have the urge to run away.

ED'S FEELING of well-being lasted until just before he left for the day. He walked past the coffee machine to see Naz and Charlotte huddled in a corner. Ed frowned, annoyed to see that slut bothering the one person Ed didn't despise. Despite his mistrust of all foreigners, Naz had the potential to go far, and he didn't want Charlotte and her ilk dragging him down. Their backs were to him and they didn't spot him as they gossiped.

"He must have got laid," Charlotte said as she poured milk into her cup.

Naz coughed. "That's a bit of a long stretch. From a smile to getting some."

"Well, how else do you explain it? Normally he's a frigid bitch, and today he's all smiles and 'Would you help me, Frankie? Thank you, Frankie.' I can't think of any other explanation."

Ed realized to his horror that they were talking about him. He was prepared to go storming over there, but something kept him where he was.

Charlotte continued, still unaware the subject of her conversation was in earshot. "I tried to get the goss out of Frankie because I *know* he knows something. You can see it all over his face."

"What did he say?"

"Nothing. Not a word. Normally you can't shut the bitch up about Winters, but now he's like a clam."

"It couldn't be... no... you don't think him... and Winters?"

Ed's eyes opened wide at the thought.

From the way Charlotte choked, she obviously had the same feeling. "God, no! Firstly, Frankie has way more taste. Secondly, Winters? And third, Al would have 'em both castrated if they laid a hand on each other. Have you seen the way he growls at anyone who comes near Frankie?"

"Possessive?" Naz asked, although from the tone in his voice he obviously knew the answer.

"Over the top. Frankie loves it. He plays on it just to get Al to tie him to the bedposts and spank his arse."

Two thoughts struck Ed as he eavesdropped. One, that he should beware of Al, and two, an image of a man tied to the bedpost, his arse cheeks red. But it wasn't Frankie with his limbs spread out. It was Ed.

And the man spanking his bare arse wasn't Al.

Ed felt his cheeks heat at the thought of Marchant doing that *perverted* thing to him. He looked up to see Frankie staring at him. From the expression on his face, Frankie had overheard Charlotte too and had a good idea what was running through Ed's mind. Please, God, he didn't think Ed wanted to spank *him*.

Frankie opened his mouth, but Ed shook his head and backed away. It was bad enough Frankie knew he'd heard this horrible conversation. Ed didn't need to face it head-on.

He quickly gathered his briefcase and bag with the shirt in it and left the office before he had to face any of the staff. He was aware of Frankie's eyes on him as he headed to the lift. Ed knew that today had been a mistake. Extending some form of friendship to Mason had led to this... this disgusting perversion. And he wasn't. Anymore.

Deviant! Abomination! Pervert!

Ed wasn't a pervert. He'd promised his mother as she beat it out of him.

THE PARK was particularly crowded, and several times he almost tripped over a small child running in front of his path. Ed wanted to scream in frustration. He just needed to reach his sanctuary as quickly as possible.

He fumbled to open his front door, but once he was inside, he slammed it, relieved to shut out the outside world. Ed leaned against the front door and looked at his hands, unsurprised to see them shaking. He didn't handle upset or change—he was weak like that. Ed sucked in a deep breath and forced himself to follow his usual routine: shoes in the cupboard, hang up his jacket, and place his briefcase neatly by the front door ready for tomorrow. He changed out of his suit and into relaxing clothes—another shirt and trousers. Ed never wore jeans or sportswear.

In the kitchen Ed poured a glass of sparkling water and sat at the kitchen table. Then he realized he hadn't put the soiled shirt in the washing machine. He took the shirt out of the bag. Something fell to the floor. Curious, Ed picked it up, a frown forming on his face as he looked at the square of card. It was a business card. "Marchant Belarus." That was all it said aside from a phone number. He looked closer at the illustration.

"That's disgusting. No way." Ed threw the card away as if it burned. "Leave me alone!"

He shoved the shirt in the machine and threw in a capsule. Usually Ed was very conscious about making sure the machine was full before he ran it. This time he didn't care. He just wanted his shirt laundered and ironed and nothing to remind him of Marchant Belarus. Slamming the washing machine door shut was a relief. He felt freed from the handcuffs that man had placed around his wrists the moment they met.

Ed disposed of the bag and sat back down at the table to drink his water. Then he got up to throw the card in the bin. He didn't need any more visual reminders of Marchant.

Unbidden, the image of the man formed in his mind: his strong body and dark hair. He was beautiful, sculpted and muscled in a way Ed had never managed to achieve. Ed moaned without even realizing he emitted the sound.

Of course he wasn't gay, but he could appreciate a well-formed body just like anyone else. Look at Michelangelo's sculpture of David, for instance.

Desperate to get away from home, Ed had spent a lot of his youth walking around museums and art galleries. If anyone had taken the time to discuss it with him, they would have considered him an expert in Renaissance sculpture. As it was, he kept his expertise to himself and took his holidays abroad to explore other museums and galleries.

"He's just art." The words broke the silence and made it more real.

Many men appreciated the lines and form of the body. He didn't need to be embarrassed by his visceral response to Marchant. It was purely appreciation for beauty.

He made his dinner and sat at the table, looking at a new book he'd received from Amazon on sculptures from Italy. He looked through the pages avidly, pausing at one or two that caught his eye. Ed ignored the mocking internal voice pointing out that the sculptures he had concentrated on had all been male and naked, and that their forms bore a passing resemblance to Marchant Belarus.

After clearing away his dinner, Ed sat down to watch a couple of documentaries he'd recorded a few weeks ago but hadn't scheduled time to watch yet. The tail end of the previous program caught his eye, and he stared wide-eyed. It was some cop show, but they were in a dungeon. Only not "ye olde English dungeon," but a modern version.

"Christ," he choked out as he watched a man tied to a cross being whipped. It was a TV show, and it was more allusion than explicit, but Ed couldn't tear his eyes away, although he was frustrated by the cast obscuring what he actually wanted to look at: the expression of the man being whipped and the strength of the man wielding the implement. "Get out of the way," he muttered.

Ed pressed down hard on his groin. He didn't want to watch this. He should turn it off. But he couldn't look away. Once, and only once, he'd given in to his perversion and visited a place like that. But it had scared him. Too many people, and no one interested in an old newbie. He wasn't young enough or pretty enough to attract anyone's eye, and then—horror of horrors—he'd actually met someone he knew from the office. The man wore little more than a harness, and he'd been collared, but somehow when the gossip got back to the office, only Ed had been perverted enough to be wearing leather. Ed had asked for a transfer, unable to deal with the gossip. He'd never dared set foot in a BDSM club again.

Deviant! Abomination! Pervert!

How many times a day did he hear his mother's voice in his head? No matter how many times Ed tried to deny it, she was right. Normal men didn't need tying up. Men didn't need to be whipped. He was weak and abnormal when he should be strong.

Then the man doing the whipping turned to face the camera, and for a split second, he thought it was Marchant. He came with a choked-off cry, his hands pressed against his pulsing erection as he proved his mother right once again.

Chapter 4

DESPITE A fluttering in his belly, Ed followed his usual routine and returned to the supermarket on Saturday at eleven fifteen. He collected one of the small trolleys and steered it into the entrance.

"Good morning, Ed."

Marchant stood by the baskets, a smile on his face. The fluttering intensified to full-on roiling at the sight of the man who had haunted Ed's dreams for a week.

"What are you doing here?"

"Shopping."

"Are you stalking me?" Ed demanded.

"I shop here every Saturday morning," Marchant said mildly. "Like you, I have a routine."

"The same time as me?" Ed's tone expressed his disbelief.

"Look around you. How many of these people shop at the same time every week? If you started looking for them I expect you'd see the same people week in, week out. We all have our routines."

Ed looked around as Marchant told him, then growled under his breath as he realized what he was doing. "Thank you for returning the shirt."

"You're welcome. Shall we get it over with?"

Ed stared at him wide-eyed. "What?"

"Shopping. Shall we go shopping?"

"I...."

No! Ed couldn't think of anything worse than having to be near Marchant. If he couldn't control himself with a mere glimpse of a look-alike, how could he manage with the real thing standing next to him?

Oblivious to Ed's turmoil, Marchant herded him toward the fruit and vegetables. "Those apples look good. I love apples. I think they're my favorite fruit."

Ed picked up a bag and placed it in his basket before he could think about what he was doing. Then he stopped. "I don't like apples."

Marchant didn't seem bothered. "That's fine. I'll have your bag." He hoicked them out of Ed's trolley and into his basket.

"Are you not buying much today?" Ed asked.

"I've been away for a few days at a conference, so I still have most of last week's shopping."

In the back of his mind, Ed had been worrying that Marchant had been stalking him. He was unaccountably relieved that it wasn't the case. "I like soft fruit," he offered.

"You like the summertime, then?"

Ed nodded. He relished the strawberries and raspberries in the summer, refusing to buy them out of season.

He collected his usual produce. Marchant proved to be a quiet companion. He didn't force Ed to buy something he didn't want, just filling his own basket where appropriate.

At the checkout Marchant unloaded his basket at Ed's insistence. It made sense for him to go first. Actually he was going to use another till, but Marchant made it clear he expected Ed to use the same till so they could continue their conversation about a museum Ed had visited the month before.

They paused as Marchant paid for his goods and resumed again once Ed had packed and paid for his food. As they got to the door, Marchant stopped. "You know, we did this the wrong way round." When Ed gave him a blank stare, Marchant said, "We should have gone for coffee first. Now we can't let the frozen food melt."

Ed hadn't contemplated going for coffee, so he wasn't sure what Marchant was talking about. "I need to get this back home."

"Of course you do. I tell you what, you take your food home and drive to my place. There's a very good place for coffee near me."

What Ed wanted to say was he was going home to spend the rest of the afternoon relaxing. What he actually said was, "I don't drink coffee."

"Oh, yes. I should have remembered. Still, you can watch me drink coffee."

"Why are you doing this?" Ed asked, bewildered.

"Doing what?"

"Telling me what to do all the time. Giving me orders."

Marchant smiled. "Because you like it. You respond so well when I give you an order."

"I'm a grown man. A manager. I give the orders, not take them."

"And it hurts your soul. Anyone can see that. You are born to serve."

Ed shook his head so hard he felt it was in danger of toppling off. "I'm not a child, and I'm not a servant."

"I don't play with children, Ed. I play with men."

Ed clutched the trolley so hard his knuckles were white. "I'm not like that. I'm not gay, not perverted, not—"

"Yes, you are. You shout and scream and stamp your foot, but you are gay, and you are deviant."

"No, not like you."

Ed walked away. He couldn't have this conversation in the middle of the supermarket. Marchant was trying to destroy his life.

"You can't keep running away," Marchant said mildly, keeping an easy pace with Ed.

"You don't understand."

"I can see you're scared. It's understandable. But I'll look after you."

"You're a deviant, a pervert," Ed spat.

"I prefer to think of myself as the former. The latter has such unfortunate connotations."

"I'm not like you."

"Well, that's true. I'm a Master and you're a sub."

"No, no, no, no—" Ed stopped as Marchant's hand pressed over his mouth.

"Stop now. I know you're panicking. I want you to take a deep breath." He took his hand away perhaps half a centimeter from Ed's mouth and waited for him to breathe as ordered. Ed sucked in a shaky breath, and Marchant stroked his cheek. "Good boy. Now, I'll give you my address, and you can come over for lunch."

"I don't want to." Ed knew that going over to Marchant's would be the worst thing he could do to maintain his control. "Please... stop, I'm not... I *can't*...."

"Lunch. Food. Nothing else."

Ed stared into Marchant's dark brown eyes. "I'm scared."

"I know." Marchant brushed his thumb over Ed's mouth. "You're doing fine."

"I'm weak," Ed admitted shamefully.

"Did someone tell you that?"

Ed nodded.

"Who?"

"My mother, my grandmother."

"What else did they tell you?"

"That I was a deviant, an abomination, and a pervert."

Marchant frowned. "They told you that?"

"Over and over."

"Where was your father?"

"He left my mother before I was born."

"When did they start telling you you were a deviant?"

"When I was little. I don't remember a day when they didn't call me perverted."

"Jesus, poor baby." Marchant sounded shaky. "We need to talk, and I'm not letting you say no. Do you know Larchmead Close?"

Ed thought for a moment. "Is it off Aspen Way?" It was an educated guess. The roads named after trees were all close together.

"Yes, it's the third on the left if you enter from the Crescent."

"I'm not sure...."

"*I* am," Marchant said firmly. "Trust me."

Ed chewed on his thumbnail. "I can't stay for long."

"Come for lunch, and then I'll let you go."

"All right."

"Good boy. See you in about half an hour?" Ed nodded, and Marchant smiled. "Great."

Ed watched him walked away. "Wait! Marchant!"

Marchant turned back. "Yes?"

"What number? You didn't give me your house number."

"I didn't, did I? It's number eleven."

"Eleven Larchmead Close."

"You've got my phone number on the card I gave you."

Ed blushed. "I haven't got the card anymore."

"Oh?"

"I... threw it away."

Marchant didn't respond and reached into his jacket for his wallet. "Did you see what was on the card?"

Ed nodded.

"I can see why you freaked." Marchant didn't seem angry at all. "I'll see you soon."

Ed packed the shopping in his car and drove away before he could think too hard.

Thinking was his problem.

BY THE time Ed had packed away the last item from the shopping, he'd worked himself up into such a state that he was incapable of driving anywhere, least of all to Marchant's.

He poured himself a glass of water and sat on the sofa. "I don't have to do this. I'm an adult. I can do what I want."

Except that he had no idea what "this" was. Sit on the sofa, drive to Marchant's. What the hell should he do?

Then his home phone rang.

"Ed? Mr. Winters?"

Ed frowned. Who on earth? It sounded like Frankie Mason. "Yes?"

"It's Frankie Mason. Marchant phoned Al for your phone number, but he wouldn't give it to him. I had your number… you don't want to know why I had your phone number. Marchant just wanted to make sure you're all right." He paused. "Are you all right?"

"I… don't know."

"Do you want me to come round? You sound as if you need a friend." Frankie sounded sincere and not annoyed at being disturbed.

"I'm all right, just a bit tired, that's all. Tell Marchant… no, I'll ring him. I'm fine."

"Are you sure?"

"Completely. Thank Al for not giving out my number. I appreciate it."

"Okay, then."

"And Mr. Mason?"

"Yes?" Now Frankie sounded wary, and so he should.

"We will be discussing how you got my number on Monday."

Frankie giggled, and involuntarily Ed grinned.

"You'll never believe it."

Ed made a disapproving hum before he said good-bye. He was going to have a long, hard talk with Mr. Mason about invading his privacy.

Now he was going to have to deal with Marchant because Frankie would ask him on Monday. He took a deep breath as he dialed the number.

"Hello?"

"Marchant?"

"Ed. Frankie got hold of you, then."

"He did, although we're going to have words on how he had my phone number."

"Thank God he did. So, were you just about to leave or had you convinced yourself that it was a really bad move?"

Ed's silence probably told far more than it should have.

"I thought so. What is your address?"

"What?"

"I'm going to pick you up, and we'll go out to lunch. Neutral territory for both of us."

"I...."

"Ed, switch off your brain and just give me your address."

"Flat 4, 2 Longdown Road."

"Good boy. Stay exactly where you are, and I'll be there in ten minutes."

ED JUMPED at the sound of the doorbell and realized he'd been staring at the blank screen of the TV since the call ended.

Marchant filled the space as Ed opened the door.

"Come in," Ed said, stepping back.

Marchant shook his head. "Let's go to lunch."

Self-conscious because he knew Marchant's eyes were on him the whole time, Ed slipped on his shoes and jacket, then picked up his keys and wallet from the shelf by the door. "I'm ready."

"Good. Let's go."

Marchant took Ed's arm as if he was convinced the man was about to bolt and led him down the stairs.

Marchant's car was a surprise. Ed had expected... Ed wasn't sure what he had expected, but it wasn't a small sky-blue Fiat 500. Marchant could barely squeeze himself in behind the wheel. He caught Ed's quizzical look and gave a rueful laugh.

"My car's in the garage, and this was all they could give me as a courtesy vehicle. I feel my nuts are going to explode every time I sit in this tin can."

Ed's lips twitched. Marchant really wasn't the right build for a car this size. "When will your car be ready?"

"Monday, hopefully. They're just waiting for a part. Something to do with the clutch. I don't understand cars."

"You mean there's something on which the great Marchant Belarus is not an expert?"

"If you were my boy, I'd punish you for that remark," Marchant said easily as he pulled out into the traffic.

"It's a good thing I'm not your *boy*, and seriously, I have to be at least a decade older than you."

"I'm thirty-two. You?"

"Thirty-seven." Ed looked older, he knew it. The silver hair and the pinched expression that usually resided on his face made people think he was nearer fifty.

Marchant shrugged. "Age is irrelevant. If you're my sub, you're my boy."

The breath caught in Ed's throat. "I'm not your sub. I'm not a sub. Stop saying things like that." In his panic he went for the door handle.

"Whoa, Ed, calm down." Marchant pulled Ed's hands away from the door. "I said *if*, okay?"

Ed snatched his hand away from Marchant's. He clasped them tightly in his lap. He felt a little foolish for overreacting. "I'm sorry."

"It's okay, but there's something you've got to understand, Ed. I'm not going to make you do anything you don't want to do." He smirked, and for the first time Ed realized Marchant had a dimple in his cheek. "I might cajole and encourage, but I can't force you to do anything. It's not the way this works."

"You beat people."

"Yes, sometimes."

"You hurt people."

"With their consent."

Ed thought about what Marchant did for a living. "Why?"

"Why?" Marchant sounded surprised. "Because I'm good at it."

"I never thought about beating people up as a job."

"It's not a job, it's my life. And flogging or whipping people is a world away from beating people up," Marchant corrected. "I've been in the BDSM community since I was a teenager."

Ed closed his eyes, not wanting to show how envious he was.

"Have you ever participated in a session?" Marchant asked.

"I went to a club once."

"And?"

"And nothing. I realized it wasn't for me, and I left." No way was Ed going to discuss what a miserable disaster it was.

"Was it a gay club?"

Ed kept his mouth shut.

"I thought so," Marchant said.

"It doesn't mean anything. It was just the nearest one to me."

Ed had looked at the het clubs, but the thought of being touched by a woman made him feel physically sick.

To his surprise he felt Marchant pat his knee. "Well done. I know it's hard to answer questions."

"I don't talk to people that much," he admitted.

"I know."

"Frankie?"

"I needed to know what I was getting into." Marchant didn't seem remotely apologetic for admitting he'd been gossiping behind Ed's back. "You've quite a reputation, Mr. Winters."

Ed looked out the window. "I know what they think of me."

"You don't care what they think?"

"I want people to leave me alone."

"That's a very lonely way of living, Ed," Marchant said gently.

"If they don't know me, they can't hurt me."

"Your mother? She hurt you?"

"And my grandmother. She beat me with a leather belt."

"Were you that naughty?"

"I was an *abomination*." Tears prickled the back of Ed's eyes, and he blinked them away furiously.

Silence in the car, and then he heard Marchant sigh. "I'm so sorry, Ed."

"But she was right, wasn't she? I am a deviant and a pervert and all those things she called me."

"They are so wrong, boy. Believe me, they are so wrong."

"How?" Ed demanded furiously, looking at Marchant for the first time. "Even you saw it the first time you met me."

"I saw that you like being played with. I saw that you took pleasure from something as simple as ice. That doesn't make you a deviant or a pervert."

"I am, though."

Marchant growled and pulled over to the side of the road. He turned so fast, Ed flinched away. "Jesus, Ed, you are such a mess."

"You think I don't know that?" Ed yelled, his voice loud within the confines of the car.

Marchant picked up one of Ed's hands and just held it, so gently that Ed was surprised.

"I knew the first moment I saw you that I wanted you as my sub."

"Why?"

"So many reasons, but I could also see how scared you were."

Ed nodded because he wasn't going to deny he was terrified.

"I know it was wrong, but I talked to Frankie and Al. I wanted to know more about you."

"They hate me."

Marchant bit his lip. "Yes… and no."

"I hate them," Ed said.

"Why?"

"Because he's everything I despise."

"Because he's gay?"

"He's so out, and in your face. He flaunts it at work. It's disgusting."

Marchant gave a little sigh. "You think he should be like you? Repressed and angry?"

Ed's brain stuttered at the thought of Frankie Mason being like himself. "Is that how you see me?"

"Christ, I had no intention of having this discussion so soon," Marchant said. "I was expecting a nice lunch and a chat about the weather."

Ed tugged his hand out of Marchant's. "Take me home."

Marchant looked at him with a serious expression. "I can drive you home if that's what you really want, but I'd like to take you for lunch. I'm hungry and I bet you are too. Let's eat first."

"I'm not hungry." Ed was, but his stomach was churning so much he was sure he couldn't force anything down his throat.

Marchant started the car and checked the mirror. "You need to eat."

"I need to be left alone."

"That's the last thing you need. Do you really want to grow more bitter and twisted as you get older?"

Ed leaned his forehead against the cool window. His eyes burned, and he was an inch away from a total meltdown. "It's too late for that."

"No, it's never too late for you to get your head straight and admit what you are."

"Gay?"

"That, and my sub."

"You never stop, do you?"

Marchant laughed. "Not when I want something. And I really want you."

"Why? Why do you want a bitter and twisted old man? Why don't you go for someone like Frankie?"

"For a start, Frankie is already taken and Al would have my nuts to decorate a collar if I laid a hand on his boy, and secondly, me and Frankie? He's a space cadet. He'd drive me insane before the end of the evening. It's you I want, and you I'm going to have."

Ed stared out the window. It was so tempting just to give up and let this remarkable man take over. But he was too old to think that people like him deserved happy endings. Once upon a time, maybe, but not now.

Chapter 5

ED'S NERVES increased as they walked into the pub. He rarely (never) went out, and being around people made him uneasy. Marchant seemed to sense that and found a corner table for them, encouraging Ed to sit with his back to the wall.

"I'll order for us and be right back. Don't run away."

It was only once he'd gone that Ed realized Marchant hadn't asked what he wanted to eat or drink. He looked around and then blinked. Two young guys on the table next to him were kissing with a tenderness that made Ed's toes curl. He looked more carefully at the other customers. There were men and women here, but it was pretty damned obvious how they were all same-sex couples. Marchant had brought him to a gay pub.

Ed curled his hands into fists. *The bastard.*

He looked at the door and contemplated making a bolt for it. Marchant had told him not to run away, but Ed was a grown man, and Marchant had no power over him. He looked at the couple again. It was disgusting. They were holding hands and kissing like there was no one else in the room.

"Deep breath, Ed."

Ed looked at Marchant, who stood in front of him with two glasses in his hands. "What?"

"You're panicking. Take a deep breath, and try to relax."

"This is a… a…."

"Gay-friendly place, yes."

"It's wrong." His voice rose in his anger and people looked around, angry expressions on their faces.

"This is a safe place for them, Ed. It's a place for me. I'm gay. It's not wrong."

"Is there a problem, Marchant?"

A large man, taller and wider than Marchant, appeared at his side.

"I don't think so, Mischa. Ed is… he needs time to adjust. He's one of us."

Ed started to shake his head, but Marchant put down the glasses and grabbed his hands.

"You're fine, Ed. No one's going to hurt you here, I promise. *They* cannot hurt you here."

Mischa's expression changed from hostility to understanding. "Ed...?"

Marchant didn't let go of Ed's hands while he performed the introductions. "Mischa Durrant, Ed Winters. Mischa owns this place, and his boyfriend, Sean, is behind the bar."

"No one causes trouble here, Ed."

Both reassurance and a warning. Ed got that. But....

"This is wrong. *They* told me that."

Marchant hung on even tighter, his thumbs pressing almost painfully into Ed's skin. Ed welcomed the pain. It anchored him to reality.

"Ed, listen to me. Your mother was wrong, evil. Here is a good place. Look around. You can see people are happy."

"Gay is—"

"What you are."

Ed's mouth went dry. He wasn't... he had *feelings*, but he wasn't....

Mischa nodded. "You're not the first, Ed. I get elderly guys in here who've spent a lifetime denying they're gay."

"My mother...."

"Beat him senseless his entire life," Marchant said to Mischa.

"Jesus fucking Christ, no wonder the poor bloke's screwed," Mischa swore loudly. "Sit down, Ed. Let Marchant hold you. Look around for a while, relax, and get used to the place."

He patted Marchant's shoulder and walked away. Marchant pushed Ed back to his seat and sat next to him on the bench.

"Drink." He pushed one of the glasses into Ed's hand.

Ed took a sip. Sparkling water. "You remembered."

"It's kind of hard to forget, considering you only drink one thing." The gentle smile on Marchant's face reassured Ed that it wasn't a dig. "I'm going to hold you now. All you have to do is lean back against me while I talk. Can you do that?"

Could he be held by a man who made him scared and horny at the same time? Ed took a breath as Marchant slid an arm around him, and he went with Marchant's gentle urging to lean against him.

"Are you okay?" Marchant asked, his breath tickling Ed's ear.

"I'm okay."

"I want you to realize that you're safe here. I don't care what your mother or any of your relatives said. They were wrong."

"But—"

"They were wrong. Look at the couples in here. Go on, look at them."

Ed cautiously looked at the couple who'd been kissing when they first arrived. They were sitting close together, one of them between the other's thighs, still holding hands as they talked. Then he saw four guys in the corner, laughing and chatting. Everyone looked relaxed.

Everyone except him. "They look happy."

"Are you happy, Ed?"

"No."

"That's why you hate Frankie so much, isn't it? Because he's happy."

"It's more than that."

"Tell me."

"He flaunts it all the time."

"Flaunts what?" Marchant stroked Ed's upper arm.

"You know." Ed really didn't want to have to spell it out.

"You mean he's out and doesn't hide the fact he's gay."

"Yes."

"Like these guys."

"Yes."

"Why can't you be like them?"

Ed stiffened and tried to pull away. "No. That would be wrong."

Marchant tugged him back, ignoring his resistance. "Why would it be wrong? And don't tell me again you're not gay, because we both know that's bollocks."

"Are you like this with everyone?"

"Like what?"

"Overbearing."

Marchant chuckled. "I've heard that before."

"Do you ever listen to people?"

"I'm listening, Ed." Marchant's voice suddenly went soft. "I've listened to everything you've said, and I want to help you be happy and find yourself."

"I'm fine as I am."

"No, you're not. You're a bitter virgin queer abused by your egg donor, and all you want to do is destroy other people. People like Frankie, who's done nothing to hurt you except be out and happy. You're crap at your job, you live on spinach salad and water, and honestly, is there one person in the world about whom you have something decent to say?"

Someone had punched the air out of Ed's chest. He couldn't breathe from the pain.

"Breathe, shh, breathe." Marchant rubbed his stomach. "I know that was hard, but you needed to hear it. You're dying inside from the poison, Ed, and trying to take others down with you."

"Hurts," Ed gasped out. He struggled weakly to get away from the person who'd inflicted such pain.

Marchant held him firmly. "I know, I know, but you've got to listen to me."

"It's not true."

"Yes, it is, but it doesn't have to stay like this. If you let me into your life, you'll be able to live again."

"I am living."

He was. He was. Since his mother died, he'd lived to the best of his abilities.

"This isn't living. This is toxic existing. Let me show you what living really is."

Ed tried to control his breathing, but all he could hear was his heart pounding and the blood rushing in his ears. Marchant was all over him, pressing against his back, his hands splayed against his belly, and God, Ed wanted more, everything Marchant had to offer, but that was dangerous, too dangerous. Ed couldn't afford to let him into his life. *Too bloody late* a small voice whispered.

"Cheeseburger and chips, green leaf salad." The waiter placed the plates on the table, seemingly oblivious to the drama of his customers at table four. "Do you want sauce with that?"

"No thanks, Sean," Marchant said, his voice steady.

"Enjoy." The waiter went away.

Ed stared after him, shocked that the man had said nothing.

"Let's eat, take a moment to calm down, and then we can talk," Marchant suggested.

It was the best idea Ed had heard all day. If Marchant let him go, then he could make his excuses and leave.

Marchant slowly unwrapped his arms, and Ed sucked in a breath. He felt more alone than before at the loss of that small moment of human contact.

"They didn't have spinach salad, so I hope this one is okay."

Ed looked at the salad without enthusiasm. "It's fine, thank you."

"Great," Marchant said cheerfully. "Let's eat. I'm starving." He tucked Ed to his left and pulled his plate toward him. "They do the best chips here ever."

Ed would have preferred to be on the other side of the table, but Marchant made it clear that he expected Ed to stay where he was. His stomach rumbled at the sight of the food, although he had a feeling it was more the pile of chips than the green leafy salad on his plate. Ed didn't allow himself chips anymore since he'd lost weight.

"Come on, babe, eat." Marchant nudged the plate toward him.

Eating so close to someone else was awkward, but Ed did as he was told and cleared the plate.

Marchant made a pleased noise as Ed ate the last scraps of rocket. "Good boy. Would you like some chips? I'm almost full."

Ed eyed the small pile of chips on Marchant's plate longingly. "No, thank you."

Marchant looked at him thoughtfully. "Were you overweight?"

"All my life until I lived by myself."

"When did your mother die?"

"Ten years ago."

"Fuck, Ed, and you're still living like she controls your life?"

"It's the only way I can stop the sickness," Ed explained. "She gave me strategies to suppress the evil inside me so that I don't infect other people."

"We keep having the same conversation. It's time you embraced it, babe."

Ed closed his eyes and leaned back against the seat, partly to shut out the chips and partly so he didn't have to think about Marchant's words.

"How long have you known you were... were...." Ed struggled to find an alternative word.

"A Master? Probably since I was a teenager and started hooking up."

"What would happen if you were told you could never dominate someone again?"

"I'd probably take that person and suggest we have a long session to cure them of that particular idiocy."

Ed snorted. "I don't have that option, but you're asking me to change my whole way of life."

"For the better, Ed. I'm not asking you to take away a part of you. I'm suggesting that you embrace what you are to make you—and others—happier."

"You don't know it will make me happy."

"Trust me, I do."

"But—" His words cut off when Marchant placed his hand over Ed's mouth.

"I scare you, don't I? Just nod."

Ed did as he was told, his eyes wide above Marchant's hand.

"I see through the bullshit of your façade to the real you."

Ed nodded again.

"And you hate that."

He hated it and loved it and wanted Marchant to leave him alone to wallow in his misery.

"Frankie…." Ed stiffened but Marchant ignored it. "Frankie doesn't deserve to be judged for being gay. You don't deserve to be judged for being a sub. Not by anyone." Marchant pressed the meaty palm of his hand against Ed's lips, but strangely, Ed didn't panic. He felt relieved, as if Marchant controlled even something as fundamental as his breathing. "I won't let anyone judge you." Marchant took his hand away and tilted Ed's face to his. "I'm going to show you how to live."

"What if I can't do it?"

"What if you can?"

"I've failed at everything I've ever done," Ed admitted, his shoulders slumping.

"You didn't have me," Marchant said.

"You really think you can help me?"

Marchant stroked his jaw. "From this moment, I make that decision."

"What do I do?"

"You say, 'Yes, sir.'"

"Not Master?"

"Not yet." Marchant looked at him expectantly.

Ed gathered up the remainder of his courage and stepped off the cliff. "Yes, sir."

"Good boy."

"What happens—"

Ed's question was cut off by Marchant's lips on his. He was being kissed for the first time in his life—in public—by a man. Ed waited for the panic to set in, but there was nothing except a fuzz filling his head where his rabbit brain normally resided.

He didn't actually kiss back, but he let Marchant take control with the kiss.

Marchant sat back with a satisfied look on his face. "Good boy," he said again.

"Are you going to keep calling me 'boy'?"

"Yep."

Nothing more, nothing less. Ed had asked the question and been given the answer. He could live with it.

Ed sat back and tried to recover his composure. "I ought to get on with my afternoon."

"What are you going to do?"

"I usually watch a film."

"That sounds like a good idea. May I join you?"

Ed looked at him dubiously. "Don't you have something you want to do?"

"You are my something," Marchant said cheerfully. "What are we watching?"

"I watch old movies."

"Like?"

"Dance movies." Ed's cheeks flushed hot.

"Like Fred Astaire and Ginger Rogers? Cool."

"You mean it?"

"I like them too. I love dancing."

Ed frowned. "Who told you?"

"Who told me what?" Marchant looked confused.

"Who told you I like dancing?"

"No one. Well, you, I guess. Ed, it's not a crime to like dancing. I like musical theater and war films."

"You do?"

"And sci-fi and mysteries. I've got eclectic interests."

"I loved dancing as a child, but my grandmother disapproved and stopped my lessons."

Marchant shook his head and rubbed his thumb over Ed's lips. "I am going to take you dancing very soon."

"We can't dance together." Ed couldn't imagine dancing with another man.

"Who says?"

"But it's—" He stopped as Marchant held up his hand.

"First rule. If I tell you we are going to do something, it's not for discussion. This is the first thing I've seen you say you actually enjoy. We are going dancing."

"Uh… okay."

Marchant looked at him.

"…Sir."

"Good boy. Now, do you want another drink?" At Ed's shake of his head, Marchant said, "I'm going to pay the bill before Mischa's head explodes."

"Why would his head explode?"

"Old story, which I shall tell you sometime."

Ed watched Marchant walk away. He'd just told Ed that there would be more than this one afternoon. "I don't know that I can do this," Ed whispered to himself.

But Marchant had told him he didn't have to know, he just had to do.

Because he was a good boy. His mother told him he could be if he tried.

Chapter 6

ED BLINKED at the sight of Marchant in his living room. He couldn't remember anyone being in his flat who wasn't a workman of some description. He'd never invited anyone into his place before, not having friends or family to invite.

Marchant looked around with interest. "How long have you lived here?"

"Nine years. I moved after my mother died. I thought about staying in the house, but...."

"Too many memories?"

Ed nodded. Too many memories, and none of them good.

"It's a nice place. You obviously have an eye for decoration."

Ed looked around. He'd never thought of it that way. He had very specific tastes, and fortunately he'd had the money to accommodate his ideas. His home was his sanctuary from the outside world.

Marchant rubbed his hands together. "So what are we going to watch?"

"I don't know. I usually pick whatever catches my eye."

"You put something on. I'm happy to watch anything."

Still dubious that Marchant would sit through a 1930s musical, Ed picked one of his favorites and slipped it into the DVD player.

He went to sit in his chair, but Marchant patted the sofa next to him.

"Another rule. I choose where you sit. If it's in a scene, you sit on the floor. If we're together you sit next to me." Ed sat down and Marchant hauled him into his arms. "Good boy. Now let's watch the film."

Marchant sighed happily as the first notes of *Swing Time* sounded. "One of my favorites. Good choice."

Ed relaxed a fraction at his words. At least Marchant wasn't going to be bored.

"Relax," Marchant said. "You're as stiff as a board."

Ed tried to snuggle into Marchant's side, but as it was the first time he'd ever done this, he really wasn't comfortable. He would have preferred to sit in his chair, but it was obvious Marchant wasn't going to let him go. Ed huffed and tried to focus on the screen. Marchant stroked Ed's upper arm as he watched the movie. The caress and Marchant's inattention seemed to do the trick, and Ed relaxed enough to concentrate.

"They look so elegant together," Marchant murmured as Fred Astaire and Ginger Rogers danced across the screen.

"She couldn't dance when they first got together," Ed said.

"You'd never believe it here. She follows him like a dream."

"My grandmother used to watch all these films every Saturday afternoon. I'd sit with her and imagine I was Ginger and in his arms."

"Is that why you like dancing so much? The chance to be close to people?"

"I haven't danced since I was a child. At least not with people. Sometimes I dance around the flat just to remember the steps."

"Do you take the role of the man or the woman?"

"The woman," Ed admitted as if it was a shameful thing.

"That's good," Marchant said cheerfully. "I don't have to learn new steps, and I do like to lead."

"You would take the woman's role?"

"Why not? It's just different steps."

Ed stared at the screen, remembering the snide comments from his grandmother. "You don't think it's weak to be a woman?"

Marchant sat up, dislodging Ed from his position. "You do?" His tone made it clear that he was distinctly unimpressed.

"They—" Ed didn't bother to say who. "—they said that women were weak and needed to be told what to do, and men should be the head of the household."

"But there was only them and you."

"I was weak. They beat it into me to make me stronger."

Deviant! Abomination! Pervert!

"There is nothing weak about being a woman, and nothing wrong in being a man who likes to be told what to do."

Ed shook his head. "You keep telling me that, but I know you're wrong."

Marchant pointed to the floor. "Sit on the floor."

Without thinking, Ed slipped down to the carpet and sat at Marchant's feet.

"Good boy. Now sit next to me."

When Ed was back next to him and resting against Marchant's side, Marchant said, "How did that make you feel?"

"What?"

"Doing what I said."

"Weak, relieved, happy, ashamed." Ed was honest about the turmoil of emotions in his head.

"My job is to make you realize you can obey my commands and be strong and in control."

"How can I be in control if I'm following your orders?"

"Because *you* choose to do it. I'm not making you."

Ed was about to point out that he didn't have a choice, but he hesitated. "If I said no, what would you do?"

"Now? I'd talk to you about why you're saying no."

"If we were at a club?"

Marchant chuckled, a wicked, dirty sound. "I'm going to make you say no a lot, but you will have your safewords, and if you use them, the scene will stop instantly."

Ed wasn't that naïve. He knew what the safewords were. He chewed on his lip.

"What are you thinking?" Marchant asked. "I can see the questions swirling around in your head."

"Why me?"

"Why not you?"

"You know what I mean."

Marchant shook his head. "No, I don't really know. You think there's some reason why I shouldn't be interested in you?"

"Look at me."

Maybe that was a mistake, because Marchant swept his gaze over Ed in a way that made Ed hot all over. "I see you."

"I'm old," Ed protested weakly.

"Bollocks. You're a few years older than me."

"I've got no experience."

"I can teach you."

"I'm a mess."

"True, but I can help you."

"I hate everyone and everything, and no one likes me."

"Only because you've never been taught how to like anything. They'll like you when you like them."

Ed scrabbled around for another reason. "I'm ugly."

Marchant gaped at him. "What the fuck?"

Now Ed was confused. "I'm ugly."

"You have no idea, do you?" Marchant got to his feet and held out his hand. "Up."

Ed placed his hand in Marchant's. "Where are we going?"

"Where do you have a mirror?"

"In the bathroom." He had a larger mirror in the bedroom, but he wasn't going to take Marchant in there.

"Show me the way."

Ed led him to the bathroom, not entirely sure what Marchant had planned.

Marchant positioned Ed in front of the mirror and stood behind him. Ed could see his own puzzled face reflected there. "Why are we here?"

"You told me you were ugly."

"So?" In all his fucked-up-ness Ed's looks weren't top of the list.

"Look at yourself."

Ed did as Marchant said. Prematurely gray-white hair, blue eyes, glasses, sharp pointy features, sour expression. He avoided looking at himself for more than the requisite "comb hair and check there's nothing between the teeth" time. "Marchant, I really don't know what you're getting at."

"Look at yourself through my eyes."

He had no idea what Marchant was talking about, but the man seemed insistent, so Ed stared at himself, framed by Marchant's taller physique. He was slight compared to Marchant with not an ounce of fat on him. He could remember a time when he'd been overweight, and he'd worked so hard to slim down, petrified of being fat again. His eyes were huge in his face, their deep blue a sharp contrast to Marchant's dark brown. His hair had gone gray in his midtwenties and now was almost white.

"From the moment we met, I couldn't stop looking at you," Marchant whispered in his ear.

"I'm nothing special," Ed insisted.

"You're blind." Marchant splayed his hand over Ed's heart, his skin dark against the pale blue of Ed's shirt.

Ed leaned back against Marchant's body only to feel a rigid length against his lower back. "I think it's you who's blind. You need a younger guy."

"I've had them," Marchant said dismissively. "So many of them, and they're all boring."

"All of them?"

Marchant smirked. "Maybe not *all*."

Jealous of the unknown men, *so many of them*, Ed pushed away. "You must have things to do this afternoon."

"I'm doing what I planned," Marchant said, following him out of the bathroom.

"Still, I have plans."

"Oh? Like what?"

Ed turned on his heel to stare at him in frustration. "Give me a break. I've played your game all afternoon. I've followed your orders. Now I need you to go. I don't know what your bloody safewords are, so I'm saying no."

To his surprise, Marchant took a step back. "All right, Ed. I'm going to go home. You have my card."

And he was gone.

Ed hadn't even blinked before he heard the *snick* of the front door. Finally he moved and collapsed onto his sofa. On the screen Fred and Ginger waltzed together, oblivious to the fact they'd been forgotten.

"It was the right thing to do," Ed said out loud. "He was pushy and too much. I don't need him interfering in my life and telling me what to do."

He sounded weak, even to his own ears, and Ed was a past master at sounding weak.

It was the only thing he was good at.

ED SAT at his desk, staring out the window at the people meandering through the park. He had a pile of reports on his desk and no inclination to look at one.

"Ed? Mr. Winters?" Frankie smiled at him, but it faded when he didn't return the smile.

"Mr. Mason?"

"What happened? What did he do?"

"I don't know what you're talking about." Ed looked away, refusing to see the pity in Frankie's eyes. "Don't you have work to do?"

"Do you need a hand with these reports?"

Ed gave him an icy glare. "I am more than capable of producing a report, Mr. Mason."

Frankie pressed his lips together and backed away.

Ed went back to looking out the window, but he didn't miss Charlotte's snide "Told you last week was a one-off. He must have got dumped or something." Ed couldn't hear Frankie's retort, but he imagined it was equally bitchy.

By the end of the day, the reports were still untouched on his desk and due in the next day. Ed knew he was going to get another dressing-down from the director tomorrow, but he couldn't bring himself to care. For the first time in his life, he considered skipping work and staying in bed.

Before he could leave, Frankie sat down in the seat in front of his desk.

"I have no idea what's happened, and I understand you don't want to talk, but whatever it is I can see you're upset, because you've not even opened one of those reports. So here is what's going to happen. We're going to work until seven and finish the reports, and then you're coming home with me and you can talk."

"Who do you think you are?" Ed snapped.

"The only bloody person who cares." Frankie took the first report off the untouched pile.

"Do I have a choice?" Even his staff gave him orders now.

"No. Where is the Trustees' report?"

"Here." Ed dug through a separate pile of files.

"Good. Naz is taking this one."

Ed's eyes widened as Naz and Charlotte came over. Charlotte looked about as happy as Ed was.

"Charlotte's taking the Liesel case, and I'm doing the Miller file with you because she's a bitch." Frankie handed out the files.

"Why are you doing this?" Ed asked faintly.

"You know why. You find the information, and I'll type."

Ed opened the file. "You and I are going to have a talk about this, Mr. Mason."

"Yes, we are, Mr. Winters. What is the title of the report?"

At five to seven, Charlotte was printing the last report while Frankie and Naz were talking by the coffee machine. Ed stared out the window again. He started when he heard a cough and realized the director was in front of his desk.

"I'm surprised to see you still here, Winters, and even more surprised to see your team."

Ed was aware of Frankie looking his way. "My team kindly helped me finish the reports you need."

The director frowned. "You asked your team to do your work?"

"We offered, sir," Frankie said cheerfully before Ed could stutter out a reply. "It didn't take long. Here they are." He took them off Charlotte and handed them to the director, who stared at them as if he wasn't sure they were real.

Ed took a deep breath. "Thank you, all of you."

Even Charlotte, who'd grumbled all evening, looked pleased with Ed's sincere thanks. "No worries. I'm going home before my husband forgets what I look like. Coming, Naz?"

"Yeah. See you tomorrow." Naz grinned and loped after Charlotte.

"I'm impressed, Winters. Keep it up." The director walked away with the reports, leaving Ed and Frankie staring at each other.

"Why did you do this?" Ed asked again.

Frankie shrugged. "Because I know what's worrying you."

"I'm not worried."

"Course you're not. That's why you stared out the window all day."

Ed tried to think of a reasonable explanation for his inattentiveness. After all, he spent a lot of time staring out the window. "He's... I...."

"I get it. He really is." Frankie didn't seem to need a better explanation.

"I sent him away."

"Did you want to?"

"He...." Ed was usually an articulate man. The lack of words to describe his intercourse with Marchant was annoying to say the least. Or should it be lack of intercourse. *Ha!*

"Earth to Ed!" Frankie clicked his fingers under Ed's nose.

Ed jumped and scowled at Frankie.

"You were away with the fairies again," Frankie explained. "Or out in the park. Which reminds me, Chinese or pizza?"

Ed looked at him blankly. "What?"

"Takeaway. I'm ordering in tonight as we're so late. Al's going to pick it up once I've called him."

Ed blanched at the thought of facing Frankie's formidable boyfriend. "I'm fine. I have dinner at home."

"What are you going to eat?"

"Spinach salad."

Frankie pulled a face. "I've never seen you eat anything different. Do you really like spinach?"

"I do now. It took me years to get used to the taste."

"What else do you eat?"

"Chicken and salmon occasionally."

"So you're not a vegetarian, then?"

"No." Ed loved meat; he just didn't indulge very often.

"Ed...." Ed raised an eyebrow, but Frankie ploughed on. "Ed, it's outside office hours now. You're Ed, not bloody Mr. Winters. And you're coming home with me."

Ed tried to find a way to let Frankie down without offending him. He appreciated the offer, but he just wanted to go home and sleep.

Frankie obviously saw his hesitation. "Come back for a while, and then Al will drive you home."

"Your... boyfriend doesn't like me." Ed still had an issue acknowledging Frankie's homosexuality.

"He's protective of me."

Ed tilted his head. "You like it, don't you?"

"What? Al's Daddy Bear approach?" Frankie smirked. "Hell, yes. At least he gives a shit if I'm dead or alive. My last guy didn't care what I did. Al's approach is a turn-on. What about you? Do you like Marchant's big-bad-Dom act?"

"I don't know what you mean."

Frankie looked at him skeptically. "Marchant Belarus. Big guy, dark hair, looks as if he wants to eat you up."

"Oh, *that* Marchant Belarus."

To his surprise Frankie burst out laughing. "You have got a sense of humor. I was beginning to despair."

"Not much of one," Ed acknowledged.

"I don't think I've ever seen you laugh."

"I don't have much to laugh about."

Frankie sighed. "You really need to rethink that policy, Ed."

"So everyone keeps telling me."

"'Everyone' being Marchant?"

Ed nodded. "He wants to change me."

"And you don't want to be changed?"

"Old dog, new tricks."

"Bollocks. My mother's cocker spaniel is twelve, and he's still learning ways to piss her off."

"That's where you get it from."

Frankie acknowledged the jibe with a smirk. "You've almost been human these last two weeks."

"Since I met Marchant, you mean."

"He's had a good effect on you. It would be a shame to lose it."

"You don't understand—"

"No, I don't. But I do know a few things about you now that I didn't before."

"Like?" Ed's heart rate increased at the thought of what Frankie could possibly know.

"You're not the sexist, racist, bigoted twat I thought you were."

"Some of it is right. I do hate curry."

"Only because you haven't had the right curry."

"And I don't like the Irish."

"What did they ever do to you?"

"My grandmother was Irish," Ed said bleakly.

Frankie's amused expression slid away. "You should talk about that."

"I've talked more in the last two weeks than I've talked in two years."

"I don't know Marchant, but Al says the man's got a good reputation."

Ed thought of the way Marchant had held him through his panic attacks. "He seems to be a kind man."

"Yeah. Scary as hell, but he looks after his subs." Frankie seemed about to say more, but his phone beeped. He looked at the screen. "The love of my life telling us to get the fuck outta here."

"You. Not us."

"He knows you're coming. I texted him earlier."

Ed frowned. "When did you do that? You haven't touched your phone while we've been talking."

"I texted him at lunchtime."

"But—?"

Frankie got to his feet. "For once in your life, stop thinking, Ed."

Ed scowled at him. "I'm still your boss."

"Yeah, yeah, tomorrow. Now you're a friend who needs a shoulder."

Frankie made off toward his desk, leaving Ed staring after him. A friend? He was a friend? Of Frankie Mason's?

Was this a nightmare or a happy dream?

Chapter 7

FRANKIE LED Ed toward a dark blue car parked on the yellow lines outside the office building. Ed swallowed nervously as Frankie opened the passenger door.

"Hey, you. Ed, get in the back."

Ed did as he was told, sliding into the vacant spot on the back seat, the rest being covered in files and boxes.

The man in the driving seat nodded at him. He didn't look welcoming exactly, but he didn't look like he was about to tear Ed's head off his shoulders either.

Frankie bounced into the front seat and waved a hand at them. "Ed, Al. Al, Ed, etc. Ed's coming home for dinner despite what he keeps saying."

"You mean you completely ignored everything he said."

Frankie grinned at his boyfriend. "There's a problem with that?"

Al stared at Ed through the rearview mirror. "Is that all right with you? I can drop you home if you want."

Frankie interrupted. "No, you can't. He's coming back to ours, and we're having pizza."

"I don't eat—" Ed started but stopped when Frankie looked over his shoulder at him and scowled.

"Stop thinking about what you don't do and start living a little."

"Pizza is living a little?"

"Pizza can be living a lot if you allow yourself to enjoy it."

Al huffed and laughed. "Give it up, Ed. If Frankie's decided what you're going to do, you may as well give in now."

They obviously thought there was no further discussion, because Al leaned over to give Frankie a kiss. Then he pulled away from the curb.

Ed thought about protesting further and gave up, staring out the window at the evening traffic. He tried not to think about the casual affection between them. The kiss made his stomach roll, but now he wasn't able to convince himself that it was disgusting. The shrill voice that had been talking at him and guiding his actions was quiet for the first time in years. Frankie and Al talked in low voices, but they weren't including Ed, so he didn't bother to listen.

They parked outside a block of flats. Ed vaguely knew the area, but he hadn't been here before.

Frankie opened the back door, and Ed got out, stretching and looking up at the flats. "We moved here about three months ago. Neither of our places was really big enough for the two of us."

"It's almost identical to my building. They are nice flats."

"Let's go order, or I'm going to starve," Al said as he locked the car.

Frankie chuckled. "We'd better hurry, or he'll get grumpy." He followed Al, and Ed followed Frankie, having nothing else to do.

The flat was almost identical to his, but whereas Ed had decorated his in minimalistic fashion, Frankie and Al's flat was a mixture of masculine leather and a riot of bright Frankie colors.

"Don't blame me for the cushions," Al grunted as they walked through the door.

"I think he can work out who's got the taste, babe," Frankie cooed. "If it was all your way, the color scheme would be brown, brown, and brown."

Al rolled his eyes at Ed and headed for the fridge. "Do you want a beer, Ed?"

Ed opened his mouth to answer, but Frankie got there first. "If you say sparkling water, I'm going to tear your arm off and beat you to death with the wet end."

Ed shrugged hopelessly. "Sure. A beer would be great."

Al handed Ed and Frankie a bottle of beer each. "We'd better order."

"I've done it already," Frankie said.

"But you don't know what we want," Al objected.

It was Frankie's turn to roll his eyes. "You always eat the same thing, and Ed only eats spinach salad. He doesn't know what he likes."

"I'm nearly forty years old," Ed said. "I think I've worked out my tastes by now."

Frankie waved it off as unimportant. "Sit down and relax. We've got fifteen minutes before the pizza arrives. I'm going to have a shower."

"How do you know the pizza will be here in fifteen minutes?" Al asked.

Frankie disappeared without answering.

Al stared at Ed and frowned. "He's up to something."

"He's always up to something," Ed said, having had more experience of Frankie's machinations than his boyfriend had.

"True, but this time he's *really* up to something. I can tell. Excuse me while I go and spank it out of my boyfriend."

Al didn't notice Ed tense up as he left the room. He probably didn't mean his careless choice of words—or perhaps he did. They all seemed to take cruelty so casually.

Left alone in a strange place, Ed wasn't sure what to do. He took a sip at his beer and pulled a face. He drank water for a reason: he thought most other drinks were disgusting. He was tempted to chuck the beer down the sink, but knowing Frankie he'd probably find out and make him drink another. Ed had to acknowledge he was scared of that idea. God, he was scared of Frankie bloody Mason.

He was scared of everything at the moment.

He could hear the low rumbling sound of Al's voice and Frankie's higher-pitched tones but not what they were actually saying. At a loss for what to do, Ed wandered over to the bookcase. Leaning up against it was an old-fashioned walking stick, the sort his grandmother had used—for more than walking. Ed tried to blink away the memory of his grandmother and mother using it to punish him. Bad memories. He knew Frankie had hurt his hip when a taxi knocked him down, but he couldn't remember him using a walking aid. That was another bad memory. He'd deliberately tried to get Frankie into trouble with the management after his accident, not explaining why Frankie was off work. Ed winced as he remembered both the act and the disciplinary action that followed when HR discovered he'd lied. Not Ed's finest hour, and in hindsight he had no idea why he'd jeopardized his own job just to take a shot at Frankie.

The doorbell rang, and Frankie yelled, "Can you get it, Ed? I'll be there in a minute."

Ed opened the front door expecting to see the pizza delivery boy.

The person was delivering pizza, but he wasn't wearing any uniform.

"Marchant." Ed stared at him. "What are you doing here?"

To be fair, Marchant looked equally shocked. "I could say the same for you, but we know what the answer will be. I should have realized from the spinach salad."

"Oh good, you're here," Frankie said from behind Ed's shoulder.

"Frankie, have you been meddling again?" Al sounded resigned and a little pissed off.

"I think he has," Marchant said. "Here are the pizzas. I think you need to spank your boy, Al."

"Again," Al said.

"We're not into that sort of thing," Frankie said loftily.

Al snorted. "If you carry on telling lies like that, I'm going to put you over my knee in front of Marchant and Ed and carry on spanking you until you're screaming."

Ed remembered being spanked like that, and it wasn't remotely pleasurable, but Frankie just looked excited.

Marchant looked at Ed and then handed the pizzas to Frankie. As if no one else was in the room, he closed the front door and gently tugged Ed to him. "It's okay," he said. "You're safe. No one is going to hurt you." He looked over Ed's shoulder. "Ed and I need a moment, as you meddled without telling us. Do you want to dish up the pizzas?" He didn't wait for a response before he focused his attention on Ed. "Do you want me to go?"

Ed tried to focus his thoughts and answer Marchant. Then he realized his hands were curled into Marchant's jacket and he hadn't let go. Marchant placed his hands over Ed's, and they stayed like that for a couple of minutes, staring into each other's eyes until Al said, "Food, beer, torturing Frankie."

Frankie snorted loudly. "In your dreams, big boy."

"They're your dreams. You told me so."

Wrapping his arm around Ed, Marchant guided them to the leather sofa. Ed just followed, trying not to think that this was probably the first social encounter in his adult life that work hadn't foisted on him.

"One pepperoni, one margherita, one meat feast, and one veggie," Frankie said.

"And a spinach salad for Ed as long as he promises to eat one slice of pizza," Marchant said.

Ed looked at the table full of temptation. "I'm going to have to starve myself."

"No," Marchant said firmly. "No way do you need to lose any weight. Which pizza do you want? I will serve you."

"Veggie, I guess." Perhaps he could eat the vegetables and leave the base.

Marchant handed him a plate with some pizza and salad. "I expect you to eat it all."

"We've got sparkling water," Frankie said. "After you've finished the beer," he added at Ed's hopeful look.

Ed took a deep breath. If necessary, he could make himself sick. later. He took a bite of the pizza, tasting the warm melted cheese and feeling the pounds plastering themselves to his waist. He forced himself to chew and swallow, even though he knew the pizza was going to rest heavy in his stomach.

"Good boy," Marchant murmured.

Marchant's praise, even using those words, warmed him. Ed nibbled his pizza slice slowly as he watched the others eat slice after slice, drink the beers, and chat. He didn't join in much, not used to small talk. He remembered training courses where he'd been forced to have conversations with complete strangers about subjects he knew nothing about—like soaps on TV.

"Hey." Marchant stroked down Ed's back. "You seem lost in a world of your own. What are you thinking about?"

"Nothing," Ed said hastily.

"Hey, Ed, you've eaten pizza." Frankie whooped and pointed at Ed's plate.

Ed looked down to see a small piece of crust left on his plate. He'd been so lost in his own thoughts, he hadn't even noticed he'd nearly finished it.

"Do you want another piece?" Frankie asked.

"No, no," Ed said hastily.

Frankie flashed a smile at him and offered him the rest of the spinach salad, which Ed accepted.

"How has your week been?" Marchant turned to Ed and smiled at him. Ed noticed that Marchant must have shaved; his chin was so smooth.

"Oh, fine," Ed said.

"He spent the week staring out of the window."

Ed scowled as Frankie tattled on him. "I did not."

"You bloody did."

"You were a little distracted?" Marchant suggested as he smiled at Ed.

"Distracted?" The rest of Frankie's sentence was cut off by Al's hand over his mouth.

"Why don't you shut up, Frankie?"

Ed noticed that although Frankie nodded in agreement, his twinkling eyes gave him away. He sighed. "Frankie and his team helped me to produce reports that I should have done during the week, but I was too busy staring out of the window."

He was pleased Marchant didn't bother to ask what he was distracted about. Instead Marchant slid closer to Ed and carried on eating.

"How's the business doing?" Al asked Marchant.

Ed looked at Marchant, unsure of what Al was talking about. He remembered Marchant mentioning something about a conference, but that was all.

"I own a club," Marchant said, "among other things."

"A BDSM club," Frankie said. "I keep trying to get Al to take me."

Al raised an eyebrow. "And you keep telling me you're not into kinky shit."

"Just because I like being tied up and spanked doesn't mean I'm into kink."

"Of course it doesn't," Marchant said with a totally straight face.

"I am so out of my depth here," Ed murmured.

To his surprise Al grinned at him. "It's simple. You listen to him." Al pointed at Marchant. "And ignore him." He pointed to Frankie.

Frankie flipped him off. "He's been trying to ignore me for years, babe. I am unignorable."

"Is that even English?" Marchant shook his head. "Do you have any idea what he's talking about?"

"*I* know what he's talking about. You guys, on the other hand, are not supposed to know what he's talking about. Frankie lives in a world of his own."

"What? It wasn't me looking out of the window all week."

"How the hell do you deal with him? He's like a flea on crack," Marchant said.

Al grinned. "God, yes. But my boy has his quiet moments. Did you know he likes chamomile tea before bed?"

Ed blinked. "He does? You do?"

Frankie stuck out his tongue at all of them. "You are all mean."

"Well, duh," Al said. "You've got your boss, your boyfriend, and a master in here. What were you expecting?"

"True, true. Did you bring ice cream?"

"I got it," Al said.

"Did you get—" Frankie started.

"Of course I bloody did. What would you guys like? I've got chocolate, vanilla, and cookie dough."

"I'll have chocolate, and Ed will have vanilla," Marchant said.

"I don't eat ice cream," Ed said automatically.

"You'll have a spoonful."

Ed shook his head. "I'll be sick if I eat ice cream as well as the pizza."

"A spoonful," Marchant insisted. "You'll be fine. I'll make sure of it."

Ed looked at him dubiously. As much as the man liked to think he was in control, Ed's stomach had its own agenda.

"I will look after you," Marchant said.

Frankie sprang to his feet. "Chocolate, a small vanilla, chunky monkey, and a cookie dough."

"And coffee," Al said. "Put the coffee machine on, babe."

"I'm doing the ice cream. You make the coffee." Frankie bounced off with a wiggle.

Ed watched him leave. "He seems to have recovered from being knocked down."

"He gets the odd twinge, but most of the time, he's fine," Al said.

"I noticed the walking stick by the bookcase."

"It was my mother's. She died just as Frankie and I got together."

"I'm sorry," Ed said sincerely. "I know how it feels to lose your mother."

Marchant growled in his ear.

Al didn't seem to notice. "Thank you. It was a relief for her. The cancer was hard." He stood, smoothing down his jeans. "I'll make the coffee."

"I don't drink coffee," Ed said quickly.

To his relief Marchant didn't insist he try coffee. Ed was going to throw the cup over him if he did.

"You can have the water in the bag."

"Ed, do you want a chamomile tea?" Frankie asked.

"I'll try it." Ed surprised himself, and he saw the look of pleasure on Marchant's face.

Frankie brought over a tray of bowls and passed them around. "Mmm, my favorite." He nestled on the floor between Al's legs and, grabbing his bowl, leaned against Al's thigh. Al combed his fingers through Frankie's hair before concentrating on his ice cream.

Ed looked down into his bowl. The casual intimacy between the couple was still hard to process. He took a small mouthful of vanilla ice cream, felt it cold and sweet on his tongue. Marchant leaned into his space and, to Ed's shock, brushed a swift, chaste kiss on his mouth. Ed licked his lips, and Marchant's gaze darkened.

"You taste of vanilla and sugar," Marchant rumbled so quietly, Ed could barely hear him. "Take another mouthful and kiss me."

Ed took the smallest of mouthfuls and leaned toward Marchant, who just waited. He aimed for the same sort of kiss Marchant had given him, but Marchant placed his hand on the back of Ed's head. Panicked, Ed stared up at him.

"You can do this," Marchant said. "It's just a kiss."

Deviant! Abomination! Pervert! Ed's mother's voice rang loudly in his head.

He tried to pull away, but Marchant wouldn't let him go. "Concentrate on my mouth, my voice," he said. "Just me. Don't listen to her."

Ed shuddered at the thought of ignoring his mother, but he did as Marchant told him and kissed him. It was barely longer than the first one, but he'd done it. He'd given his first kiss.

Marchant's hands tightened around him and then let go. "Good boy."

"You taste of chocolate."

"I like chocolate. Maybe a bit too much." Marchant patted his belly.

Ed looked at Marchant's belly. He wasn't skinny, but he didn't seem to be sporting a potbelly. "You must work out a lot."

Al chuckled. "Beating those subs into submission keeps you fit."

Ed panicked. He tried to keep calm, but the thought of being beaten made him feel sick.

"Come with me." Marchant pulled Ed to his feet and took him into the hallway. "I know what he said, and that is what I do, so people are going to make comments like that all the time. Can you deal with it?"

Ed scrubbed through his hair. "You're all so casual about it."

Marchant pressed his lips together. "You were mentally and physically abused by your family. I don't abuse people."

"You hurt people."

"Because they want me to."

"How can anyone want to be hurt?" Ed remembered the lash of the belt and the hard *thwack* of the stick against his back. He remembered the tears and the pain and the humiliation as he crawled to his bedroom to get away from them.

"You went to the BDSM club."

Ed nodded.

"What did you see?"

"Men."

Marchant rolled his eyes. "Doing what?"

"Blowjobs. Being whipped."

"And?"

Ed shuddered as he thought of the dark dungeon where men did things he'd never dreamed of. "Being fucked."

"And?"

"Why are you making me say all this?"

Marchant gathered Ed against him. "You've never touched a man. You have no idea what hurts or what is pleasurable."

Having Marchant hold him was pleasurable even if he was scared out of his mind. "I'm so fucked-up."

"Yes. But you don't have to be."

"Promise?" Ed needed the reassurance, desperate to know that the way he was feeling wouldn't last forever.

Marchant leaned against the wall and pulled Ed against him. Ed listened to the steady beating of Marchant's heart. "You're not the only screwed-up bloke I've met, Ed. I keep telling you to trust me."

"It's not easy."

"Trusting me is easy. I won't let you down."

Marchant sounded so confident. "What do I have to do?"

"I told you before. Stop thinking, and just do as I tell you."

"Yes, sir."

Marchant massaged his head. "Good boy. Our ice cream must be melted. Let's hope the coffee is still hot."

"I don't know how you can drink coffee. It's vile."

Marchant snickered as he took Ed's hand. "You wait. I'll get you drinking it before the summer is over."

"No chance."

"Want a bet on it?"

"I never bet on a certainty," Ed said solemnly.

"You've probably never bet on anything, have you?"

"Do you want to bet on that?" Ed raised an eyebrow, challenging Marchant to answer.

Marchant pursed his lips. "You know what? I don't think I do."

"Wise move," Ed said, although he was a little disappointed.

Ed did like a small flutter.

Chapter 8

BEFORE THEY left, Ed had something to say to Frankie. He could have taken Frankie aside, but he chose to do it in front of Al and Marchant.

He swallowed hard to gather his courage. "Frankie. You've been really nice to me, and you had no reason to. I know I've been a complete shit to you."

Frankie chewed on his lip, and Ed could see his urge to say what he really thought. "Yeah, you were, from the day I started."

Ed nodded. "I hated you. I owe it to you to tell you why…." He took a deep breath. "But I can't. Not yet. It's still too raw." He looked at Marchant. "One day I hope you'll be able to forgive me."

Frankie rolled his eyes. "I've forgiven you already. I wouldn't have spent hours doing those damn reports if I didn't realize you were a decent person under that shitty exterior. Even if you don't like curry."

But Ed hadn't finished. "I'm sorry for trying to get you into trouble when you hurt your hip."

"Yeah, that was an arsehole thing to do. Don't do it again."

Ed nodded. "I won't. I won't get the chance. I'm handing in my resignation tomorrow."

He took pleasure in seeing three jaws drop.

"*What?*" Frankie exclaimed.

Marchant looked at him, a furrow between his brows. "What are you doing?"

"I hate that job. I've always hated it, and I know I'm crap. Frankie does a better job than me without even trying."

"So what are you going to do?" Frankie asked.

Ed shrugged. "I've no idea. I have savings, so I can survive for a while. I think I'd like to take dance lessons again." He thought about Frankie and Charlotte dancing together. "I used to dance a paso doble that would make you cry."

He clapped his hands over his ears as Frankie squealed. "I love dancing. We could take lessons together."

Al and Marchant let out remarkably similar growls.

"Ed will dance with me," Marchant said.

"You stay out of it," Al said, grabbing Frankie by the waist. He waited until Frankie had settled before he spoke to Ed. "I think that you need to learn to live for you, Ed."

Frankie stepped forward and hugged him. "You do that, and when you want to talk, I'll be here."

"So will I," Al added.

"Thank you." Ed smiled at them and looked at Marchant. "I'd like to go home now."

Marchant held out his hand. "Let's go."

His hand was warm and strong around Ed's, giving him courage when all he was thinking was *What the hell have I just said?*

Ed was lost in thought as they walked down the stairs, and he didn't hear Marchant's question.

"Ed?"

"Huh?"

"Do you want to go home or come back to my place for a nightcap?"

Ed blinked. "Your place?"

"Yeah."

"I...." *Shit!*

"For a drink. Nothing else."

Ed nodded and held Marchant's hand a little tighter as he jumped off the cliff again.

ED STARED up at the outside of the club. "You live here?"

"Above the club, yes."

"I thought you lived in a house."

On the corner of the road, 11 Larchmead Close had been an old pub, and now it was something else entirely.

"What do your neighbors think?" Ed blurted the first thing on his mind.

Marchant didn't seem offended by his question. "We had a struggle when we first proposed the club, but the place is fully soundproofed, and there is a car park at the back. We also accommodate some of our neighbors a couple of nights a week."

"You do?" Ed did not want to think about it.

"There's a reason the club is in this area." Marchant didn't elaborate as he led Ed into the flat.

Ed looked around Marchant's home with interest. "It's larger than I expected."

"It was mainly small rooms when I moved in, but I knocked them through, so the living area is open plan. I like my space." Marchant filled the kettle, and then he sat down next to Ed, who was perched on the edge of the sofa.

"Is there any point me asking you to relax?" Marchant asked as he lounged in one corner of the sofa. Ed gave a startled chuckle, and Marchant's expression softened. "I like seeing you laugh."

"Frankie said the same thing tonight." God, was it still only the same evening? It felt like years.

"You don't do it enough."

"He said that too."

"I bet he didn't say he really wanted to kiss you." Marchant growled a little. "At least, he'd better not."

"He didn't," Ed said breathlessly, still perched at the edge of the couch.

"I'm going to kiss you," Marchant said.

No "please" or "may I." Just an acceptance that Ed was going to let him.

Marchant took Ed's glasses from him and placed them on the side table. Then he cupped the back of Ed's head with one large hand and tilted his jaw until he was satisfied, his mouth came down on Ed's, and Ed stopped thinking.

There was nothing chaste about this kiss. Marchant's lips were warm and dry, and he was sucking the breath out of Ed.

Ed moaned and curled his fingers around Marchant's shirt. This time Marchant didn't allow Ed to be passive. He demanded Ed respond with every part of him, pulling Ed's hands away from his chest.

For one awful moment, Ed thought Marchant was trying to get away from him, but then Marchant took Ed's hands and held them behind his back in one strong hand.

For the first time in his life, Ed felt what it was like to be overpowered by someone who wanted to bring him pleasure instead of pain. Marchant was forceful, taking Ed's kiss as if it was his right. Ed willingly gave him his submission, closing his eyes as he followed Marchant's lead. Marchant growled under his breath and pulled him even closer, bending him back until Ed was only held up by the force of Marchant's arm.

Ed only opened his eyes when he realized Marchant had stopped the kiss.

Marchant was staring down at him, a fierce look in his eyes. "You are perfect."

Ed shook his head. "I'm broken, useless."

"You aren't broken."

"But…."

Marchant's hand tightened around Ed's wrists, and Ed hissed at the sudden pain. "If I tell you you're perfect, then you are perfect. I will tell you what to think."

Ed stared at him, dazed. "Promise?" He knew he sounded like a child.

"I will give you exactly what you need."

"Nobody has ever done that for me before."

"You're mine." Marchant growled and kissed him again.

Ed closed his eyes again and let himself sink into Marchant's will. Marchant demanded that he open his mouth and let him explore. He could have been in Marchant's arms for minutes; he could have been there for hours. He had no way of telling time.

Eventually he became aware that he was free and pressed against the sofa, Marchant stroking his cheek.

"Here, have a drink of water." Marchant pressed the glass against Ed's lips.

Ed drank the water obediently, choking a little at first as he tried to drink too fast, then slowing down at Marchant's growled command to be careful.

"What happened?"

"You did exactly what I told you to do. You stopped thinking."

"I'm so tired." Ed felt like he was incapable of standing, let alone thinking.

"I know, but you won't be tired anymore."

"What do I have to do?"

Marchant pinched at Ed's cheek, the nip of pain helping to focus him. "You keep asking me, and you're not listening to the answer. Do what I tell you to do."

Ed sighed. "Keep telling me."

"That's not the way it works. There is a punishment if you disobey me, and not listening to me is disobeying."

Tension flooded Ed's body. "Punishment?"

"I know what was done to you," Marchant said carefully. "You were abused."

"They punished me for not listening."

"By beating you."

Ed shuddered. He lived through the beatings in his nightmares.

"I'm not going to beat you."

"You're not?" Bewildered, Ed looked at Marchant. Beating was a part of BDSM, wasn't it?

"I want to explore your sensory side."

"What do you mean?"

"I saw how you reacted to the ice. I want to explore that side of you."

"You're not going to hit me?"

"Not yet. Not until I know you can handle it."

"But you said you'd punish me for disobeying you."

Marchant caressed Ed's cheek again. "There's more than one way of punishing someone. It doesn't have to involve pain."

Not really understanding, but wanting to appear willing, Ed murmured his agreement.

Marchant narrowed his eyes. "Oh, baby. You have so much to learn."

"I'm too old. You need a young sub to train."

"Are you trying to give me an order?"

Ed caught the dangerous edge in Marchant's voice. "No, no, I'd just understand if you didn't want me."

Marchant placed his finger over Ed's mouth, and he stopped talking. "I want *you*," he said and followed up his actions by kissing Ed until Ed was limp in his arms again.

Ed knew at some point he was going to have to go home, but until Marchant released him, he wasn't going anywhere.

And Marchant didn't seem in any hurry to do that. After the kiss ended, he rearranged Ed so that he lay with his head on Marchant's lap and his feet on the sofa. Marchant's fingers idly tangled through his hair.

"I'm going to fall asleep," Ed murmured, breaking the silence after long minutes.

"It doesn't matter if you do. I can take you home tomorrow morning in time for work."

Ed thought for a long while about the decision he'd made. It was the right decision, he knew that, but the thought of losing one of the things in his life that gave him structure was frightening to contemplate. "What shall I do?"

"Learn to dance, train to be my sub, and understand what it means to enjoy life."

Marchant sounded so firm, so sure, that Ed relaxed, knowing that for once he didn't have to make another decision until he was ready. He closed his eyes, Marchant's firm thighs under his cheek and his hands in Ed's hair. He was safe for the moment.

ED COWERED away from the leather belt, anything to avoid the sharp lash of pain as it struck his spine.

"How dare you go back to the ballroom!" His mother lashed out again, and Ed screamed in pain. "Shut up. Shut up! I don't want to hear your excuses!" She hit him again. "Dancing is perverted. You're perverted. My son is a deviant."

He tried to curl up away from the belt, but it struck him across the face. She normally avoided his face, arms, and hands, anywhere visible. She only struck him where no one would see, and he had learned to avoid the questions by hiding from everyone—teachers and kids. No one knew. No one cared.

"ED, SHH, it's all right. You're safe, shh. I've got you."

Ed opened his eyes, but he still saw his mother screaming in his face. He didn't remember her ever saying he was safe. "I'm sorry, I won't go back there. I'm sorry, I'm sorry."

"There's nothing to be sorry for, baby, you're fine. We're all fine, here, in my bed. You'll always be safe here."

Still unsure who was talking to him, Ed closed his eyes again and rested against the solid bulk propping him up.

Gradually the soothing circles traced on his back and the masculine scent permeated Ed's consciousness, and he opened his eyes. A lamp on the bedside table bathed the room in a pale glow. "Marchant?"

Marchant tightened his embrace. "Yeah, I'm here. You're safe, love."

"I'm sorry."

"What for?"

"Waking you up." Another thought struck Ed. "Where am I?"

"In my bed."

"How did I get here?" He looked down at himself. "You undressed me?"

Marchant snorted. "You were out like a light, so I carried you to bed. I couldn't let you sleep in your suit."

"I didn't wake up?"

"You grumbled a bit when I undressed you."

Ed flopped back onto the pillow. He never slept well—another hangover from his childhood—and yet he'd slept like a baby in Marchant's arms.

"Are you ready to sleep again?" Marchant asked.

"I think so."

Marchant turned out the light and tugged Ed back into his arms. "You okay?"

"I think so." Ed lay with his head on Marchant's chest, listening to the steady beat of his heart.

"What did you dream about?"

"The usual. Being beaten with a belt."

"You...." For once Marchant seemed lost for words. "Do you dream about it often?"

"Most nights."

"Have you ever thought of getting a therapist?"

"Once or twice."

"What stopped you?"

"I was afraid they might tell me my mother was right."

"I can introduce you to someone who understands people like you and me."

Ed stopped the protest on his tongue. He was tired of denying it even to himself. He *was* like Marchant, even more than Frankie was.

"I like Frankie," he said.

"He's a brat," Marchant said easily, and Ed understood it was a term of affection. Marchant had probably known many brats like Frankie Mason.

Ed buried his nose against Marchant's T-shirt and inhaled the scent of him beneath the flowery smell of the detergent. Unlike Ed, Marchant was wearing a T-shirt and pajama bottoms. "Take off your T-shirt."

"Ed?"

"Please."

Marchant still waited.

"Sir."

Ed found himself dislodged as Marchant sat up and pulled the T-shirt over his head. Then they were back in the same position again, and Ed's cheek tickled as he lay on Marchant's hairy chest. Part of him wondered why he wasn't panicking, but the other part realized he'd come to associate Marchant with "safe."

"That's better," he said and yawned, his jaw cracking with the force of his tiredness.

"Go back to sleep."

The order rumbled above him, and Ed obeyed.

ABOUT FIFTEEN minutes after Ed arrived at work, the admin director called Ed into his office. "Would you come to my office, Winters?"

Ed had been expecting the call. In fact he'd been staring out at the park waiting until the moment his phone rang.

The admin director looked up as he entered his office. "Morning, Ed."

Ed nearly tripped over his step. This was the first time the director had shown him any sign of friendliness. In the three years he'd worked there, they'd exchanged as few words as possible.

He sat down where indicated and waited.

The director tapped his desk for a moment before he spoke. "I received your resignation."

Ed nodded. He'd sent it as soon as he'd woken up, in case he lost his nerve at work.

"I'm amazed. I thought you'd be carried out in your box. Where are you going now?"

"Nowhere. At least I haven't got a job planned. I'm going to take some time to do other things."

The director looked curious. "Like what?"

"Oh...." Ed was purposely vague. He didn't think the director would understand if he said he was learning to live like a man for the first time in his life. "I'd like to learn to dance."

"You're giving up a job to learn to dance?"

Ed smiled. "Among other things."

The director shook his head. "You've shocked the hell out of me. We'd better start looking for your replacement."

No "sorry you're going" or "you'll be irreplaceable." Ed nodded. He'd long made peace with himself with the knowledge that he was as bad in the job as the job was bad for him.

"Train Frankie Mason to do the job."

"Bloody hell, Winters, have you hit your head?"

"Not lately."

"One minute it's handbags at dawn, and the next you're in bed together. You're not a poofter as well, are you?"

Ed stared at him in dislike. He was beginning to understand why Frankie had taken the piss out of him all the time. "I thought I was the only one with outdated views."

"Good Lord, man, don't be so touchy."

"Frankie's the best man for the job, even better than Naz or Anne-Marie."

"He's inexperienced."

"Then train him."

"We still need to interview. You'll need to set that up with the coven—I mean Human Resources." The director sighed. "I'm not handling this too well, am I?"

"No, sir, not too well." The anger drained out of Ed. He'd been that man two weeks ago. God, was it that short a time? He smiled at the director so brightly the man blinked. "I call them that too." Ed got to his feet. "Mr. Mason *is* your man."

The director leaned back in his chair. "Why now?"

"Why am I leaving?"

The director nodded.

"Someone finally convinced me to live a little."

"You've found a woman."

"Good God, no. I am a poofter too. But I still don't like curry—or women."

Ed walked out of the office with his head held high.

Chapter 9

MARCHANT LOOKED at Ed over his plate of ham and chips in the supermarket café. "So when are you leaving?"

He had phoned Ed the previous evening and said he was busy, but could he catch up with him at the supermarket for an early lunch. Ed had agreed, and they'd met at eleven thirty in the café. The place still made Ed's skin itch, but he wanted to see Marchant, and Marchant wanted to meet him there.

Ed paused before he ate a mouthful of salad. Then, "Next Friday. I've got so much holiday left I could go now, but they refused to let me go before I tentatively train up a successor."

"Do they have anyone in mind?"

"I suggested Frankie, but they have to interview people first."

Marchant choked on a chip. "You suggested Frankie?"

"Well, yeah. He's kept the team together recently." Ed pulled a face. "He's always kept the team together. I just didn't notice."

"But there's a huge difference between being team clown and team leader."

"You don't think he's up for it?"

"I don't know him well enough," Marchant said.

"I do," Ed said firmly. "They'll have to advertise the job, but Frankie is right for the role."

"What changed your opinion?"

Ed paused before he answered. "Someone opened my eyes to the world around me."

Marchant smiled at him. "Good boy."

Rather than saying what was on his mind, Ed ate another mouthful of salad. "What are we going to do today?" he asked.

"After we've finished shopping, I thought I'd show you around my club."

Ed's cutlery clattered to the plate. "What?"

"You haven't seen the place, and I'd like to show it to you."

"I don't think I'm ready for it." His heart raced and his hands were suddenly clammy.

"Ed, calm down. I'm asking you to look around a few rooms, not tie you to a cross and whip you bloody."

"Oh." Ed looked down at his near empty plate, his cheeks flushing as an elderly couple at the next table looked over at Marchant's words.

"Shall we get going?"

Ed pushed away his plate and stood. "Sure. Why not."

Marchant looked at him suspiciously. "You mean it?"

"I've been kissed by a man for the first time in my life, slept with him, and resigned from my job. I can handle a little shopping and an afternoon trip to a BDSM club."

"Jesus, Mary. You never promised me anything like that if I endure the shopping trip," the man at the next table said.

"Your heart couldn't stand it, Alf," Mary said. "Football's enough excitement for you."

"Still...." He sounded wistful.

Marchant bowed to the couple and handed his card to the woman. "You are more than welcome for a tour."

She read the card and then stared a little closer. "You want to kill him off? He hasn't had that much fun in years!"

Marchant winked at her and then looked at Ed. "Are you ready?"

Ed nodded speechlessly, and he followed Marchant toward the lift.

"Wait, young man, is it really that big?"

Marchant looked over his shoulder at Mary. "I promise you, madam, it's perfectly in proportion."

"Oh dear God," Ed muttered, his cheeks ablaze.

"Don't get any ideas, Mary. These... gentlemen prefer each other." Alf sounded a little worried.

Marchant snorted and kept going.

Ed brushed past him and stabbed at the lift button.

"Don't you want to take the stairs?" Marchant asked mildly.

"No," Ed growled.

He stepped into the lift, almost bowling over the woman coming out with her toddler.

"Watch it," she said sharply, holding her kid close to her side.

Marchant apologized to her and stepped in after Ed. "Do you want to tell me what that's all about?"

The door closed before Ed answered. "Why did you do that?"

"Do what?"

Ed could scream at Marchant's mild tone. "Talk about it as if it's normal."

"As if what's normal?" A frown had settled between Marchant's thick brows.

"*It*. You know!"

"No, I really don't know what you're talking about, Ed."

The lift doors opened way too early for Ed's liking. He stalked out with Marchant hard on his heels. He could have screamed as he stood in the supermarket. Ed clenched his fists in frustration at having nowhere to go to work through his deep-rooted feelings of unease and anger.

Marchant curled a hand around his bicep. "I'm not letting this go until we've talked it out."

Ed refused to look in his eyes. "There's nowhere to go."

"We'll find a quiet corner somewhere in the car park."

"It's not important." Ed tried to tug his arm away, but Marchant held on to it firmly.

"You're wrong." Marchant forced Ed to look at him. Ed cringed away at the disappointment in his eyes. "This isn't just about a silly conversation. It's about us, who we are. This is very important." Then he let go of Ed's arm and walked out of the exit.

Ed had a choice. He could follow and endure an excruciating few minutes, or he could walk away. He had a feeling that if he walked away, Marchant wouldn't follow him—this was too important to Marchant. And Marchant was too important to lose just because Ed was embarrassed. He rushed to catch up with Marchant and heard him exhale sharply. Marchant had been waiting for his decision.

At the far corner of the supermarket building, Marchant spun on his heel to look at Ed. The movement was so sudden, it made Ed rock back on his heels.

"Are you embarrassed by what I do?" Marchant asked.

"It's not the sort of thing you talk about in public, is it?"

"I do."

"You tell people you own a gay BDSM club?"

"I tell people I own a club, and if they ask for details, I tell them more."

"But—"

"I'm not embarrassed by what I do, Ed. I thought you understood that."

"But it's not right to talk about it."

"Who says?"

Ed stared at a pile of misshapen cardboard boxes rather than look in Marchant's eyes. "I told you I went to a BDSM club once."

"I remember."

"One of the subs, a young guy from my old office, spotted me. He told everyone at work. He made it sound as if *I* was the pervert rather than him. It didn't seem to occur to everyone that he was there too. I had to transfer to get away from the rumors."

"Bastard. I wish I'd been there to help you. Can you remember the name of the club?"

"Dungeon something or other." Ed had tried to put the whole experience out of his mind.

Marchant's lips twitched. "They're all called that."

"They talked about me like my mother did," Ed whispered shamefacedly.

"I'm so sorry, Ed."

"They were right. It is—"

"Don't say it. Whatever was going to come out of your mouth, don't say it. I am proud of my club and proud of my life. Don't make that something dirty."

"I'm not like you."

"You're not like that either," Marchant pointed out. "You'd have never left your job three weeks ago."

"One kiss and I'm turning my world upside down," Ed said. "I must be insane."

"More than one kiss, and you're not insane. Happy. For the first time in your life you're tasting happiness because you're allowing yourself to be who you are."

Ed shook his head. "It was a kiss, nothing more."

"You have got so much to learn about submission and BDSM, Ed. Yeah, ropes and flogging is part of it, but submission is so much more." Marchant hesitated. "Today that was just some fun. They overheard something, and I ran with it. I wasn't trying to embarrass you or hurt you. None of us were. It was a passing interaction between strangers. You should try it sometime."

"You mean I need to lighten up?"

"A little, yes."

"It's not easy for me."

Marchant stepped closer and placed one hand on Ed's hip. "What do I keep telling you to do?"

"Stop thinking."

"What did you do?"

"Think."

Marchant nodded. "You broke the rules, and there is a punishment."

Tension flooded Ed's body. "Punishment?"

"Not a beating. Your punishments aren't beatings."

"What, then?"

Marchant dug in his pocket and handed Ed a piece of paper.

Ed frowned. "What's this?"

"My shopping list. You can get my shopping as well as your own."

Ed stared at the paper with its neat list of items and then back at him. "You're joking."

"I don't joke about punishments. Instead of us sharing time together, you get to do both lots of shopping."

"And what are you going to do?"

"Me? I'm going to have another coffee."

Ed glared at him.

Marchant raised an eyebrow.

"Fine." Ed stomped back to the supermarket entrance. He checked just once to make sure Marchant was following him. He was, slowly, and Ed breathed a little easier.

It didn't stop him huffing as he went around the store, careful to keep their respective shops separate. Marchant was very clear about what he wanted, brand and size, and Ed started to get a suspicion that he'd planned for Ed to do his shopping.

"It won't happen again, bastard," he hissed under his breath.

He hoped Marchant didn't expect him to pay for his shopping. He was going to be unemployed very soon, and he needed to save every penny.

The young man at the checkout chattered away to him about nothing in particular, and Ed listened with half an ear. Before he would have ignored the boy, but Marchant's lessons about interacting with strangers rang in his ears. He smiled and wished the assistant a good day as he finished and received a dazzling smile in return. Ed's limited gaydar pinged, probably for the first time in its life.

Marchant joined him as he reached the entrance.

"That was good timing," Ed said.

"I watched you from the top. Pretty boy."

Ed flushed. "Yes, he was. Here's your shopping."

"You can push the trolley until we reach my car," Marchant said easily. "And I meant you."

He didn't know what to say to that. Ed resisted the urge to shove the trolley into Marchant's groin. The man left him speechless whichever way he turned.

Marchant didn't wait to see what he'd do, just led the way to his car. Ed followed him. It started to rain, light drops, but from the dark gray above threatening to get heavier. Pausing to wipe his glasses, Ed then had to dodge a car, and Marchant was some distance away. Ed gritted his teeth as he saw Marchant get into his car and shut the door. He had no choice but to follow him, because Marchant had given him a lift to the supermarket.

Doing his best to ignore the rain, Ed loaded the shopping into the boot and disposed of the trolley. Finally able to slide, dripping and pissed off, into the car, Ed sat down next to Marchant, who smiled at him.

"Ready to go?"

"Is that all you can say?"

"You took your punishment. Good boy."

Ed exploded. He hadn't intended to say anything, but he opened his mouth and nearly forty years of resentment and misery came flooding out—again.

"Don't you fucking dare call me that ever again!"

"Call you what?" Marchant's expression was a mixture of anger and confusion.

"Good boy. I'm not a good boy. I'm not a fucking *dog*."

"Ed." Marchant gentled his voice. "I've called you that many times when you've done something good."

"I know, and I hate it. It's wrong and demeaning, and it just means *hurt*." Ed ended on an indrawn breath and a sob.

Marchant turned in his seat to look at him. "Ed, who called you a good boy?"

"My mother."

"But not to praise you."

Ed shook his head.

"Did she sexually abuse you?"

"God, no, no. She never did that."

Marchant exhaled noisily. "Thank Christ for that. So when did she call you a good boy?"

Ed pressed his flushed cheek against the cool glass of the window. "When I'd taken my punishment like a good boy."

"When she'd beaten you."

"Yes. As long as I kept quiet, I was a good boy."

Marchant was quiet for a long time, and Ed didn't feel like talking.

"We can make that term one that you want to hear because you know I'll be pleased with you, or I can use something else."

"Like what?"

"I don't know. I'd have to think."

"I would be happy never to hear it again."

Good boy. You took your punishment like a good boy.

Marchant squeezed Ed's knee. "Then you won't. I will never say that to you again, love."

Ed looked at him. "You called me love."

"You are my love."

"So soon?"

"From the first moment I saw you getting turned on by the ice on your skin. You were covered in Coke, and all you could think of was the ice trickling down, down, down." Marchant's voice was almost hypnotic.

"I was a mass of goose bumps," Ed admitted.

"I wanted to rip off your shirt and see your nipples, see how hard they were."

"I would have screamed... or fainted."

Marchant pressed his finger against the pulse point at the base of Ed's neck. "I would have caught you. I will always catch you."

It sounded terribly formal, like a vow.

"Promise?"

"I promise."

"Thank you," Ed whispered.

"I love you, baby."

Ed pulled a face. "Seriously, I'm older than you. 'Baby' is off the table."

"Oh?" Marchant queried. "And who makes the decisions around here?"

"You do, son."

"Baby is off the table, and if you ever call me son again, I'll...."

Ed could see Marchant biting back the words he wanted to say. "You'll spank my arse?"

"Is that off the table?"

"Not if you spank me with your hand."

Marchant nodded. "We'll negotiate your limits, bab… Ed."

"Thank you." Ed lightly brushed Marchant's pulse point just as Marchant had done to him. The throb of blood under his fingertips felt as intimate as a kiss.

Chapter 10

ED HAD to gird his loins to step over the threshold of the club. "Girding one's loins" was a phrase that had always made Ed blush, but in this instance, it was very appropriate. Ed's loins were primed and willing, even if his brain was not so cooperative.

Marchant waited patiently for Ed to process this and take the step into the club. He didn't nag or tug, for which Ed was very grateful.

Having only had one ill-fated attempt at going to a club, Ed had very little to compare it with. Marchant's club seemed full of light and space compared to the other place, but Marchant assured him there were dark places. The room they were in was just the bar area. Ed would be very content to stay in the bar, but he had a feeling Marchant wouldn't leave it there.

As expected, Marchant led Ed into the farther reaches of the club. Ed wasn't naïve; he recognized most of the equipment.

"What do you think?" Marchant asked as he led Ed back to the bar and the comfort of daylight.

"It's very… nice," Ed said lamely.

Marchant snorted. "You sound like you've been shown around the vicarage."

"What do you want me to say? It scares me? It turns me on? I have no idea what I'm doing here? All of those things and more."

"That's better. I can see you're turned-on." Marchant was almost purring.

Ed blushed, but in the loose fit of his trousers, his arousal was hard to hide.

Marchant grabbed Ed's hand and pressed his palm against the bulge in Marchant's jeans. "You're not the only one."

Closing his eyes, Ed squeezed gently, feeling a man's erection beneath his hand for the first time. A lifetime of guilt threatened to overwhelm him, but he pushed it back and sunk into the feel of Marchant.

"Ed. Ed, open your eyes." Marchant's firm voice interrupted his thoughts. "If you want to stop this at any time, you say stop, and everything comes to a halt. Say yes if you understand. I need to hear your words, not your thoughts."

"Yes." Ed left his hand where it was because Marchant's hand was still on top of his.

"Unzip my jeans." As Ed's eyes opened wide, Marchant said, "Don't think. Just do it."

Ed's hands shook, but he did as he was asked, undoing the button and unzipping Marchant's jeans.

"Careful," Marchant murmured.

Ed flushed as he realized what Marchant meant, but he slid his fingers into the opening to stop anything being caught in the zip. Crinkly hair and hard, sticky heat grazed his knuckles. He paused and then took a deep breath. He could do this. Girded loins, remember?

"Take it out."

Carefully Ed wrapped his hand around Marchant's dick and exposed it. He didn't look, not yet. He kept his eyes on Marchant.

"Goo… well done. Make me come. You can jack me off or suck me, I don't mind."

Ed sucked in a breath. Marchant didn't say anything else, and Ed realized he'd been given an order. Marchant expected him to obey unless Ed called a halt.

Biting his lip, Ed looked at Marchant's cock for the first time, noticing how the large, bulbous red head glistened and a drop of liquid was trapped in the slit. He captured the drop with the pad of his thumb, eliciting a hiss from Marchant. He wanted to suck his thumb, learn Marchant's flavor, but that was a step too far. He held out his thumb to Marchant, who swiped the drop away with his tongue.

"Make me come."

"Yes, sir."

Ed jacked Marchant's cock, watching the tip weep again. He wanted to sink to his knees and give his first blowjob. He wanted to, he was desperate to, but…. Ed yelped as he felt a sharp pain on his arse.

"You're thinking again. What did I tell you to do?"

"Stop thinking," Ed said, his cheeks flushed with embarrassment. At Marchant's raised eyebrow, he added a hasty "Sir."

"Follow the order. Make me come."

Ed gave up and sank to his knees to take the first taste of Marchant. Bitter flavor burst on his tongue—bitterness mixed with something else.

He licked again, and again. Marchant groaned, and Ed felt triumphant. He sucked on the spongy head and then deeper, unable to take more than an inch or two into his mouth before gagging. It was awkward and uncomfortable, he hated the drool, and his jaw ached quicker than he expected, but he refused to give up. Marchant hadn't asked for perfection, just for Ed to have a go.

"Use your hands as well," Marchant said, his hands resting lightly on the back of Ed's head.

Ed did as he was told, jacking the shaft as he sucked on the head. Marchant groaned again, and then he pushed in farther, making Ed gag. Determined to hear Marchant make that groaning noise again, Ed sucked harder. Marchant stiffened, his hands clutching, and he came, flooding Ed's mouth with creamy, bitter fluid. Ed found it hard to swallow and suck at the same time, but somehow he managed it until Marchant was still and spent in his mouth.

"Beautiful boy, well done." Marchant's fingers carded through his hair.

Ed sat back on his heels and wiped his mouth with the back of his hand.

Marchant stared down at him, looking sated. "You've done so well, boy."

"That wasn't easy," Ed admitted.

"You'll get better with practice, and I intend to make you practice a lot. Tuck me away."

With some regret Ed hid Marchant's half-hard cock behind denim and zipped him up. He went to get to his feet, but Marchant stopped him.

"You have no idea how beautiful you look on your knees like that." The fierce look in Marchant's eyes made Ed glow. "I've imagined you like this since we first met. On your knees in front of me, hard as a rock and desperate to come."

Ed had been trying to ignore his own erection, but Marchant's proud voice made him harder still.

"Show me," Marchant said.

Ed fumbled at the fastening of his trousers, but he got them open and pushed them down along with his boxers. He was nothing special, at least in his own eyes, but Marchant didn't look disappointed.

"You're stunning."

Ed whimpered, a knife-edge from coming over himself.

"Stand up."

"Yes, sir." Ed managed, although it wasn't that graceful as he tried not to trip over his trousers.

Marchant wrapped his warm large hand around Ed's dick, and Ed's control failed; he came in hard pulses over Marchant's hand. Ed's legs almost failed him, but Marchant held him up with a strong arm around his back. Ed was mortified, but there was nothing he could have done to prevent his orgasm.

Marchant maneuvered Ed against the wall. "Stay there, I'm going to get a cloth to clean us up."

"I don't think I've got the strength to walk anywhere," Ed confessed.

"Job done." Marchant grinned at him. "You're even more beautiful come-drunk."

"You make me sound like a girl."

"I would never say that to a woman." Marchant looked so horrified, Ed started laughing.

"You're worse than I am where women are concerned."

"You don't like women?"

"I have never found a woman who wasn't a slut or a bitch."

Marchant frowned, but he said, "I guess you haven't had the best role models."

"You think?"

It was only when Ed caught the expression on Marchant's face, he realized how rude that sounded. "I'm sorry, sir."

"Apology accepted. I have a good relationship with my mother and my sisters. They are neither sluts nor bitches."

Ed could hear the edge in his voice. "I will treat them with respect, sir." Then he frowned. "You want me to meet your family?"

"Of course I do." This time Marchant frowned. "Why wouldn't I introduce my partner to my family?"

Ed choked. "Your partner?"

"My family are open-minded, Ed, but even they might find it hard to be introduced to my sub at the first meeting. They'll *know* you're my sub, of course. We just won't talk about it."

Partner! Ed blinked at the thought. Three weeks ago he'd been alone.

Three weeks ago he'd been slowly dying.

"Isn't it a bit soon to be your partner?"

Marchant shrugged. "I don't care what I call you to the outside world. The only titles that count are the ones we use together."

"Dom and sub?" Ed hazarded.

"Master and sub," Marchant corrected.

Ed nodded, more to himself than Marchant. "I am your sub."

"Hello, anybody around? Marchant?"

Ed panicked at the rattle of keys. He'd hadn't even cleaned up yet, derailed by their conversation about women.

Marchant stepped in front of him. "It's okay. This is Tony, one of my barmen. He's working tonight." Efficiently he tucked Ed back into his boxers and zipped him up. "In the bar, Tony."

"Okay, see you in a minute. I need a wazz."

Marchant stared at Ed. "Are you all right? Are you going to panic?"

"Probably." Ed hadn't decided what he was about to do. He wasn't sure he had the energy to panic after giving his first blowjob and coming so hard.

"You're not sure? Tony's a great guy. He's been with me from the start."

"As your barman?"

"He's done most things. He's a great sub and very efficient at running the club."

"A sub?"

Marchant chuckled at the edge in Ed's voice. "Not my sub. Tony's never been my sub."

"Fuck, no, we'd kill each other." Tony walked in, shaking his hands.

Ed's jaw dropped. The man was the size of a small house and furry—really furry.

"You see?" Marchant murmured in his ear.

"You must be Ed. Markie's not shut up about you since he covered you in Coke."

Tony bounded over and shook Ed's hand. Still holding hands, Ed looked at Marchant. "Markie?"

Marchant shot his barman a sour look. "Don't even think about calling me that. He hasn't learnt the meaning of respect."

Tony snorted. "I've seen you weeping into your beer, remember?"

"What happened?" Ed asked.

"Bad breakup," Marchant said shortly.

Ed laid a hand on his arm. "Are you still hurting?"

Marchant smiled at him. "Not since I found you."

"Oh, how sweet." Tony's voice dripped sarcasm. "I'll just puke in the bucket, shall I?"

"You can fuck off," Marchant said, not taking his eyes off Ed.

"In other words, go away while you make goo-goo eyes at each other?"

"Please," Ed said.

Marchant gave him a broad smile. "You're going to get on just fine."

Tony huffed. "Fine, fine, at least this one has manners. I'm going, but if you're going to fuck, don't do it here."

Before Ed could panic, Marchant said, "Not here and not in front of other people, okay? I'm not expecting you to do anything like that."

"But that's what you do here." Ed waved a hand to show he meant the club.

Marchant nodded. "Yes, some do. Some guys come here for other things than sex. It depends on the guy and the situation."

"If I asked you never to have sex with me in a public place, you would do that?" Ed wondered if it was odd to be negotiating sex when they hadn't actually had sex yet.

"It's your limits, Ed."

"Will you still have sex with other people?" He'd worried about that too.

Marchant scrubbed a hand through his hair. "We really need to talk about this in a formal setting."

"What does that mean?"

"It means that as Master and sub, it's one of the things we negotiate."

"Do you have sex with other subs here?"

"Yes, sometimes. Not very often now."

"Why not?"

Marchant shrugged. "I tend to do the demonstrations with the whips and floggers. I don't have so many sessions as I used to."

"Why not?" Ed asked again.

"Because he's bored with all the subs," Tony answered before Marchant could respond. He disappeared through another door.

"Oh." Ed thought about it, and then he smiled.

"You're all right with that?" Marchant asked, a cautious note in his voice.

"You're not bored with me. Of course I'm all right with that."

Marchant yanked Ed into his arms. "Of course I'm not bored with you. God, you're the most exciting man that's come into my life for years."

Ed thought that was probably exaggerating a little, but then Marchant was kissing him, and his brain decided it had something better to do.

Like switch off and enjoy the ride.

MARCHANT HAD to work, so Ed left the club for an evening with a spinach salad and Fred and Ginger. Marchant had invited him to stay, but he wasn't ready, and he knew that. Marchant had looked disappointed, but he nuzzled Ed's neck and nipped it—which made Ed gasp—and said he'd see him the following day.

Ed parked himself on the sofa with a large glass of sparkling water and a fresh spinach salad. He hesitated over which film to choose but eventually picked *Follow the Fleet* and sat down to an evening where he could lose himself in another world. He'd always felt he'd been born in the wrong era. This world was too loud, too brash, too *lacking* for him. Now, though, Ed thought about Marchant. There was nothing lacking about him, or the way he made Ed feel.

He was so lost in his thoughts, he jumped when his mobile phone beeped. The phone was a relatively new acquisition. He'd never bothered before. He didn't have friends or family to call, he didn't play games or listen to music, and he didn't go anywhere. There didn't seem much point in getting one. Marchant had looked incredulous when Ed said he didn't have one and the next day had presented him with a phone. Ed was still trying to work out all the functions—like how to turn it on.

He picked it up and looked at the screen. There was a text from Marchant. Gingerly he pressed a button, hoping he wasn't going to delete anything. To his relief he saw a photo of Marchant and the text.

Bored missing u

He grinned and then tried to respond.

Wishing I was dancing with you.

He felt inordinately pleased that he'd managed his first text. Even though it had taken fifteen minutes.

Me 2. C u 2moz.

"2moz"? Ed frowned for a long while before he puzzled out that it meant "tomorrow." Sometimes he felt like an alien in the modern world.

Goodnight.

The response was immediate.

Love you.

No textspeak, for which Ed was thankful.

I love you too.

There. He'd said it for the first time in his life—about anything.

"I love you, Marchant Belarus," Ed said out loud.

It didn't sound so frightening now. Now he had to be brave enough to say it to his love.

Chapter 11

MARCHANT HAD been suspiciously quiet about their destination since Ed had got in the car. Ed was used to a peaceful drive, but normally he got a kiss that made his knees tremble and a suggestion of what they were doing that day. Since he had left the insurance company, he spent most days in Marchant's company, even if only an hour. Today he'd received a kiss that had made his cock rise and his toes curl, but nothing else, not even when Ed tried to question him.

Neither was the route familiar. In the time Ed had lived in the area, he'd not explored it much beyond finding the supermarket and the basic amenities. After half an hour, Marchant pulled in behind some shops.

Ed looked at him. "Are you going to tell me what we're doing here?"

"Not yet, pretty boy, you have to wait."

Ed growled, both at being called "pretty boy" and at being fobbed off again, but Marchant ignored him.

"Come on. We're expected." Marchant got out of the car.

"By whom?" Ed muttered, not loud enough for Marchant to hear him. He had swiftly learned that his master did not like backchat. Marchant was his master even if they hadn't ventured into the world of kink. Ed was really sick of shopping and cleaning for Marchant as his punishments.

To his surprise, Marchant held his hand. "Come with me, pretty boy."

Ed slipped his hand in Marchant's, feeling grounded and safe as he always did when Marchant touched him. "I don't suppose you're going to tell me where we're going?"

"It's a surprise. You'll like it."

Marchant's surprises weren't always pleasurable, but Ed knew better than to point that out.

They went up the outside staircase to the first floor above the shops. Ed blinked as his eyes adjusted to the dim light, then Marchant led him into a brightly lit room, and Ed stopped breathing.

It was a dance studio. Marchant had brought him to a dance studio. From the size, it obviously stretched the length of the row of shops underneath.

A young woman came toward them, dressed in a leotard and a silky skirt. "Master Belarus, about time you visited me."

"You knew I was coming, Maisie," Marchant said mildly as he gave her a hug.

She punched him on the bicep as they stepped apart. "But it's been too fucking long, dipshit. I have missed you at my lessons."

Ed watched the byplay with some bemusement. They obviously knew each other well, and Marchant had kept that quiet too. He took dance lessons?

Maisie turned her attention to Ed. "And this must be your new sub."

Ed tried not to flinch at the term. He was getting better, but it still caught him by surprise to hear it mentioned so publicly.

Maisie didn't seem to notice as she shook his hand. "Hi, Ed, pleased to meet you at last. I knew Master Belarus must have found a new guy when he called me out of the blue."

"He makes a habit of bringing them to you?" he asked.

Marchant sighed and hugged Ed to him. "Way to go, Maisie. Now Ed's all suspicious and thinking I bring a string of guys here. I should get Joanne to spank your arse for putting doubts into my new sub's mind."

"She'd enjoyed it too much, Belarus, you know that."

Ed looked around to see the new speaker—a woman dressed similarly to him in trousers and masculine-style shirt. Her hair was blonde and so closely cropped to her head that for a moment Ed thought she was bald.

"Hi, I'm Joanne." She held out her hand to Ed.

"I'm Ed."

"He's pretty," Maisie said.

Marchant smirked at Ed. "You see. I'm not the only one who thinks so."

Ed blushed.

Maisie snickered. Then she yelped as Joanne swatted her backside.

"I'm sorry for the behavior of my sub, Master Belarus. After our lesson I will punish her by making her wax the studio floor."

Ed winced, suddenly feeling very sorry for Maisie. The floor was huge. She didn't seem that bothered, though, and Ed had the feeling she'd done the job many times before.

"So what are you here for, Belarus?" Joanne asked.

Marchant hugged Ed closer to him. "My boy danced when he was younger, but he hasn't had the opportunity for a long time. I want you to teach him the steps, so I can dance with him."

Ed frowned, not getting what he meant.

"You want him to learn the woman's steps?" Joanne asked.

Marchant nodded. "I want to lead."

Maisie snorted loudly. "You always lead. I'm surprised you didn't teach him yourself."

"I want Ed to learn on a proper dance floor, and I thought it would be good for him to meet you."

"Someone else in the lifestyle, you mean?" Joanne asked.

Marchant inclined his head.

Joanne looked at Ed. "When was the last time you danced, Ed?"

"Over twenty years ago." Two decades of wishing he could find a man like Fred Astaire to take him in his arms and lead him in dance.

"I assume you learned the male steps."

Ed nodded. "I wasn't allowed to learn the female steps, but I've picked them up by myself."

"Of course." Joanne turned to Maisie. "Take Ed to the other end of the ballroom and take him through his paces. I don't expect too much, Ed, so don't get embarrassed about what you don't know. It just gives us a baseline to work from."

"Sure. Come on, Ed." Maisie grabbed his hand and tugged him away from Marchant.

"Wait!" Marchant stopped them before they'd got too far and looked at Ed. "Are you all right?"

Ed swallowed hard. "Nervous of making a complete twat of myself, but I know it's got to be done."

"You'll be awesome, pretty boy. I love you." Marchant bent to kiss Ed on the lips. Then he looked at Joanne and Maisie. "Neither of you are to call him a good boy under any circumstances or to threaten him with a beating. Do you understand?"

Maisie looked curious, but she said, "Yes, Master Belarus."

Joanne just inclined her head.

Ed gave Marchant the biggest smile he could manage and followed Maisie down the studio.

At the end of the room, Maisie turned to him and said, "You don't know how lucky you are."

Ed had a very good idea of how lucky he was, but he asked, "What do you mean?"

"Not all of us find Doms and masters who have the skills to care for us. You have one of the best."

"You haven't been so lucky?"

Maisie looked down the studio to where Marchant and Joanne were talking. "My mistress is all I could wish for, but it took me a long time to find her."

"How long have you been a sub?" Maisie didn't look more than twenty-five.

"Ten years. I'm nearly thirty."

"I've only been involved for a few weeks. We haven't even done much yet." Ed blushed again.

"Take your time. There's no need to rush, Ed," she said earnestly. "I know there's a temptation to rush into everything, but Master Belarus can wait. He's a good man. He'd rather train you slowly than break you quickly."

Ed looked at her. "Could… we go for a coffee sometime? I'd really like to have someone to talk to." He had a feeling he could talk to Maisie in a way he couldn't with Frankie.

Maisie looked pleased. "Sure, I'd like that. At the end of the session, I'll give you my number." Then she looked over at Marchant and Joanne, who were giving them twin frowns. "We'd better get a move on, or they'll be yelling at us. Let's start with a waltz. Do you need the music, or can you do it from counting?"

"Let's try just from counting." He took Maisie into his arms. She barely came to his shoulder.

"I'll lead first of all, and then you can have a go."

"Yes, ma'am."

Maisie grimaced. "That sounds all wrong. Call me Maisie."

"Yes, Maisie. Sorry."

"No worries. Now one, two, three, and…."

THEY CAME to the end of the paso doble, and Maisie stared up at Ed with wide eyes.

"Holy fucking shit, Batman. Where did you learn to dance like that?"

Ed smiled. "Madam Julie was a good teacher."

"You should have become a professional."

"I always wanted to, but my mother wouldn't let me."

"What a terrible waste."

"Ed."

He turned to see Marchant staring at him, his eyes glistening with unshed tears.

"You were amazing," Marchant said, sounding completely choked up.

"Fucking brilliant," Joanne said. "The best I've seen walk through the door, and that includes the two people standing next to you. I can't believe you haven't danced for twenty years."

For the first time since he'd left Madam Julie's class for the last time, Ed smiled at them with utter confidence. "Dancing is the only thing I've ever been good at."

"We'll see how good you are when you dance backwards," Joanne said brusquely.

"He dances with me." Marchant's tone left them in no doubt that if anyone tried to stop him, he would dismember them limb from limb.

Marchant held out his hand. "Dance with me, boy."

"Yes, sir." Ed placed his hand in Marchant's.

"You'll follow my lead."

"Yes, sir." Ed had to think about where his arms were meant to be as Marchant pulled him against him. "But you know I've never taken the lady's role before."

"I know, just follow me. We will start with a foxtrot," Marchant said and counted them in.

As Marchant counted slow, slow, quick, quick, Ed realized he had imagined this moment his entire life, being in the arms of the man he loved. It wasn't perfect, but it was everything he'd wanted—the strength of Marchant carrying him through the rough spots. He had enjoyed dancing with Maisie, but dancing with Marchant was like being home.

"Woo-hoo. You are welcome here anytime, Ed," Maisie said when they'd finished.

"We could do with someone like you at our group lessons," Joanne said. "Belarus said you're free at the moment. How would you like to help us, and in return we'll teach you to be even better?"

Before Ed could answer, Marchant held up his hand. "What do you mean? What lessons?"

"We offer group lessons during the week."

"To whom?"

Marchant sounded deeply suspicious and Ed was confused. They were asking *him* to dance and learn. What was the problem? For the firs time in his life, he was in a position to do the one thing he really loved.

"Mainly the old ducks, who come here for the tea dance, and the kids. Neither of them are particularly stimulating, Ed, but we're always short of men. The senior citizens aren't looking for expertise, just a fur time to dance."

"Would he be expected to dance with any men?"

"Down, boy," Julie said drily. "He won't dance with another Dom I'll make sure of it. Most of the time it's strictly man-woman here. You are both welcome to the LGBT dance classes, but you can dance together."

"He's allowed to help you, but only if he doesn't dance with any other men."

Ed opened his mouth, but Marchant just scowled at him. "It's a harc limit, Ed. I won't let you do this any other way. You are mine, Ed, and will not let another man touch you without my permission."

"*You* won't? *Your* permission?" Ed glared back. "I'm not your slave Marchant. You don't own me."

"You haven't got a contract yet?" Joanne looked at Marchant ir surprise. "That's not like you, Belarus. What were you thinking?"

Marchant groaned and tugged at his hair. "I've been taking things slowly. We are not at the contract stage yet, but that doesn't mean you're not mine and that I'm not desperately possessive about you. I will kill any man I see leading you in a dance."

"That's really hot," Maisie whispered to Ed.

He had to agree. That was really hot. "I promise not to let anothe man lead me in a dance. You are my Fred. No one else even comes close."

"Good." Marchant took a noisy breath. "But we really need to talk about a contract and limits."

"Let me dance at least once with your boy," Joanne said. "I've neve seen Maisie melt like that about anyone."

"Except you," Maisie said.

"Except me," Joanne agreed.

Ed glanced at Marchant to get his consent, and he nodded. "Joanne is a beautiful dancer. You will look good together."

"We'll dance a rumba," Joanne said. "Maisie, love, put number three on."

"'Kay."

As they waited for Maisie to sort the music, Ed held out his arms.

Joanne raised her eyebrow. "You really think I'm going to dance the female part?"

"But Marchant just said—"

"He didn't want you dancing with a man. I'm all woman. You're safe."

He looked at Marchant, who just shrugged. "You do as she wishes."

In less than an hour, Ed found himself dancing with a third partner. It wasn't the same as dancing with Maisie or Marchant. Maisie had swiftly given up the lead when she realized how skilled he was, and as in all things, Ed had followed Marchant's lead. Joanne may have been the woman, but she was definitely in control of the partnership.

At the opposite end of the room, she led Ed through a complicated series of steps that tested his skill.

"Fallaway, promenade rock step, side position, rumba box, rock step."

After Ed tripped over his feet for the third time, Joanne stopped and grinned at him. "Thank Gawd for that. I was beginning to think you were better than me."

"I couldn't keep up with you."

"I wouldn't expect you to. You did great, Ed. Let's get you back to Belarus before he bursts a blood vessel."

As they walked together, Ed asked quietly, "How long have you known each other?"

"Belarus? We went to school together. It wasn't much of a shock when we discovered each other on the scene."

"You never thought about, um…."

She looked at him. "Me and him? Christ, no. He got my share of dick loving. Besides which, we're both so dominant, we'd kill each other."

"Me and Jo?" Marchant laughed. "She's my best friend, but Jo's right. Two Doms is a recipe for disaster."

"Unless you find a cute little twink who loves his daddies."

Jo and Marchant laughed at each other in some unshared memory.

Ed tried to smother a yawn. "Sorry, I'm shattered."

"I'm not surprised," Marchant said. "Let's go home and relax."

"See you next week, Ed," Joanne said. "Three o'clock, Monday afternoon. Bring dancing shoes with steel toecaps and your A-game. The women in this class can sense fear."

Ed stared at her in alarm. "I'm not sure this is such a good idea. I'm not ready to be eaten alive."

Marchant slung his arm around Ed's shoulders. "You'll be fine. Joanne will protect you. You will, won't you?" He frowned at Joanne, who shrugged.

"You'll learn."

Ed raised his eyebrow. "Or...."

She grinned wickedly at him. "Come here on Monday and find out. I dare ya."

Chapter 12

"HEY, I didn't expect to see you up still," Marchant said, throwing his keys onto the table. "It's gone three. You should be in bed." He yawned noisily and rubbed his eyes. "God, what a night."

Disturbed from his thoughts, Ed smiled at his lover. "I hadn't even noticed it was that late, love. Are you okay?"

As Marchant had been at the club all evening, Ed had spent the whole evening curled up on the sofa. Ostensibly he'd been reading, but in reality he'd been staring out the window lost in his thoughts.

Marchant sat down next to him and kissed Ed's cheek. "It was fine. Just long. You've been thinking? Sounds ominous. What have you been thinking about?"

Ed sighed and pushed his feet under Marchant's thighs. "I helped the old-age pensioners' session today." He sighed again.

"What happened?" Marchant looked fierce. "Did anyone try to hurt you, baby?"

"No, nothing like that. There was a couple there. They'd been together for sixty years." Ed stared at Marchant. "Can you imagine being together that long?"

"Does it scare you?" Marchant pushed back Ed's hair, longer now since he left the office.

"I'm jealous," Ed admitted. "And angry."

"Why are you angry?"

"Because they took it away from me," Ed said, his voice harsh and raw.

Marchant knew better than to ask who "they" were. "Your mother and grandmother?"

"Yes."

"What did they take away from you?"

"The chance to have a lifetime of loving." Ed knuckled at his eyes. "Instead I've spent most of it being bitter and twisted."

"How old are you, Ed?"

"Nearly forty."

"How old was your mother when she died?"

"Seventy-eight, and my grandmother was ninety-five."

"So assuming you go somewhere around eighty, how long will we have been together?"

"Forty years."

Marchant raised an eyebrow. "So? Is that long enough for you to become unbitter and less twisted?"

"I hate you."

"Course you do." Marchant patted his head. "And I love you too." He kissed Ed. The angle was wrong and sloppy, but Marchant was hard and forceful enough to leave Ed breathless and wanting.

Marchant traced the pad of his thumb over Ed's lips. "Want to take you to bed, Ed."

Ed pressed his lips together, and then he shook his head.

"You don't want to fuck?" Marchant sounded shocked, and Ed couldn't blame him. After a lifetime of suppressing his needs and desires, Ed was always willing for whatever Marchant wanted to do in the bed or out of it.

Ed shook his head again and slipped to the floor, kneeling in front of Marchant with his head bowed and his wrists clasped behind his back.

"Ed?"

"Sir?"

"Are you sure you know what you're asking?"

Ed couldn't blame Marchant for his uncertainty. Six months after their relationship began, Ed was still refusing to explore his submissive side beyond light play.

"I'm sure, sir."

"Boy, look at me."

Ed raised his head, and Marchant stroked his cheek.

"My love for you isn't conditional on your submission. I won't leave you just because you're not kneeling for me."

Trust Marchant to understand his concerns.

"You can't deny you think something is missing, though." Ed didn't mean to sound challenging. It was just an observation after months of living with a dominant man.

"I think we can have something more," Marchant said carefully.

Ed smiled at him despite the nerves roiling in his stomach. "So do I, and I'm ready, sir."

Marchant took so long to answer, Ed started to think he'd made a dreadful mistake. But then Marchant sat up, his face stern, and with a thrill, Ed realized that he was seeing the Dom, who rarely appeared in their home life.

"Take off your clothes, boy."

Ed knew this was a test. Getting undressed in front of Marchant wasn't an issue, but being ordered to strip—that was a different matter. Ed's inborn need to submit welcomed the order, but the hurt caused by years of abuse insisted he stayed where he was. Marchant knew all of this, of course, which is why he'd said it.

If Ed rebelled at this simple command….

With shaking fingers, Ed undid his shirt buttons one by one, knowing Marchant's hot gaze was on him. He pushed the shirt off his shoulders.

"Wait!" Marchant stared at him closer. "You weren't wearing that earlier. I recognize this shirt. It's the one you were wearing the first day we met."

Ed bowed his head. "Yes, sir."

"You put it on deliberately."

"Yes, sir."

"You wanted my attention."

"Yes, sir."

"To tell me something."

Ed breathed out slowly. "Yes, sir."

"Take it off, and give it to me."

"Yes, sir." Ed handed the shirt to Marchant, who folded it neatly in his lap.

"Now the rest of your clothes."

Ed stripped slowly until he was naked in front of Marchant.

"On your knees."

Marchant stood as Ed sank to his knees. The difference in their positions was never more obvious. Ed kept his head bowed, his eyes trained on Marchant's boots.

"Look at me," Marchant ordered.

Ed looked up at him, strong and tall, staring down at him with fierce, possessive eyes. Ed reacted to the sight, his cock filling and a flush spreading down his body. Marchant couldn't fail to notice how turned-on he was.

"You have my attention, boy," Marchant said, so softly Ed could barely hear him. "You always have my attention."

"I know, sir."

Marchant yawned suddenly, and Ed felt guilty for springing this on Marchant after a long night at the club, but he knew he'd have lost his nerve if he'd waited until morning to offer his submission.

"I'm tired, boy, and when we have our first session, I want to be fully in control. For now I expect you to start thinking about your limits, because we're going to be writing that contract." Ed felt Marchant's fingers in his hair, and he leaned into the touch. "You make me very proud, Ed."

"It's all thanks to you, sir." Without Marchant, Ed would have been slowly withering away from his own person. "You saw something in me I didn't even see myself."

"It was all there, waiting to be tapped. It just needed sunlight." Marchant tugged Ed's head back.

Ed gasped at the sudden pain, and his cock filled even more.

"Suck me off," Marchant ordered, "and then we're going to bed. You need a good night's sleep, boy. Tomorrow is going to be a long day."

"Yes, sir."

"And make sure there is ice in the freezer. We'll need lots of it."

Ed's hands shook as he did as his master told him. "*Yes*, sir."

ED SETTLED on the leather sofa and looked up at Marchant. Butterflies raced around his stomach as he waited to find out what his master had in store for the session. He'd been relieved to find that Marchant wanted to conduct their initial sessions outside of his club.

"I'm going to blindfold you," Marchant said as he tied the cloth over Ed's eyes. "I won't leave you alone at any time."

Ed didn't like being deprived of his sight, but he didn't give his safeword or make Marchant promise. Marchant had never broken his promise. He opened his eyes, but he couldn't see anything behind the blindfold.

"Shh, calm yourself." Marchant stroked Ed's cheek, his usual method of calming him.

"I'm trying, sir." Ed took a deep breath, and another.

"My boy." Never *good boy*.

"Always yours, sir." Ed received a pat on his shoulder.

"All I want you to do is listen to my voice and focus on what I'm doing to you. Stay completely still, but don't hold back your noise, and you can come when you need to."

"Are you going to hurt me, sir?"

"Not today, my boy."

A whisper of a kiss passed over Ed's mouth, which settled him more than anything. He took another deep breath and waited for Marchant's touch. Marchant didn't make him wait long.

"Cold!" Ed yelped as something ice cold traced the line of his jaw.

"Stay still," Marchant reminded him.

"Sorry, sir."

Ed relaxed, until Marchant used an ice cube on his left nipple, circling the nub until it was stiff and cold. "Fuck, fuck, fuck," he swore under his breath. He clenched his fists as he tried not to arch his back. Cold water dripped down his side as the ice cube melted, sending its own set of goose bumps.

"Not yet," Marchant said. "I'll fuck you—or not. My decision, not yours."

"Yes, sir!" Ed gasped. "God!"

The ice cube torture/pleasure resumed on his right nipple, making it as hard and wanting as its companion. Ed had never realized his nipples were so sensitive, but Marchant played them like they were musical instruments.

The cold was followed by warmth—Marchant's breath as he blew and then sucked each nipple into his mouth.

Marchant had known from their first meeting that ice and cold aroused Ed. Ed was hard, his cock weeping against his stomach, but although his hands were free to touch himself, just resting by his side, he left them there, not wanting to disappoint his master.

Ed gasped as an ice cube slid down onto his stomach, coming to rest near his navel. Then he moaned loudly as Marchant pushed the cube around with his tongue. He wanted to grab Marchant's hair and shove him toward his cock, and his fingers flexed restlessly as he forced himself to stay still.

His eyes flew open as melting ice trailed down the length of his shaft. "Can't... got to move... now!"

"Stay still, boy! I know you can do it."

Ed groaned as Marchant wrapped his cold hand around Ed's shaft and sucked the tip into his hot-and-cold mouth. The urge to shove up into Marchant's mouth was huge, but Ed stayed with his arse on the sofa, the leather sticky under his sweaty back. Marchant sucked until the cold had gone and only heat remained.

"Sir, sir, need more."

Ed yelled louder as Marchant took him at his word and sucked him to the root. Ed felt his orgasm racing down his spine and pushing through his cock. Each spasm was like a hot wave, and he shuddered for a long time through the aftershocks.

He was almost dozing as Marchant unwrapped his eyes. Ed blinked sleepily as he looked up at his master.

"You did well," Marchant said tenderly.

"Thank you, sir." Ed suddenly remembered Marchant hadn't come. "Oh God, I'm sorry."

Marchant frowned. "Who is in charge of the session?"

Ed's heart started pounding in fear. "You, sir."

"What are you apologizing for?"

"You're still hard."

"Not everything is about coming, Ed."

"But—"

Marchant placed a finger over Ed's mouth. "What makes you think the session has ended?" Ed's eyes opened wide and Marchant nodded. "Exactly. On your knees."

Trying not to grimace as he peeled himself off the sofa, Ed slipped to the floor, his wrists crossed and his head bowed.

Marchant grunted. "The first time we met, I imagined you like this."

"I wanted to run away," Ed admitted.

"I know." Marchant tangled his fingers hard in Ed's hair. "Thank you for staying."

Ed pressed a kiss against Marchant's foot. "Thank you for allowing me to dance."

"Oh baby, I showed you how to live. The dance was still inside you."

SUE BROWN

ANTHONY
& LEO

To my kids, still coping with me working all hours. You rock, guys.

Dear Reader,

By now, you Cock must be HORNY. I wish I were with you to Suck your Cock.

How big is your Cock?

7" 8" ——— 10"

I want you to Fuck me.
I have lots of CONDOMS

How does your CUM taste?

Sweet, bitter, Sour?

My cum tastes Salty.

Prologue

ENDLESS CARS ahead of him. Endless cars behind him. Tony Drake was stuck in the worst traffic jam on the M25 since the last one—yesterday or the day before. Two lorries had collided just before junction 12, and Tony was still halfway between junctions 10 and 11. The report on the radio said they were diverting vehicles as fast as they could, but there would be a long delay.

Once it became clear no one was going anywhere for the foreseeable future, Tony sat back, thanked his lucky stars he'd picked up a couple of bottles of water and a large packet of Doritos, and stuck on his headphones to listen to Tom Goss. Around him, people were getting out of their cars, but he had no intention of doing anything. He'd worked in the club where he was a barman until four that morning, and as it was only lunchtime, he was knackered. If it hadn't been for his mum begging him to come and look at her boiler, he'd have still been in his bed, fast asleep.

Tony opened his eyes as something thumped his car. A man ran up and claimed the large beach ball, mouthing an apology. Tony was tempted to scowl, but the man was hot, even if he was straight and on the short side. Tony liked his men—his Doms—tall, dark, and loving dick. This guy was five ten, if that, and very blond. And okay, he had a nice arse, Tony had to give him that. Tony watched the man run back to the wife and kids and resume their game. The kids were young enough that their kicks went wild, and the bloke spent most of his time retrieving the ball from under cars. Eventually the urge to sleep overcame the desire to watch the eye candy, and Tony fell asleep.

A rap on the window made him jump. He opened his eyes to see the blond guy grinning at him. Tony turned the key and opened the window.

"Hey, sorry to wake you, but the police just told us we'll be moving in a few minutes."

He had a nice voice, low and rumbly.

"Thanks." Tony rubbed his eyes. "I must have fallen asleep for a few minutes."

The man chuckled. "Nearer an hour. When I saw you were still sleeping, I thought I'd wake you up before you became very unpopular."

"God, really? An hour? Thanks." Tony looked at the time and winced. "I ought to call my mum. She'll be frantic."

"Do it now," the man suggested. "I can hear engines starting in the distance."

Tony watched him—well, his arse—walk away for the second time before he reached for his phone. He was listening to the dial tone when there was another rap at the window.

The man was back again, this time sporting a blush and holding a business card. Tony lowered the window.

"You don't know me," the man started, "and I don't even know if you're... but if you are... here's my number." He threw it at Tony and jogged away.

"Hello, hello?"

Tony suddenly became aware his mum was talking in his ear. "Mum?"

"Tony? Where've you been? I've been worried sick."

"I'm sorry. There's an accident—"

"An accident? What's happened? Are you all right?"

Tony cut across his mother's worried babble. "I'm fine. The motorway is closed, and we've been stuck here for nearly two hours."

"And you couldn't have called me sooner?"

"I fell asleep. I was working last night, remember?"

"You should have told me."

"I did. You made me feel guilty, so I agreed to come over."

"Anthony Drake, I did no such thing."

"Yes, you did." Tony grinned as he heard his father in the background.

"Hush up, Martin," his mother snapped. "You should have told me how tired you were."

"I did that too, Mum. I've got to go. We're finally moving. See you hopefully by three."

Not giving his mum a chance to reply, Tony threw his phone on the seat next to him and switched on the engine. It was only as he went to pull away he realized he was clutching the blond guy's business card. He looked at it briefly before he threw it next to his phone.

Leo Markus. It was nice to put a name to the butt. So he was gay. At least Tony was pretty sure that was what he was stammering about. No wife and kids, then. Or ex-wife? Tony shrugged. He'd been pretty, but he wasn't going to call.

Tony was looking for a Dom, not a boyfriend.

Chapter 1

MARCHANT BELARUS sat in his customary place at the end of the bar in his BDSM club, sipping at his ice-cold Coke. He frowned as Tony spilled another drink across the polished wood. "What's with you this evening? That's the fourth drink you've spilt in the last half hour."

Tony growled under his breath as he mopped up the mess and dropped the sopping cloth next to the others behind the bar.

"Stop growling and tell me the problem."

"You wouldn't understand."

"Try me." When Tony hesitated, Marchant said, "Let's put it another way. Tell me, or I'm going to start charging you for all the wasted drinks."

"I need a session with a Dom." Tony felt ready to crawl out of his skin. He needed something—or someone—to steady him.

"That's easy enough to arrange."

Tony shook his head. "I don't want another flogging."

"What do you want?" Marchant asked.

"I'm lonely," Tony finally admitted.

"You want a Dom of your own."

"I know I should be grateful I can get flogged or spanked anytime I want, but it's not enough." It hadn't been enough for a long, long time.

"I understand." Marchant's tone gentled as if he realized Tony's issues couldn't be cured by the simple lash of the leather.

"Do you?" Tony looked at him sadly. "You have Ed."

"I've only just met Ed, and I'm older than you," Marchant pointed out. "I waited a long time to find someone who suits me the way he does."

"You think I'm being impatient."

"I think you look around you and see all these young subs coming through the doors, and none of the Doms give you a second look because you're just Tony, the man who pours their drinks and deals with their problems."

"Are you trying to make me feel better?"

"Is it working?"

"No," Tony said shortly.

After he'd taken another sip of his drink, Marchant said, "What else? Are you hacked off with me?"

It was still early and no customer in earshot, so Tony decided to be honest. "Yep."

"Want to talk about it?"

Tony bit his lip. He liked working for Marchant, but the guy didn't take fools gladly and staff had been sacked for dissing his subs, and Ed wasn't just any sub, he was *the one* for Marchant, anyone could see that.

Evidently his feelings were written plain on his face because Marchant snorted. "Talk. I'm not going to take your head off."

Tony considered his words carefully. "You've not been around recently."

Marchant inclined his head. "I've been training Ed."

"Not in the club."

"He's not ready for it."

Tony knew Marchant was handling Ed with kid gloves and with good reason. It had been a long time since he'd seen anyone as vulnerable as his boss's new submissive. "The club has missed you."

Marchant sighed. "I hear you, Tony. You don't need to say it. I've been neglecting the business."

"You're a great Dom and the best master Ed could have."

"But a lousy boss."

"You've been… distracted since he agreed to be your sub." Tony didn't want Marchant to think he was jealous of Ed, because he genuinely liked the fragile man, and he and Marchant had never been interested in each other.

"But I've got a business, and it's not fair to expect you to run it."

"Members have been missing you," Tony said. "I'm only the barman and a house sub. They don't see me in the way they see you."

Marchant frowned. "Have the Doms been giving you trouble?"

"Not as such," Tony lied. "Although you can tell they think I'm just a sub and I've got no real authority."

"Perhaps we need to change that."

"I may be built like a brick shithouse, Markie—Marchant—but I don't think I can be a Dominant."

"Call me that again during work hours, and I'll put you over my knee." Marchant's tone was mild enough, but Tony knew he'd overstepped the line.

"Sorry, boss."

Marchant acknowledged his apology with a nod. "I'll talk to Ed."

"He's your priority," Tony said.

"I love Ed, and I want to train him, but my club is my life, and you are important to me too, Tony. I have invested too much time and trouble to lose you."

"You need an assistant manager."

Marchant hummed. "I've been thinking...."

"Careful."

"Heh. What about you?"

"What about me?"

"Do you want the job?"

"Assistant manager?"

"Call girl." Marchant rolled his eyes. "You said no one treated you with authority. How about you have the title to go with all the responsibility I've heaped on your shoulders?"

Tony was about to respond when a Dom with a shock of red hair approached the bar, closely followed by a young sub.

"Two waters, please, Tony. Hey, Marchant. I thought you'd been abducted by aliens."

Marchant sighed. "I haven't been gone that long." He glared as Tony opened his mouth. "Hush, you."

"Yes, boss." Tony gave him a mocking salute. He tipped ice into the glasses and poured the water.

Marchant studied the young man hiding behind Jordan. "I don't know you. I'm Marchant Belarus. Welcome to my club."

Tony looked at the sub as he shyly greeted Marchant. Slim, pretty, and typical of the subs Jordan and most of the Doms liked. He sighed inwardly.

"I'm going to make Tony the assistant manager of the club," Marchant said to Jordan.

"'Bout time. He's been doing the job for years. Mike, this is Tony. He knows everything and everyone here."

"I guess he has," Marchant agreed. "You don't think the Doms will give him any trouble?"

Jordan looked between Marchant and Tony. "No more than usual. It might make things easier for him than it has been lately."

Marchant sighed. "I really have taken my eyes off the ball, haven't I?"

"You've had your hands full," Jordan said, "but Tony's man enough to deal with the idiots."

Tony concentrated on stocking the water. Yeah, he was more than capable of dealing with a few overbearing Dominants, but no one ever thought he might like someone to deal with the idiots for him.

"Well, now we have an assistant manager, I'll pass the word around," Marchant said.

"I haven't said yes," Tony protested.

"But you're not going to say no, are you?"

Jordan snorted. "I think we'll leave you to discuss this. My boy and I have a date with a flogger."

Tony watched the sub fall into place behind Jordan as they walked away, and something inside him ached fiercely for that kind of commitment.

"How long has it been?" Marchant's question disturbed Tony's attention.

"Huh?"

"How long has it been since you submitted to anyone on more than a one-off basis?"

"Two years." Tony thought about it. "Probably nearer three."

"That's too long."

"What can I say? Doms aren't looking for subs who could make mincemeat out of them. I'm too old, too big, and too hairy. I should be a bear, except I'm not."

Nope. He was a little guy inside a big guy, waiting for someone to realize it.

"Not every Dom is looking for the same thing," Marchant said. "Why the hell would I have taken on Ed?"

"Because you like a challenge?"

Marchant's new sub was nearly forty and had spent his life being an obnoxious jerk to everyone. Tony was sure there was a whole other side to Ed, otherwise why would Marchant be bothering with him. The one thing Tony knew about his boss was that he didn't like arseholes, and he insisted on well-mannered subs in his club.

Marchant snorted. "You got that right. Listen, we'll talk tomorrow about the new job. In the meantime, if anyone gives you trouble, send them to me."

"Yes, sir." Tony saluted him again.

"Smartarse."

Tony grinned at him. It was good to have Marchant back, and hey, he'd got a promotion. "Do I get a pay rise along with the extra work?"

"Tomorrow. We'll talk about that tomorrow. Now we need to concentrate on your love life."

"I thought we'd just established I don't have a love life." Tony wanted to discuss extra pay, not the lack of a Dom in his life.

"You need to get off your arse, Tony. Master Right isn't going to walk through that door, declare undying love for you, and whip you into subspace. That's a dream for the newbies. You've got to get out into the real world and find that man."

"You don't find your Dom in the outside world," Tony scoffed.

Marchant raised an eyebrow. "We have to eat and drink like everyone else."

Tony remembered that Marchant had met Ed by tripping and throwing a large cup of Coke over him in a supermarket car park.

Marchant leaned forward and took the cloth out of Tony's hand. He'd been wiping the same patch of bar over and over again. "Tony, you're looking in the wrong place. Go and have some fun. Go to a gay bar. Hell, go to a straight bar. Just do something instead of moping in here."

"When do I get the chance to go out? I work every weekend."

"Where's that card?"

"What?"

"The man who gave you the card on the motorway."

Tony had told Marchant about the blond guy on the M25. "In my car." He'd not thrown it away even though he had no intention of phoning the man.

"Go and get it."

"What? Now?"

Marchant nodded.

"I'm working. The boss gets pissed if I slack off."

"I'll make your excuses. Now hurry the fuck up. It'll be busy soon."

Tony shook his head and made for the door, only doubling back when he realized he'd left his car keys under the bar. Marchant opened his mouth to shout at him, but Tony said, "Keys," and he shut it again.

Tony shivered in the winter air as he jogged to the car. It took him seconds to find the business card. He'd shoved it in the glove compartment when he'd reached his parents' house. As he walked back to the club, he turned the card over and over in his fingers.

"Tony?"

He looked up to see Jordan smiling at him. "Hey. Where's...." Tony struggled to remember Jordan's new sub's name. "Mike?"

"He's talking to a couple of friends. I came out for a smoke. What are you doing?"

"To be honest, I've no idea. The boss wanted me to get a business card from my car."

"Why?"

Tony hesitated a fraction too long, and Jordan arched an eyebrow, obviously expecting an answer. Tony was tempted to tell him to mind his own business, because Jordan was his mate, but in the club, he was an employee and Jordan was a client and expected Tony to treat him as such.

"Marchant thinks I need to get out into the world."

"Find yourself a Dom, you mean."

"Is it that obvious?" Tony asked bitterly.

"Only to those of us who watch you. We can all see you're not happy."

"I'm—"

"Lonely and looking for the right Dom."

"Yeah."

Jordan guided Tony through the double doors of the club. "I know it's not easy for you."

"How the hell do you know that?"

"I see you look at each Dom who comes through the door."

Tony pulled back in horror. "Are you all pitying me?"

"Don't be ridiculous."

"Then what?"

"Is everything all right?"

Oh great, now Marchant was involved, a frown between his brows.

Jordan didn't seem fazed. "Sorry, Marchant. I've stuck my nose in where it's not wanted."

"Oh?"

Tony gritted his teeth. "Apparently everyone thinks I'm a fucking loser, boss."

Marchant looked at the card in Tony's fingers. "Don't swear at me. Call him."

"I don't want to call him."

"Call who?" Jordan asked.

"No one," Tony said.

Marchant ignored Tony. "A bloke Tony met a few days ago. He gave Tony his card in case he was interested."

"I'm not interested."

Marchant and Jordan ignored him.

"A perfect distraction," Jordan agreed.

"But I'm not interested in him." It was true—kind of.

"You said he was pretty and had a great arse," Marchant pointed out.

"But he's not a Dom."

Jordan looked at him seriously. "Not everything is about BDSM, Tony. Sometimes a hookup is just about having fun."

"He's right," Marchant agreed.

Tony suppressed a growl. "You're both involved with your subs."

"Yeah, but I've had plenty of outside hookups. Variety makes for an interesting Tony." Marchant plucked the card out of Tony's fingers. "Go and have some fun with—" He looked at the card. "—Leo Markus."

"I'm not calling him."

"Give me your phone." Jordan held out his hand.

Tony cursed himself for handing it over meekly. Marchant gave Jordan the card, and before Tony knew what he was doing, he was listening to the ringtone and praying Leo wouldn't answer.

"Hello? Who's this?"

"H-hi," Tony stammered. "My name is Tony. You gave me your card." He was acutely conscious of Jordan and Marchant watching him, so he walked away from the peanut gallery.

"I don't remember… oh! The hot guy on the M25. I wondered who was calling me at this time of night."

Tony flushed. "I don't know about the hot guy, but yeah, the M25."

"I'd given up hope you were going to call me."

"I'm sorry."

"No worries. Now you have, what can I do for you?"

Tony looked at Jordan and Marchant in panic. Jordan rolled his eyes, but Marchant said, "Invite him out for a beer."

"Beer?" Tony managed.

"Cool. Are you free tomorrow night?"

"I'm working tomorrow—"

"No, you're not," Marchant said.

"I get the feeling you're not on your own," Leo said, but Tony was relieved to hear he sounded amused rather than pissed off.

"My boss," Tony said. "He says tomorrow is fine."

"I like your boss already. Where do you live?"

"Sutton. But I'll be in Wimbledon tomorrow."

"Even better. I've got a meeting near Wimbledon at five o'clock. See you at the Wetherspoon's at seven. Is that okay?"

"See you then." Tony put his phone away and scowled at Marchant and Jordan. "Happy now?"

"See," Jordan said. "That wasn't so hard, was it?"

Tony stalked past them and relieved the sub who'd taken his place behind the bar. He was all kinds of pissed off at this interference in his life, but even more annoyed that he'd let it happen.

Marchant slid into his usual seat at the bar. "I know you're pissed off with us."

Tony served a sub and took the ten-pound note. He handed over the change before he spoke again. "Why did you do that to me? It was humiliating."

Marchant sighed. "Working here can skew your thinking. It's easy to think your whole life has to be about kink."

"Yours is," Tony snapped.

Marchant shook his head. "My life is about Ed, not kink. I want to make him happy. I also have a club to run. You've worked for me for five years, and this is the first time I've seen you so unhappy. Look, go on the date, maybe get laid, and enjoy yourself."

"It's not what I want," Tony said miserably.

"I know, but unless you try something different, you might not find what you really need."

To Tony's relief, a couple of Doms wandered over to chat to Marchant, and the lecture was over. Tony dug the card out of his pocket and placed it on the bar. He didn't have to keep the date.

"If you even think of cancelling, I'll smack your arse so hard, you won't sit down for a week," Jordan said.

"That's not really a threat," Tony pointed out.

"I guess not." Jordan grinned at him. "Go on the fucking date. What have you got to lose?"

"My dignity. Oh wait, I already lost that."

"Tony, I hate to burst your bubble, but you're not some dewy-eyed virgin. I've seen you being lashed and fucked against the cross, and you weren't protesting about your dignity then. Go on the date, and we'll arrange a session. Mike's been desperate to see you in action ever since he met you."

Tony looked at him skeptically. "Mike? Your Mike?"

"Yep. The kid who looks like a puff of wind would blow him away. Turns out he's got a thing for big bears."

"What's he doing with you, then?"

Jordan shrugged. "He needed a sir, and I was there."

Tony frowned. "That doesn't sound like you."

"It doesn't have to be. We're both young and learning. Anyway, go on the date tomorrow."

"Do I have a choice?" Tony asked sourly.

"No." Jordan beamed at him and wandered away.

Tony grimaced and shoved the card back in his pocket. He'd go because Leo seemed like a good guy and Tony really needed a night out. Then he'd demand his flogging, and they could leave him the fuck alone.

Chapter 2

BY EIGHT o'clock Tony realized he'd been let down. He finished his beer and headed for the exit of the pub, only to collide with someone in the doorway. Automatically he grabbed their arms to steady them.

"Sorry. Oh, Tony, thank God. I thought I'd miss you." Leo grinned at him. "The meeting overran, and my phone died. I really need a new battery."

He looked tired, and he had gingerish stubble he hadn't had the first time they met.

Tony waited for Leo to stop babbling before he spoke. "I was about to give up."

"I'm glad I caught you. Let's get a beer."

Leo headed for the bar, looking expectantly at Tony. "Heineken?"

"Thanks."

Leo paid for the two beers, and Tony followed him to a corner booth. He could have found the table, but he enjoyed watching Leo's arse as he walked.

"So what do you do?" Tony asked when they sat down.

Leo slurped a mouthful of beer before he answered. "I'm in sales."

"Oh? What do you sell?"

"Toys."

Tony raised an eyebrow. "Toys? What kind of toys? Dolls and stuff?"

"Yeah, kind of. What about you?"

"I'm a barman."

"Which pub?"

"Not exactly a pub. It's more of a club."

"A dance club? I love dancing."

"It's a private club."

"Oh?" Leo narrowed his eyes as he looked at Tony. "You're prevaricating."

"So were you."

"True. So do we 'fess all or keep our secrets?"

Tony shrugged. This was one date. It didn't matter if Leo was shocked. "I work in a BDSM club."

"No! Really?" Leo sounded like a small boy in a sweetshop.

"Really. So what do you really sell?"

"Sex toys."

Tony slammed down his glass, the beer slopping over the side. "You're joking."

Leo's eyes twinkled in obvious amusement. "Nope. I sell dildos, vibrators, cock rings, butt plugs…."

"Male toys?"

"Both. I sell a great masturbator." He chuckled as Tony made a face. "You don't like the thought?"

"I don't like any thought of women's parts." Tony liked women in theory. He just didn't want much to do with the practical.

"Not played with the fairer sex?"

Tony shook his head. "I knew I was gay early on. There was no way I was going near a woman."

"I like a man who knows his own mind. I groped a few girls, but it didn't do too much for me. I only realized I preferred guys when I got a dick in my mouth."

"And what did you do with the dick?"

"Gave it a really bad blowjob." Leo chuckled, his blond curls shaking. "I used way too much teeth."

"Ouch!" Tony winced at the thought.

"Yeah, the man on the other end of the dick wasn't impressed."

"What happened?"

"He didn't have a happy ending."

"Have you improved?"

"Since the first time? I bloody hope so."

"Do you still use teeth?" Tony loved a touch of teeth. *A touch!*

"Only if they ask me nicely."

Tony tried to hide his shudder, but from Leo's smirk, he wasn't entirely successful. "And do you like receiving blowjobs?"

"I'm a bloke." Leo's tone made it obvious he thought that was a really stupid question.

"What else do you like?"

Leo tilted his head. "Are we talking about sex or kink?"

"Both."

"Is it important?"

Tony looked down at the table. "Yes, it is."

"Tell me why."

"I'm a sub… submissive." Tony's gut cramped with nerves, but he was going to be honest.

"I know the terminology." Leo leaned back in his seat. "So you're a sub and you're what? Looking for a Dom?"

Tony fixed his gaze on a beer ring on the table. "Yeah."

"Is that why you didn't ring me?"

"I'm not comfortable with people outside of the scene." Tony chanced a look at Leo. He didn't look pissed off, just curious, and Tony relaxed.

"So why did you call me?"

"I didn't," Tony admitted, feeling his cheeks heat up.

"So who did?"

"A Dom at the club. He's a mate. He thought he was doing me a favor."

"But not *your* Dom?"

"No, he likes twinks."

"And you're not a twink."

"Hardly."

"Thank God."

That caught Tony's attention. He looked at Leo fully. "You're not into twinks?"

Leo shook his head. "Not my type."

Tony had seen that look before. "I suppose you're into bears."

"I'm… let's just say I'm into you."

Tony tried to suck in a breath. "Even though I'm a sub."

Leo leaned forward so far, Tony felt the oxygen leave the room. "*Especially* because you're a sub."

"Are you a Dom?" Tony asked hopefully.

"I'm a top."

Tony tried to suppress a twinge of disappointment. Top was okay. At least he wasn't going to expect Tony to take the dominant role. "That's a relief."

Leo smiled at him, and for the first time, Tony noticed he had dimples under the fuzz.

"You really do look tired," Tony said, more naturally than he had since Leo had burst through the doorway.

"My boss has been working me hard."

"I never thought of sex toys as being a high-pressure industry."

"It's my dad's fault."

Tony raised an eyebrow. "Your dad?"

"He's my boss."

"A family business?" Tony burst out laughing.

Leo smiled. "You have a great laugh."

Tony grinned back. "How old are you?"

"Twenty-four. You?"

"Thirty in a couple of months." Tony was trying hard not to think about his impending birthday.

"We'll have to celebrate."

"I'm trying hard to ignore it."

"Bollocks, you've got to celebrate."

"Leo, my idea of a good night is being lashed to a cross with a plug up my arse and being whipped and fucked until I come."

Leo's eyes widened. "Wow."

"Thanks for the beer." Tony got to his feet.

Leo frowned. "Where are you going?"

"I think I ought to go."

"Why?"

Tony looked down at him. "I'm sorry, but I can't pretend I'm like every other guy you've gone out with."

"No," Leo agreed, "you're certainly not like them."

"It's best I leave before I make a bigger twat of myself."

"Tony, sit down."

Tony hesitated.

"Sit. Down."

Leo's tone was firm, and Tony obeyed because it was such a relief to do as he was told.

"I'm going to get a couple more beers, and you can tell me more about the club."

Tony sat in a whirlwind of confusion while Leo went to the bar. The sound of his mobile phone penetrated his confusion.

"Hello?"

"Do I have to come and rescue you?"

"Jordan?"

"Yeah. Are you okay? Do you need me to intervene?"

"Uh… no. Where are you?" Tony looked around, expecting to see Jordan's bright red hair, but he wasn't in sight.

"In the pub down the road. I can be with you in two minutes."

"I'm fine."

"You don't sound very convincing, mate. I'm coming over."

Tony could hear him talking to someone, but he didn't recognize Mike's voice. "No! Honestly, I'm fine. I just told him about me, and he took it so well. It's just thrown me."

"Are you sure?" Jordan sounded worried.

"I'm sure. Gotta go, he's coming back."

"Okay, but remember, if you need me—"

Tony cut the connection before Jordan finished the sentence. He knew he'd pay for that sooner rather than later, but better that than be caught having this extremely embarrassing conversation.

Leo grinned at him as he sat down. "Someone checking to see if they need to make an intervention?"

Tony flushed. "Jordan. He worries too much. If it hadn't been him, it would have been my boss. In fact, he probably will ring."

"You've got good friends."

"Yeah." Tony smiled. "I have. Even if they're interfering bastards most of the time."

"My mate Charlie will probably call," Leo admitted.

"Is he doing the same thing?"

"She. She was the one you saw me with on the motorway. I was out for the day with her and her nephews. The fact my phone is out of charge is going to drive her nuts."

"I thought you were a lovely family."

Leo smirked. "I wanted to ditch them and do wicked things with you in your car."

Tony's dick twitched at the thought. "You did?" To cover the fact, he grabbed his glass and took a long slug.

"I did."

"What sort of things?"

"I could show you if you want. I've always been more of a show, rather than tell, guy."

"You want to have your wicked way with me?"

"Fuck, yeah." Leo arched an eyebrow. "Are you on board with the idea?"

Tony considered it. He could give the guy a kiss good night and go home to porn and his right hand, or he could get laid for the first time in far too long. "I could be persuaded." Then he looked over to the door. "Oh fuck."

"What's the matter?" Leo looked confused.

"Jordan is coming over."

The Dom was striding over as if he owned the bloody place, closely followed by a young blond guy Tony recognized.

Leo looked around. "Frankie? What are you doing here?"

"Jesus Christ." Tony wanted to smack his head against the table.

"You know him as well?" Leo asked.

Jordan reached the table and smiled at them. "Tony, what a—"

"I told him all about you," Tony said, cutting off the lie.

Leo looked at Frankie. "Where's your guard dog?"

Frankie bent down and kissed Leo on the mouth, the act making Tony twitchy for some reason. "Al's having a night out with the boys. Jordan and I are catching up, except he got all worried about Tony, so here we are. Hey, Tony."

Leo turned to Tony. "Do you know Frankie? Charlie works with Frankie."

Tony sighed. "My boss's sub used to be Frankie's boss. Hey, Frankie." He lifted his face up for a kiss.

"Really? Damn, it's a small world." Leo whistled through his teeth. "Wait! Do you mean the prick with a stick up his arse? That boss? Charlie hated him."

"Yes, that prick, and never, ever let my boss hear you say that," Tony said. "If you think Al is a guard dog, you need to meet Marchant."

"We'll go away now," Jordan said. "I just had to check for myself you were okay."

"I told you I was fine," Tony managed through gritted teeth.

Frankie sniggered. "You should have seen Jordan. He would have been here an hour ago if I'd let him."

And he would have seen Tony sitting here alone like a fucking sad sack. Tony thanked God Leo had eventually turned up.

"I'm fine, so you can go now," Tony suggested helpfully to Jordan.

Frankie wound an arm around Jordan's neck. "Come on, big boy. Tony wants alone time with his cutie, and you can see he's fine."

Leo made the decision for him. He stood and looked hopefully at Tony. "Shall we stick to our original plans?"

If it got him away from Jordan, Tony thought that was a brilliant idea. He pushed back his chair and stood up. "Jordan, I'm fine. I'll call you later, okay?"

"Tomorrow," Leo said. "You can call him tomorrow."

When Jordan looked as if he was about to protest, Frankie dragged him out of the pub. Tony expelled a deep breath, and Leo snorted.

"Are you sure he's not interested in collaring you?"

Tony shrugged. "I don't care if he is. Still interested in having your wicked way with me?"

"Sounds good.... Your phone is ringing."

"Shit, shit." Tony looked at the screen. "It's my boss."

Leo leaned forward and plucked the phone out of Tony's hand. "He's fine," he said and switched it off. He handed the phone back to Tony. "Ready to go?"

Tony nodded mutely.

"Your place or mine?" Leo asked as he steered Tony through the pub, one hand resting on Tony's back.

"I don't mind. I start work at three tomorrow, so I'll need to be back by two." Tony suddenly realized that sounded as if he was inviting himself for the night. "I mean—"

"I know what you mean."

Leo smirked at Tony, who groaned. "I'm not very good at this," he admitted.

"What?"

"Dating. I'm really crap at dating."

Leo stood back to let Tony go through the door. "Oh. It's probably hard to do the dating thing when you're being spanked." Two women walking in at the same time shot Leo a startled look, but he ignored them and continued. "Good thing you're going to get some practice, then."

"You want another date with me?"

Leo nodded. "If we can do it without your bodyguards running interference."

"I'll warn them off."

"Tell them I'll bite if they interfere."

Tony choked. "Are you sure you're not a Dom?"

"Dominant with a small d, perhaps. My car's over here."

Leo led the way to his car, a bright red Mini. He grinned at Tony. "I live about half a mile away. Do you think you can squeeze in for a short drive?"

Tony gave the inside of the car a dubious look. "Doubtful, mate, but I'll have a go." He squeezed into the front seat and shoved it back as far as it could go, which wasn't very far.

"Hmmm." Leo looked at him. "I'm going to have to change my car if we stay together."

Tony's stomach flipped over, but he said, "The car suits you." He was dazzled by the intensity of Leo's beaming smile.

"You're a doll." Leo leaned over and gave him a kiss on the cheek.

Tony didn't know whether to growl at being called a doll or touch where Leo had kissed him.

"I love the car," Leo admitted as he pulled out into the traffic. "She's the first car I bought myself."

"I've only had the one car. It's a Land Rover. It's twenty years old, but I love it."

"Suits you," Leo said, and it didn't sound like a criticism.

Tony looked out of the window, feeling very vulnerable sitting so low down compared to his car. "Where do you live?"

"Poplar Road. I still live with my parents." At Tony's startled look, he said, "I have my own flat. I'm not expecting you to have a night of wild sex with my parents in the house."

"Thank Christ for that." Tony was relieved. "You're not far from the club."

Leo snapped his fingers, startling Tony. "It's the old pub in Larchmead Close, isn't it? I remember my dad talking about it when it first opened."

"It upset a lot of the locals." Tony remembered the petitions that went around to prevent the club opening.

"My dad didn't give a shit about that. He wanted to see if he could get some business."

"And did he?"

"I don't know. So do you live close by?"

"I live in Sutton. It's a bit of a trek, but I'm usually traveling outside of rush hour."

Leo snapped his fingers. "You said that before. So is your car nearby?"

"I left it behind the club."

Poplar Road was about halfway along the Crescent, the long arcing road from which all roads named after trees started. As they turned in, Tony took a look at the large houses and wondered what a huge mistake he'd made. He'd been brought up by his mum on a council estate and left school at sixteen with two GCSEs. Tony had worked as a barman since he was eighteen.

"I can see what you're thinking," Leo said, "and I know it looks like I'm a middle-class spoiled brat working for Daddy and still living at home, but I'm not like that."

"What I was thinking was that I'm a working-class kid with no qualifications and I'm not good enough for you."

Leo slowed down and turned into a driveway, waiting for the gates to open. "Well, that's bollocks for a start."

"Seriously—"

"Tony, shut up. *I* decide who's good enough for me. I'm not a bloody snob. I don't care if you're a chief exec or a dustman." Tony subsided as Leo drove behind the big house to a garage. He cut the engine and looked at Tony. "I live above the garage."

Tony wriggled out of the car and stretched his cramped muscles.

Leo raised an eyebrow. "In pain?"

"Next time we take my car."

"Deal."

Leo took his hand and led him up the stairs to his living space.

Chapter 3

TONY LOOKED around the living room. It was hard to really tell what the room was like under all the clutter, but it looked homely rather than full of designer furniture.

Leo caught his gaze. "Yeah, I'm not the tidiest person in the world." He didn't seem that bothered.

"Your car is tidy."

"I've only just got that. Haven't had time to make it a tip yet." Leo dismissed the state of his car as unimportant and turned to Tony, his gaze intense.

Tony licked his lips nervously.

"You're a real contradiction," Leo said, reaching up to run his hands through Tony's thick hair.

"A big girl," Tony said bitterly. He'd heard that one before.

"Big, sexy, soft, adorable." Leo brushed his hand over the mound in Tony's jeans. "All man."

Tony hissed and pushed into Leo's hand, his cock stiffening at the touch.

Leo squeezed it again. "Let's go to bed." He took Tony by the hand and walked him into the bedroom. "I'm going to fuck you."

"I'm very happy with that idea."

"Thought you might be. You stay there."

Tony stood patiently as Leo stripped off his own clothes, appreciating the lithe body that came into view. His shoulders were broader than Tony expected, and he was covered in strawberry blond hair over his chest, narrowing down to a vee and a small patch around his cock.

"Now you," Leo breathed, slowly opening the buttons on Tony's shirt. "God, you're so—"

"Hairy? Yeti?" Yeah, Tony had heard that one before too. He got his back, sac, and crack waxed, and that was it.

"Yes." But Leo didn't sound repulsed and his hands were all over Tony's chest. "Fuck, you feel wonderful."

Tony shivered as Leo thumbed over his nipples, his cock fully hard now and desperate to be free of the restricting denim. "Fuck! Ditto."

Tony ran his hands over Leo's chest, expecting Leo to tell him to stop at any moment, but the order didn't come. He swallowed. Leo's knuckles had grazed his belly as he slipped his hand inside Tony's jeans.

"I'm going to cream myself if I don't get naked soon," Tony warned. He was a submissive with plenty of experience, but somehow one touch of Leo's hands, and he was ready to blow.

Leo snorted in amusement. He undid Tony's jeans and slid them over his hips and down his legs, together with his jock. "God."

Tony held back the obvious comment as he rested one hand on Leo's shoulders and stepped out of the clothing.

"You are built like a god." Leo's hands were busy again, exploring Tony's arse, hips, and legs. Everywhere except where Tony actually wanted him to touch. "Get on the bed."

Stretched out on Leo's bed, Tony waited, but Leo didn't seem to be in a rush. He took his time staring at Tony in open admiration. Tony flushed, but he lay passively beneath Leo's intense gaze.

Eventually, just as Tony began to think Leo was never going to actually *touch* him, Leo climbed on the bed and straddled his hips. He leaned forward, and their cocks slid together as if they were joined seamlessly. Leo obviously hadn't finished exploring Tony, because he caressed his neck, running his fingers over the stubble Tony perpetually sported unless he'd just shaved. He pushed Tony's arms over his head, so he could touch his armpits and slide his hands down his torso.

"You're lucky I'm not ticklish," Tony pointed out, when the touch threatened to get—maybe—a little sensitive.

Leo grinned mischievously. "You're not ticklish anywhere?"

"No one has found a ticklish spot." Tony knew that was a mistake the minute he saw the challenge in Leo's eyes.

"I see." Leo swept through the fur on Tony's chest, flicking at his nipples. He looked pleased as Tony arched up underneath him. He flicked them again, and Tony moaned.

Tony's dick leaked onto his belly, the drips getting caught in the fur. Leo licked them off and swirled his tongue into Tony's navel. Tony closed his eyes, relishing the sensations provoked by Leo's skillful tongue. Leo kissed ever downward until he reached the base of Tony's dick, then he paid the same careful attention to Tony's balls, taking each one into his mouth, rolling it around with his tongue.

"Leo, please," Tony begged, sliding his hands through Leo's thick hair. He wanted to tug Leo's head, force him to put his clever mouth where he really wanted it, but he wasn't confident enough to do that.

Leo raised his head, his mouth and chin glistening. "Hmm? What do you want, Tony?"

"Suck me, fuck me, do fucking something!"

"I *am* doing something."

"I need you in me."

"Roll over and get on your hands and knees," Leo said as he got off the bed.

Tony rolled over and got to his knees. Before he'd had a chance to settle, Leo was pressed up against him, his hard shaft slipping between Tony's arsecheeks. Tony rested his head on his fists, gasping as Leo penetrated him with slick fingers. It had been a long while since he'd been fucked.

"God, you're tight," Leo said.

"Yeah?" Tony was on the receiving end of the fingers. He could work that out for himself.

"Yeah." Leo breathed out. "You feel so good."

Tony closed his eyes and concentrated on the feeling in his arse. It didn't take long before he needed more than just fingers. He threw his arm back and grasped Leo's thigh, digging in his nails in desperation. "I need you."

The fingers disappeared. Tony mourned the empty feeling until he heard the snap and crackle of a condom wrapper and a blunt head pushed in, filling that loss and replacing it with something much better. Leo's hands settled on his hips, and Tony pushed back until Leo rested against his arse again. Tony took a deep breath, reveling in the feel of Leo in him and around him.

"You're tight." Leo sounded strained, as if he was holding on to his control by a mere thread.

"Been a while," Tony said simply.

Leo thrust a couple of times, too slowly for Tony's liking. He pushed his arse against Leo, silently begging for more. Leo stroked his hand down Tony's back and did as he asked, setting up a pounding rhythm that took Tony's breath away. The room filled with grunts and the slap of flesh against flesh. Tony wanted to jack his cock, but Leo didn't give him a chance, and he had to just hold on as Leo pounded into his arse. There was no noise except their bodies meeting in passion. Tony felt Leo's rhythm faltering as he poised on the brink of orgasm, then his own climax swept over him and he came over the sheets, taking Leo with him.

Tony's arms gave way and he faceplanted onto the sheet, grimacing as he landed on the wet patch. Leo grunted, and he went with Tony, collapsing on his back.

"Jesus." Leo's breath ghosted across Tony's sensitized skin. "What have you done to me?"

Sated and shattered, Tony lay among the wreckage of the bedcovers, smothered in come, with Leo prostrated across his back. "I don't think it was me," he managed.

Leo pressed a kiss into the sweaty nape of Tony's neck. "Believe me, it was all you, sweetheart. That, whatever it was, was all you."

Unable to move, Tony stayed where he was, a stupid grin on his face. He would have to ask Leo to get off him eventually, but right now, Tony was happy for the man to remain just where he was.

After several minutes Leo rolled off Tony with a loud groan. "You have a shower, and I'll change the sheets."

"I can help," Tony protested, even though he was covered in come and sweat and really needed a shower.

Ignoring him, Leo shoved Tony into the bathroom and got the shower started. "I like it hot, so turn it down if you need to. Here's a towel."

Tony took the towel and looked at Leo. "Are you sure you don't want me to do the bed?"

Leo patted Tony's arse. "Not this time, mate." He kissed Tony on the cheek and bounced out of the bathroom.

Tony shook his head. Jesus, where did the man get his energy from? He stepped into the shower and yelped, fumbling for the knob to turn down the heat before it peeled the skin from his body.

"I did warn you," Leo yelled.

Once the water had cooled from volcano to pleasantly warm, Tony relaxed, enjoying the pounding spray against his skin. It took Tony a minute to realize most of the bottles of shower gel were empty. He shook them until he found one half-full. Tony sniffed it cautiously. He had deep-seated issues about flowery shower gel after living with his mother. This one smelled of watermelon. He could live with that.

Leo was fighting with the duvet cover as Tony wandered into the bedroom after his shower. Leo was engulfed by dark blue fabric; the only parts of him visible were his calves and feet. After a couple of minutes listening to Leo curse the bedding, its mother, and the horse it rode in on, Tony decided the duvet cover was winning.

"Would you like a hand?" he asked. He didn't bother to hide his amusement. Leo couldn't see his face.

"I've nearly got the sucker under control," Leo panted from within the cover.

"Really? Cos from where I'm standing, it looks like it's got the upper hand."

"A-ha!" Leo emerged from the duvet, his face bright red and his hair sticking up like a mad shaggy dog. "Got the bastard."

"I'll take your word for it."

"I have! See?" Leo held out the corners of the duvet to show that it was tucked inside.

"Well done," Tony said solemnly.

Despite Leo's assurance that he could make the bed, Tony helped him finish it off. Then Leo had a shower, and Tony sat on the bed, not sure whether to climb into it or get dressed. It was still early, and he wasn't sure what Leo expected him to do.

When Leo returned, he looked surprised. "I expected to find you passed out in the bed."

"I wasn't sure if you expected me to stay or not."

"Get into bed. I sleep on the left." Tony obediently rolled onto the right-hand side. Leo beamed at him. "Do you want a cup of tea? It's still early. We could watch TV for a while."

It all seemed very domestic to Tony. He wasn't used to postcoital company, but he murmured his agreement because that seemed to be what was expected. A few minutes later, Leo returned with two mugs of tea. Tony had spent the time staring at the ceiling, wondering what the hell he was doing.

"Do you want any sugar?" Leo asked as he put the tea on the bedside table.

"No, thanks."

Leo got into bed, plumped up his pillows, and sighed happily. Then he handed one tea to Tony and grabbed his mug and the remote. "What do you want to watch?" He flicked through the channels.

"Pick what you like," Tony said. He slurped his tea. "I don't watch much TV. I work most evenings."

"What do you do on your time off?" Leo settled on some documentary with David Attenborough and turned to look at Tony.

"I'm at the club. I spend most of my time there."

"I can see why whatshisname thought you might need a break."

"Jordan," Tony said. "His name is Jordan."

"What do you do for fun?" Leo huffed out a laugh when Tony took a long time to respond. "The fact that you really have to think of the answer is kinda sad, Tony."

"I used to go paintballing at the weekends until my mates got hooked up. Then they weren't interested anymore."

"I love paintballing. What about bowling?"

"Bowling's okay."

"We'll go—" Leo frowned. "When are you next off?"

"I'll talk to Marchant. See if I can get next weekend off if you're free."

"I am. I spend most of my weekends sleeping."

Tony finished his tea and leaned back against the pillows. They were softer than he expected, and he wriggled before he found a comfortable position. "Why aren't you with a guy?"

"I don't think I've found anyone I've been interested in for a long time." Leo gave a half smile. "Also I work crazy, silly hours. Dad is a slave driver."

Tony took the mug out of Leo's hands and pulled him down so he was half resting on Tony. "You're an oddball, Leo Markus."

Leo cupped Tony's face. "You've only just realized?" He scraped his stubble down Tony's cheek.

"I can do that to you," Tony pointed out.

"Shut up and enjoy it," Leo said, using his chin again for greater effect.

Tony shut up, because he did enjoy it. Especially right—*ahh!*

TONY WOKE with the realization he was comfortable and in no rush to move. Warmth pressed into his back, and something hard prodded against his arse. It didn't take him long to work out he was in a strange bed and the warmth wrapped around him was Leo. He lay for a few minutes, enjoying the feeling of being the little spoon. It had taken a minute last night to realize that Leo was the one who wanted to do the hugging. Tony had rolled over and let Leo snuggle around him, and he woke up in the same position.

"Morning." Leo pressed a kiss between Tony's shoulder blades, his voice low and growly.

Tony shivered at the scrape of Leo's stubble, fast turning his body into one big erogenous zone. "Morning." He had to cough a couple of times to get the word out. "What time is it?"

Leo raised his head. "Eight thirty. You don't have to get up yet, do you?"

"Nah." Tony sighed and relaxed back into Leo's arms.

"Good. Let's go back to sleep." Leo sounded as if he was half-asleep already.

Tony contemplated getting up, but he was content to stay where he was, and he closed his eyes.

THE NEXT time Tony woke up, he was aware of two sensations. One, his bladder was screaming for relief, and two, he was being kissed sweetly and tenderly. He opened his eyes, blinking a couple of times to focus on the giver of the kisses.

"Hello, sleepyhead."

"Hey." Tony smacked his mouth a couple of times. "You're better than a sleeping pill."

"Do you have problems sleeping?"

"I don't sleep well," Tony admitted. "I keep odd hours compared to most people." His first problem made itself known, and he fidgeted. "I'm sorry, I need a pee."

Laughing, Leo pulled back and let Tony escape to the bathroom.

It took a minute or two for Tony to relax enough, and then he sighed in relief as the yellow stream arced into the pan.

"Feeling better?" Leo asked when Tony returned to the bed.

"Much."

Leo welcomed Tony back into his arms. "Hmm, you took the time to clean your teeth."

"Finger and toothpaste," Tony admitted.

"You don't like morning breath?"

"It doesn't bother me." Tony proved it by kissing Leo deeply. When he pulled back, Leo was flushed and panting, and both of them were half-hard and grinding against each other.

"It's nearly twelve," Leo said. Tony yelped and tried to sit up, but Leo wasn't having any of it. "I'll drive you home to get changed, then I'll drive you to work."

"That doesn't make sense," Tony pointed out. "The club is within walking distance. I can pick up my car and drive home to get fresh clothes."

"But I want to see where you live," Leo admitted.

"And where I work?" Tony laughed at the flush that stained Leo's cheeks. "Fine, but we have to get moving soon if I'm going to get home in time."

Leo pushed Tony down into the bed. "We have an hour to fuck, shower, and eat before we have to go."

"We can do that." Tony wrapped his arms and legs around Leo and groaned as Leo's cock slid behind his balls.

"Of course we can." Leo reached over him to grab the lube and condoms.

"How do you want me?" Tony whispered.

"Like this, babe." Leo plopped a kiss on the end of Tony's nose. "Just like this."

Tony watched as Leo rolled a condom down his dick and slicked himself. Leo prepared him without finesse, then he was pushing into Tony, his eyes fixed on him, so loving and intimate it took Tony's breath away. This was new, just a hookup, too much too soon. Then Leo thrust hard, and Tony forgot about his worries and concentrated on the one thing that made sense—Leo's body giving him pleasure. Tony pushed up, needing more, and Leo grunted hard and pinned Tony to the bed, fucking him as hard as he could. They came together, panting out their pleasure into each other's mouths.

Leo slumped on Tony until Tony had to push him off before passing out through lack of oxygen. Leo thumped onto the bed beside Tony and sighed. "You're just...."

"Yeah," Tony agreed. He tilted his head to grin at Leo.

"I'm keeping you," Leo declared. "Just so you know."

Tony waited for the panic to set in. The panic was there, coiling its way around the edges of his postcoital euphoria, but it didn't make any incursion into his pleasure.

Leo rose up on one elbow and looked down at Tony. "Is that okay?"

"Ask me again later," Tony suggested. "It's unfair to expect a decision when you've nailed me to the mattress."

"Fair enough," Leo said. "Just thought I ought to warn you."

Tony stared up into Leo's huge eyes, noticing for the first time the flecks of gray and blue. "Don't say it if you don't mean it," he begged. "I know I look tough, but I'm not as strong as I seem."

"I get that." Leo pushed Tony's dark hair away from his face. "The thing is, I always say what I mean. To a fault. My dad is always having a go at me for lack of diplomacy. So if I say I'm keeping you, I am."

He kissed Tony hard on the mouth and bounced out of bed before Tony could respond. "You have a shower while I make the tea and toast."

"Did your dad say you were a bossy bastard too?" Tony grumbled.

Leo chuckled over the sound of him filling the kettle. "That might have come up once or twice."

Chapter 4

AS LEO drove Tony home, Tony tried—and failed—not to worry about the comparison between the area he lived in and Leo's. The contrast was stark, and despite Leo saying he didn't care, the fact was—Tony sighed—the fact was he was embarrassed. Leo lived in a tree-lined road with huge houses and gates. Tony's flat was on a main road near a row of shops, which he'd picked because it was all he could afford. He considered himself lucky to be able to buy a place at all. His income from the club wasn't large, but he'd received an inheritance from his grandmother.

"Turn down the road just before the shops," he said as they approached his house. "I park in an alleyway that runs behind the shops."

Leo did as he asked, negotiating the bags of rubbish dumped near the start of the alleyway. Tony pointed out where he could park. He was lucky to have a space behind the flat, which was really a house converted into two flats. The nice elderly couple downstairs who actually owned the house didn't have a car, so they let him park there. They were grateful for the odd jobs he did for them, and they closed their eyes to the occasional man he brought home.

"You can stay here if you want," Tony said. "I've only got to change my clothes."

"And miss the chance to be nosy?" Leo smirked at him. "Don't be an idiot."

Cursing inwardly for not sticking to his guns and getting Leo to drop him at work, Tony led the way up the stairs and into his flat.

Leo looked around with bright, curious eyes. "It's nice."

Tony followed his gaze, viewing his flat with critical eyes. It was about the same size as Leo's place but much, much tidier. He'd made an effort to decorate his home and kept it as tidy as he could.

"You've got a lot of DVDs." Leo wandered over to look at the shelves of DVDs lining one wall.

"I'm either working, sleeping, or watching films."

Leo looked at a couple of DVD boxes on the coffee table. "Ginger Rogers and Fred Astaire? Really?"

Tony shrugged. "My boss's sub is a huge fan of old movies."

"These people are a large part of your life, aren't they?" Leo asked.

"I spend most of my life at the club. All my friends are there." He caught sight of the time. "Sorry, but I've got to get moving."

Without asking if it was all right, Leo followed Tony into his bedroom and sat on his bed while Tony found the tight black T-shirt and black trousers that was his uniform.

"You don't believe in personal space, do you?"

Leo didn't seem the least bit bothered. "I had my dick up your arse. I think we bypassed personal space a long time ago. Come here." He held out his hand.

A little confused, Tony walked over. He gasped as Leo slid chilled hands under his T-shirt to find the warm skin underneath. Then Leo lifted the T-shirt over Tony's head. Before it had even dropped on the floor, Leo was stroking the fur on Tony's chest.

"I have to get to work."

"I know," Leo said. "I was just reminding you how I felt about you." He briskly stripped Tony of his jeans, but he seemingly couldn't resist a grope of the bulge in Tony's briefs.

"Need… clean… underwear," Tony gasped out.

He bolted for his chest of drawers, Leo's smug chuckle following him. He grasped a fresh pair of briefs and wondered if he could make an excuse to go to the bathroom.

Leo took the matter out of his hands by coming up behind him and pressing against his back before removing Tony's briefs. "Clean pair."

Tony handed them over.

Leo drew the clean pair up his legs, covered his arse, and kissed each cheek through the soft white fabric. "Okay, you can dress the rest of you." He stepped back to give Tony some space.

Tony meekly put on his clothes, conscious of Leo's eyes on him. "Shall we go?" he asked quietly. He took Leo's hand, and they left the house, pausing only to let Tony lock the door.

At the bottom of the stairs, Tony's landlord smiled at him. "Tony, my boy, how are you?"

Tony held on to Leo's hand. "I'm fine, Mr. Griswold. How are you?"

"Fine, son." Mr. Griswold leaned heavily on his stick. "Mavis wondered if you'd come in and check to see if we have a leak under the sink."

"Course I will. I'm going to work now, but I could pop in tomorrow lunchtime."

"See you tomorrow." Mr. Griswold looked at Leo. "Sorry to interrupt you."

Leo stepped forward and held out his hand. "I'm Leo Markus. Pleased to meet you."

"Benjamin Griswold. Pleased to meet you, young man."

"I've really got to go," Tony murmured to Leo. "See you tomorrow, Mr. Griswold."

Mr. Griswold waved at them and shuffled back to his flat. "Good-bye."

Leo slapped an arm around Tony's waist, and they headed out the door. "He's nice," he said as they got in the car.

"Mr. Griswold? Yeah, he is. They've been good to me over the years." Tony sighed as he tried to lean back in Leo's Mini, and he closed his eyes.

"Babe?"

"Huh? Are you okay?" Tony opened one eye.

"I kind of envy you."

Tony furrowed his brow. "You envy me? What the hell for?"

"You live your own life. Mine is dependent on my father."

"Are you good at your job?" Tony asked.

Leo nodded. "Bloody good at it. I'm amazed, but I really enjoy selling sex toys. My previous job was at McDonald's. I was convinced I was going to work my way up and end up owning a franchise."

"What happened?"

"The smell. My boyfriend at the time couldn't stand the frying stink in my hair and on my skin. He moaned so much that I quit. My dad was furious and made me work for him. He thought I'd be so embarrassed about selling dildos to women that I'd find another job."

"But you loved it instead?"

Leo snickered as he signaled to turn onto the main road. "Dad was furious and proud all at the same time. He thought he'd be teaching me a lesson, and instead I increased his business, especially when I suggested we market our products to the gay sector as well as straights."

Tony shook his head, stunned by the sheer energy from Leo. "You're amazing, you know?"

Leo shrugged. "Like father, like son. I've got mild ADHD, so I never rest for more than a minute or two."

"You hide it well."

"Years of practice."

"Do you take medication?"

"Not if I can help it. I did at school because it was the only way I could get through the day, but it dulls my senses. Now I'm working, I can be doing something all the time."

Tony stared out of the window. For the first time in his life, he might be able to admit something to a guy and not have it held against him.

"What's the matter?" Leo asked. "Do you have a problem with me having ADHD?"

Shocked, Tony stared at him, horrified Leo had got that impression. "No, no, not at all. I'm more...." He huffed in frustration. "I'm dyslexic. It was diagnosed really late, and I still can't read very well. I left school at sixteen with two GCSEs, and that's why I'm still a barman at nearly thirty." He refused to think of the promotion Marchant had offered him.

Leo made a noise, a sort of "ah" and "I understand" sound at the same time. "Must have been hard for you."

"School sucked. It got easier when I met Marchant. He took me under his wing and gave me a job."

"You've known each other for a long time, but he's never been your Dom?"

"We'd kill each other. You need to meet him and Ed to understand."

"Fair enough."

Tony was relieved Leo seemed content to let it go. He did have a relationship with Marchant, but it was more like guardian and protector than Dom-sub—or even boss-employee—and somewhere there was a long-term friendship thrown in. Leo was going to have to realize Tony was in more than one relationship if they stayed together.

He looked at the clock on the dashboard. "Do you want to come in and meet Marchant if he's there?"

"Are you ready for that?"

Tony thought about it for a minute because he wasn't really sure.

"You don't have to." Leo reached over to squeeze his hand, and Tony couldn't hear any edge to his voice.

"Not today," Tony admitted. "Marchant will be there, and Ed, and half the staff who probably already think I'm a loser for not having a Dom. I'm not ready for the whole world to know about us yet."

"Do you really believe they think you're a loser?"

"I guess not, but I just need more time."

"Does it bother you that I'm not a Dom or a Master?"

Tony chewed on the inside of his cheek, welcoming the bite of pain. "It would help if you were."

"You know I'm no sub, right?"

Tony's arse took that moment to make the ache known. "I think I worked that out when you pounded me into the mattress."

"You enjoyed it, though."

"I loved it." Tony hadn't been nailed like that for months.

"Me too."

Tony wasn't surprised to see the smug look on Leo's face. "I could go off you, you know."

"Then you wouldn't have my dick in your arse."

True. Tony sighed as he fidgeted, because his arse was really making its presence felt.

Leo turned into Larchmead Road. "Where do you want me to drop you?"

"Just behind the green van. I'll walk in from there." Tony sighed as Leo pulled in to the curb. "Thanks for a great night."

"No worries. See you again soon?"

He sounded really hopeful, and Tony leaned over to kiss him. "I'll give you a ring."

"You this time, rather than the other guy?"

"I promise," Tony said, heat filling his cheeks.

"Uh." Leo looked over Tony's shoulder. "We've got company."

Tony sagged, refusing to look over his shoulder. "Big guy, thirties?"

"Yup."

"Marchant." Tony sat up and looked out of the window. Yep, his boss was grinning at him. He pressed the button for the window, which didn't work because the car was turned off, so he opened the door. "What do you want?"

"An introduction?"

Tony rolled his eyes at Marchant. "You couldn't have waited?"

"I *know* you," Marchant said. "If I'd waited for you to be ready, I'd never meet him."

Tony heard Leo snickering in his ear. *Bastard!*

Marchant leaned into the Mini and held out his hand. "Hi, I'm Marchant Belarus. You hung up on me yesterday."

"Leo Markus. Sorry about hanging up. I've heard a lot about you."

They shook hands over Tony, ignoring him completely.

"Come into the club, Leo. Have a drink," Marchant said.

Leo laid a hand on Tony's arm. "Is that all right with you, Tony?" At Tony's shrug, he frowned. "No, I mean it. I won't come in if you don't want me to."

Tony looked at him and saw the sincerity in his eyes. "Thanks, but that horse has bolted now you've met Mister Nosy." He tilted his head at Marchant.

"That's Master Nosey to you," Marchant growled.

"Yeah, yeah. Bog off, Markie, we'll be in shortly."

Leo raised an eyebrow. "Markie?"

"It really pisses him off," Tony confided. "I call him that as much as possible."

"He's lucky I don't sack him."

"Sack Tony? Don't be ridiculous. You'd be lost without him." A new voice joined the conversation.

Tony looked over his shoulder to smile at the small silver-haired man smirking at him. He felt very protective toward Marchant's sub. "Glad that someone knows my use."

"Ed is just deluded," Marchant said.

"You did not just say that about your sub," Jordan said.

Tony banged his head against the dashboard as Jordan joined them.

"Okay, if I'm coming in for a drink, perhaps we could meet you all inside?" Leo said firmly.

Tony caught the unspoken conversation between Marchant and Jordan, and he huffed. Ed must have caught the expression on Tony's face because he herded Marchant away from the Mini. Jordan shot Tony a knowing look, but he followed Marchant and Ed into the club.

Leo huffed out a laugh. "They're like a bunch of overprotective aunts."

"You have no idea," Tony murmured.

"Come on, you need to get out of the car, and I want to take a look at the club."

Tony stretched as he got out of the car, wincing as his back, shoulders, and arse protested.

"Hmm, something hurt?" Leo squeezed Tony's arse, smirking as Tony yelped. "I guess it does."

Tony poked his tongue out at Leo even as he leaned into his touch.

"Get in here," Marchant yelled.

"You'd better do as the boss orders," Leo said.

"He's worse than my bloody father," Tony grumbled as he led the way. "Marchant is convinced the whole world will fall apart unless he controls it."

"That's because I know best," Marchant insisted as he guided Leo into the club. "And don't let Tony tell you any different."

Tony watched anxiously for Leo's first reaction to the place that had become his whole life. It shouldn't matter to him that Leo approved of it, but for some reason he needed that.

Leo turned to Marchant with sparkling eyes. "Would you give me a tour?"

"Are you sure you don't want Tony to show you around?"

"We might get distracted," Leo confided, smirking at Tony.

There was no *might* about it. Tony sighed. "I'll make coffee for us all, and I'll use the time to find out why Jordan is here."

"There was a good reason," Jordan protested.

"And I can't wait to hear your explanation," Tony said. "Have fun." He grinned at Leo.

Leo rocked on his heels. "Oh, I will. I really will."

Tony watched him depart, then fixed his gaze on the Dom who shouldn't have been there so early in the day.

"Now, you can tell me all about why you're here, and believe me when I say 'looking after Tony' is not the right explanation."

Chapter 5

ED'S LIPS twitched as he grinned at them. "I can't wait to hear this." For a man that would barely say boo to a goose a few weeks ago, he was oozing amused sarcasm now.

Jordan glared at them. "Fine, fine, I won't *say* I was worried about you."

Tony scowled back. "Thinking it loudly is the same thing. I'm old enough to look after myself."

"You really think age makes a difference to these guys?" Ed asked.

"You're not helping," Tony snapped.

Jordan frowned at Tony. "Marchant will have your head if he hears you talking to Ed like that."

Ed held up his hand. "It's fine. I'll make the coffee. Jordan, make your peace with Tony before Leo comes back, otherwise he might have *your* head."

Jordan huffed, but he guided Tony to a corner of the bar, and they sat down. Obviously deciding offense was the best form of defense, Jordan launched into his explanation. "I pushed you into this date. I just wanted to check you were all right."

"You did that last night when you gate-crashed the date."

"I'm sorry."

"No, you're not."

Jordan huffed again. "No, I'm not. Look, I pushed you into going on the date. You're not only my friend, you're also one of the subs here, and I feel protective toward you."

Tony shook his head. "I'm grateful, but—"

"It's smothering?" Jordan asked.

"Just a bit." Tony smiled. "Marchant's bad enough. I don't need another one who isn't my Dom, no matter how well-intentioned."

"But maybe your protectiveness could be channeled into looking after all the subs." Ed placed a tray full of empty mugs on the table.

Jordan looked curious. "What do you mean?"

"Let me get the coffee, and I'll tell you my idea."

Tony stood. "You sit and discuss it, and I'll get the coffee."

Tony was anxious to escape before Jordan thought he could get involved again, and he pretended not to see Jordan's knowing look. Ed managed to keep the smile off his face as he slipped into Tony's seat, but Tony could see it in his eyes.

Marchant and Leo came back as Tony brought the coffee to the table. They both looked excited, and that made Tony suspicious.

"What are you two plotting?"

Leo waited until Tony put the tray on the table, and then he pulled Tony in for a hug. "We were just talking business."

"And was I part of the business *discussion*?"

"You were," Marchant said, "and no, I'm not telling you what we said."

Tony looked at Leo, who just shrugged and reached up for a kiss, which rapidly turned passionate. Tony tried hard not to let his knees buckle under the force of Leo's kiss.

Leo pulled back and licked his lips. "Is there a coffee for me?"

"If you put your boy down for five minutes. Sugar?" Marchant handed Leo a cup.

Aware he was blushing, Tony grabbed his own mug and sat down. Leo sat next to him. Really close. Like no-personal-space close. Marchant and Ed sat that close, but that was only because Marchant was stupid in love and there was no way he was giving Ed the potential to bolt for the door. Tony also knew Ed was long past those days, but as Ed was also stupid in love, he didn't bother to tell Marchant.

Leo took a long chug of coffee, and then he said, "I told Marchant about the business, and he's going to look at some of the toys we sell."

"I've been thinking about replacing some of the toys for a while," Marchant agreed. "They do good work. I've bought from them before."

Tony leaned into Leo, pleased that he was fitting in so well. Leo kissed his cheek before drinking more coffee. Then Tony caught the smug expression on Jordan's face.

"Ed has a new idea for Jordan to keep him from interfering in my love life."

"Oh?" Marchant looked at his sub.

"I'm not sure anything will stop him doing that," Ed said, "but his overprotectiveness gave me an idea. Who looks after the subs?"

"I do," Marchant said.

Ed shook his head. "You look after the club."

"And all the people in it."

"But you can't pay attention to all the people all of the time."

"That's why I've promoted Tony to assistant manager."

Jordan leaned over and kissed Tony on the cheek. "You've actually said yes now? Congratulations." He turned to Leo, who'd made a distinctly growly noise. "Just a peck on the cheek, okay?"

"The subs need someone to take care of them. Someone they can bring their problems to," Ed said insistently.

"Why can't they talk to me or Tony?" Marchant growled as everyone burst out laughing except for Leo.

"They're all scared of you," Ed said. "And they see Tony as part of the club."

"Great. I'm part of the furniture," Tony said.

"You're an extension of Marchant. Even the Doms who give you a hard time still come to you with their problems. The subs need someone of their own, especially new subs."

Tony nodded. "It wouldn't be a bad idea, boss. Jordan's a Dom, so he's got authority, but he's not so scary that people are afraid to approach him."

Marchant wore his "thinking" face. If he'd thought it was a stupid idea, he'd have said so immediately, so he obviously thought it had merit. "Let me think about it, and I'll talk to you and Tony," he said to Jordan.

"You didn't tell me about the promotion?" Leo said to Tony.

"Because it was new. Marchant and I still haven't discussed it. And I've had other things to talk about with you."

Leo hummed in Tony's ear. "You do have other ways to use your mouth."

Heat flared in Tony's cheeks.

Marchant sighed. "Are you going to be able to keep your mind on work today?"

"Like you did?" Tony snarked.

Marchant scowled at him, but he couldn't say anything in his defense because since he'd met Ed, his mind was definitely elsewhere.

Leo just snorted and hugged Tony. "I have to go anyway. It may be the weekend, but I've got reports to write. I'll give you a ring tomorrow, Tony."

Tony nodded, hoping that his heart and insecurity weren't written plain for everyone to see.

"I'll walk you out," Jordan said.

"Why?" Tony asked suspiciously because he wanted to walk Leo out.

"I think he wants to ask my intentions," Leo said, obviously not fazed. "Let me say good-bye first." He pulled Tony up and dragged him into a corner. Tony went, because honestly, Leo had such a grip on his hand that he didn't have much choice, and whoa! that was a rush. Leo pulled Tony against him and looked up. "Listen, I get how it is here now, and I want to know if you still want to see me."

"Yes," Tony said without hesitation.

Leo gave him an almost shy smile. "Okay, then. I'll call tomorrow, and we'll arrange another date."

They kissed, which turned into more of a grope when Leo grabbed Tony's arse and molested it. Tony was left hard, flushed, and wanting when Leo let go.

"Ready?" Leo said to Jordan.

Tony watched Leo saunter out of the bar. All eyes were on him. Bloody hell, the guy might not be a Dom, but he knew how to own a room.

"I need more coffee," Tony muttered.

"Good idea," Ed agreed. "I'll make it." He sounded a little breathless.

Tony collapsed onto his seat. It felt lonely without Leo next to him. Alone at the table, Marchant gave him a knowing look. "He's got a possessive streak, hasn't he?"

"I'm beginning to realize this," Tony said.

"He told me to butt out, and I bet he's giving Jordan the same lecture."

"I really hope so."

"He'd make a great Dom."

"He could make a great boyfriend," Ed said as he sat down.

Marchant frowned. "Is that enough?"

Tony kept quiet, but Ed said, "What do you mean?"

"Tony's a born submissive even if he is a hulk. He likes pain and control. A hookup for some vanilla fun is one thing, but giving up the way you are… can you live with that?"

Ed scowled at Marchant, which almost made Tony laugh. The man really was coming out of himself. "He's had one date with the guy, and you're already writing him off?"

"All I'm saying is that Tony is a beautiful sub who deserves the right Dom, not a hot substitute."

"You think he's hot?" Tony grinned at Marchant.

"I'm not blind," Marchant snapped. "And you can stop looking worried, Ed. I think he's hot, but I'm not planning on making any substitutions in my life."

"Thank fuck for that," Tony murmured, "because Ed and I would have your balls strung up."

"Yes, I would." Ed did not look pleased at Marchant's comments about Leo.

At that point Jordan walked back into the club, and Marchant looked relieved at the distraction.

"Is that more coffee I can smell?" Jordan asked.

"I'll get it." Ed jumped up.

Tony looked cautiously at Jordan. "Are your balls still intact?"

"After the chewing he just gave me? Boy, for someone you just started going out with, Leo has a clear idea of your relationship."

"He told you to butt out too?" Marchant asked.

"Yep." Jordan looked positively gleeful.

"So you'll leave us alone?" Tony asked.

"Not a chance." Jordan looked at him seriously. "But I might just watch from a safe distance."

Marchant snorted loudly. "That's the best you're going to get, Tony. I'd accept it and move on."

"But he's not a Dom."

"So? He's as dommy as all shit even if he doesn't realize it yet. Train him."

Tony gaped at him. "What?"

Jordan shrugged. "You want a Dom. He's dominant. Train him to be the sort of Dom you want."

"I can't do that."

"Why not?" Marchant said. "You're an experienced submissive. You know what you want."

"I want him." At least Tony was sure about that. He definitely wanted Leo.

"Now that's sorted, do you feel like doing any work?"

Tony caught the edge in Marchant's voice, but before he could answer, Ed brought the coffee over.

"He gets to have his coffee in peace," Ed said firmly.

"You do remember I own the club?" Marchant said.

"Yes, dear." Ed petted his cheek and sat down.

Marchant huffed and muttered about bratty subs, which might have been convincing but for the soppy look on his face.

"I think I'll go home," Jordan said. "I've done my work for today."

Tony stood and gathered Jordan in for a hug. "Thanks for looking after me."

"You're welcome. He's a keeper."

Jordan kissed Tony on the cheek and left them, heading off to enjoy the rest of his Sunday, which he said involved tracking down his errant sub and paddling him senseless. Mike was going to be in heaven. Tony couldn't help feeling envious.

THE BAR heaved with men in various amounts of leather, and Tony was kept busy with orders, mainly for nonalcoholic drinks. The other barman and he worked well as a team, and they worked their way through the crush at the bar.

"Hey, beautiful."

To Tony's surprise, Leo leaned over the bar and kissed him. Tony had spoken to him earlier in the day, but as Tony had been woken from sleep and Leo was at work, it wasn't a long call.

"What are you doing here?"

"Marchant invited me over to see the club in use and get an idea of the toys we need to provide."

Tony looked at him suspiciously. "Are you sure that's what he invited you for?"

"Sorry, love, this is strictly business. I even brought my dad." Leo beckoned to the man standing behind him. "Dad, meet my boyfriend. Tony, this is my father, Jim, who runs the company."

Leo's father was an older, grayer, slightly taller, and—Tony had to acknowledge—still very hot version of his son.

Both of them were dressed in jeans and T-shirts, looking out of place among all the leather.

Tony held out his hand. "Pleased to meet you, Mr. Markus."

"Call me Jim. Good to meet you, Tony."

"Tony?" The other barman looked over.

"Sorry, Will." Tony smiled apologetically at Leo and Jim. "I've got to work. It's busy tonight."

"No worries," Leo said. "Is Marchant around?"

"He's in the back room."

"Tony!" Will snapped.

Leo's frown at the poor barman shouldn't have made Tony quite so happy as it did. "I'll be back later."

Tony went back to work, with an apology for keeping people waiting, but he couldn't quite keep the grin off his face.

The happiness he was feeling must have showed, because Tony noticed people studying him during the evening, and more than one man commented on the smile.

Partway through the evening, Jordan and Mike appeared, although they just waved at him and disappeared into the back room. Tony groaned inwardly at the thought of Jordan and Leo together again.

When Tony finally got a break, he went in search of Leo. He found him and his father watching a paddling in the back room. Marchant was discussing the paddle with Jim, but Leo's eyes were fixated on the scene before him.

Tony stood behind Leo and whispered into his ear. "It's pretty intense, isn't it?"

Leo nodded and leaned back into Tony's space. Tony put his arms around him and savored the feel of Leo's hard body pressed against his.

"I keep thinking of you and me," Leo said.

The breath caught in Tony's throat. "You and me?"

"You over the bench and me paddling your arse until it's as red as that guy's."

"Would… would you like that?"

"If it was you? Yeah, I'd like that."

Tony's cock liked that idea as well, and by the way Leo ground against him, he was just as aware of Tony's erection.

"I think we're done," Jim said. "Hey, Tony."

"Hi, Jim." Tony went to stand back, but Leo grabbed his arms.

"Give me five, Dad, and I'll be there."

Jim rolled his eyes, but he turned back to Marchant. "I think I'll have a drink."

"Come with me," Marchant said, clapping him on the back. "Scotch?"

"Sounds good to me."

Marchant looked at Tony. "Fifteen minutes max."

"Yes, sir."

The second the two men walked away, Leo backed Tony up against a wall, pulled his head down, and kissed him like he was a starving man and Tony a luscious steak dinner. He didn't let go until they were both breathless and hard enough to pound rock. Then he kept their mouths close together while they dragged in shaky breaths.

"Fuck, Tony, you make me want to take you here."

Tony gave a shaky laugh. "No one would care if you did. Except perhaps your dad."

"Ugh, no. Just *no.*"

"Fucking me here?"

"In front of my dad." Leo pushed his fingers through Tony's hair. "I've got to go. See you tomorrow."

"I ought to hate you, leaving me like this."

Leo cupped Tony's hard cock. "Keep this sweet, and tomorrow it will get all the exercise it needs."

Tony tried to thrust into Leo's hand, but Leo took his hand away. "You bastard."

"I know! See you tomorrow."

With one last kiss, Leo left Tony propped up against the wall. Tony's only consolation was that Leo was trying, and failing, to hide a large erection.

Chapter 6

WHEN TONY opened the front door, Leo pushed off from the wall he was leaning against. "You look all soft and warm," Leo said.

"Hey." Tony blinked sleepily. He'd been dreaming about Leo, and here he was, standing in front of him. Tony wasn't quite sure what was reality and what was the dream.

"I'm sorry. Did I wake you?"

Tony stood back and let Leo into the flat. "I'd better give you a spare key. I keep strange hours."

"Do you want me to make you a coffee?" Leo asked.

"Please." Tony knuckled his eyes and headed to the bathroom. He doubled back and dug into the key pot by the front door. "Here. Take this one."

Leo hefted the key in his hand. He looked down, a thrilled look on his face. "You trust me with your door key?"

"If you're a serial killer, I'm really going to regret this," Tony said as he shuffled to the bathroom.

"Yep, you are."

"Oh well." Tony shut the bathroom door. He looked at himself in the mirror and groaned. He had bed hair, thick stubble, bags under his eyes, and a broad, soppy grin on his face.

"Bacon sandwich?" Leo yelled.

"I will have your babies if you promise to make me breakfast every day," Tony muttered. Then in a louder voice, "Yes, please. I'll be out in ten."

He managed to shower, shave, and clean his teeth in ten minutes, which was some kind of record, then wandered into the kitchen.

Leo was cutting the bacon sandwiches in half, humming under his breath and looking like he belonged there. He looked up as Tony walked in. "Just in time. Coffee for me, tea for you, and bacon sandwiches for both of us."

"Fuck me," Tony moaned.

Leo paused as he was about to bite into the sandwich. He looked at him over the edge of the bread. "Now?"

Tony had to think about it. "After breakfast."

"Fair enough."

They finished the sandwiches and topped up their drinks before cuddling up on the sofa. Leo draped his legs over Tony's and rested his head on Tony's shoulder.

"You smell nice. Bacon and shampoo."

"That sounds…." Tony couldn't think of how it sounded.

"What time do you start work tonight?"

"Seven."

"Can I stay with you till then?"

Tony sighed and settled comfortably against the sofa, pulling Leo closer. "Shouldn't you be at work?"

"One advantage of being a salesman, I can set my own hours. At the moment I'm meeting with the assistant manager of a BDSM club."

"You don't think your dad will know exactly where you are?"

"Of course he does." Leo finished his coffee and placed it on the table. "Have you finished your tea?"

Tony looked at the small amount of liquid in the mug. "Yeah, more or less."

"Good." Leo took the mug and looked at Tony. "Can we do the 'fuck me' part of breakfast now?"

"You want me to fuck you?" He could, if pushed, but….

"Heh. Nice try." Leo placed Tony's mug next to his and pulled him up. "Come on, baby."

Tony's bed was just as he'd left it to answer the door. Leo stripped Tony of his joggers and T-shirt and pushed him onto the bed. Before Tony had a chance to breathe, Leo had straddled his hips, looking down at him with a twinkle in his eyes.

"What shall we do?"

"You could cuff me and I could suck you off, or you could fuck me."

"Where are the cuffs?"

Tony reached up above his head and rattled the cuffs around the metal bedstead, seeing Leo's eyes light up.

"Why didn't I see these before? Where's the key?"

"On the shelf." There was also a spare key taped to the back of the bedpost, which Tony could reach even if he was cuffed. He never told anyone about that one.

Tony was locked into the cuffs before he'd drawn the next breath. "Are you sure you haven't done this before?"

"Played with cuffs? Oh yeah, I've played with handcuffs."

"Which end?"

Leo's lips twitched. "Let's just say I'm *always* the one with the key."

"Figures." Tony tugged on the cuffs. They were reassuringly tight.

"All right?"

"Fuck, yes." Tony took a deep breath and relaxed into the familiar headspace. This was where he was happy, where he was content.

Leo leaned over him and looked into Tony's eyes. "I'm going to fuck you now."

Tony felt he was going to drown in Leo's gaze. "Do it."

Leo sat back on his heels and took the lube from the bedside table. Tony settled and spread his legs, giving Leo easier access. Leo kissed Tony's knee, an oddly tender gesture, then kissed down his thigh.

Moaning, Tony arched up, wanting Leo to put his mouth to better use, but Leo took Tony's legs in a tighter grip.

"Wait."

Tony forced himself to stop moving at Leo's firm command and wait for Leo to do whatever he wanted to, because Leo was working to his timetable and not Tony's. Leo smiled approvingly and pressed his fingers against Tony's hole. It took only a few minutes to prepare them, then Leo's dick kissed against the muscle and he pushed in.

Leo shuddered as Tony's body closed around him.

"You feel so fucking good," Leo gasped.

Tony breathed out. "Likewise."

"I'm going to take you until you're screaming."

"I can scream loud."

Leo gave him a wicked smirk. "Loud enough to wake the downstairs neighbors?" He rammed in hard and without warning.

Tony yelled loudly at the pain of muscles not prepared enough.

"Sounds good, but not loud enough."

Tony gritted his teeth. "Do it again, arsehole." He was going to have to apologize big-time to the Griswolds.

Leo obliged. He set up a rhythm that set Tony rattling on the cuffs. Beads of sweat broke over Leo's brow, and he caught his bottom lip between his teeth. Between each bone-shuddering thrust, Tony watched him.

"You're not screaming," Leo gasped.

"Want to watch you."

"Another time." Leo hauled on Tony's hips, and Tony yelled as Leo's cock brushed his prostate. "That's better."

"Again."

Leo obliged, fucking Tony until he was mindless, yelling, babbling, begging Leo to let him come.

"Almost, almost." Leo punched in short, sharp thrusts, selfish fucking that did nothing for Tony except drive him out of his skull.

Tony lay back and let Leo use him. Leo's eyes closed as he got closer and closer to climax. Then Leo came with a yell rivaling Tony's. Tony felt Leo's dick swell and pulse inside him, and he wished there was no barrier between them. Perhaps it was something he could discuss later. He whimpered in discomfort as Leo pulled out.

Leo disposed of the condom and rolled back to Tony. "Your turn."

Without warning, he sank his mouth over the head of Tony's cock and sucked hard. Tony screamed and came, thrusting up into Leo's mouth without regard. Leo sucked him through his orgasm, and then Tony flopped back onto the bed. His cock gave one last, weak pulse, and dribbled onto his stomach.

"Fuck." Tony stared up at the ceiling.

Leo groaned. "You're going to have to wait at least an hour. My balls just turned themselves inside out."

He managed to uncuff Tony's wrists before flopping onto the bed. Tony tried not to wince as he moved his arms, flames shooting through his shoulder joints, but Leo gave him a knowing look.

"Do you need a massage?"

"I'll be okay." Tony rolled over and placed his hand on Leo's chest. "Wish I could have felt you inside me for real."

"Me too, babe." Leo looked at him. "We need to get tested."

Tony hummed his agreement and curled around Leo. "Soon, babe. Damn, who the fuck is that?" Growling at the disruption of his postcoital peace, he fumbled for his phone on the bedside table. "*What?*"

"Tony, I need you in here now."

"Marchant? What's happened?" Tony frowned at his boss's terse voice.

"Who is it?" Leo mouthed.

"Marchant," he murmured and tried to concentrate on what Marchant was saying, but Leo looked edible and was really distracting.

Leo smirked as if he knew what was running through Tony's mind.

"Tony, are you bloody listening to me?" Marchant snapped.

"I'm sorry, boss. What did you say?"

"Jordan and Mike got attacked in town last night."

Tony sat bolt upright. "Are they okay?"

"No, they're not bloody okay. Mike's dead. Jordan's hanging on, but he's critical."

"What the fuck happened?" Tony leapt out of bed, looking for his boxers. He could see Leo looking at him in alarm, but he couldn't spare any concentration for him.

"Just get in here, and I'll tell you what I know."

"What the hell's happened?" Leo asked as Tony disconnected the call.

Unable to comprehend the question, Tony just stared at him.

Leo stood up, walked to Tony, and put an arm around his shoulders. "Tony," he said carefully, "tell me what's happened, sweetheart. Is Marchant all right?"

Tony tried to find the breath to get the words out, but everything seemed jammed in his throat.

"Can I use your phone to call Marchant?" Leo asked.

When Tony handed it over, Leo punched in a couple of buttons. "Marchant? It's Leo. What's happened?" Tony leaned against Leo as Leo listened to Marchant. "We'll be there in half an hour."

Leo threw the phone on the bed. "Get dressed. I'll drive you."

Tony shook his head. "I'd better take my car in case I need to drive anywhere."

"Then we'll take your car, and I'll drive. You're not driving while you're in shock. I can walk home and if necessary get a cab back to pick up my car."

"I'm fine."

"Yeah, yeah. Humor me. Here's your pants."

Tony didn't have the energy to argue, so he got dressed as Leo did the same. He brushed his hair and splashed water on his face in lieu of a shower. The news had shaken him to the core. He didn't have the energy to do anything more than follow Leo's orders until he was standing by the front door, watching Leo put on his shoes.

"Give me the keys." Leo held out his hand.

Tony handed them over and followed him down the stairs.

As Leo drove to the club, Tony stared out of the window. All he could think of was some nameless, faceless thugs touching his friends, hurting them, killing Mike and Jordan, fuck, *Jordan.*

"Baby, are you okay?" Leo squeezed his thigh.

Tony made a sound. "Not really."

"Not surprising. You're very fond of Jordan, aren't you?"

Tony looked over to see if there really was an edge to Leo's voice. "We've been friends since he joined the club."

"Just friends?"

Tony leaned back against the seat and closed his eyes. He couldn't deal with the weight of Leo's unasked questions. Not now. Not when he didn't know if Jordan was alive or dead.

"I'm sorry, Tony. I know the answer to the question, and it's stupid of me to throw a jealousy fit now."

Leo patted his leg.

"I wanted him, but he never wanted me as a sub. I made my peace with that. He was still a good friend."

"He's *still* a good friend, and he may not have wanted you, but he's very possessive about you."

"Yeah." Tony's phone rang again, and he answered it. "Hi, Frankie? Yeah, Marchant told me. We're on our way to the club. Yeah, see you there."

"Frankie's heard the news?" Leo asked.

"They're going to the club."

"We'll be there soon."

It was midafternoon, and the schools were just coming out. It seemed to take forever to negotiate the traffic, but eventually they pulled up outside the club. Tony pointed his lover to his usual parking space.

As Tony got out of the car, a jeep pulled alongside. Frankie sprung out of the passenger seat, rushed around to Tony, and clung to him.

"Hey." Tony patted Frankie's back.

"Hi, Tony."

Al, Frankie's boyfriend, got out of the car. He was a member of the club, although he spent less time there since he'd met Frankie.

"Hi, Al. Have you heard anything new?"

"Not yet." Al looked at Leo, who'd been waiting patiently by the car. "Hi, Leo."

Tony held out his hand for Leo. He felt like a giant compared to the three men, even though Al and Leo weren't that short. He sighed inwardly. It wasn't the first time, and it probably wouldn't be the last time he felt his height was a disadvantage.

Inside the club, the men were greeted by Ed. He looked gray and drawn. Frankie rushed over to give him a hug, which he gratefully accepted.

"Marchant's gone to the hospital to see if he can get any more information. He asked if Tony could run the club while he's gone."

"Sure. Have we got anyone to mind the bar?"

"Yes. Gary is coming in."

"I'm going to the hospital," Ed said. "Marchant's distraught. He needs me."

"We'll take you," Al said. "Tony, can you get us all a drink first?"

Infuriated by the way they'd made plans without even discussing it with him and then just casually threw an order at him, Tony stalked off to the bar. He knew he had to step up and look after the place, but he was closer to Jordan than probably anyone there except Al. No one seemed to give a shit about *his* feelings.

"Are you all right?" Leo's soft voice sounded behind him.

"I'm going to be busy, Leo. Probably best if you went home." Tony refused to look at him as he went behind the bar.

"You're angry."

"I'm fine."

"Bollocks. I saw what just happened there."

Tony finally looked at Leo. "I'm the barman. I take orders for drinks. What do you want?"

Leo grabbed his wrist, pressing into the marks left by the cuffs. "You're not the barman, you're the assistant manager."

"Tell them that." Tony cocked his head at the small group still chatting by the door.

"Why don't you tell them?"

As if on cue, Al looked over and frowned. "Everything okay, Tony?"

Leo pressed a little harder against Tony's wrist. "You need me to deal with it?"

"I'll get the drinks. Then I'll discuss it."

Al came over. "What's happening?"

"Nothing." Tony said shortly. "What do you want to drink?"

"Sparkling water and two Cokes. Leo, do you want one?"

Leo huffed and let Tony go. "No, I'm going home. I'll call you later, Tony." He walked out without giving Tony a kiss.

Al watched him go. "What was all that about?"

"Will Pepsi do?" Tony asked as he poured out a sparkling water for Ed.

"Tony."

Al sounded really annoyed at Tony's prevarication.

"Look, Leo's pissed off because I'm angry that you all just told me what to do without considering I might want to see Jordan. I know someone has to mind the club, and I know it has to be me, but you didn't discuss it. You just told me what to do. I'm the assistant manager, but you just treated me like the barman and a sub."

Al just stared at him. "I think that's the most I've ever heard you say."

Tony shrugged.

"We're all stressed. You're right. We didn't think about the fact you're close to Jordan. I could manage the club while you go to the hospital."

Tony was tempted, but he knew it was his job. "I'll stay, but can you phone me when you know what's happening? Have Mike's friends heard the news? He's new, but a lot of the subs know him."

"I don't know. Who are his friends?"

Tony started to make a mental list. "I'll deal with it."

"Good man." Al looked at the marks around Tony's wrists. "Leo's not so vanilla, then?"

"Not so vanilla," Tony agreed and handed Al two Pepsis.

"Do you want to join us? Ed can tell you what he knows."

Tony poured himself an apple juice and wandered over to the small group.

Ed smiled sadly as he sat down. "What did Marchant tell you?"

"Just that they were attacked."

"Outside the club on George Street. Cinderella's."

Tony frowned. "That's not a gay club."

"Mike wanted to go somewhere different."

"But Cinderella's? Jesus, that's a shithole." Frankie leaned into Al, who put his arms around him.

"I wouldn't go there if you paid me," Tony agreed. He sipped at his juice. "What time is Gary coming in?"

"He'll be in by five," Ed said.

"Okay."

"I'll stay and give you a hand if you want," Frankie offered.

Tony smiled gratefully at him. "I'm fine. It'll be a quiet night tonight. It's just the bar open, not the club. Gary and I can manage."

Al got to his feet. "I'll phone you as soon as I know what's happening."

Tony cleared away the glasses after they left. Gary joined him, and they got the bar ready for the evening trade. The first telephone call came half an hour after they opened. Gary answered the phone, but he handed it straight to Tony.

"It's Chaz."

Tony frowned, but he took the phone. "Chaz?"

Chaz was one of the subs. He'd been around almost as long as Tony, but they weren't particularly close. Chaz was petite and pretty—everything that Tony wasn't.

"It is true? About Mikey?"

"I'm sorry, Chaz, mate. It's true. I don't know too many details." He heard Chaz sob. "As soon as I know more, I'll call you."

"How… how is Jordan?"

"I don't know. Marchant has gone to the hospital."

"I know you and Jordan were friends."

"*Are* friends," Tony said fiercely. "He's still alive." Tony hoped and prayed he was still alive.

"Are friends," Chaz said. "I don't know what to do. About Mikey, I mean. He was friends with a lot of people."

"Tell everyone to come here. I'm not opening the club tonight, but people can come here to grieve. All of Mike's and Jordan's friends are welcome."

"I'll let them know." Chaz sounded exhausted and distressed.

"Chaz, I'm sorry about Mike." Tony could look after everyone here. It was easier than endless phone calls.

"Me too. I'll be there soon."

Tony looked over at Gary. "Club members and subs we know as friends only, Gaz. No public. Tonight's for remembering Mike and Jordan."

Gary nodded in approval. "I'll put a note on the door."

One by one, submissives and some of the younger Doms filed through the front doors. Tony looked after them, making sure everyone had a shoulder to cry on and plenty of tissues. One or two local people huffed as they were asked to leave, but Tony explained the situation, and they agreed to come back another day.

It was nearly nine before Marchant returned, with Ed, Al, and Frankie. He paused just inside the door as he looked at the crowd. Tony caught his eye. The nod of approval was enough. Marchant wasn't annoyed with him.

Marchant came over to the bar. "Everyone okay?"

"As well as they can be. Jordan?"

"He's still alive. He's still critical."

"Oh thank God." Tony slumped against the bar.

Marchant looked around. "Leo not here?" he asked casually. Too casually.

"I sent him away."

"Why don't you go and see him? Take an hour's break."

"He might not want to see me."

Marchant had perfected the "you're talking bollocks" look over the years. Tony huffed. "Fine, fine."

"Don't rush. There's enough of us here."

Tony grabbed his keys from behind the bar. He wasn't convinced this was a good idea. Perhaps he could just wander around for an hour.

Marchant stopped him as he walked out of the door. "I called him. He's expecting you."

"Sometimes I really hate you," Tony muttered.

"Suck it up, big man."

Chapter 7

THE IDEA of walking around for an hour was still appealing. Tony needed to get away from the grief inside the club, and he wasn't sure he could handle any other form of emotion. He hesitated on the corner of the Crescent, and almost turned on his heel to walk away from Leo's house. But then he saw a familiar figure crossing the road a hundred yards away.

Tony waited for Leo to reach him, as running clearly wasn't an option.

"Hey." Leo reached up for a kiss.

"Hey."

Leo studied him carefully. "You look like shit."

"I feel like it," he admitted.

"Come back with me?"

Tony agreed, following Leo. They walked in silence, Tony too exhausted to try and think of something to say.

In Leo's flat, Tony stood, not sure what to do.

"Come here." Leo held out his arms.

After an evening being everyone's support, Tony finally got a chance to mourn for his friends. Tears slicked down Leo's neck, but Leo just stroked Tony's hair and made soothing noises. Tony wept for a long time until he'd cried himself out and all that was left were shudders, sore eyes, and a raw, painful throat. Eventually Tony raised his head.

"Oh God." Tony cringed as he saw the mess he'd made of Leo's neck. He patted his pockets but came up empty-handed. "I need to... clean...."

"Here." Leo offered him paper towel and submitted to Tony's embarrassed cleaning.

"Sorry."

"Just shut the fuck up," Leo said easily.

"But earlier—"

"You were angry and upset. Anyway, what the hell could I do?"

"You're being too good to me."

Leo trailed his fingers down Tony's swollen cheeks. "Stop. Okay? You were dealing with a lot of shit. I get it."

Tony subsided because he didn't have the energy to argue. "What's the time?" he said, searching for a clock. "I ought to get back to work."

"Not for another half an hour. Sit down, and I'll get you a cuppa. I'm assuming you don't want a beer?"

Tony shook his head. Despite his size, he was a lightweight when it came to alcohol. "Tea'll be fine." He scrubbed his hand through his hair.

"Now it's sticking up all over the place." Leo came over with a brush, put a finger under Tony's chin, and tidied him to his satisfaction. "Much better."

As Leo poured the tea, he said, "What's happened since I spoke to you? I know Jordan's still hanging on."

"The subs started calling, so we shut the bar to the public and opened it up to the members and friends. Mike's friends needed somewhere to come and cry. It was okay, but full-on."

"Was that your idea?"

Tony wrapped his hand around the cup and nodded. "Marchant approved, so no shit there. Have you put sugar in this?"

"A little. It was a great idea."

"Sugar in tea? It's a disgusting idea."

"Opening the club to the subs, idiot. Just drink it. You need the sugar."

"As long as you pour me one without so that I can get rid of the taste." He pulled a face. The sugar was foul, even if it was making him feel warmer.

"Deal."

Leo poured him another cup, sans sugar, and sat down next to Tony on the sofa. He twisted his body and sat facing Tony, with one leg tucked up underneath him. "I had a chat with my dad earlier."

"How is he?"

"He's fine. He's got friends at the local cop shop."

Tony looked at Leo. "Oh?"

"He heard a rumor they know who did this to your friends."

"Have they arrested them?"

Leo shrugged. "Don't know as yet, but watch this space."

"Have they beaten up other guys?"

"They target gays in the area," Leo said.

"What a surprise." Tony ground his teeth together.

Leo squeezed Tony's forearm. "Dad wanted to warn me to be careful. He didn't realize the victims were connected to you."

"Jordan and Mike. Not victims," Tony snapped.

"I'm sorry," Leo said soothingly. "That was crass of me."

Tony took a deep breath, trying to recover his composure. "I'll let Marchant know. We can put out a warning to the club."

"At least they're taking it seriously," Leo said.

"The cops are pretty good around here. I know a few of them through the club."

"You've got cops who are Doms?" Leo huffed. "That figures."

Tony smirked. "Most of them are subs."

Leo choked on his tea. "You're joking!"

Tony crossed his heart. "No lie. At least three of the guys are subs, and one who says he's a Dom isn't, really."

"I guess I shouldn't be surprised. Looks can be deceiving." Leo winked over the top of his mug.

Tony gave a weak smile. "I ought to get back."

"I'll drive you."

"Your car is at my place."

"My dad drove me back to pick it up."

Leo grabbed his keys, and within a couple of minutes, Tony was outside the club. He looked at Leo.

"I'd invite you in, but—"

"Tonight is for members to mourn." Leo reached over to kiss Tony. "I get it. Come back to mine when you've finished. Here's a key. You can let yourself in."

"I don't know what time I'll be done. It could go on all night."

"It doesn't matter what time you turn up. I want you in my bed."

Tony closed his fingers over the key. "Thanks. I'll be there."

He got out of the car and watched Leo drive away. A warm place in his heart spread out to the rest of his body. For the first time in a long while, someone cared about him. It was a good feeling.

Marchant looked at him when he walked into the club. "Everything okay?"

"It's fine, except he has a horrible habit of putting sugar in tea."

"He probably thought from your stupid behavior you were in shock. So did you try to run in the opposite direction?"

Tony tried really hard not to flush guiltily, but from Marchant's sigh, he was busted. "I thought about it. He walked here to meet me."

"At least one of you has some sense."

"Leave Tony alone," Ed scolded. "He's kept it together this evening."

"Thank you, Ed. At least *one* of you notices."

Marchant flipped him off and served the next customer. Ed winked at Tony and wandered off to talk to a group of young subs in the corner. Tony watched him for a moment, struck by how much the man had come out of himself in the short time he'd known him. Ed had been a mess, fragile and tetchy, yet a few months of Marchant's patient care and he was taking his first steps into the BDSM world. He still wasn't ready to take part in the club as an active member, but people liked him. The subs welcomed him into their group, and Ed put his arms around the youngest member, who was barely old enough to be there. The kid started crying, and Ed petted and soothed him.

"He's a different man," Marchant said.

"Thanks to you."

"Thanks to all of us. I don't think Ed would have dared to dream about being happy if everyone hadn't shown him he was allowed to be."

Tony looked at his boss. "But you gave him permission to be happy."

"True." Marchant tilted his head. "Has Leo given you permission to be happy?"

"I don't need permission," Tony protested.

"Don't you?"

Tony growled at Marchant and started work. *Damn the man.* He was too bloody perceptive sometimes.

It wasn't until they were locking up, having finally shoved the last member out at four in the morning, that Tony remembered to pass on the news about the attacks.

"Sorry, I should have told you earlier."

"Damn! Never mind, I'll e-mail it out to everyone."

"Do you want me to do it now, before we forget?"

Marchant shook his head. "Go home. Are you going home?"

"I'm going back to Leo's."

"Okay. Get some sleep."

"If I can, I'd like to visit Jordan tomorrow."

"Call ahead. They weren't letting visitors in yesterday. I only managed to see him because I know the staff nurse."

"One of us?"

"Mum of a member. She recognized me and let me in for two minutes."

"Okay." Tony yawned. "I've got to sleep. Night, boss."

"Night, Tony."

Tony left his car at the club and took a slow walk back to Leo's. He was exhausted, but he needed the fresh air to clear his head.

At Leo's house the locked gates foxed him momentarily, but then he realized the key had a tag with the keypad number on it. As he walked around the building, he prayed Leo's parents didn't look out and think he was a burglar. However, he reached Leo's flat without a problem. It was dark and quiet inside. Tony wondered if he should sleep on the sofa rather than wake Leo. Then the man himself appeared, wearing nothing but a pair of baggy boxer shorts, yawning and scratching his chest.

"Get naked, and come to bed."

Tony blinked at him, then he did as he was told, stripping off where he stood and following Leo into bed. He sighed as he settled, Leo wrapped around him.

"Go to sleep," Leo said, wafting morning breath over him.

Tony closed his eyes and did as he was told.

"RISE AND shine, big man."

Tony groaned. Leo was too fucking cheerful for arse o'clock. He flapped his hand in front of his face. "Tired. Too early."

"It's three in the afternoon."

"You're lying." Tony opened his eyes and wished he hadn't. His eyes were itchy and raw, and he just wanted to die quietly in a corner.

"No, I'm not. Now get the fuck up. I've promised Marchant that if I take you to see Jordan, you'll be back for work tonight."

"I can see Jordan?"

"Five minutes only. Marchant's cleared it with Jordan's parents and the hospital staff. Hurry up and get dressed. Your clothes are washed and dried. Go me for being organized."

"Dial back the happy, and I'll think about it," Tony grumbled, forcing his unwilling body to sit up.

"Okay. Tea and toast in five."

Thankfully Leo left the room before Tony worked up the energy to throw a pillow at him.

TEARS WELLED in Tony's eyes and spilled over onto his cheeks. "God, Jordan, what did they do to you?"

He sat down next to Jordan, fluttering his hands, unsure where to touch him that wouldn't hurt him. Jordan was sedated and didn't respond to Tony's question. He lay still, which was as frightening to Tony as the injuries. Jordan was always on the move. The man couldn't stay in one place if he tried.

If it hadn't been for the red hair, Tony wouldn't have believed the man in the bed was Jordan. His friend was unrecognizable. Jordan's cheeks were swollen and bruised. His cheekbones and jaw were fractured, both eyes swollen shut. Both arms were broken, and his groin bruised from the repeated kicking. He was lucky that his kidneys weren't permanently damaged from the assault.

According to the nursing staff, they were less "concerned" than they had been. They had moved Jordan from intensive care to the high dependency unit.

Tony wanted to run out to Leo and beg for his comfort, but he knew that Marchant had pulled strings to get him in here, and he wasn't going to waste time. He held Jordan's hand as gently as he could and told him about last night. He didn't say Mike was dead, in case no one had told Jordan, but he talked about the subs and their need for comfort.

After five minutes the nurse poked her head around the door. "Time's up."

Tony dried his eyes and squeezed Jordan's hand. "I'll be back tomorrow, mate."

Tony kissed Jordan on the forehead and left the room.

Leo stood up as he came out, concern written all over his face. "How is he?"

"He looks like he's gone ten rounds with a heavyweight."

The nurse was still nearby, and Tony swallowed hard to keep it together.

Leo patted his arm sympathetically. "Let's get out of here. Five minutes to my car, and you can let go."

The nurse looked over. "You're on the list of visitors now."

Tony nodded. "He's my best friend."

"Jackie knows you. That's good enough for us."

Tony frowned, not having a clue who Jackie was.

The nurse must have seen his confusion because she said, "Her son knows you all. I'm not sure of his name. Tall lad with freckles and ginger hair."

"Callum?"

"That's him."

Tony finally managed a smile. "I know Jackie, although I didn't know her name. She insists we call her Mum."

"That sounds like Jackie."

An alarm sounded, and the nurse snapped back into professional mode. "See you again, I expect."

Heart pounding in fear, Tony waited to check the alarm wasn't coming from Jordan's room before he followed Leo down the hall. Leo held his hand all the way back to the car, despite Tony's protests.

"What time have you got to go back to work?" Leo asked as they got in the car.

"Marchant texted to say I could have the day off. I'm on at eleven tomorrow."

"Good." Leo was driving Tony's car. Tony wasn't quite sure how he'd been relegated to the passenger seat again.

"You ought to get to work." Tony was going to go home and sleep for a lifetime.

"I worked until you woke up. Now I'm going to take you bowling, then we're going back to your place."

Tony looked at him dubiously. "I'm really tired."

"I know you are, but you need exercise and sleep. As I hate the gym, we're going bowling."

"Do I have a choice?"

"You can always give me your safeword."

Tony shook his head. "You were a hookup."

"Of course I was, but you got something so much better."

The fecking man sounded like he believed it too.

Tony thought about the plan. Bowling and sleep. "Can I have nachos?"

"Well, duh!"

Tony assumed that was a yes.

THEY WERE evenly matched at bowling. So evenly matched that it turned into a more serious competition. Tony took the first game by a point, but Leo thrashed him in the second game—Leo got two strikes. They paused for beer and nachos and contemplated whether to leave or to stay. It wasn't that busy, so they booked another two games.

By the time they walked out, Tony was exhausted but on a high. For a couple of hours, he'd thought about nothing except having fun.

"You're amazing, do you know that?" Leo said as they walked toward the car.

Tony grinned down at Leo. "Back atcha."

"Why don't you come back to mine tonight? You can sleep until half ten."

It was tempting, and Tony almost said yes. "I could really do with a night in my own bed."

"Alone?"

Leo looked resigned rather than angry, and that gave Tony the courage to say yes.

"Just for tonight. Do you mind?"

Leo shook his head. "I'm going to miss you, but it's okay. Can I see you in the morning?"

"Sure." Tony was exhausted now. Even being civil was hard work.

Leo took Tony home, steered him into his bedroom, stripped him, and put him to bed. "Night-night, lover."

"You do this a lot," Tony mumbled.

"Say good night?"

"Put me to bed."

"I enjoy it. Go to sleep." He pressed a kiss to Tony's temple.

Tony relaxed as he heard his front door close. Leo was a fucking keeper.

Chapter 8

TONY LOOKED up at the new U-bend. "'Kay. Turn the tap on, Mr. Griswold."

He held his breath and looked up at the plumbing, praying he wasn't about to get a face full of water. The water swirled down the tubing, and he remained dry.

Tony took another breath and smiled. "I think it's fixed."

"That's good news, Anthony." His neighbor sounded pleased. "Mrs. Griswold has tea and cake ready for you in the living room."

"I'll just finish up here, and I'll be in." Tony groaned at the twinges in his back as he wriggled out from under the sink.

Mr. Griswold frowned at him. "When are you going to get your back looked at? I've been telling you for months to visit my chiropractor."

"I think it's spending so much time in Leo's Mini. It's an instrument of torture not designed for a guy my size."

"That's true. If you're going to stay together, he'll have to get a bigger car."

"I think he would cry. He loves it with a passion."

Mr. Griswold leaned on his stick. "More than you?"

Tony's stomach rolled over. "It's a bit too soon to be talking about love, Mr. G."

"It's never too soon to admit you love someone. I told Mrs. Griswold I loved her the first day I met her."

"He did," she agreed, shuffling in from their living room. She was a tiny woman, barely reaching Tony's chest, but she ruled the household with a rod of iron. Her husband adored her, and Tony made it his life's mission to keep her happy. "I thought he was mad, and I told him so, but he insisted he loved me and he would wait for me to catch up with the program."

Tony grinned at the old woman. "How long did you make him wait?"

"Three months."

"Twelve weeks and five days," Mr. Griswold corrected. "It was the longest wait of my life."

She smiled at her husband. "I had to be sure."

"What made you realize he was the one?"

"I told him my worst secret, and Arty told me he loved me for me, not for what I'd done in the past."

Tony wanted to ask, but at the naked pain in her expression, he kept his mouth shut.

She smiled at Tony shakily. "I knew he was a good man and one I should hold on to."

"You were very lucky," he said.

Mr. Griswold hugged his wife. "We both were. I've never regretted a moment of our life together."

She hugged him back. "Let's have some tea."

Tony followed them into the living room, envying their long-term relationship.

Mrs. Griswold handed him a cup of tea and fixed him with her piercing gaze. "Tell me about your boy."

"Leo?"

"He seems like a nice boy. He always says hello to me when he meets me."

"He is nice," Tony agreed.

"What does he do?"

"He's in… sales." Tony prayed she wouldn't ask what Leo sold.

"Arty used to be in sales."

"I sold used cars," Mr. Griswold said. "I was bloody useless at it."

"He was," she agreed. "You were much happier at the library."

"You were a librarian?" Tony asked.

"For thirty-five years. I was very happy there." He sighed as if recalling happy memories. "Are you still working at the club?"

"I am." Tony had been sparse with information about exactly where he worked. "I got a promotion, though. I'm the assistant manager."

"Congratulations, Anthony." Mr. Griswold got to his feet, rocking a little as he tried to steady his balance. "Let's have a celebratory drink."

Tony groaned inwardly. He knew what was coming next.

Mr. Griswold shuffled toward the dresser. "Let's have a sherry."

Tony hated sherry, but he didn't want to upset his landlord, so he accepted his glass and Mr. Griswold's toast to his new job.

SIGHING HAPPILY, Leo wriggled back against Tony's chest, putting pressure on Tony's cock, trapped between their bodies. "Harder," he ordered.

Tony wrapped his hand around Leo's cock and slowly jacked him off with firm, hard strokes that made Leo's toes curl.

"So good. So good." Leo breathed out. "Now what were you telling me?"

"My neighbors really like you." Tony squeezed as he reached the head.

"Good!" Leo gasped. "They seem like a lovely couple."

"He told me…." Tony stopped, not wanting to have this discussion while they were making love.

Leo tilted his head to look up at Tony. "What did he tell you?"

"Not now. I'll tell you later."

Leo frowned at Tony's deflection. "You'd better. Ahh!" He arched his back. "Christ, need to come."

"Is that an order?"

Tony held Leo firmly against him, one large hand splayed against Leo's flat belly, and the other pumped Leo's dick, feeling it harden and swell against his palm.

"It's an order, babe."

Leo arched his back, spraying over Tony's fingers. Tony held Leo through his orgasm, feeling each pulse, each shudder.

"God!" Leo subsided against Tony, letting out a long breath.

"You feel so good," Tony said.

"So do you. I can feel you poking my back."

Tony wriggled, making sure he poked Leo a little more.

"Do you want to come?" Leo asked, making sure he applied just the right pressure to make Tony gasp.

"Stupid question."

"Mouth or hand?"

"Your mouth."

Leo turned in Tony's arms to give him a kiss, before kissing down Tony's neck and stopping to play with his nipples. He kissed very slowly down to Tony's hard cock, leaking against his belly. Leo sucked the tip of Tony's cock into his mouth.

Tony closed his eyes, his hand around Leo's head, as Leo swept his tongue across the slit. He clutched Leo's hair and then realized what he was doing.

"You taste so good." Leo pulled off briefly to praise him and then went back to exploring the head.

Tony was so aroused that it took little more than Leo's expert tongue to have him spilling into Leo's mouth. Then Leo was kissing him to share his taste, and Tony sank into the feel of the man in his arms.

Leo rubbed his head against Tony's furry chest. "Do you want me to remove the plug?" He had insisted on inserting the largest plug his company sold before Tony jacked him off.

Tony licked his lips as Leo jostled the plug. "I want you to play with it."

"Fuck, yes."

Leo obviously liked the idea from the way his cock was showing interest. "I can't believe the effect you have on me."

He cupped Tony's balls, then slipped his hand back to nudge the black plug, and grinned as Tony's dick showed its appreciation. Leo tugged on the plug, and Tony groaned.

"Want me to do that again?"

"Stupid fucking question." Tony hissed.

He'd asked for it, and Leo was obliging, and the way Leo's attention fixed on his arse swallowing the plug, he was finding it just as exciting as Tony.

Leo traced a finger around the muscle. "I want to fuck you."

Tony spread his legs even wider in answer.

"On your hands and knees."

Tony rolled over and rested on his forearms, arse begging for Leo's attention. He felt Leo press against him. Then the plug was gone, and he felt empty until Leo's sheathed cock replaced it.

Leo shoved his cock in until he was resting against Tony's back. "Mine."

"Possessive git." Tony grinned into the sheet.

"Just stating a fact."

"Do I have a say in the matter?"

"You say 'Yes, sir.'" Leo said it so matter-of-factly.

"Yours forever?"

"Until death do us part and all that bollocks."

Tony blinked back sudden tears. Leo was offering him all he'd ever wanted. "Yours," he agreed, his voice shaky.

Leo ran his hands down Tony's flanks. "No more talking," he ordered.

"Whatever you say." Tony yelped as Leo slapped his thigh. "Sir. Whatever you say, sir!"

"Better."

"Mine," Tony whispered. He felt a featherlight kiss placed in the center of his spine.

"Yours. Just yours."

"ARE YOU going to see Jordan this afternoon?" Marchant said.

He'd been perched at the end of the bar with his laptop and calculator, growling over the accounts. Tony was perched at the other end growling at the staff rotas.

Earlier that morning Marchant had handed over the rotas with a wicked grin. "They're all yours, assistant manager."

Tony scowled at him. "I'm going to hate you for this job, aren't I?"

"You're welcome to do the accounts."

"Fine." Tony gave him a long-suffering sigh.

Three hours later, Tony was ready to do unspeakable things to Marchant's genitals. Every single one of the staff seemed to have issues working with other people except him.

He looked up with annoyance at being disturbed. "What did you say?"

"Jordan? Are you going to see him?"

"Yep. This evening. Leo's working, so it seemed a good time to go."

"Do you want a lift?"

"It's okay. I promised to get some things from B&Q for Mr. Griswold. I can stop off on my way home."

"'Kay. I'm going to take Ed to see him earlier, and I think Al is popping in as he's back from the course."

"Jordan's going to be tired from all the visitors. I won't stay long."

Two weeks after the attack, Jordan was conscious, although he'd worried the doctors by how long it had taken him to come round. He still wasn't in a position to be discharged, and even when he was, he would have to go home to his parents rather than his own flat because he wasn't able to take care of himself as he was still in plaster. Jordan had made it very clear how unimpressed he was about that.

Marchant had arranged for a couple of subs to take care of Jordan while he was in hospital and to go to Jordan's parents' house when he was there. They were happy to look after him even if he was deeply miserable. Mike's death had hit Jordan hard. Although they'd been new together, Jordan's feelings for Mike were strong, and now suddenly Mike had been ripped away. Jordan wasn't even well enough to go to the funeral, and Mike's parents had made it plain that no one from the club was welcome.

"They washed away the gay," Jordan had said bitterly on the day of the funeral.

Tony had stroked Jordan's hair, trying to comfort him, but Jordan had turned his head away.

Marchant had made his feelings about Mike's parents known and had told Jordan he would arrange a memorial service for Mike when Jordan was out of hospital. A club memorial service with kink. Tony's mind boggled at the thought.

"Okay, done," Marchant said. "What about you?"

Tony looked at the rows of days and staff for the next month. "I think I'm done." If the buggers weren't happy, they'd have to suck on it.

"I need a drink and something to eat."

Tony yawned loudly. "I need fresh air."

"It's an hour before we open. Go for a walk."

"Yes, boss."

Tony grabbed his coat as it was drizzling outside. The weather had taken a downturn over the past week, and the temperature had dropped too. He grimaced as the wind and rain blew in his face, and nearly abandoned the walk.

"It's shite out here," he yelled to Marchant. "I'll get in the car and go to Tesco. Do you want anything?"

"Chocolate, as long as you promise not to tell Ed."

Ed was still trying to convince Marchant to give up sweets and eat spinach salad. Marchant had growled more than once that it would be a cold day in hell before he gave up chocolate.

"Deal."

The car was parked near Leo's house because Leo had been molesting him in the car on the drive to work, and he'd pulled over to let Leo complete the job and then left it there. Tony cursed now as he ran toward the Land Rover.

By the time he reached it, he was soaking wet. He got in the car and stripped off his jacket. As he looked up, the gates of Leo's house opened and a familiar red nose poked out. Tony grinned as the Mini pulled out and stopped, but then the smile slid off his face. Leo hadn't stopped for the traffic. He'd stopped because he was kissing someone. A man.

Leo was kissing another guy.

Then he pulled out into the road, driving past Tony's car without even noticing.

Tony switched on the ignition. The windows had steamed up, and he had to sit for five minutes, waiting for them to demist. It took a long time. Like Tony's brain took a long time to process what had just happened.

Leo, the man who'd said only the previous night that they were together forever, was screwing around.

Chapter 9

THE FAN blasted hot air and eventually the mist cleared from the windscreen, if not from Tony's head. He turned the car around and drove back to the club, parking in his usual place.

As he walked in, Marchant said, "That was quick. Did you forget my chocolate?"

Tony hesitated on the doorstep. "I… yes…. Sorry. I'll go and get it."

"Typical. You send someone out to do one job…." He grinned, but when Tony didn't return it, the smile slid off his face. "Tony? What happened?"

"Leo."

Marchant looked confused. "What about him?"

"Just seen him kissing another guy." Tony tried not to show any emotion.

"I'm going to kill him."

Tony smiled sadly. "Thanks, but it's okay. Guess it wasn't meant to be. It's no big deal."

Marchant came over and hugged him so tight, Tony couldn't breathe. He was big, but Marchant was strong, and he only offered dominance. "I'm going to kill him," Marchant repeated. He held Tony for a long time before guiding him to the bar.

"Drink this." He poured a brandy and made Tony knock it back.

Tony gasped as the spirit burned down his throat.

"Another?" Marchant raised the bottle.

"Gotta drive later." Otherwise Tony would have quite happily taken the bottle and drunk himself into a stupor.

"Tony, are you sure you saw what you think you saw?"

"My boyfriend sticking his tongue down another man's throat? Yeah, I'm pretty sure I saw that."

"What are you going to do?"

"Today?"

Marchant nodded.

"I'm going to work now, visit Jordan for a couple of hours, and then I'm back here this evening."

"You know what I mean. What are you going to do about Leo?"

"Nothing. I'm going to forget he exists."

"Are you going to speak to him?"

"I don't see the point."

Tony was useless at handling confrontation in his private life. He was crap at handling confrontation anywhere, despite his size. Faced with a lover who messed with Tony's heart? Tony didn't have a clue.

Marchant poured him another brandy. "Drink that. I'll drive you home. You can see Jordan tomorrow. Go and check all the stock for tonight. I think we need to replace the lube in rooms two and six."

"Sure." Tonight the club was open for members only. It was the sort of night he'd been planning to introduce Leo to his world. He shook his head. He should have known it wouldn't work. His world and Leo's? Poles apart.

He went through the checklist for each room, but it was mindless and gave him too much time to think.

Tony was lost in his own thoughts when he heard a commotion out the front. He rushed out in case Marchant needed help, only stopping short when he realized who was at the door. Knowing it was cowardly, he slunk behind the door so Leo couldn't see him.

Marchant held out his hand, preventing Leo from entering the bar. "I'm sorry, Leo, you can't come in today."

"But why?" Leo looked genuinely confused. "You've let me in at other times. I'm here to see Tony."

"Because you were with Tony then."

Leo frowned. "I'm with Tony *now*. Isn't he working today?"

Marchant shook his head. "Please leave, or I'll be forced to call the police."

"Jesus, Marchant. What the hell have I done?"

"You really need to talk to Tony about that."

"Then let me in to talk to him."

"Not today," Marchant said firmly.

"So I *have* done something?"

Marchant herded Leo away from the entrance, and Tony couldn't see them anymore, but he could still hear them.

"Leo, I'm only going to say this once more. Please go. Tony will talk to you when he's ready."

"Fine," Leo snapped, and Tony flinched at the harshness in his tone. "But tell Tony I expect an explanation."

"I think you owe him one," Marchant said sternly and slammed the door shut.

Marchant walked back into the bar and saw Tony looking at him. "You heard?"

Tony gave a nod.

"I'm not going to do that again, Tony. Next time you talk to him. Are you sure you couldn't be mistaken?"

"Do you want me to kiss you to show you what I saw?"

And, of course, at that point Ed chose to make an appearance down the stairs. He looked between the two of them. He raised one silver eyebrow. "Did I hear you mention you want to kiss my boyfriend?"

Marchant let out an explosive breath. "Long story short, Tony saw Leo kissing another man and instead of confronting him and then punching his lights out, he's avoiding him. So I've had to ban Leo from the club."

Ed still looked confused. "So you want to kiss Marchant?"

"Hell no!" Tony wanted to bash his head against the wall. "Marchant didn't believe me when I told him what I saw, so I offered to demonstrate."

Ed nodded as if that was reasonable. "Fair enough. Leo, though, he's a good bloke. He wouldn't kiss another man."

Tony gritted his teeth, because he knew from long experience with Marchant he shouldn't lose his temper with Ed if he wanted to keep his job and his head on his shoulders. "He was kissing another man, Ed. I saw it."

"All right," Ed said, and Tony could hear his dubious tone. "You know you're going to have to face him sometime."

"Not today. Just not today."

Marchant pursed his lips. "Not today. But soon. I won't allow disruptions at the club."

"Fine, fine." Tony turned on his heel and stalked away. God forbid the precious club got fucking disrupted.

"Tony, stop!"

Tony ignored Ed. Job be damned. He could feck off.

"Tony!" Marchant bellowed at him.

"What?" Tony snapped. "I've got work to do."

"You're behaving like a three-year-old."

"I'm trying to get ready for tonight." He shut the door to the back room with an irritated *click* and leaned against the wall. Tears streamed down his face. "Why wasn't I enough for you?" he muttered.

The door opened behind him. Tony wiped his face, prepared to snap again, but the two men pressed up against him, one almost as tall as him, the other slim and short. Tony rested his head on Marchant's shoulder, and Ed stroked his back.

"I'm all right," he said eventually.

"No, you're not, but you will be." Ed hugged him a little closer. "Don't give up on Leo until you've spoken to him."

Marchant growled in his throat. "And then I'm going to rip off his balls."

Tony laughed shakily. "Deal."

"Do you want to talk to him now? You can get it over with before the club opens."

"Not now." Tony would rather have his teeth pulled. "I'd rather work and sleep on it."

Marchant gave him a knowing look. "Yeah, yeah."

"Don't you dare put it off," Ed scolded.

Tony knew better than to snap at Ed, so he just nodded. "Got to get the rooms ready, or the punters'll be complaining."

Marchant slipped his arm around Ed. "Ed's staying this evening."

"Really?" Tony grinned at Ed. "He's finally persuaded you?"

Ed huddled into his Dom. "He's promised if it gets too much I can leave."

"I'll look out for you," Tony promised.

Marchant frowned. "I was going to ask you to take over for the night so I can focus on Ed, but we could delay it for a while."

"No way." Tony knew how much this step meant for both Ed and Marchant. "My failed love life does not trump your relationship." He bent down and kissed Ed's cheek. "We're all here for you."

Ed held Tony's hands and reached up for another kiss. "You have a big heart."

"Do you two want a room?" Marchant asked sourly.

"He'd like that," Tony confided. "He's got this thing about watching." He chuckled as Ed whipped around to stare at Marchant in alarm.

Marchant scowled at Tony. "I'm going to get one of the Doms to spank your arse. He's taking the piss, Ed. I'd never allow you to have sex with anyone else."

"Me and Tony? And you'd be watching?" Ed really looked as if he was thinking about the idea, and then he giggled. "Oh, boys, your faces are priceless."

Marchant slapped Ed's arse, grinning wolfishly at his squeak. "Tony's right. I do like watching guys take pleasure in each other."

Ed tilted his head and stared at Marchant. "No promises, but never say never. I never thought I'd get this far."

Tony looked away as Marchant stroked Ed's cheek. "Baby, you constantly amaze me."

"Thanks to you." Ed pressed his mouth into Marchant's palm.

The moment was too private to share. Tony left them to go and finish the rooms. Their tenderness rubbed salt into the open wound in his heart.

Chapter 10

"I'M FUCKING coming. Hold on!" Tony yelled as some bastard did a number on his front door. He was very pissed at being woken up at seven in the morning, just two hours after going to bed, especially as he'd spent an hour and a half alternately sobbing and punching his pillow. He had a hangover from the booze Marchant had forced down his throat.

Tony unlocked the door and threw it open, narrowly missing a punch in the face from the man about to pound on the door again. "What?"

Leo pulled his arm back just in time. He shoved his hands in his jacket pocket and glared at Tony. "What the hell happened last night?"

"Go away." Tony attempted to slam the front door, but to his annoyance it didn't shut in Leo's furious face.

Leo shoved it open with his foot. "Not until I know why you dumped me. I thought you were better than that."

Tony snorted derisively. "That's rich." He turned on his heel.

"Where the hell are you going?"

"Back to bed."

Leo grabbed him by the arm. Tony tried to shake him off, but the bastard had a tight grip and he dug his fingers into Tony's bicep.

"Tony, tell me what I've done. I was awake all night worrying about it."

"You should've got him to fuck you till you slept."

"What? Got who? What the hell are you talking about?"

Leo sounded so genuinely confused, Tony would have believed him if he hadn't seen the evidence with his own eyes.

"I saw you," Tony hissed, and this time he found the strength to shake Leo off. He made a bolt for his bedroom.

"Jesus, stop behaving like a fucking three-year-old. Saw what?"

Tony climbed into bed and pulled the covers over his head. "You! Now fuck off."

"Not until you talk to me."

Knowing that Leo was going to outstubborn him, Tony sat up and stared at him, noting that the infuriating bastard really did look like he'd been up all night. Dark circles ringed his eyes and his normally tousled hair lay flat and lifeless. Tony wanted to wrap the lying traitorous bastard in his arms until they fell asleep.

"I saw you," Tony said quietly.

"You already said that. Saw me doing what?"

"Kissing that bloke. I took a break and drove past your house. You were kissing a bloke by your gates."

Leo looked puzzled first of all, and then his eyes opened wide. "Yesterday?"

Tony nodded.

"Yesterday afternoon?"

"How many other times did you kiss a bloke yesterday?" Tony asked sourly.

"You—lots. The other bloke—who is a friend by the way, but thanks for bothering to ask before you flounced off in a huff—once, like we always do."

"You kiss all your friends by sticking your tongue down their throat?"

"Only when I want to piss him off and make his girlfriend laugh. She was in the car too, but you probably didn't see her."

Tony opened his mouth and then shut it again.

"If you'd come over and shouted at me, then I could have introduced you to Malcolm and Jenny. But you didn't, did you?"

"I saw you kissing another man," Tony said miserably, fixing his gaze on the stripy pattern of his duvet.

"I wouldn't do that to you, Tony," Leo said, and Tony really wanted to believe him because he said it so fiercely. "I would *never* do that to you. I'm not like that."

"I thought—"

"I know what you thought, you fucking idiot, but you should have trusted me." Leo sat on the bed, but he made no attempt to hold Tony. "I don't fuck about, Tony. If I'm with someone, that's it. I thought you knew that."

"That's what you said, but then I saw you, and it wasn't a little peck on the lips."

"Nope. It was a full-on tongues and too much spit. But it was for a laugh, and he hated it, and his girlfriend thought it was hysterical."

Tony stared at him blankly. "It didn't mean anything?"

"Nothing at all."

"Oh." Tony looked at Leo. "Are you really pissed at me?"

"I'm more than pissed, mate. You've really fucked up. One, for not believing in me—" Leo counted them off on his fingers. "—two, for running away instead of confronting me. Three, for hiding behind Marchant. Four, for not trusting me—"

"You already said that." Tony felt like a naughty kid being scolded by the headmaster.

"I said 'believing' first of all." Leo frowned at Tony, his eyebrows furrowed together. "I told you I was yours. You should have believed me. And you didn't trust me."

"You were kissing another man," Tony protested. "What was I supposed to think?"

"You weren't supposed to run away before you'd even spoken to me." Leo's expression softened. "I'm sorry, babe. That kiss was just a joke to piss off Malcolm. I wasn't trying to hurt you."

"That's all?"

"Just a stupid joke to wind him up."

"Next time you do that, I'm gonna punch your lights out."

"There won't be a next time, but understood." Leo leaned forward and pressed their foreheads together. "The only person I'm going to kiss is you. I'm yours."

"Mine." The knot inside Tony's chest that had been there since he'd watched his lover kiss someone else eased, and Tony took a deep breath for what felt like the first time in hours, which turned into a yawn.

Leo chuckled. "Let's sleep for a while." He sat back and stripped off his jacket.

Tony flopped back onto his pillows and watched Leo strip down to his boxers. Leo climbed into bed, nudging Tony onto his side so that he could wrap around him. Once settled, Leo sat up again briefly to turn the pillow over.

"It's wet," Leo said. Then he hugged Tony close to him and placed his hand over Tony's heart.

"Go to sleep, sweetheart." He pressed a kiss on Tony's shoulder blade. "We'll talk later."

"Yes, sir." Obediently Tony settled down, brushed his lips against Leo's fingers, and closed his eyes. He was on the brink of sleep when Leo spoke again.

"I like that."

"Huh?"

"You calling me sir."

"Oh. Me too." Tony yawned. "G'nite."

"Night, babe." Leo held Tony close as they fell asleep.

LEO WAS asleep when Tony woke, bodily needs warring with his desire to stay right where he was, still in Leo's arms. Tony had stirred a few times, the noise of the commuter traffic on the main road outside disturbing him. Once or twice he'd tried to roll away, find another position to sleep in, but Leo had pulled him back into his arms with a grumble. Tony understood. In Leo's arms was where he was meant to stay. But as cute as it was to feel Leo's rolling snorts and snuffles across his back, Tony really needed a pee. He gently extricated himself from Leo, who grumbled and tried to grab him back.

Tony bent down to kiss his cheek. "Shh. I'll be back soon. I need to take a wazz."

Leo smacked his mouth a couple of times and fell straight back to sleep. Tony looked at the clock on his phone. Jesus, it was nearly one in the afternoon and he had three missed calls from Marchant.

He took care of needs first, sighing in relief as he emptied his bladder. Then he called Marchant.

"Yeah?" Marchant sounded as if he'd been asleep.

"Markie, it's Tony. You called me?"

"Oh hey, just checking you're okay."

"I'm fine. Now." Tony hesitated, but Marchant was going to find out sooner or later. "Leo came by after I got home."

"Oh?" Marchant was more awake now, and he sounded wary. "Do I need to hang him up by the balls?"

"Lay off his nuts. They're mine. He explained the kiss. A joke with a friend."

"And you believe him?"

Tony smiled at Leo, who'd just walked into the lounge wearing only his boxer shorts, looking sleep mussed and frankly edible. "I believe him."

Marchant huffed. "If you're sure."

Before Tony could respond, Leo plucked the phone out of his hand. "Marchant, it's Leo." He listened for a long while before he spoke.

Tony could hear Marchant bellowing down the phone. He decided not to interfere. Instead he wandered into his bedroom to get dressed. As he tugged a T-shirt over his head, fingers tweaked his nipples. He emerged from the T-shirt and looked indignantly at Leo.

"What was that for?"

"For leaving me to get my arse chewed by your boss."

"Did he shout?"

"I'm surprised you couldn't hear it in here," Leo said sourly.

"Marchant does get overexcited when he's angry."

Leo placed his hands on Tony's hips. "Much as I love the fact you have protective friends, I could have done with waking up first before he had a go at me."

"You took the phone away from me," Tony pointed out, acutely conscious of Leo's warm hands under his T-shirt, pressing into his skin.

"He said if I hurt you again, he would take steps to make sure I never do it again."

"Oh?" Tony was less interested in his overprotective boss and more concerned with the way Leo was making circles with his hands, moving in closer to Tony's dick, which was taking an interest in proceedings. Tony hissed as Leo's fingers brushed over the head of his cock.

"I promised I would keep you safe forever."

That caught Tony's attention, and he looked Leo in the eyes. "You can't make those sorts of promises."

"Yes, I can."

"You never know what's going to happen."

Leo caught Tony's hands and brought them up to his mouth, pressing a kiss into each palm. "We make the future for ourselves, Tony."

Tony didn't believe that—even less since Jordan and Mike's attack—but he was willing to let Leo believe it for him. "What now?"

"Where're the cuffs?"

"In the top drawer of the bedside table."

Leo licked his lips. He seemed nervous. "A flogger?"

"Same place."

"I'm going to cuff your hands and flog your arse. Then you're going to suck me off. And if you're a good boy—*a really good boy*—I might let you come." Leo brushed Tony's dick again by way of emphasis.

"Yes, sir."

"What are your safewords?"

Tony sucked in a breath. Handing over his safewords made this real—official. "Red for stop and yellow for slow."

Leo cupped Tony's jaw. "Marchant told me to step up or fuck off. He said you deserved better than a play Dom. He said—and I agree—that we could make it work, but only if I became part of *your* world. I am dominant, but I need to become *your* Dominant. He's going to train me."

"He's good at that."

"He also said that I could easily lose you to Jordan if I wasn't careful."

Tony frowned. "That's... not right. I'm not the right sub for Jordan."

"Jordan's too fucking possessive over you for that to be true. I know he thinks he wants a twink, but the way he looks after you, I think he's kidding himself." Leo kissed Tony's mouth with an arrogance that went straight to Tony's core, right fucking Dominant with a large *D*. Tony melted into the kiss, holding on until Leo drew back. "He's not fucking having you. Understand?"

Tony nodded, suddenly speechless.

Leo waited, looking expectant.

"Yes, sir," Tony managed.

"Good boy. Strip and lie over the end of the bed." Tony didn't obey immediately, and Leo raised an eyebrow. "Didn't I make myself clear?"

"Are you sure you don't want a young guy. Nearer your age?"

"Small and pretty like Mike? Bratty like Frankie? Vulnerable and needy like Ed?"

"Yeah," Tony whispered.

"Hell no. I want a big man, with dark fur I can lick and smell. A man I can pull and push, that I can fuck, and he'll take it all and give back more. I don't want a kid. Don't you understand? I'm doing this because of you. I want you, no one else."

"You don't think I'm weak?"

"I think you're tired of trying to be something you're not. You're a submissive, Tony, and that's the core of you."

"I should have been a little man."

Leo huffed and pushed Tony flat onto the bed, straddling him before Tony drew breath. "You're submissive. Not little, not weak."

Tony laid his hands on Leo's thighs, feeling the fine hair tickle his palm. "Are you—?"

"If you say 'sure,' I'm going to have you," Leo warned.

"You're going to have me anyway." Tony smirked at him.

"True, true. Now, cuffs, flogger, bare arse, bed."

"You're sitting on me," Tony pointed out.

"Don't be cheeky." Leo twisted one of Tony's nipples.

Tony arched up and yelped. "Sorry, sir."

"Better." Leo climbed off him and looked in the bedside table, giving a low whistle at the toys jumbled in the drawer. "We sell some of these."

Tony flushed. "They are yours. I wanted to know more about your company."

"Thank you." Leo bent down and kissed him. "Now, end of the bed. I'm not asking again."

Tony shuffled down until he sat at the end of the bed and rolled over to display his arse. Leo threw him a pillow.

"Shove that under your hips." Leo waited for him to get into position, then cuffed Tony's wrists.

The moment the leather encased his wrists, Tony relaxed. This was *his* world, something he understood and embraced. Tony knew Leo was inexperienced with the flogger, but he knew a lot about being flogged and could stop the scene if he was in any danger.

"Do you need me to secure your ankles?"

"I can stay still," Tony promised.

"Spread your legs more. What are we going to do?" Leo asked, his voice low and steady.

"You're going to flog me, then I'm going to blow you, and if I'm a good boy, you'll let me come."

"Good. Now, don't keep quiet. Tell me how it feels for you."

"Yes, sir."

Tony's eyes closed as he felt the leather strands of the flogger trail over his back. He moaned in appreciation. It had been too long. Leo brushed the flogger over each knob of Tony's spine, from his neck to the base, and dragged it between his arsecheeks and over his balls. He teased and tormented until Tony was a quivering wreck as he lay on the bed.

"Please," Tony begged, sticking his arse out.

"Please what?"

"Hit me. Please, sir. I can take it."

A pause. Too long. Tony waited, his breath held for what felt like forever... then *oh yes* the smack of the leather across the meat of his arse and the burn that followed was like coming home.

"Okay?" Leo's inexperience showed in his hesitant question.

"More than all right." He pushed his arse out again.

Leo flogged him again—and again. Tony moaned loudly and heard an answering moan from Leo.

Tony dropped his head between his shoulders and reveled in the burn. His dick leaked steadily from the pleasure.

"Ten more," Leo panted.

Tony turned to look at Leo, seeing the strain in his face. A sheen of sweat spread across his chest, and the hair in his armpits was dark and damp. He was naked and hard, his cock sticking out proudly.

"*Do it.*"

Tony groaned at the first one across the bottom of his thighs and didn't stop as Leo worked up, the last one a mere flick that caught the back of his balls. Tony roared, pain layered with pleasure until he didn't know which was which.

"Don't come," Leo barked.

Tony sucked in a noisy breath as he tried to hang on to his control. He took strength in Leo's hand on his shoulder.

"Okay. Okay." Leo stroked his back until he'd calmed. "God, you look amazing."

"Got...." Tony swallowed to get some saliva in his mouth. "Want to suck you off, sir."

"Can you kneel?"

Marchant would have had Tony's hide for the lack of grace as he slid to the floor, but Leo didn't correct him. Tony hissed as his arse connected with his calves.

Leo settled in front of him and spread his legs. His dick was flushed dark red, the head sticky with precome. Without finesse, Tony leaned forward and sucked the head of Leo's cock into his mouth.

"Fuck!" Leo clutched Tony's hair, tugging on it painfully. He thrust up, but Tony was ready, taking Leo's cock to the back of his throat. His throat muscles opened up around the head of Leo's dick, and Leo groaned.

Tony looked up at him, seeing his teeth caught in his bottom lip. It wouldn't take much to push Leo to his climax. Tony pulled back to use more tongue, to explore the shaft in his mouth, but Leo's hands tightened in his hair, and Tony took the hint. He set up a rhythm, tight and fast until Leo let out a choking noise and Tony's mouth flooded with semen. Tony swallowed around the shaft, working Leo through his orgasm and not letting him go until his dick had softened in his mouth. Then he pulled away and knelt before Leo, his head bowed.

"Well—" Leo coughed and tried again. "—I think you've been a good boy. Stand up." Tony got to his feet, feeling the sparks fly through his arse and thighs. Leo pulled him closer and looked up. "What would you like? My mouth or my hand?"

"Your mouth, please, sir." His voice was hoarse, his throat sore.

Tony closed his eyes as Leo took him into his mouth. For his first time out as a Dom, Leo hadn't done badly at all. And this time, Tony wouldn't sleep alone.

Epilogue

EVERY TIME the door of the club opened, Tony looked over, only to be bitterly disappointed when it wasn't Leo. Leather-clad club members streamed through the door, all of them waving at him as they passed through. But none of them were his.

"Patience," Ed murmured.

Tony had been so intent on the door he hadn't even realized Ed was by his side. "I've been patient. Now I want my Dom here."

Ed smiled up at him. "Is this the first time he's been here as a member?"

"Yep. Up to now he's been my guest. Now he's a full member, and I'm taking the night off to play. Only I stupidly said I'd work until he arrived." Tony worried his bottom lip. "Perhaps I should call him."

The door again. It still wasn't Leo, but to Tony's surprise, Frankie bounced through the door, closely followed by Al.

"*Tony!*" Frankie squealed loudly and rushed over to the bar.

"Hey—" Tony managed before Frankie plastered his mouth against his.

"Put him down." Al tugged Frankie back to his side of the bar. "He needs to breathe. Tony's got a big night tonight."

Frankie licked his lips and smirked at Tony. "Nice lip gloss. Cherries."

Tony sighed. He'd put that on for Leo. "What're you doing here?" Frankie rarely came to the club even though Al was a member.

"Marchant invited us."

Tony frowned. "He did?"

Frankie looked at him uncertainly, then at Al, who shrugged. "Yeah."

"Look." Ed pointed to the door.

The one time Tony had taken his eyes off the entrance, Leo walked in. Tony nearly swallowed his tongue. Leo wore a tight black shirt and equally tight leather trousers that outlined his dick perfectly.

Leo smiled at him, but to Tony's surprise, he didn't come over immediately. The reason became clear when a man with a familiar shock of red hair appeared.

"Jordan?" Tony swung to Ed. "Did you know he was coming today?"

Ed rolled his eyes. "Of course I did. Marchant asked Leo to bring him to the club. Jordan can't drive yet, and you know he's shaky on his feet."

"Why didn't he ask me?"

"We offered to bring him, but he'd already made arrangements with Marchant and Leo," Al said.

"Jordan wanted it to be a surprise for you," Ed said.

His arms still encased in plaster, Jordan made his way slowly to the bar. Leo and Marchant, who'd also arrived, hovered by his side. Marchant moved his stool for Jordan to sit down and helped him onto it. Frankie and Al shuffled down the bar.

"You're honored," Tony said. "He never lets just anyone sit in that stool. I swear the seat is molded to his arse."

"No wonder it's so bloody uncomfortable," Jordan huffed, then grinned at Tony. "Hey."

"Welcome back. You look like shit."

"Thanks."

Tony studied Jordan carefully, noting the loss of weight and the dark marks under his eyes. He went to hug Jordan, pausing to look over at Leo for permission. Leo rolled his eyes, and Tony enveloped Jordan in a hug, grieving at how fragile he felt. "God, I'm pleased to see you back here."

Jordan leaned against his shoulder for a moment. "I'm pleased to be back. Now put me down before your man gets jealous, and get me a drink. With a straw."

Tony hugged him gently once more and stepped back. "Gary can do it. I'm off the clock now my Dom is here." He beamed at Leo.

"Why did I agree to this?" Marchant grumbled.

"Because it's about time you let Tony have some playtime," Al said.

Ed slipped under Marchant's arm. "Go and have fun, kids."

"Who's in charge of this club?" Marchant asked, but his tone held no heat and he pulled Ed back against him.

Jordan chuckled. "Whipped!"

"So whipped," Tony agreed.

Marchant scowled at him. "I could sack you."

Tony raised his eyebrows.

Marchant sighed. "I'm not that stupid."

"Good to hear," Leo said. "In which case, my boy and I are going to play in your fine establishment, and if anyone approaches Tony with a query or a problem or a request to fucking scratch their arse, I'm going to string them up by the nuts."

Tony dipped his head to kiss Leo's cheek. "You're my hero. Did I ever tell you that?"

"Not today."

Leo kissed him back, but it was a whole different kind of kiss, and Tony pulled back, gasping for air.

"Get in the back with you," Marchant growled.

Tony caught Jordan's sadness as he looked away. He would take time to sit and talk to his old friend, but not this evening. Now was for him and Leo. Frankie caught his eye and gave the slightest of nods. They would look after Jordan for the evening.

"Do you want a drink?" Tony asked Leo. He was anxious to get started but mindful of his Dom.

Leo shook his head. "I've got other things to do right now." He looked Tony up and down. "You're overdressed for what I have in mind."

"What do you want me to wear?" Tony's breath caught in his throat as Leo pulled out a thick strip of leather and held it out. A collar. Tony touched it with one finger. "You want to collar me?"

"Yes."

"Are you sure?"

"He's bloody sure," Marchant said. "Now get out of here."

"I'm going to collar you, but in peace, away from this lot telling me what I'm doing wrong."

Marchant and Jordan snorted, and Ed burst out laughing.

Tony and Leo left them behind and headed to the changing room. As Leo opened the door, a Dom walked out, his expression clearing. "Tony, just the man. There's no towels in the john."

"Tell Marchant," Leo growled. "Tony's busy."

Tony's dick stiffened at Leo's dominant tone.

The Dom looked down his nose at Leo. "But—"

"*Busy*," Leo said and pushed past.

Tony gave the Dom an apologetic smile and followed *his* Dom. Tonight he was there just for Leo.

Leo scanned for an empty locker. "Strip."

"I have my own locker," Tony pointed out.

Leo raised his eyebrow, and Tony undid the top button of his shirt. It didn't matter. Nothing mattered. Except the two of them. He stripped off his clothes and knelt before Leo.

"I never thought a game of football on the M25 would lead me here." Leo traced a finger around the bare skin of Tony's neck.

"Do you regret it?" Tony had spent more than an hour or two worrying about Leo having to adjust to his world.

"I have the sexiest man at my feet, and you're asking me if I regret it?"

"Er. Yes?"

"Shut up, Tony." Leo buckled the collar around Tony's throat, checking to make sure it was comfortable. "That's better."

"Why do you want to me to wear a collar?"

"Because you're mine and you submit only to me. Marchant suggested it."

Tony blinked as he looked up at Leo. "No one wanted me until you."

Leo pulled Tony to his feet. "You really have no clue, do you?" He smoothed his hands over Tony's shoulders and arms, his touch possessive and stimulating Tony's already tingling nerves.

"Clue about what?"

"Tony… no… just watch the Doms tonight."

"What are you talking about?" Tony asked, exasperated.

"You think no one wanted you?"

"You know they didn't."

Leo dragged Tony against him, cupping his arse. "Marchant told me there were half a dozen Doms wanting to collar you."

Tony shook his head. "He's just yanking your chain."

"They wanted you, but they didn't think they could handle you."

Tony just stared at him. All this time, and no one had approached him just to fucking *ask*?

Leo kissed him fiercely. "The difference is I *know* I can handle you. I may lack in experience, but I can manage Anthony Drake."

Tony's head was a swirling mix of emotions, but Leo didn't give him time to overthink. "Let's go and play," he said. "I want to try some of the paddles."

"You do?"

Leo smirked at him. "Do you remember you told me how you spent your birthdays?"

Tony vaguely remembered their discussion on their first date. "Lashed to a cross, plugged, and being whipped and fucked until I come?"

Leo leaned into him and licked his lips. "It's your birthday soon. I don't think I'm up to whipping you, but what do you think of a flogger?"

Tony felt his dick rise to the promise. He couldn't think of anything better. "Practice makes perfect, sir."

Keep reading for
an exclusive excerpt from

Jordan & Rhys

A Novella in Frankie's Series

Eight months after the assault in which his sub and lover was killed, Jordan Nicholls isn't making much progress in his recovery. Marchant and Ed, Jordan's friends from the BDSM club, stage an intervention.

They employ a carer to look after Jordan. Rhys may be a sub, but he's forceful, making Jordan eat and exercise, rather than live on coffee and cigarettes. Despite Jordan's protests, Rhys slowly forces him back to life.

But Rhys wants to be Jordan's sub, and despite being protective of Rhys, Jordan's not sure he can ever return to the BDSM lifestyle. In order for their relationship to continue, they'll need to find a compromise that meets both their needs.

Coming soon to
www.dreamspinnerpress.com

Prologue

"THE NEXT time you tell me the music's great, I'm going to remind you of tonight." Jordan Nicholls laughed at the disgusted expression on his submissive's face. "You've got to admit it was crap."

"More than crap," Mike agreed. "Even that bloody awful club Frankie insisted we tried was better than this one."

"He only likes it because he finally got to grope Al there."

"Which is more than we did tonight. Next time I mention going to a straight club, remind me that we won't be able to snog."

"Yeah, I didn't like that." Jordan slipped his hand into Mike's. "Next time, you listen to your Dom, okay, or I'm going to spank your arse. I hate going someone where I can't touch you and kiss and…."

"You can tease me with a butt plug?" Mike asked hopefully.

Jordan chuckled as they walked down the side road toward his car. "You're so predictable."

"Yep," Mike said happily. "We could go home and do that now."

"Yeah. I'm going to cuff you to the bed and drive you insane until you beg for mercy."

"You always think that's a threat."

Jordan turned and raised an eyebrow at Mike.

Mike hissed. "You just do that because you know it makes me hard."

Oh yeah. Mike was very predictable.

"Oi! Poofs!"

Jordan rolled his eyes as someone shouted behind them. "Great. Just the end to the evening we needed."

"Ignore them," Mike said. "We're almost at the car."

They sped up, anxious to reach the car before the confrontation turned to violence.

"Fuckin' homos!"

Mike snorted. "Well, at least their gaydar works."

"We were holding hands. It's not like we made it difficult." Dammit. He should have known that any sign of affection in a public place was a stupid idea. Now they were in deep shit. Jordan fumbled in his pockets for the car key.

"We can get married, but we can't bloody hold hands in the street," Mike said bitterly.

"Gonna take it up the arse, fucking fudge-packers! You should all be shot."

Mike spun on his heel. "Fuck off, arseholes!" he yelled.

Jordan tugged on his arm. "Leave it, Mike. Look, we're at the car."

"Faggots. Gonna bend over for him later?"

"Why? Are you jealous?" Mike said. "No one wants to fuck you?"

Jordan groaned. "Leave. It. Mike."

Jordan had barely spoken before thudding pain spread across his back and he landed hard on the ground. He smacked his head on pavement, leaving him dazed and confused. Jordan tried to take a breath, but it hurt too much. He felt the rough tarmac beneath his cheek and a trickle of blood by his ear. Jordan couldn't see anything, but then he realized his eyes were closed. He forced them open to see Mike on the ground too, so close to him, quiet and still. Mike was never still. Jordan reached out to try and touch him, but someone stamped on his arm. He shrieked with the pain as he felt his bone snap, but Mike didn't react.

"Fucking faggots. Gonna kill you."

Jordan could hear them laughing as if this were a joke. Unable to draw breath, unable to get away from the vicious assault, Jordan focused on Mike. The green flashing light from a nearby shop window shone on Mike's face. He lay unmoving, his eyes wide and unseeing. Jordan tried to get to him, to see if he was all right, but then agonizing pain splintered through his head, and he remembered nothing more.

Chapter 1

Eight months later

JORDAN SAT alone at the end of the bar, nursing a Coke and pretending not to notice his best friend Tony, who was pushed up against the wall, his hands pressed flat against rough plaster as Leo kissed him.

"Wishing it was you?" Marchant Belarus sat on the stool next to Jordan. He was the owner of the BDSM club and too fucking perceptive. There was nothing he didn't see or interfere in when it came to his club.

Jordan couldn't take his eyes away from the couple, watching with a sad envy that didn't come naturally to him.

"Leo's not my type." Jordan's lame attempt at a joke fell flat when Marchant didn't chuckle.

"I never thought he'd be Tony's, but look at them now."

Finally Tony had a Dom of his own, and he exuded happiness. Despite the fact that Leo was younger and shorter than Tony, it was clear who was dominant in their relationship. For the first time, Jordan *saw* Tony, watched how beautifully he submitted—and Jordan was too late.

"Tony waited for years for you to notice him," Marchant said quietly.

"You think I didn't know that? I just thought…. Leo's better for him than I am." Jordan turned his head as Tony sank to his knees. The couple weren't bothered by an audience. They never seemed to notice anyone else when they were in a scene. Jordan gave Marchant a wan smile. "What do you want? Apart from reminding me what I've lost."

"Ed's worried about you." Marchant waved his hand at the barman. "He sent me to talk to you."

"I'm fine." Jordan gritted his teeth as Marchant raised an eyebrow. Could you raise a derisive eyebrow? Marchant possessed eyebrows that conducted whole conversations, particularly when he thought someone was being an arse. "It's taking time."

Marchant patted his back, not requiring more explanation. It had been eight months since Jordan had been badly injured in an assault in which his sub, Mike, had been killed. Jordan was still recovering from the physical injuries, and the mental trauma was like a scar to his soul. Once outgoing and gregarious, now Jordan shuffled through the day, feeling like he was wrapped in layers of gray wool that muffled him from the outside world. Marchant's sub, Ed, had once told Jordan that he breathed for the first time the day he met Marchant. Jordan had stopped breathing the day three drunk thugs used their fists to tear his world apart.

Jordan swallowed hard at the memory, and then he noticed Marchant had put his arm around him and Tony was pressed against him, also holding him. He was crowded by solid walls of men. "What?"

Tony gently swiped a tear from Jordan's face. Jordan hadn't even realized he was crying, but his nose was blocked and his throat tight. He rested his head on Tony's chest and let the tears flow. Finally he raised his head, suddenly feeling claustrophobic. "Shit, I'm sorry, Tony. You—"

"Shut up." Tony hugged him even tighter.

"Get off." Jordan tried to bat them away. "Christ, you're going to suffocate me."

They stepped back, to his relief, but they didn't leave his side—which was also a relief, even if he'd never admit it.

"Why don't you go upstairs for a while?" Marchant said. "Ed's working, and the place is empty."

Jordan pushed back his hair, grimacing at the greasy feel. He'd let himself go recently, finding even washing his hair was a battle. His arm had taken a long time to heal, and he struggled with even basic motor skills. "I'll go home before I make a bigger idiot of myself." He loved his friends, but suddenly their concern was too much. It pressed down on him, and he needed to get away.

"I'll run you home," Tony said, looking over to Leo to check if it was all right.

"It's okay, I can get the bus." Jordan hadn't been able to drive since the assault. A blow to the head had left him with intermittent seizures in the early stages, and he was banned from driving for a year.

"I'll drive Mr. Jordan home."

Jordan turned to look at the unknown speaker. He was young and slim, maybe Leo's age, maybe younger, with a shock of dark hair that looked as if he'd stuck his finger in an electrical socket. "Thanks, but I'm okay."

"Sorted," Marchant said with satisfaction. "Jordan, this is Rhys. He's new to the club. Thank you, Rhys."

Jordan opened his mouth to argue, but then Leo appeared with Jordan's leather jacket, and Marchant ushered Jordan out of the club, Rhys leading the way.

Jordan scowled at Marchant and Tony as they waited for Rhys to bring the car around the front. "I'm not a fucking invalid."

Tony stepped forward and hugged him close. It was like being mauled by a bear. "Look in the mirror, Jordan. You look like shit, and you need a fucking shower."

"Rhys will look after you."

Jordan narrowed his eyes because Marchant sounded too damned smug, but then a Prius pulled up in front of them, and Rhys hopped out.

"Ready?" he asked Jordan.

Jordan held back a growl but got into the passenger seat. He was grateful to sit down again. His bones ached all the time since the assault.

"Where do you live?" Rhys asked, looking at him expectantly.

"Worcester Park. Look, you can drop me off at the bus stop or the station."

Rhys drove out of the club car park, ignoring him. "I said I'd take you home. I was about to leave."

"That's early. You don't want to stay for the evening?"

"Not this evening."

Rhys didn't say any more, and Jordan was left frustrated as they drove toward his home.

"Rhys? Like Jonathan Rhys Meyers?" Jordan asked to break the silence.

"Yeah. Except it's my surname."

"Oh? What's your first name?"

There was a pause, long enough for Jordan to turn to look at Rhys.

"Everyone calls me Rhys."

From out of nowhere, Jordan managed to summon his inner Dom. "That's not what I asked."

"My name is Richard," Rhys said reluctantly.

"What's wrong with Richard?"

"I spent my entire childhood being called Dick or Faggot. Now everyone calls me Rhys."

"You could be called Richard, Rick, Rich—"

"I know the alternatives."

Rhys sounded angry, and Jordan didn't have the energy to deal with someone else's anger. He found it hard enough to handle his own. He subsided against the door and watched the scenery go by.

"Mr. Jordan?"

"Huh?" Jordan opened his eyes to see Rhys peering at him.

"I need you to tell me where we need to go."

Jordan held back the sarcasm forming on his lips. "Turn right near the station. Third lamppost on the left," he said as Rhys pulled into his road. "Yeah, just here."

Rhys stopped the car and looked at him. "I can help you if you want."

"I'm more than capable of walking into my house." Jordan stepped slowly out of the car, but before he could say anything, Rhys came around to join him.

"You need a shower."

"Yeah, thanks, I got that."

"I can help you." Rhys looked at him kindly, and Jordan bristled at the implication he couldn't manage.

"I'm more than capable of taking a shower." Jordan wasn't going to do anything except collapse into his bed. He could sleep in his own stink. He fumbled in his pocket for his keys.

"Keys." Rhys held out his hand.

"I'm fine," Jordan said sharply, just about at the end of his tether.

"I promised Master Marchant I would look after you."

"You promised to drive me home. You've done that. Good to meet you… Rhys."

Rhys stayed exactly where he was. "Mike was my friend."

Jordan swayed, the shock hitting him. "You knew Mike?"

Rhys grabbed Jordan's arm and took the keys from him in one motion. "He was my best friend from school."

"I never met you."

"He never shut up about you," Rhys said. "You didn't know him very long. Not long enough to meet the friends and family."

Jordan pressed his lips together. "Not nearly long enough." He swayed again, and Rhys slid his arm around him.

"Come on. You need to sleep. You're dead on your feet."

Too tired to argue, Jordan let Rhys lead him into the house. Jordan leaned against him, thinking that even if he didn't, Rhys smelled good. "Mike is dead. I should have died."

"That's bollocks, and you know it. Mike would've kicked your arse if he'd heard you say that. Now where's the bathroom?"

"I just want to sleep." Jordan yawned and headed for the stairs.

"Shower first, then sleep." Rhys kept pace with him up the stairs.

"Go away, Rhys."

"Nope. You stink worse than my teenage brother's trainers."

Jordan managed a weak laugh and figured that if he had a shower, Rhys might leave him alone.

In the bathroom, Jordan held on to the sink and looked at himself in the mirror. He'd aged considerably since the accident: deep lines etched his eyes and his once-vibrant red hair had shots of silver through it. "I look like shit."

"Yeah, you do. Here, let me help." Rhys was incredibly gentle as he helped Jordan strip.

"Anyone would think you'd done this before," Jordan remarked.

Rhys quirked one side of his mouth. "Once or twice."

"I'm so fucking tired." Jordan pushed down his once-tight black jeans. Now they hung loose on his hips.

"Ten minutes, and I'll have you in bed."

"Not today," Jordan murmured.

Rhys gave him a startled laugh, and Jordan laughed in return. It felt good. It felt *strange*.

After Jordan had come home from the hospital, they'd fitted a seat—for an old man, he'd grumbled—into the shower so that he didn't have to stand for too long. He sat there and let Rhys wash his hair, then Rhys left him, and Jordan finished washing in peace. Normally he would just let the water run over him for five minutes and then get out of the shower, but he was damn sure Rhys would sniff him to make sure he was clean, so Jordan scrubbed and rinsed until he was exhausted. Then he sat there, eyes closed and half-asleep, until Rhys turned off the water.

"Come on," Rhys murmured, "the sheets are clean."

"You made my bed?" Jordan couldn't remember the last time his sheets were changed.

"Yep." Rhys wrapped Jordan in a towel and roughly dried his hair. He eyed Jordan's hair with amusement and took his time combing it to his satisfaction. "I thought my hair was crazy. You need a shave, but you can do that in the morning."

Grateful that Rhys didn't expect him to be clean-shaven in bed, Jordan submitted meekly to his attention and then followed him into the bedroom, crawling gratefully into his clean—smelling like lavender fields—bed.

"Do you need to take any painkillers?" Rhys asked.

"Downstairs," Jordan mumbled.

He was asleep before Rhys returned and didn't appreciate being woken up.

Rhys ignored his grumbling. "Take your pills and shut up."

"Are you sure you're a sub?" Jordan muttered as he subsided onto his pillows.

Rhys gave him a peculiar look. "Very sure." He stroked Jordan's damp hair back from his forehead. "Go to sleep, Sir."

Jordan was about to make some comment about not being Rhys's Dom, but sleep tugged him into oblivion, and he gratefully gave in.

Did you come?

Yes

SUE BROWN is owned by her dogs and two children. When she isn't following their orders, she can be found with her laptop in Starbucks, drinking latte and eating chocolate.

Sue discovered M/M romance at the time she woke up to find two men kissing on her favorite television series. The kissing was hot and tender and Sue wanted to write about these men. She may be late to the party, but she's made up for it since, writing fanfiction until she was brave enough to venture out into the world of original fiction.

Sue can be found at:
Website: www.suebrownstories.com
Blog: suebrownsstories.blogspot.co.uk
Twitter: @suebrownstories
Facebook: www.facebook.com/suebrownstories

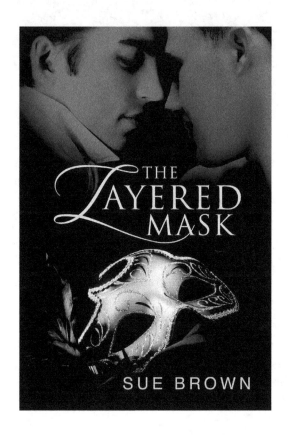

THE
LAYERED
MASK

SUE BROWN

Threatened by his father with disinheritance, Lord Edwin Nash arrives in London with a sole purpose: to find a wife. A more than eligible bachelor and titled to boot, the society matrons are determined to shackle him to one of the girls by the end of the season.

During a masquerade ball, Nash hides from the ladies vying for his attention. He is discovered by Lord Thomas Downe, the Duke of Lynwood. Nash is horrified when Downe calmly tells him that he knows the secret Nash has hidden for years and sees through the mask Edwin presents to the rest of the world.

And then he offers him an alternative.

www.dreamspinnerpress.com

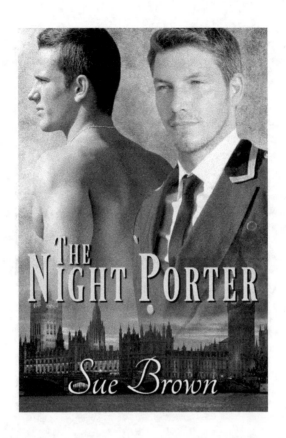

The first time Max lays eyes on Robert Armitage, he knows exactly what he wants to happen. Tall, broad, and gorgeous, Robert pushes all his buttons. When Robert asks Max to show him around town, the attraction between them only intensifies. But Max is just a night porter and Robert a guest at his hotel before his wedding, and Max knows even as they sleep together that in the morning he'll have to send the groom on his way.

www.dreamspinnerpress.com

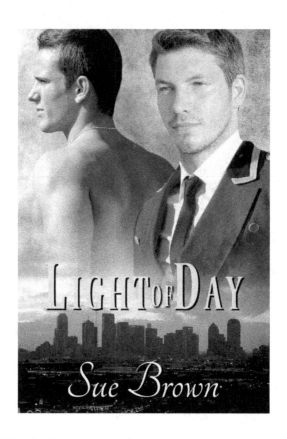

The first time Max laid eyes on Robert Armitage, he knew exactly what he wanted to happen. But Max was just a night porter and Robert a guest at the hotel before his wedding, and Max knew even as they slept together that in the morning he'd have to send the groom on his way. Max's heart was broken when Robert left, and so he ran home to Texas. When Robert's marriage failed, Max waited for Robert to come looking for him, and waited....

A year later, Max's dreams come true and Robert finds him, but there's a catch, and Max has to decide if he wants Robert enough to be satisfied with hiding their relationship.

www.dreamspinnerpress.com

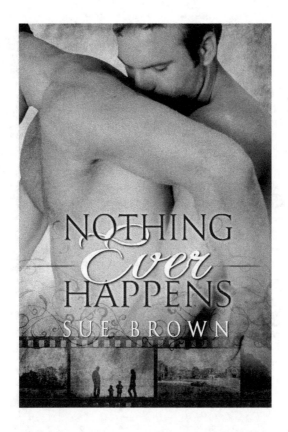

Andrew's life is a cliché: he's a gay man trapped in a loveless marriage, thanks to his religious, overbearing mother. Then a new couple moves in down the street, and Andrew finds himself falling for Nathan in a big way. Nathan is straight, married, and just about to be a father, but after one fateful night out together at a club, Nathan has to face the fact that his feelings for Andrew go way beyond that of a friend and neighbor.

When Andrew's wife asks for a divorce, both men's lives are thrown into disarray. Arguments about their responsibilities to their wives and children, doubting themselves and each other, and some harrowing lies pull them apart… but they never leave each other's thoughts.

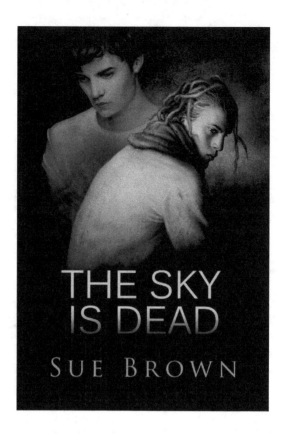

THE SKY
IS DEAD

SUE BROWN

Danny is young, gay, and homeless. He lives in the park, preferring to avoid attention, but when thugs confront a stranger, Danny rushes to his rescue. He and the would-be victim, Harry, form a cautious friendship that deepens months later, when Harry persuades Danny to visit his home. Daring to believe he has found happiness, Danny finds his world turned upside down yet again when tragedy strikes.

Until he runs out of options, Danny won't trust anyone. Finally he has to accept the offer of a home, and Danny becomes David, but adjusting to a new life isn't easy. When he meets the mysterious Jack, it stirs up feelings he thought were long gone. Can David dare to allow himself to love? Or will the truth bring his new world tumbling down around him?

www.dreamspinnerpress.com

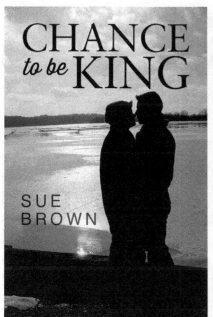
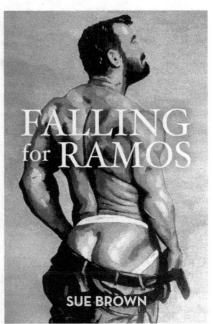

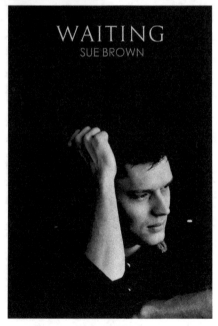

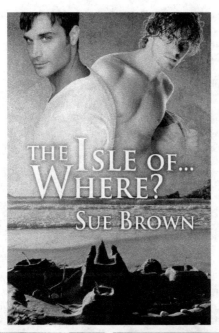
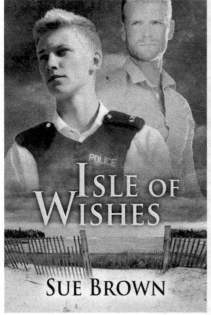
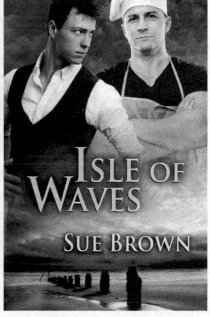

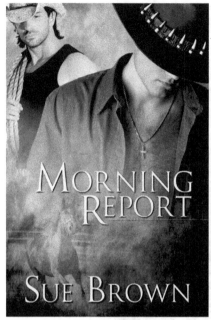

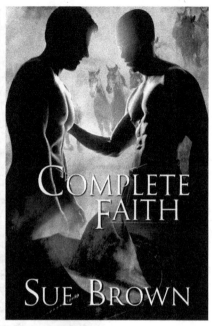

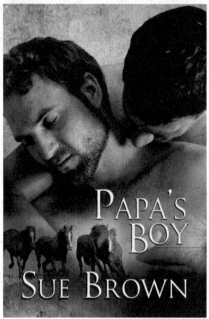

www.dreamspinnerpress.com

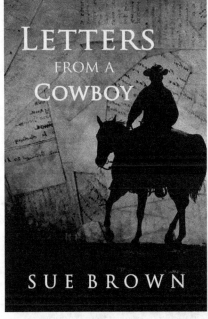
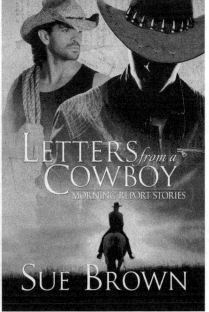

FOR **MORE** OF THE **BEST GAY** ROMANCE

DREAMSPINNER
PRESS
dreamspinnerpress.com

CPSIA information can be obtained
at www.ICGtesting.com
Printed in the USA
LVHW080509101220
673815LV00025B/372